GODS *of*
GIFT *and* GRIEF

THE SECOND VOLUME OF
THE DIVINER'S CHRONICLE

FRANK DUPONT

authorHOUSE®

AuthorHouse™
1663 Liberty Drive
Bloomington, IN 47403
www.authorhouse.com
Phone: 1 (800) 839-8640

Published by AuthorHouse 01/29/2019

ISBN: 978-1-5462-7766-8 (sc)
ISBN: 978-1-5462-7764-4 (hc)
ISBN: 978-1-5462-7765-1 (e)

Library of Congress Control Number: 2019900930

Print information available on the last page.

*Any people depicted in stock imagery provided by Getty Images are models,
and such images are being used for illustrative purposes only.
Certain stock imagery © Getty Images.*

This book is printed on acid-free paper.

*Because of the dynamic nature of the Internet, any web addresses or links contained in
this book may have changed since publication and may no longer be valid. The views
expressed in this work are solely those of the author and do not necessarily reflect the
views of the publisher, and the publisher hereby disclaims any responsibility for them.*

TABLE OF CONTENTS

NAMES OF CHARACTERS

Aga	Only son of Erra-Imitti, former king of Isin
Alim	A lead gardener for the temple of Ninisina
Ansar	A lead household guard for the king of Isin
Aruru	A slave acquired by Enmerkar
Asgi	Chief Counselor of Nur-Adad, king of Larsa
Ashgi	A retired Isin general
Azuru	Lith-el's aunt, Nani's great aunt
Banda	Chief Priest of Ninisina's temple, *Egal-mah*
Dagan	Friend and former co-worker of Enlil-Bani
Enlil-Bani	King of Isin, formerly a lead gardener
En-me	Enlil-Bani's personal healer, an *a-zu*
Enmerkar	Chronicler of the story, Enlil-Bani's son
Enmul	Successor to Banda, Chief Priest of Egal-mah
Ezina	Zambiya's wife
Gibil	Suba and Nani's daughter
Ibbi	One of General Ashgi's sons
Ila	Sister of the Director of Trading in Manjadar, a trader
Indur	The son of Zambiya and Ezina
Kulla	Enlil-Bani's barber
Kusu	Tikal's wife, Neti's mother
Mas	The son of Kulla, Enlil-Bani's barber

Muda	A Gutian, former slave of Enlil-Bani
Nabi	A palace guard and friend of Zambiya
Nani	Daughter of Enlil-Bani, wife to Suba
Naram	An *ummia*, Enmerkar's mentor and adoptive father
Neti	Son of Tikal and Kusu
Ninegala	Younger daughter of Nisaba, also known as Nina
Ningal	A priest of Ninisina's temple who studies the stars
Ninlil	One of General Ashgi's twin daughters
Ninmah	Priestess in *Egal-mah*
Ninmul	One of General Ashgi's twin daughters
Nintud	Dagan's wife
Nisaba	Widow of Erra-Imitti
Nur-Adad	King of Larsa
Rangu	An interpreter for the caravan to *Meluhha*
Sherida	Daughter of Nisaba, also known as Rida
Sigsig	One of General Ashgi's sons
Suba	Husband of Nani
Sud	Slave to Ezina
Tikal	Chief Advisor to Enlil-Bani
Uttu	Naram's wife
Zambiya	Stepson of Enlil-Bani, formerly named Iskur
Zid-tara	Chief Steward to Enlil-Bani

DECEASED CHARACTERS

Erra-imitti	Deceased king of Isin
Indur	Lith-el's father
Lith-el	Enlil-Bani's deceased wife
Isme	A palace guard, murderer of Lith-el
Nanse	Deceased daughter of Dagan and Nintud
Saman	Rogue palace guard, leader of robber gang

PLACES AND GODS, TITLES AND OBJECTS

Adad	Sumerian god of weather
Akitu	Akkadian word for the New Year ceremonies
Akkad	The Northern part of Mesopotamia
Akkadian	A Semitic language
Aruru	Possibly a birth goddess
Asag	A monster from Mesopotamian literature
Ashipu	A healer who uses herbs, potions and entreaties to the gods
A-zu	A healer who employs physical treatments
Buranun	Euphrates river
Corvee	Labor owed in lieu of taxes or payment
Damu	One of the gods of healing, son of Ninisina
Edubba	A school for scribes
Egal-mah	The temple of Ninisina in Isin, atop the zigurrat
Ensi	One of many terms for a city's king
E-sig-mese-du	The temple of goddess Inana at Isin, also atop the zigurrat
Ganzer	The gate to the underworld
Idiglat	Tigris river
Id-kura	The river of the underworld
Inana	A female goddess, sexually insatiable and promiscuous
Isin	The Sumerian city where Enlil-Bani reigns

Ki-en-gir	The Sumerian's name for Sumeria
Kirsig	A major canal near Isin
Larsa	A Sumerian city to the southwest of Isin, a competitor of Isin
Lulal	A warrior god
Manjadar	A city along the Indus Valley, part of the Meluhhan trade network
Meluhha	Akkadian word for the Harappan culture of the Indus Valley
Mutanu	The word for plague
Namtaru	The god of plague
Nergal	A warrior god
Ninisina	A goddess of medicine and chief protector deity of Isin
Ningirama	A god who provided protection from snakes
Ninkasi	The patron goddess of beer
Nisaba	The patron goddess of scribes and writing
Orant	An effigy of a worshipper
Sangu	A High Priest
Shurruppak	A neighboring city to the south of Isin
Ummia	The title of a teaching scribe in an edubba
Ur	A southern Sumerian city, ally of Isin
Uruk	A neighboring city south of Isin, north of Larsa
Utu	Sun god, protector of Larsa
Zid-abzu	The household god for Enlil-Bani's family
Zigurrat	A monumental structure made of mud bricks, with one or more temples on the uppermost level

INTRODUCTION

It was in Mesopotamia that the underpinnings of human civilization were invented or developed, arguably the first. These included monumental architecture, writing, the plow, the wheel, the potter's wheel, kingship, formalized law, history, fired bricks and even a form of democracy. Metallurgy, including the creation of beautiful jewelry and useful objects, was refined there.

Cuneiform writing was on clay tablets, starting with pictographic representations of transactions and land-holdings and culminated in representations of spoken sounds. The first recorded Hero epic, the story of Gilgamesh, gives a pre-Biblical account of the flooding of the earth. Some of their cities had populations exceeding 20,000, with large-scale agriculture and domesticated herds for feeding the people, even producing an abundant surplus. Agriculture was possible due to the creation of extensive canals and tributaries for irrigating fields of grain and date palm orchards, and to accommodate the annual floods of the Tigris and Euphrates rivers. Irrigation and flood control had commenced at least 3 millennia before the Common Era; maintenance demanded constant and exhausting labor in extreme heat by large crews of workers.

Flax, wheat and barley were exported great distances as a medium for trade, north to the Mediterranean and even into the Indus Valley, now the border area dividing modern Pakistan and India. Imported were stone, hardwood, precious metals and gems, which were absent from most of Mesopotamia. What Mesopotamia had was abundant water and fertile soil.

Over time, ancient Mesopotamia became two sections, with Akkad in the north, Sumeria in the south.

FOREWORD

This is a work of fiction intended for adults. The beginning times of civilization contained all the seeds and examples of love and compassion, brutality, vengeance, and love of family as now. Some of each will be found in the following pages.

This story is centered primarily in the city-state of Isin. At its apex there were about 20,000 residents living inside its walls with most males required to work in the fields of the temples and palace to grow crops and water the fields. For their labor, they received rations of grain and beer. Isin had become the seat of power in Sumeria in about 2000 B.C.E. after its founding by Isbi-Erra. Lipit-Ishtar established a system of uniform laws, many of which were included later in the Code of Hammurabi. Over time competition erupted between Isin and Larsa, another city to the Southeast. Vying for control of trade routes, access to ore and raw materials, and arable land to put under cultivation became an ongoing source of contention and occasional warfare between the two cities.

The story is told from the perspective of a scribe who refers to himself as Enmerkar the Diviner. He commences each chapter with a comment on the gods or his people. The scribe's account begins:

I am writing this tablet myself. I am now known as Enmerkar, although my birth family called me Bani-mur. I am an <u>ummia</u>, a teacher of student scribes in a civil school, an <u>edubba</u>. I was not born to this role, but earned it by excelling when I was learning the system of writing as a student. Within my family I became known as a diviner of future events, and was therefore called to the service of the Ensi on occasion. I do not claim that gift, which some would call witchcraft, and therefore a curse.

No one has seen all the events of which I speak. This accounting tells of things I know and have seen; others I believe from what has been revealed to me. *My best students in the edubba* prepared *most of these tablets; no one has read all the texts except me, as I had them prepared over time by a series of accomplished scribes as they completed their final exams. Lest I be accused of witchcraft, I inscribed those tablets that suggest the diviner's gift. Under my direction, the texts have been removed far from our land to preserve them; no city remains ascendant forever, and even mine, Isin, will fall eventually. The pride of conquerors leads them to erase the memories of prior kings. My Ensi, Enlil-Bani, is also my father; like the immortal gods, he should be remembered forever. I expect this chronicle to remain hidden for longer than the city walls will stand.*

Signed: Enmerkar, the Diviner.

CHAPTER ONE

TRANSPLANTED

The requirements of the gods for service and entertainment do not cease, not even for grief. This is true for exalted ones as well as commoners; each must serve the gods as their roles demand.

King of Isin for barely five months, Enlil-Bani chose to walk instead of being carried in a palanquin; he intended to inspect the fields of barley owned by the palace and also inspect a newly-constructed wall. He felt most comfortable in this activity, since he had been a supervising groundsman for the temple of Ninisina before he became king.

Six guards surrounded him: two in front, two in the rear, and one at each of his sides but slightly behind him. Each guard bore a shield and wore a sickle sword, as well as carrying a short spear. One of the two front guards led, with the other immediately in front of Enlil-Bani by little more than a pace.

The mid-morning summer air was already sweltering. The king wore a light-weight white linen skirt; a dark maroon shawl was draped over one shoulder, symbolic of wealth, as it sported gold beads along the fringe. His shawl covered a canvas shoulder bag holding such personal items as a knife, a horn cup and his personal drinking straw.

They had exited the main gate of the city well after the throng of field workers had left to tend the fields and ditches. Dust rose from their sandals laden with the odor of pulverized dung from the many dray animals, sheep, and goats intended for market. Enlil-Bani noted a rut in the track that featured a pronounced drop to one side; he started to reflect on all that had occurred to him since his son had suffered an accident at this very spot over a year before.

They had progressed but a little distance from the massive cedar city gate when Enlil-Bani stopped abruptly and called to the lead guard, "Wait, Ansar." The group of guards all stopped short.

Precisely at this moment an arrow angled down past the king's head and pierced through the inner thigh of the guard just ahead of him. The man screamed and pitched face down onto the dirt track. Rolling onto his shoulder, he reached behind him seeking the cause of his torment.

The other guards surrounded Enlil-Bani, holding their shields over him as a barrier, but looking about for the source of their mate's injury.

"Look!" one said pointing over the gates, "There he is!" A dark brown common cowl was seen briefly behind the corrugated brickwork of the city wall before disappearing from view.

Shocked though he was, Enlil-Bani grabbed Ansar's shield and pushed it away. "Help him right now!"

Seeing no threat, Ansar stepped back from the group of guards and dropped his shield to the ground, kneeling to assist the injured guard, who writhed on the ground trying to reach the arrow in his leg.

"Turn to the side, Gula. I'll get it out," Ansar declared. A large pool of blood spread across the ground and was soaking into the soil. The arrowhead had penetrated clear through the man's thigh and was protruding out the front. Blood spurted rhythmically from both front and back of the wound.

Ansar turned Gula onto his back and grasped the shaft as close to the arrowhead as he could manage and used his other hand to brace Gula's thigh. He pulled the arrow out whole through the puncture wound in the front of the leg. Gula screamed again, using both his hands to try to staunch the blood.

"Here! Use this to stop the bleeding!" Enlil-Bani insisted. He thrust the shawl from his shoulder to Ansar, then stood between Gula and Ansar, searching along the length of the city wall while his order was being obeyed.

Nevertheless, within the time it took Gula to take another ten breaths, he was lying pale and lifeless in the dirt.

———————— • ● • ————————

The sentries standing guard in the front of the palace had no reason to even notice a boy carrying his long bundle wrapped in dark cloth. He posed no obvious threat. No one else in the market area paid any attention to him either; he skirted the temporary vendors on their colored mats as he strolled toward the broad avenue that led to the neighborhood where wealthy citizens lived.

———————— • ● • ————————

Tikal entered the palace throne room with an air of authority. He had been Chief Counselor to Erra-Imitti, the former king, for all of that ruler's reign, and considered himself indispensable to Enlil-Bani. Squat in build and free of hair above his waist, even his eyebrows were shaved off. A faint aroma of wild roses emanated from him due to him being rubbed with scented oil each day. Only Tikal himself knew how much responsibility he bore for the ascension of Enlil-Bani to the kingship of Isin, he had become disgusted with Erra-Imitti's selfishness and depredations and poisoned him.

"Shalamu [a greeting meaning 'Peace'], *Ensi.* I've already made inquiries about this aborted attempt on your life." He kept his voice low, noting the locations of the guards in the room, all six of them at some distance from where Enlil-Bani sat on the high-backed, ornately carved throne. Tikal held two arrows in his right hand, down along his thigh; neither held an arrowhead any longer.

Enlil-Bani abruptly held up his hand to stop further conversation. He announced to the guards who were closest, "You two. Go to the entry door and stop anyone from interrupting the Chief Counselor and me. These are private matters." The guards hastened to obey, and Enlil-Bani sat forward on the throne and addressed Tikal.

"Don't try to sweeten the garlic. Are people so afraid of my inexperience they want to prune me away like a sucker growth? Do you think it was really an attempt to kill me?" He indicated with a wave of his hand that Tikal should sit on a close-by bench.

"*Ensi*, only the gods know what they have in mind for you, but I will always give you honesty in my opinions." He looked directly into Enlil-Bani's eyes and continued, "I don't know who shot at your group, but I've not found that the dead guard had enemies. So, yes. I think the arrow was meant for you." Tikal waited just a moment before looking directly toward the doorway and declaring, "I don't think the people of Isin are afraid of you, and few are grieving the death of Erra-Imitti." He hesitated, then added with a sardonic grin, "In my opinion, not even his widow." He waited a moment before continuing, "You agreed early on to start building projects that would protect the city and honor the gods, and the people know that. They've been much impressed by the wall you ordered to be built to divert the spring flood waters from striking the northwest city wall directly, so they know you're thinking of their safety, too."

"That's where I was going when we left Isin this morning; I wanted to see how it was progressing, and to be certain about how high it should be."

The Counselor's forehead wrinkled in response to the king's statement, and said, "How will you know how high it should be, *Ensi*?"

"There's a clear mark on the wall where the last high flood came at us. That should be our guide. The mark's about my height, as I recall."

Tikal nodded, then stood back up and walked toward the ceremonial entry with its full sized *lamassu* looking toward the throne, a deity with a man's head on a winged bull's body, always lighted with a wall torch. He looked out, assuring himself that there was still no one within earshot. He returned and sat back down with the arrows held on his lap.

He continued with another thought, expressed almost off-handedly, saying, "I don't think it's connected, but the one constant question I have heard the people ask about you is why you've not taken another wife. Some think you should do so to create an alliance with another city, but everyone knows your wife was murdered only months ago."

The king frowned and made a gesture with his hand, as if pushing an object down, and said with finality, "I'm not interested, Tikal, you know that." He hesitated before adding, "I wanted no other wife than Lith-el. Still don't."

Tikal responded by holding up both hands and saying, "Understood,

Ensi." He waited a moment before continuing the previous conversation, pointing to the arrow and adding, "I can't deny the danger, Enlil-Bani. I just don't think it's a citizen of Isin. You allowed Erra-Imitti's widow and daughters to stay in the city so her daughters could find suitable husbands. That's all Nisaba cares about, and if there were some plot from her, I'd know it. There's a new boy in the household, probably a slave in training." He looked away before continuing. "Don't concern yourself with how I know."

"I know you're well informed, Tikal, and I trust you. Who does that leave, then? We sent Aga to Larsa, so he's not a threat."

"I don't agree and this is why." He held up the two arrows. "This one's made for a short bow, not battlefield use." The second arrow was longer by as much as the length of a man's open hand from the wrist to the end of the middle finger. Tikal placed the long arrow on the floor and held up the shorter, which still showed blood on its shaft. "This's designed for short range, like an assassin would want. There're no marks to tell us who made it, but," running his finger along the pink cock fletching, "there're no pink ducks. One of my stewards says it comes from a large bird that lives in the marshes south of Ur. No help." He hesitated before continuing, "I apologize for asking, but do you have enemies from your days as lead gardener?"

"No, none I can think of." Enlil-Bani unconsciously felt the twin scars that stood out between his neck and his shoulder, a souvenir of his first battle against Larsa. "When he's feeling better I'll ask Dagan if he knows anyone from my field crews who harbors a grudge, but I was thinking it might be a guard who was friends with Lith-el's murderers. If so, they waited near six months to strike."

"I doubt it. Saman wasn't well liked; the other guards say that crew kept to themselves."

"If this is an attempt on my life, my children may be in danger as well. Send for Nani and Enmerkar at once, so I can be sure they're safe and they can be warned to be especially cautious."

"I'll order it at once, *Ensi.*" Tikal turned to leave through an open portal located behind the throne. With a gesture of his hand he directed the two guards who had been waiting by the *lamassu* to return to their post by the throne.

"Go in peace, Tikal. I'll think about anyone who might want me dead."

"I'll do the same, *Ensi*."

———————————•●•———————————

Nani, Enlil-Bani's daughter, heard the sounds of several people walking in the narrow street in front of her home. She was kneeling in her courtyard grinding barley and listened for them to pass, gladly straightening her back and easing the weight from her knees. After rubbing the fine dust of the ground meal from her hands onto her skirt, she pulled some errant strands of curly black hair back into place under the plain narrow linen headband that served to keep sweat from dripping into her eyes. Her physique was more slender than the typical Sumerian, in keeping with her mother's Semitic heritage, but she was already showing her pregnant state. She became pregnant within a month of wedding her husband, Suba, soon after her father had become the king, and was now a bare five months along.

"Please come to the door." The shout from the street startled her, and she had to remember that both the houses next to hers were empty.

Nani rose to her feet, adjusting her sandals as she walked toward the rear door of her home. She stepped over the worn clay bricks that kept the rains out during the winter season and made her way to the front of the house. She arrived at the door just as the voice sounded again, "Lady Nani, please. I've come from the palace to escort you there."

Nani stepped onto the brick bench that ran along the inside of the front wall of her home, having to angle to one side to avoid her cat, Bibi, who shifted one ear toward her owner, then resumed sleeping. Nani pulled aside the cloth insect barrier and looked out the narrow opening at the alleyway in front of her home; she saw four men in palace uniforms gathered close to her door, each with a shield and spear. A moment of fear tinged with anger sent a clenching gripe into her innards.

"Who wants me? What is wrong?" she inquired, listening closely to assess the tone of the guard's response.

"Your father, the *Ensi*, has sent for you. He sent for your brother as well. Other guards have gone for him, Lady. We weren't told why. Just to bring you."

"Step to the other side of the street, so I can see you all," she ordered. The guards looked at each other in wonder at hearing instructions from the house. The guard who had been speaking to her nodded his assent to the others, and they obeyed.

"Wait there," she demanded.

Nani scooped Bibi into her arms and carried her into the interior of her home, putting the pet down in the doorway of her bedroom. She then stopped briefly in the doorway of the family chapel, the location of Zid-abzu, the household god. The room also held the graves of both her mother and her paternal grandfather. She bowed toward the effigy and with both her hands cupped over her abdomen, murmured, "Zid-abzu, protect me and my child." She then went to the kitchen prep area just inside the courtyard door and selected a medium-sized bronze knife which she slid into a leather scabbard.

She went to the small extra bedroom at the rear of her home and spoke to an elderly woman. "Azuru, auntie, please come to the front door with me."

The crone rose from her bed where she had been sorting linen skeins by color and weight into separate palm baskets for future use in weaving, an activity both she and Nani shared to add to the household income. Azuru had taught Nani's mother, Lith-el, how to weave, and Lith-el had done the same for Nani.

While she led the way through the dark hallway to the entryway, she told Azuru she had been called to the palace. She slipped the knife into a fabric shoulder bag with a green and black beaded design, and then draped a light beige shawl over her shoulders and across her bosom. She hoisted the strap of the bag over her shoulder so that she could reach into the bag easily, and then placed a veil over her lower face, symbolizing that she was a respectable married woman.

Before she opened the door, she picked up a stout hardwood walking stick that could also serve as a cudgel. She opened the door and said to Azuru, "Look at these men, Auntie. Remember their faces. Bar the door behind me until I return. Open it only for me or Suba." Nani was well aware that Azuru could only see clearly close up, but was relying on the likelihood that the guards wouldn't know that.

She stepped out into the lane and closed the door behind her, insisting, "I'll follow you. Proceed."

———— • ● • ————

Enmerkar was flagging in the heat of midday. The strain on his right leg was only moderately helped by the walking sticks he'd been using since his accident two years earlier. He attended with forced interest to the sounds from the homes on both sides of this lane in an upper level residential district, mostly to distract himself from a growing ache above his knee.

Son to Enlil-Bani and Lith-el, he'd been called Bani-mur by them, but his mentor Naram retired from teaching scribes at his *edubba*, and gave those duties over to Enmerkar when he and his wife Uttu adopted him. Enmerkar had been the name of their deceased son, who had died along with his sister during one of the pestilential illnesses that devastated whole cities.

He rested the two canes against his waist while he wiped the sweat from his palms onto his dark green linen skirt and took deep breaths. He was surprised to see six palace guards approaching him at a trot, carrying a litter with a light cane chair and a dusty white canopy, with another guard leading them. He stepped to the side of the residential path to allow them to pass by, but once the lead guard saw him, the men slowed and then halted, placing the litter on the ground after turning it around. Enmerkar recognized the guard in front as one he had seen several times at the palace.

"Shalamu, friend. Where are you going?"

"For you, Enmerkar. The *Ensi* sent for you and wants no delay. Please get into the litter and we will return."

"I was already on my way to see him. Has something happened?"

"I don't ask; when the *Ensi* says go, I go. Tikal said this was his wish, so we're here." The leader plucked a dark gray leather-wrapped bladder full of beer off of the litter and drank from it, placing the wooden plug back into its opening before passing it to the bearers, all of whom drank from it. It was offered to Enmerkar, who accepted it gratefully but drank sparingly before responding.

"My leg is already aching, so blessings on you all." All too aware of his tendency to drag his right foot, he concentrated on lifting it with each step as he got into the long divan chair, placing his canes along the side. The bearers hoisted the litter up to shoulder height and started toward the palace at a trot. Relieved of the grueling walk to the center of Isin, Enmerkar sighed deeply. 'En-me would tell me to welcome the walk to strengthen my leg,' he acknowledged to himself ruefully. His mood brightened at the prospect of seeing En-me, his lover as well as the king's physician, while at the palace.

• ● •

Enmerkar sat sideways to the banquet table on a dining chair facing his father, the king. Supported on another chair, his right leg was elevated on a plain beige bolster. Steaming mugs of antelope broth near both of them, Enlil-Bani's chair was also placed sideways to the table. "I'm told you were already on the path to see me; what would have caused you to make that trip? I know you can't walk for long."

"You know about the dream I had before mother was killed. When I have dreams that seem like warnings, I always wake up with an ache behind my right eye. That happened this morning, and I wanted to tell you about it. I didn't know what the dream meant, and I usually don't. Now that an attack has happened, I understand the dream better."

"Tell me, son."

"I was on the path outside the gates, at the same place where my accident happened, and at first it was just like that time. But then all the workers suddenly changed into soldiers walking in ranks but not marching. You were there, too, but you were between two ranks of soldiers. Then a child in a hooded cape flew over your head on a large heron and tried to drop a spear down on you." Enmerkar thought about the dream a moment before saying, "I woke up when the spear dropped toward you. I couldn't tell if you were hurt, so I needed to come to the palace to see you."

Both Enmerkar and Enlil-Bani sat thinking about the dream; neither spoke for a while.

"I've never had this broth before, father. What makes it different?"

"Zid-tara told me he uses a spice from far south of here along with mashed carrots mixed in. I thought you'd like it, too." The king drank another sip, then added, "I should let you know I've arranged for palace guards to pass by your *edubba* four times a day, and Nani's house as well."

"I do. Like the broth I mean; not as spicy." He thought about the dream again before asking, "Has there been any progress toward finding the archer?"

"No, not yet." Enlil-Bani mused a while, then asked, "Do you know when you started having these dreams?"

"I don't have them often. But I'm sure I never had one before I had that injury when I was a child. I don't actually remember it, but Mother told me when I was eight a donkey broke loose and knocked me into a group of soldiers while one was showing a new knife to his friends. She said it went into my head." Enmerkar pointed to a place at the side of his head above his right ear, now covered with hair. "You were in the temple gardens and she had gone to the market with her father. He took care of the wound himself. As I say, I don't remember it."

The king's brow furrowed as he tried to recall an event that had only been reported to him. Then he lowered his voice and addressed his son, saying, "I had two other reasons for wanting to see you, and the first will have to be just between us. I don't want you in any danger and I'm mindful of your reputation." Enlil-bani looked toward the passage to the main hall to be certain there was no one there. "I know you've had other dreams that foreshadow events that actually occur, like you did when your mother was killed. You had no time to report that then, and I doubt we would have understood it." His voice dropped even lower in volume as he continued, "And now this time. You know as well as I do that there are some priests who would consider your ability sorcery. Sorcery is punished by death! So no one else, even En-me, can know if you have a dream that you think would be warning me or your sister about some danger. But I need to know right away if you have another."

"But Father, I don't live here at the palace and I can't abandon Naram's students, so how can I tell you quickly?"

"I know how it could work." Enlil-bani watched his son's face to gauge his reaction. "I want you to teach me to read. Not like a scribe, of course, but well enough to tell what a palace scribe is doing. So I want you to visit in the morning of every third day and teach me." Enlil-bani reflected a moment, then asked, "Can you do that? I know it will be a hardship, but I'll make it easier by sending a litter for you each way."

"That will be a blessing, father. My leg has never gotten strong, despite the things Muda taught me to do. If I think a dream is urgent I'll send an older student to tell you."

"I'll arrange with Zid-tara so the student can get in quickly." The king stopped and held his palm forward to signal his son to not speak, and then said, "We'll need a reason for these events; no one can know about your dreams."

"I'll say my leg is hurting me cruelly, and I need to see En-me." Enlil-Bani smiled and nodded slowly in assent.

Enmerkar looked toward the ceiling, trying to get a memory to focus in his mind, then said, "I recall that we spent some time teaching you numbers years ago when I'd just started my studies with Naram. Do you remember them?"

"A lot of water has flowed by Isin since then, so I can hardly see those marks in my head. I'll have to start over, I'm sure."

"Then that's what we'll do, father. Start in three days. I'll spend that time planning what you should learn first." He closed his eyes briefly as he thought, then said, "Probably numbers again. When I return, you can tell me how to get my student in to see you without delay."

"I think another factor will speed up your visits if you want to see me in a hurry. I will have the litter stay at your home, so that the bearers only have to carry it one direction. That will look normal since you will visit me regularly anyway."

"Good! It can be kept in the front courtyard."

• ● •

The 'boy' lived in the home of Nisaba, the widow of Erra-imitti, and her two daughters. A very small man, he had arrived several days earlier from Ur, home of the Chaldeans. He placed the bundle just inside the front gate of the front courtyard before entering the house's foyer, whereupon he immediately called out, "I need a servant."

One of Nisaba's male slaves responded from the interior, asking as he approached, "What do you require, Chaldean?"

"I've left a package by the front gate. Carry it carefully and put it in my room."

"What is it?"

"None of your business! Bring it in; I'm tired and will be in my room resting."

The slave watched as the Chaldean left for the sleeping area and waited until he was no longer visible before uttering in a low voice, "Pig turd!"

STAKES

There is a strange habit in how people see the world, both of things and other people; we seem to be ready to see only what we have seen before, so that anything new or different isn't recognized immediately.

Next morning Enlil-Bani woke from a troubled sleep, as he had done ever since he had been thrust into the kingship of Isin. He lay on his back, his hands balled into aching fists crossed tightly across his chest. He tried to ease them by clenching his fists even harder, then relaxing them, repeating the ritual again and again until he felt his fingers respond with less pain.

With his eyes still closed, he unconsciously reached over in the bed to seek the comforting presence of his wife, Lith-el, but found only an empty space. He turned toward where she should have been, but the memory of her murder flooded in on him again, and he woke fully. He shook his head to reject the knowledge of what he knew to be true.

Lith-el had been murdered months before by rogue palace guards during a robbery. The guards had blamed Enlil-Bani's slave Muda for the robbery and murder. As Muda's owner and therefor responsible for his actions, Enlil-Bani was also blamed and condemned to die. All this had happened just before the New Year's celebration. Because the priests had predicted a tragedy would befall king Erra-imitti, Enlil-Bani had been appointed the substitute king of Isin. By hanging the substitute at the end of the day, the gods were supposed to be fooled into thinking the tragedy had occurred, and the king would then resume his normal life. Instead, Erra-imitti had died during the day of the celebration. Tikal, with the support of the high priests of Isin's two temples, announced Enlil-Bani to be the new king, asserting that the gods, who cause everything, willed it so.

Enlil-Bani still felt some satisfaction from having sent the guards who had killed Lith-el to their slow deaths. It had been established during their trial that they had robbed other citizens, and killed at least one other person, by chance Enlil-Bani's elderly neighbor. Despite the recurring ache of grief in his throat and chest, he wondered about what his vengeful reaction meant about the kind of person he truly was.

At times Enlil-Bani still felt like a condemned man, on an endless quest to learn the civic and religious rituals of kingship. He sighed, thinking to himself, 'Lith-el, why aren't you here beside me?'

He had declined to sleep in the bedroom that Erra-imitti had used; instead he had taken as his royal bedroom that of the former queen, Nisaba. The bedchamber was nearly dark as he wakened, with two wall torches close to guttering in the windowless room. They threw dim, flickering light onto the wall with its painted figures of the healer goddess Ninisina, the protector and patron goddess of Isin, with her husband Pabilsag and their son Damu.

After throwing off his linen covers Enlil-Bani swung his feet over the edge of the bed and onto a rug made from a lion's pelt. He reached for the goblet of water on his bedside table and took a sip. Then he rose and walked to a niche in the wall by the doorway; using a splinter from a pile of dried palm frond ribs, he lit two additional oil lamps, holding his breath and fanning the acrid smoke away from his nostrils. He then went into a small alcove, where he urinated into a bitumen-coated basket. Returning to the bed, he sat back down and stretched his back to ease its stiffness.

He resumed drinking while he reflected on a second dream Enmerkar had told him the previous day before returning to the *edubba*. In the dream, which his son had experienced just one night before, Enlil-Bani had been flying like a bat, looking in the streets of Shuruppak, then Uruk, then Larsa, cities he knew to exist south of Isin, but which he had never seen. He was seeking an elusive person, whose form was vague and indistinct, but menacing. Then, as he was hovering over the market of Larsa, a clear voice announced, "Turn back. Turn back." Enmerkar reported at that point he had wakened, feeling more puzzled than threatened.

"Guard, enter," he said loudly. Shortly, a household guard pushed the curtains to the side of the portal, stifling a yawn with the back of his other hand.

"Yes, *Ensi*. How may I serve you?"

"I'm ready to eat." He rubbed his pate and chin and noted the stubble on both, then added, "Send for my barbers, too. They're probably waiting at the palace door. And Tikal will want to know when I'm ready, so ask him to come in when he's ready."

"I'll send the other guard to attend you while I go to the kitchen. Is there anything else?"

Enlil-Bani thought a moment, then replied, "Yes. Send for my physician to see me later."

"Yes, *Ensi*, right away." The guard spun on his heel, rehearsing his tasks as he went.

Enlil-Bani settled himself to wait, leaning against a large bolster he propped against the head of the ornately carved cedar frame of the bed. He sipped wine-infused water while he again reviewed his transformed life, shaking his head slowly. He was still not reconciled to Tikal's speculation that someone had tried to assassinate him the day before.

A guard approached the portal and called him from the hallway. "*Ensi*, your barber is here now and Zid-tara sends word that your meal will be served shortly." The guard who delivered the message remained outside the tightly woven dark maroon curtain. "Is there anything I can do for you right now, *Ensi*?"

"Yes, guard. Bring in Kulla and Mas."

The guard pushed the curtain aside and admitted the two men who accompanied him.

The barber, Kulla, was shorter than the average citizen, dressed in a drab sleeveless tunic that ended at mid-thigh. His stubby fifteen-year-old son Mas was dressed similarly. Both were striking for their complete lack of body hair, with no evidence of nicks or cuts, a testimony to their barber skills. Already an accomplished barber, Mas was still learning the skills for dentistry, a common expectation of the role.

Upon entering both Kulla and Mas bowed, as did the guard, who then took up his post at the doorway. Without further pleasantries, Kulla spread a tightly woven square cloth over the floor tiles about a long stride from the foot of the bed then moved a wooden stool from near the wall by the alcove to set it on the middle of the cloth.

The guard watched the setup, then asked, "What can I do for you, *Ensi*?"

"I won't need protection from Kulla. Add some oil to those two lamps, guard, then send someone to Dagan's quarters and ask if he and Nintud would join me for breakfast. I'd like to see them." Dagan was the king's friend of many years, who had moved into the palace at Enlil-Bani's invitation; Nintud was his wife. They were now childless, since their one daughter had died in a bizarre accident during the previous year.

"Nintud told the other guard that Dagan's affliction has returned and he is suffering again this morning, but hopes to be better later on. She humbly asks to be excused."

"Then go and be sure the kitchen is providing whatever food they'd like."

Enlil-Bani was already sitting on the stool Kulla had moved onto the drop cloth, and closed his eyes in appreciative anticipation of this service.

Using sesame oil to lubricate the face and head, Kulla used a slender yellow obsidian blade to start removing Enlil-Bani's head hair and facial stubble, intending to leave only the eyebrows. His son watched attentively, and as soon as his father was done with a section, he used a clean soft linen cloth to wipe off the remaining oil. Leaning close to the king's ear, Mas then volunteered in a low voice, "I am hearing more talk about Larsa, *Ensi*. People know you sent Erra-Imitti's son there as an emissary. Nevertheless, most of Isin thinks the Larsan merchants who come here are spies, reporting to their *Ensi* on our city." Larsa, a city to the south and east, was a generations-old contender for supremacy in Sumeria, and Isin's recurrent foe.

"What do you hear from the people in the square, Kulla? And Mas, if you've heard something different, tell me." He kept the volume of his voice low, and refrained from mentioning the theoretical attempt on his life from the day before, as Tikal was opposed to letting that prospect be known to anyone else.

Kulla answered in a similarly low voice, paying close attention to the working of his blade as he considered his response, while listening for sounds in the hallway.

"What I've heard is that there are people who're anxious that you've become *Ensi*. Since you weren't born to lead a city and have no experience at it, they're afraid you'll make some awful mistake. Others are pleased that the maintenance of the walls and temples aren't being neglected. Some fear that we will be surprised by an attack, and there are still some who worry about angering the gods with the trick that was played on them during the New Year celebration." Kulla was noted in the square for his garrulous manner and ready wit, and had been Enlil-Bani's barber for years. Now that Enlil-Bani was king, he was more reserved with him, but felt honored by being used to keep Isin's ruler informed about his fellow commoners. His compensation by the palace was a consideration, plus he was now getting more business from other wealthy citizens, serving them in their homes and being able to spend less time in the heat of the market square.

Kulla had just finished shaving the back of Enlil-Bani's neck when Zid-tara arrived, followed by three male kitchen slaves carrying trays of food, plus an attendant steward, a commoner but not a slave. The slaves waited in the hallway while Zid-tara, who was both the Chief Steward and supervisor of the palace kitchen entered, bowing. Zid-tara was bare above the waist except for a gold medallion worn as a necklace, which signified his rank. He, too, was clean shaven all over his upper body and head. The slaves were equally bare, except for their hair, shaved except for the topknot that signified their slave status. Each wore a uniform dark walnut brown work skirt that ended just above the ankles.

"May the gods be with you, *Ensi*. Where would you like to be served this morning?"

"Shalamu, Chief Steward. One moment, please." Mas finished wiping off Enlil-Bani's neck and shoulders while his father shaved off the sparse hair on his chest.

The King got up from the stool and walked over to the bed to wait while Kulla and Mas gathered the drop cloth and their tools. "Thank you," said Enlil-Bani. "Come back in five days, Kulla. Bring Mas with you."

Enlil-Bani turned to Zid-tara as the barbers left the room and said, "I want to eat in sunlight, Zid-tara. I'm like a date palm; I need light. Where's that possible, Zid-tara?

I'm in the palace all day long most days, and I'm used to working outside. It's cool in the palace, but dark. I'm like a prisoner, except for the food."

Zid-tara was nonplussed at this request, but recognized that Enlil-Bani was asserting his new status more and more, and becoming more confident that such minor preferences would be taken as commands. He thought quickly about the physical structure of the palace, which he knew intimately, and knew that Tikal would object to the only possible solution to this request.

"*Ensi*, the palace has only one courtyard, and that's the one next to the kitchen, where the ovens and fruit trees are. You'd have to go through the kitchen where the slaves and stewards work to get there. It wouldn't be proper."

"I understand your point. Well, today's food's here already, so I'll eat here today. Nevertheless, I'll talk with Tikal about how to create such a place."

Zid-tara directed the slaves at setting up the meal on a table near the doorway. Once the food was set out, the slaves withdrew, squatting along the wall outside in the hall.

The steward picked up an armless chair and brought it to the table. Spreading a cloth over the back and down onto the seat as a cushion, he then waited for Enlil-Bani to sit. As soon as the king started eating the steward went to the bed, where he levelled and smoothed the barley-hull stuffed mattress and the covers. He said nothing, but returned to the table, trying to anticipate when to re-fill the King's goblet with hot spiced broth or serve more of the wheat cakes and honeyed dates that his lord wanted each day for his first repast. Despite the abundance of food that had been prepared and brought to the bedroom, Enlil-Bani ate but little, and only held onto the goblet, waving away the balance of the food after only a few bites.

"Is Tikal here yet, Zid-tara?" he called.

"I hear someone, *Ensi*, but I don't know who it is."

Rather than Tikal, En-me, the king's personal *a-zu*, approached the doorway from the end of the hall near the entrance to the royal quarters, having just returned from breakfast with the household stewards. He waited for the steward to remove the remains of the king's repast before he stepped inside the bedroom and bowed.

En-me had the typical large Sumerian nose and was of ordinary size, but his arms and fingers were unusually long and he favored his right ankle due to a childhood accident. His complexion was vaguely lighter than the typical tan, hinting at a Gutian in his distant parental forebears, and his eyes were chronically bloodshot.

"Shalamu, *Ensi*. Tikal told me to tell you he'd be here soon. Are you in pain, *Ensi*?"

"No more than usual, En-me. That's not why I wanted to see you." Enlil-Bani stood up from the chair, raised his arms over his head and stretched, arching his back, then walked back over to the bed and sat back down, leaning against the bolster propped against the wall. Holding them out to demonstrate to En-me, he noted, "My hands have served me in the gardens and the fields every day of my thirty-eight years, and they complain." He examined his hands, front and back, but then shrugged his shoulders with acceptance and re-affirmed the common explanation for the cause of both human and natural events, though without conviction, "The gods so chose. No, I wanted to ask whether there is anything wrong with Enmerkar. He seemed in a hurry yesterday, as well as being tired from starting the unexpected walk. I know you love my son and spend many nights together."

En-me sniffed and swallowed before explaining, "This is the time for testing the senior students at the *edubba*. After yesterday's attack, he may not have mentioned that. I've barely spent any time with him for the last eight days, and I miss him, too."

"How long 'til the tests are done?"

"Another couple days, I think. Naram's wife is still running the household, but Naram has given up teaching students and is working on a catalog of all our gods and goddesses." He hesitated before emphasizing, "Really! All the gods and goddesses! I would have thought the temple scribes would do that. So the teaching's all on Bani-mur now." He let a frown pass over his face, recognizing that he had used Enmerkar's original family name, then brightened and said, "I'll visit him today and tell him he's missed by both of us. How is Nani? I didn't have a chance to see her yesterday."

"Nani's settling in to married life but she still misses her mother." The king massaged his hands before adding, "I'm glad she has Azuru to keep her company while Suba works at the market."

"We all miss Lith-el, *Ensi*." He hesitated by sniffing and swallowing again, but then inquired, "How is Azuru? I last saw her at Nani's wedding and she looked frail."

"I think she's fading, as we all do when we get to her age. She's seen over sixty summers, now." Enlil-Bani looked down at the reed covering on the floor, and sighed. "Lith-el loved her like a mother, and she was very kind to me."

The guard at the door stepped just inside the passage and announced, "*Ensi*, Tikal approaches."

"Thank you, guard. Send him right in." Rising from the bed, Enlil-Bani placed his hand on En-me's chest saying, "Invite Enmerkar to join me for a meal as soon as he can get free. May the gods give you peace, En-me."

"And also to you, *Ensi*," replied his *a-zu*. He exited just moments before Tikal entered.

"Shalamu, *Ensi*," Tikal said, bowing automatically. "I've already spoken with Zid-tara about your desire to have a space where you can enjoy your first meal in the light of the sun." He hoisted the chair that the king had used at his breakfast and pulled it to where he could sit facing Enlil-Bani. The king became conscious of Tikal's scented body oil.

"Erra-Imitti was usually too hot to voluntarily spend any time outside the palace that he didn't have to, so he would never have wanted such a place. It would have to be protected, of course, especially since we don't know the source of the threat to you."

"Of course. But even if it's temporary, I'd be grateful. With all the official requirements, I'm like a slave to the role of *Ensi*."

"You've always been a responsible person, *Ensi*. I learned that about you after the gods put you on the throne." Tikal was being less than forthcoming; he had learned much about Enlil-Bani prior to Erra-Imitti's death. "They recognized that you would accept your position with the diligence that is needed." He rose and stepped toward the doorway and offered, "I'll take a look about the palace with your desire in mind."

"There's another thing on my mind, if you will listen, Tikal." Enlil-Bani's brow was furrowed with lines, and he crossed his arms over his chest.

"I am always at your service. What's troubling you?"

Enlil-Bani went to the doorway and sent the sentry down the hall before he settled back down on the bed. "Sit with me, please."

Tikal did as he was asked, accepting it as an order from his king. Enlil-Bani started his comment slowly, taking care to express his exact feelings and concerns.

"It's been over four months since Lith-el was murdered and I was given the throne of Isin. I've done my best to do what the gods and the people expect of me, and with your guidance I've been pleased to be able to make some improvements to our city. What weighs on me is how I dealt with my wife's murderers." He paused, looking first toward the ceiling, then at the floor, then abruptly looked straight into Tikal's eyes before continuing.

"I think of myself as a gentle man. I don't make rash decisions, and I'm not easily offended. I try to think out what will be the results of my acts. As much as I was grieving at the trial of the robbers, I tried to distinguish between those two that were just there for the robbery and the two who were responsible for killing Lith-el. They all deserved to die, and I don't regret that. But…" The king hesitated and his voice dropped in volume before he declared, "Isme and Saman died horribly by my sentence, confirmed by the Council. But I know that Lith-el wouldn't have approved of what I did." He paused with his brow creased and his mouth turned down at the corners and made himself remember the sight of the two murderers, staked in a seated position, their hands cut off then seared, both to stop the bleeding and so they couldn't defend themselves. Their bellies had been cut open to allow the pigs and dogs to feed on their entrails easily. What had sickened Enlil-Bani at the time was the sight of the birds feeding on the men's faces.

He shook his head to dispel the vision he had conjured, then added, "So I wonder about myself, what I'm really like. Am I truly fit to be *Ensi*? When we say, 'The gods so chose,' aren't we just excusing ourselves, claiming it's the gods who're responsible? When are we responsible? Should I have blamed the gods for her death?" He put his hand on Tikal's shoulder and implored, "Tell me, honestly, Chief Counselor. What do you think?"

Tikal had asked himself the same questions before he poisoned Erra-imitti, and had arrived at decisive answers for himself, so he was prepared to respond without revealing too much.

"My *Ensi*, let me say when I give you advice, I hold myself responsible for what I say. Do I think some god has put words in my mouth, and so I'm not really to blame if I'm wrong, the god is? No. I make choices based on what I know. Or what I think. Or what I believe is so. What else do we have to go on in life? The priests tell us all the time that the *igigi,* the ancient gods, set the world into motion and control the events of men and the natural forces of the world they created." Then he lowered his voice and said earnestly, "Too many gods!" he declared. "I know I'm speaking blasphemy when I say that the priests use the gods to explain what they can't predict or control, so 'the gods' interfered. That's really how you became *Ensi,* because the priests didn't get their prediction right!"

The Chief Counselor made a sweeping motion with his hand that was closest to the king and then asked, "Is that why you climb the zigurrat steps every evening? The people believe you're very devout, though I've never asked you. Ningal the priest told me you've passed him and his helper several times when they were on their way up to study the stars' movements and you were going back down."

"Yes, in part," the king answered. "If I can serve Isin better by conferring with the two goddesses in their temples, I'm happy to do that, plus it keeps me active. I used to walk long distances when I was a temple groundsman."

Satisfied, Tikal settled back on the bed, as he had been hunched forward during the conversation. "As far as Isme and Saman are concerned, no one is blaming you for seeking righteous vengeance. They were evil men, and your sentence showed the city that evil will be dealt with decisively, without mercy. Be merciful on another occasion, if you wish. I'm confident that you'll choose some citizen who is deserving of mercy, but those two weren't. The decisions are yours; you're the *Ensi* of Isin."

* ● *

After leaving Enlil-Bani, En-me the *a-zu* went as directly as possible through the maze-like hallways of the palace to the quarters that had been granted to Dagan and his wife, Nintud. The royal household area contained a set of four halls branching off from the king's living space, each with its own variety of suites, some small, a few others quite elaborate.

Dagan had been Enlil-Bani's best friend and co-worker for many years, and the two families had recently lived next to each other for several months after the accidental death of Dagan and Nintud's daughter, and until Lith-el's death. Upon becoming king, Enlil-Bani had elevated

Dagan's status to that of a site inspector for the palace's grain fields. Dagan was well experienced due to his years as assistant to Enlil-Bani, supervisor of Ninisina's temple's wheat, barley, and flax holdings. Dagan had lately had a relapse of an affliction to his legs and insides, worse than the first bout he had suffered the previous year. He suffered severe itching from lesions on his legs and cramps in the lower abdomen.

En-me called his greeting to Dagan's wife at the entrance to their apartment before entering, "Shalamu, Nintud," expecting her to be awake, while Dagan might have gained merciful sleep.

"Shalamu, En-me. Please enter, quietly." Her voice was just two notches above a whisper, signifying to En-me that Dagan slept.

He entered and without preamble asked, "Did Dagan sleep last night?"

"But little," she responded, "despite the lotion you gave him. Itching was less, but the gods afflicted him in the belly, and his piss is dark. He drinks little; it hurts him to pass water. Do you know what causes it?"

Seated on a small cot in the anteroom to their chambers, Nintud was a slender woman with dark eyes; they were puffy and the corners of her mouth were turned down. Her simple tunic was a demure dark brown. She had been sitting up leaning against the wall, listening for any sound from her husband, not lying down.

En-me placed his hand on Nintud's shoulder and sighed sympathetically in response to her report, then walked over to a rough clay pitcher sitting in its three-legged wooden support stand on a nearby table; he hefted it by its hatch-marked neck, since there was no handle.

"When he wakes, tell him he must drink the contents of this pitcher not less than twice a day. It will probably ease the griping in his belly after a day or two." He turned to leave her, but turned back at the doorway focusing on the seemingly permanent wrinkles etched into the woman's forehead and around her eyes, warning, "You need sleep as much as he does, Nintud. And food, too. Even if he doesn't want to eat, you need to. You're a good wife, but Dagan won't be helped by you wearing yourself out." Then he added, "Ask your gods for help, but after you've slept."

He could hear her crying softly as he re-entered the hallway.

— • • —

The Chaldean looked like a muscular boy, with typical dark skin. A braided beige headband held his matted hair in place and an ordinary ankle length tunic covered his body. Even those near him could not tell that his facial hair had been plucked out and the hair under his arms burned off to hide his age, a full twenty-three summers. As tall as a girl of eight years, his nose was a bit smaller and his lips fuller than that of a typical male of Isin; his forearms showed the sinewy definition of rigorous use.

Early in the morning, five days after the attack on the king, many city vendors were arranging their foodstuffs and hard goods for easy viewing, and some traders were still arriving from outside the city walls. Some early patrons were starting to bargain in the coolest part of the morning, though the day was already quite warm. The locations of the butcher shops, the bakeries, and the spice and oil merchants were familiar to the wives and slaves who milled about, each seeking an advantageous position to start negotiating for what they wanted. Many shoppers carried packets of grain of variable sizes for paying, others had small purses holding silver coils or discs.

Human voices mixed with the bleats, cackles and brays of creatures in the square. Except for some crones, each veiled woman was accompanied by a male, often an older man or a boy still too young to work in the ditches, fields, or gardens.

The diminutive man stood with his back to the corner of a stall that sold baskets and small rugs made of palm fronds. Shielding his eyes from the sun rising in front of him, he looked about as if searching for someone in the growing throng of shoppers. In reality, his eyes frequently shifted to watch the front of the palace across the square, noting the positions of the guards although their placement seldom changed. The sentries made their observation of the market throng obvious, and they had a clear sight advantage due to their height above the square; this was especially so for the archers who watched from the balcony over the ceremonial entrance door.

The man maintained his gaze toward the palace with difficulty due to the glare of the risen sun, so he moved to his right and closer to the palace, the object of his interest, being careful to avoid contact with anyone. Once he reached the edge of the growing collection of patrons, as if he had remembered something, he moved with a purposeful stride to the steep stairway leading to the first level of the zigurrat. Treading carefully to avoid tripping on his tunic as he mounted the steps, he moved upward alongside a few worshippers intent on making sacrifice to one of the two goddesses whose temples graced the top of the man-made mountain that was the zigurrat. Ninisina's temple *Egal-mah* shared the top with that of Inana, called *E-sig-mese-du*.

He stopped and feigned breathlessness once he had attained the first level of the mount, allowing those ascending the stairs to move past him. From there he looked to his right toward the front and side of the palace, memorizing the path that led around the south-east side of the two-story structure. He paid close attention to a courtyard with fruit trees along the outer wall. He remained in place long enough to note that palace workers occasionally entered the area but none remained for long, skirting the edges to remain in the shade as long as possible.

Seeing no one else ascending or descending toward him at the moment, he made sure he wasn't being watched, then sat on a step and re-positioned the bronze dagger in its sheath that was cinched close to the inside of his lower right leg. Its blade no longer than his diminutive hand and fingers, it was slender and sharp on both edges.

"Make way! Step aside!"

A young scribe called out to those below him on the stairway. He carried a heavy bag on his back, and was leading an older man who wore a conical hat on his head and a robe with painted stars and moon phases. Clearly a priest, he followed the scribe with one hand on the youngster's shoulder; it was then that the small man noticed that the priest was blindfolded with several thicknesses of dark cloth around his eyes. The priest followed the scribe to the last set of stairs, staying well away from the edge of the steps as they were without rails or walls; the two made their way down to ground level, and then turned left toward the administrative compound for their temple.

The man intercepted a young woman who was carrying a bundle before she reached the second level of stairs and, keeping his voice high to simulate his pretended youth, asked her, "Who is that, lady?"

"That's Ningal, the priest." She sat her burden on the brick landing, glad of the chance to rest. She wiped her brow and adjusted her veil and then continued, "He goes to the top of the zigurrat every night, attended by his scribe. The scribe's an apprentice priest. They watch what the stars are doing. Sometimes that's how we mortals can learn what the gods are planning. The scribe records all the changes they see on his tablets, I'm told, and that's what's in the bag he was carrying."

"But why's he blindfolded? That's dangerous. Can't he see, or does the scribe tell him what he sees?"

"Oh yes, he can see. I asked my brother, who's also a priest of that temple, that same question. He told me Ningal believes that his vision is better at night if he hasn't been out in the sunlight, so he blindfolds himself as soon as the stars disappear when the sun god comes up in the morning. He takes the blindfold off once he is down below and back inside."

"Thank you, lady. I just thought it was curious." He shook his head in wonder.

Having gained as much information as he felt was possible on this foray, he carefully made his way back down the stairway. Once he reached the ground, he made his way through the crowd to exchange two packets of barley the size of a grown man's fist for two cold boiled duck eggs, a fried barley cake and a serving of beer. He moved over to the shade of the zigurrat and sat, eating, thinking and watching the crowd.

Nani sat on a brick bench in her home chapel, naked above the waist, her back against the cool wall with her bare feet on the floor mat, facing her household god, Zid-abzu.

Shorter in height than a woman's forearm, the effigy had a rudimentary human body. Formed from a light gray smooth clay, with arms at the sides and an ochre-colored cloth garment, the god's oval eyes were the most arresting feature. Carved from mother-of-pearl and set into the clay forming the head, the eyes dominated the god's face, expressing the ability to see into the family's situation and know what gods could intervene in any matter of difficulty. Glittering from the light of the ceremonial flame, with holes representing the irises, the eyes were set over a hollowed out portion of the head, giving the illusion of concentration and innate wisdom. The carved headdress was like a flattened turban, completely circling the head, and was painted the same yellow color as the robe. The ears were also dominant, overly large for hearing the pleas of the family members; ear holes pushed into the clay promised attentiveness by *Zid-abzu*.

Nani's fingers were interlaced across her swollen belly, and she spoke aloud to the effigy on its altar.

"What can I do to help father? He has an enemy, as you must know, and what if there's more than one? He asked for your help with the gods, but is there something I can do? Iskur should be with him, he's a warrior, but an arrow from afar could reach him without warning. I feel like I'm doing less than nothing, just waiting. Bani-mur must feel the same way even though he's started visiting to teach father to read. I'd do something like that, if I could think of something. Please guide me, Zid-abzu. Please." She never thought of her brothers Zambiya or Enmerkar by their adopted names; she still thought of them by their original names, Iskur and Bani-mur, respectively.

She wiped a tear of frustration from her cheek with the back of her hand. It was then that she noticed that her hands were still powdered with barley that she had ground earlier. She rose and bowed slightly to the god, then turned toward the place in the floor where her mother Lith-el was buried, and spoke again. "I miss you so much, mother. Be at peace."

She left the chapel and slipped back into her sandals, then went to the pantry room next to the courtyard and poured herself a draught of warm beer, her second since her husband Suba had left for his pottery shop in the merchant square. It was still midmorning and she had already ground the day's grains into meal. She sucked up the beer with her silver straw until it was gone; Enlil-Bani had given her and Suba matching silver straws as part of their wedding gifts.

Before she had become aware of her pregnant state and until very recently, she would kneel on the ground to grind grain, but recently had begun using the gritty solid brick table next to her cooking oven and hearth to do that work, hoping that her ankles would not swell as much. Now she stood in the doorway to the courtyard, still in the shade of the interior but with much better light, and appraised the swelling in her hands and fingers. With a sigh, she clenched her fists and raised her hands high over her head, waiting several moments before putting them down and observing with some satisfaction that they were returning to their normal slender state. She pushed aside the heavy woven doorway screen and entered sideways, letting it fall back across the frame to reduce hot air from entering her home.

With an almost instinctive knowledge of the time of day, Nani started ambling toward her craft room, formerly her bedroom. She and her husband now shared the larger bedroom that had been her parents'. Then she continued on to the last room at the end of the short hall. "Auntie," she called. "Feeling better?"

"Don't worry about me, little one. I'm just resting; I didn't sleep well." Azuru's voice was weak and tremulous, but she made an effort to sound strong, adding, "I'll join you if you have a midday meal. I'll be better then, I'm sure."

"If you're not feeling better by then, I'll ask Suba to have En-me come by tomorrow, if he can. Rest now."

Nani returned to her craft room and lit two wall torches using a sliver of palm frond to transfer flame from the one in the hallway, then sat and resumed weaving on a backstrap loom. She wanted to complete another colorful fringe strip, her specialty, to be bartered at the market stall run by Suba and his father. She sighed again, refreshing her prayer to Zid-abzu.

• ● •

The former king's widow, Nisaba, called to her first daughter. "Rida, where is your sister? And where is that stunted Chaldean?" She left the central public room of her home and walked into the dining area.

Sherida, sixteen years old and buxom like her mother, came into the room from the hallway that led to the bedrooms, trying to tame her thick, curly hair with a dark tortoise-shell comb and said, "I don't know where he is now, mother. I heard him tell one of the slaves he was going to the square for some food."

"We have food here, lots of it," the portly woman responded irritably. "I still don't know why your brother sent that runt of a man to stay with us. But it was good to hear from Aga. I'm glad he's being treated well in Larsa. And your sister?"

"Nina's in the courtyard by the duck pen. She's taking care of that blind duckling, because the other ducks get its food. I think she treats it too much like a pet."

Scowling, Nisaba retorted, "And I think you spend too much time thinking about your sister and not enough practicing the lute. I heard you playing yesterday, and it wasn't pretty." She waved her hand in dismissal, causing her daughter to sigh and leave the room, walking toward the food prep area. At that moment, the Chaldean came into the room from the front entry; he removed his headband and greeted Nisaba, who had her back to him.

"Shalamu, lady. Sorry to miss breakfast with you. I enjoy your genteel manners, and your daughters', too. They remind me of the Larsan palace. My stay here has been most pleasant. I had hoped to end my visit soon, but it's not looking so." The Chaldean's vocabulary was ordinary with formal phrasing but with an exotic character to his spoken inflections and pacing.

Nisaba turned toward him and started at his appearance. "Why are you dressed like a waif? You have fine clothes, I've seen them. What are you up to?"

"Aga has given me duties in the city while I'm here, but once they're concluded I will return to Larsa. He told me not to bring attention to myself nor to your family. I'm just following his orders."

"What are you doing that I couldn't arrange?"

"He insisted that he wanted to surprise you, so I can't say. Please excuse me, lady, and I'll get into my regular clothes before the midday meal."

Just then Ninegala, the twelve-year-old daughter came into the home from the courtyard, pausing in the doorway long enough to let her eyes adjust to the dimmer light of the interior rooms. Unlike her sister, she was slender and long-legged, with delicate features and long straight hair, held in place by two tortoise-shell combs just behind her ears. Her arms revealed muscles that showed the definition of regular and specific exercise. The light of the outdoors behind her made her filmy white tunic almost disappear, displaying the shape of her newly adolescent body.

The Chaldean paused before exiting to watch her surreptitiously; he greeted her with a throaty, "Shalamu, young lady."

Nisaba had been watching her daughter; she adjusted her pendulous gold and lapis necklace higher on her neck but turned to watch the short man exit the room. Still musing about Aga's assignment to the Chaldean, she murmured to herself, "Mysterious."

———◆●◆———

Nani and Suba sat on the mud brick bench along the exterior wall of their courtyard. It was after their evening meal, and both were sipping beer through long reed straws since their silver ones were shorter; the dull gray earthen jug of beer rested between them on the bench. Suba was a lean young man, serious of mien and well-respected as a craftsmen and artist in his father's pottery shop.

Suba slapped a mosquito that had settled on his forearm and wiped away the carcass along with the blood the creature had extracted. He turned his body to face Nani more directly and commented, "When we were courting, in the early days, I told my mother that I must be favored by the gods, because you liked me as much as I liked you." He watched carefully to appraise Nani's expression before continuing. "But I've not felt that way as much since your mother was killed during the robbery. With a baby on the way, I wish I could get that feeling back."

Nani adjusted her position as well, and put her hand on his, saying, "I've been the same. When I was just a daughter in my parent's home, and the youngest child as well, I believed our family was blessed. Father was a lead gardener for a temple, so he could bring home the same kind of vegetables and fruits that the priests were served, even if they had blemishes. And mother's father and her brothers were doing well as traders, so they often gave us exotic foods from afar, like real grape wine. We always had honey, and mother was given fine imported fabrics for her weaving projects." She looked pensive, then added, "I think I will always miss my mother, and sometimes even now I'm shocked when I think I hear her in another room and have to remember it's Azuru, not mother." Quickly wiping away tears from her eyes, she forced herself to smile at her husband and patted her abdomen. "You're a blessing to me, and I want our child to feel the same joy in life that we had back then."

Suba looked out toward the direction of the western city wall and the diminishing light in the sky, and hoped aloud, "Perhaps the feeling will return to us, dear wife." He put his straw down into the pot and caressed Nani's cheek, then her hair, then raised her hand to his mouth and kissed it.

CHAPTER THREE

INFERTILE SOIL

People think their last memory of a place or a person will be what they find when they meet them next. Everything is changing, yet we expect constancy.

Zambiya, Enlil-Bani's step-son, strode along the dusty and rutted track that paralleled a nearly unbroken thicket of tall dust-clad green reeds twice the height of a man. Closer than the reeds, low tan bushes grew on the east side of the trail. He could hear the constant sound of rushing water from the swift-flowing, tumultuous *Idiglat* (Tigris) river just past the reed forest and noted with satisfaction the accompanying variety of bird songs and cries.

He was followed at a distance of several yards by the contingent of guards and merchants who comprised the caravan. They had left Isin shortly after the vernal equinox with a dual charge from Enlil-Bani: first to return a former slave, Muda, to his Gutian home across the river, and second, to renew partnerships with traders in manufactured and raw materials far to the north. Having completed both, the caravan was now returning. Within less than a month the caravan members expected to return to their home city.

To his rear Zambiya could hear the barrage of sounds from his caravan, the men and their beasts as well. They disturbed the dry ground beneath their feet, which rose into the air like a fine dry mist to settle onto everyone. By walking in front, Zambiya avoided much of the dust. Looking as far as he could down the trail, he noted how groups of birds launched themselves off the reed shafts as the sounds of metal weapons and dray animal hoofs reached them. Reminded of how his mother had enjoyed watching the birds around their home, he felt a pang of sorrow on recalling her murder. Lith-el, his mother, had been the last person who called him by his birth name of Iskur. Once he became a palace guard, Enlil-Bani, his half-brother Enmerkar, and half-sister Nani had acquiesced to calling him by his new identity of Zambiya.

Even after these months, he found himself marveling at the sudden transformation in his circumstances. Within a day he had changed from being a lower-level guard in the palace of Erra-imitti to being step-son of the new king, Enlil-Bani. Within days after that he had married Ezina, a novitiate priestess, after finding that she was pregnant with his child. By now she was about seven months along.

Zambiya slowed his pace as the heat of the day rose, observing with fascination a newly formed dust-spirit dancing across the ground in the middle distance. Myth held these to be drunken lesser gods that visited the world of people but, uncomfortable with the solidity of earth, they lurched along the ground from one side to the other and returned again, finally dissolving into non-corporeal essence. Such visitations were common enough, but always drew Zambiya's attention. He breathed in deeply, appreciating the aroma of the nearby reeds, like a mix of dust and spice.

Initiated by Zambiya, every day's travel started as soon as it was light enough to see, with even their first cold meal deferred until mid-morning so they could travel as far as possible in cooler temperatures. Now it occurred to him that it was time for the first food break. He looked past the river vegetation, seeing the low hills rising above the plain on which the caravan walked. He remembered that they were nearing the river crossing they had used to escort Muda to his winter village.

A hint of movement to his right caught his attention, and he looked closely toward the sandy plain beyond the irregular path on which he walked, at first detecting nothing that was moving. Caution and vigilance were like second nature to him now, as this arid country held dangers from both creatures and people.

He moved slowly in the direction of the motion he felt he had seen, and was about to dismiss his perception as nothing more than morning wind blowing the dun-colored sand.

Just as he was about to abandon his search, not more than three yards away, a full-grown horned viper the length of a man's arm raised up from the loose grains of the ground, almost indiscernible from the black-speckled sand in which it lay.

Without further thought, he dried his sweaty left hand on the skirt at his hip and reached for the leather-wrapped hardwood handle of the sickle sword that hung from his belt, its bronze blade projecting from the dark wood to behind his body. Keeping the serpent in his sight, he removed the sword from its carrier with his right hand.

He moved in a closing circle around the creature. With two black spiky horns protruding from above its round eyes as if the spikes grew from the eyes themselves, the viper turned toward him.

Zambiya took two swift steps to get behind the snake, and with a practiced move, swung his sword in an arc, severing the head and a handspan of the stout body from the rest; both parts immediately commenced writhing as if trying to find the other to re-connect. Satisfied, Zambiya returned to the middle of the track and continued on.

After only another dozen yards progress he raised his his right hand to signal those behind him to pay attention, but instead of stopping and turning around, he slowed his pace and continued to fix his gaze on the track ahead, seeing a man in the distance. He heard the men behind him slow their approach, then saw the distant figure on the trail move in his direction.

Zambiya turned around and beckoned one of the guards to join him at the front of the caravan.

"Look down the trail, Nabi. Do you see anyone but him? If he's a scout for a bandit band, I want to be ready for them."

Nabi shielded his eyes with his hand to his forehead to reduce the glare of the sky and stared down the track, trying to detect any movement in the brush that would indicate more than the one man. Nabi was a short, squat and husky guard who had been part of the palace crew before joining this trek. His neck was short and his nose was bulbous; he had a reputation for preferring beer to food, though he partook of large quantities of both whenever he could. Satisfied that there were no obvious disturbances in the reeds, he replied, "No, Zambiya. He's walking toward us, but he's pretty far. Shall I go ask him his business?"

"No. Wait here and watch, and get our group in a defensive formation.

Get an archer up here, ready to cover me if there is trouble. If nothing's wrong, we'll eat here."

Zambiya walked slowly toward the man while Nabi followed orders; moving among the members of the caravan, he alerted them that it was time for their meal, but that someone was approaching them from further down the trail. Nabi was the only other sentry who bore a sickle sword, as he and Zambiya had been palace guards. There had not been any trouble with raids from Hurrians or other scavenging tribes during this trip, but it was not an uncommon danger along this route. Although they weren't soldiers or guards, the merchants and pack leaders were all armed with axe or spear or cudgel, and expected to fight if attacked. Everyone carried some form of knife, bronze or obsidian, for use as a tool or weapon. Two men in addition to Nabi were known to have some skill as archers.

Once the pack animals had been corralled into a central area, the men arranged themselves so that one would be getting their trail food together, (cold flat barley cakes baked the night before, and either dried fish or meat, plus water or beer), while another stood watch. There was no point building a fire at this time of the day.

The eight guards assembled toward the front of the group; Nabi remained in front of the formation, awaiting further instructions from Zambiya, who still stood observing the distant figure. Though Nabi remained alert, he took a palm-sized fine grit stone from his waist bag and used it to sharpen the blade of his sword as he rejoined Zambiya. He had acquired the stone on this caravan, in the northern country, and was proud of how sharp he was able to make his blade. Stone was absent from Isin and the southern part of the land.

"Nabi, look closely, now. Does he look familiar to you?"

"Yes, but I don't know why. He's taking his time to get here. I still don't see any sign of anyone else, and the birds don't seem disturbed. If there were men in the brush, the birds'd be flying about."

"Right. Still seems familiar. You stay here; I'm going to go talk to him."

Zambiya retrieved his hiking staff from Nabi, who had been carrying it over his shoulder via a looped leather sling attached to the shaft, and propped it against his shoulder. Lifting both his hands to shield his eyes as he peered down the trail he suddenly laughed and said to Nabi, "I'm pretty sure that's Muda. That's his red hair, I'd bet a night with Inana," he said, referring to a goddess known for her sexual appetites. He hoisted his staff and said, "I'll go greet him and find out why he's here. Tell the others to relax and eat their meal."

Zambiya moved down the trail at a half trot, covering most of the distance in a short while, and quickly confirmed that the man was his family's former slave. When he thought he was at a point where he could be heard he shouted, "Muda. I'm happy to see you, my friend."

Muda continued toward Zambiya, trudging along the trail and waving his staff. The two men finally were close, and each put a hand on the other's breast in greeting.

Zambiya started to smile at his Gutian friend, but stopped when he saw the expression on Muda's face: his mouth was turned down and his eyes were puffy.

"What's happened, Muda? Why're you here instead of with your family?"

Instead of answering, Muda knelt in the dust of the trail and took a deep brown cloth bag off of his well-muscled shoulders, placing his staff across the bag before standing back upright and facing Zambiya. He wore little more than a worn plainspun workskirt around his waist and sandals with leather bindings that laced up to his knees. A headband made of plaited leather kept his red hair in check; around his neck he wore a necklace of black hematite beads with reddish streaks, with a matching carved hematite eagle as a pendant. His expression was one of despair, and his deep voice betrayed sorrow with a quaver and lack of energy.

Muda's knowledge of the common Akkadian language was far less than complete, but he was able to express himself. Hesitantly he explained, "Was long time for bring home. Too late for Muda. No family now." He paused and looked east over the reeds toward the distant hills, his voice catching in his throat before he continued. "Muda gone over four years as slave in *Ki-en-gir*. Wife think Muda dead; whole village think Muda dead. Muda father dead. Wife have new husband. Son not know Muda." He sighed. "Can't stay, Zambiya. Muda not know where else go, maybe Isin." "Muda warrior, good worker. Can go Isin with you?"

Zambiya's brow showed furrows below the simple linen headband that held his gently curled black hair in place. He was used to Muda's blue eyes and reddish hair, common to the Gutians, but not the morose cast to his countenance. He picked up the bag and staff at Muda's feet and handed them to him. "You'll be welcome, Muda. I know my father will be sad to hear that your family was lost to you. Even though you're Gutian, you're now freed and you have skills. Come," he said, putting his hand on Muda's shoulder, "let's eat with the rest of my troop up there. We'll talk about your future during our return to Isin."

———————— • ● • ————————

That night Zambiya slept poorly, recalling a conversation with his wife Ezina the night before he had left Isin.

Ezina and Zambiya sat alone in their bedroom in the palace. Situated at some distance from the suite of Enlil-Bani, it had been the quarters of Aga, the son of Erra-imitti. It was a spacious room, with a smaller one adjoining for Ezina's newly assigned personal slave, named Sud.

Ezina sat on the edge of the bed, dabbing at her puffy eyes with a cloth to absorb her tears, occasionally pushing her thick black hair back from her face. Zambiya stood frowning near the doorway.

"You didn't want to marry me!" she accused him again with an imploring tone. She sniffed and wiped her nose again. "Now you're leaving me here alone while you go off on a journey that could take many moons." She tugged her shawl more tightly to her shoulders impatiently, adding, "I should never have listened to Ninmah. I could still be a priestess, but now I'm pregnant.

Zambiya's attitude swiftly changed, his tendency to anger rising to the fore. He held his arms down with his palms forward, stating huskily, "We've been over this, Ezina; most of the day, in fact. There was no real choice. If you had started showing, all three of us would've been burned alive. Marriage was the only way out, and that was only possible because my father is now the Ensi." He continued defending himself by saying, "You hadn't gotten pregnant before your husband died; I thought you were barren." Going on the offensive, he added, "You wanted to enjoy Inana's ecstasies as much as I did."

"But you don't love me," she retorted. "I could tell you really wanted Ninmah, but she wouldn't let you have her fully." Looking up at him she softened her response, admitting, "And yes, I did enjoy our coupling. I was already starting to love you." She shook her head and then held her hands up to her temples, asking, "What kind of marriage can this be, starting like this?"

"You're bearing my child, Ezina." Zambiya took a step toward her, stated

as a matter of fact, "We will do what the gods demand of us: become a family. It wasn't what either of us expected, but what other choice do we have now?"

"But will you ever forget Ninmah and finally love me?" She wiped her nose and eyes and looked straight at him, searching his face for truthfulness in his response.

Zambiya stepped away from the door to kneel in front of her and took both her shoulders in his hands. With a mixture of tenderness and resignation he looked into her eyes and spoke again, reasoning, "Many couples marry who've barely met. At least we know one another, so we have a better chance to be happy." He stood up and sat close to her on the bed. "We didn't expect to marry but I believe I can be a good husband to you." He knew better than to respond again about Ninmah.

Ezina chose to accept her husband's statement as sufficiently hopeful, and reached a hand up to his smoothly shaved face.

"You're a most attractive man, and many a woman would be pleased to be with you. I intend to be a good wife to you as well." She recalled the primarily erotic nature of their relationship up to this point and added, "In every way." She shrugged her shawl off her shoulders and guided his hand to her bosom, saying, "Let us begin by making each other happy this night, then I'll be more patient as I wait here for you to return."

*　　　　　　　　　　• ● •*

In the days following, Zambiya encouraged Muda to look for a hopeful future when they returned, reminiscing about their last days in Isin before starting out to find the Gutian village. He even offered vague speculations about the possibility of meeting a Gutian woman that Muda would like.

Though he spoke little to the other travelers, being self-conscious about his limited command of Akkadian, Muda was nevertheless a help to everyone in the company, loading and unloading the burdens from the donkeys and onagers, finding fuel for the evening fires and standing sentry duty more often than anyone else. Mostly he spent his time in work or solitary vigil.

Only when alone would he allow his sorrowful gaze to turn from the foothills of the Zagros Mountains across the river to the southward track that would return the caravan to Isin and, according to Zambiya, hope.

• ● •

The Chaldean lit both of the wall sconces in the room formerly occupied by Aga, his employer. Just before dawn, using a fine-grained hand stone, he put a new edge on the blade of his knives. Once finished, he again dressed in the garb of an urchin and left the home after telling the night guard to tell Nisaba he would be returning about midday. Working on his knives was precautionary; today was another scouting mission.

When he arrived at the zigurrat the sun had risen to the point that the steps were in shadow, but clearly visible. He intended to mount the stairway to the second level to get a better view of the city and especially, the palace. While his body was proportioned like an adult, his legs were nevertheless short, and the zigurrat stairs were a challenge for him, so he wanted to make the ascent in the relative coolness of the day.

He had just arrived at the second tier of stairs when he heard Ningal and his servant/scribe making their painstaking way down. The Chaldean stepped to the western shadow side of the staircase and crouched there. He had previously observed the process by which the scribe backed down first, his supplies on his back in a pack, holding one of the priest's hands.

As soon as he was sure the pair had started on the last stairway and were concentrating on that, he stepped to the eastern side. From this vantage point high above Isin, he could discern activity in the palace courtyard, which he already knew was attached to the kitchen since it held the two round-topped ovens and large grill. He was further rewarded by observing a dozen guards round the far corner of the palace from their barracks on their way to relieve the night sentries and start civil neighborhood patrols. The guards had just entered the market square when a slave arrived next to the courtyard wall and picked up a wooden rake with a long handle that had lain next to the wall. He used the rake to gather smoldering ashes into the center of an area next to a pile of rubble and discards, and then added dry material. He squatted next to the ash pile and blew into it until something ignited and flames appeared.

The Chaldean still had not seen anyone ascending the stairs, so he determined to make note of where the guards were stationed on the city walls. He saw that there were now two guards posted above the city gate from where he had made his first attempt to kill the king. Starting to move to the other side of the stairs, he heard people down at the ground level in front of the zigurrat. Looking over the edge by the stairs he saw two groups coming toward him: a set of priests in the lead, with a set of priestesses following. Crouched in deep shade at the corner of the stairs and the support wall and breathing shallowly, he made a decision. Once the groups had reached the topmost level where the temples were, he would descend before worshippers started arriving. He sighed with satisfaction at all he had observed.

<hr />

En-me arrived at the *edubba* a few days later in the late afternoon, just as the students were leaving for their respective homes; the older boys left on their own, but the youngest were met by servants or older siblings. Some carried dry clay tablets in wooden frames, to be studied and re-traced over and over by hand that evening. Student scribes in the civil *edubbas* were often the younger males of artisan families, deemed unlikely to succeed at the craft trade of their fathers but talented enough to become successful in the scribal arts. Like those attached to the temples, civil scribes were in great demand by the largest estates and craft businesses, to keep records and contracts and to write letters to their counterparts in distant cities.

The sound of the exiting students was not remarkable by itself, with a murmur of voices as greetings and farewells mixed together. But En-me was surprised when he saw two girls at the outer edge of the group being greeted by a burly male attendant, apparently a servant as he had no topknot. Seeming to be about the same age, the girls were dressed alike, with matching slender plaited leather headbands that sported a row of short gold beaded strands hanging; matching bracelets encircled their left wrists. They wore identical dresses, made of a high quality ankle-length creamy white linen with a simple yellow waist belt. The girls held out their tablets to the servant, who accepted them and held them back-to-back by one arm as he led them away, so as to keep the cuneiform script intact.

Always alert to clues that revealed emotional tone, En-me noted that both girls seemed subdued, with matching affect, their shoulders rounded forward and their heads inclined toward the ground, looking just a few yards ahead of them.

He was admitted to the home immediately, since he was a frequent and welcome visitor. "Shalamu, En-me," said the ancient door attendant as he gave way before the guest. "He's in the courtyard. You're expected."

"Are the gods favoring you today?" The healer's inquiry was as much concern for the servant's age as politeness, since he had been aware for a long time now that the attendant could no longer stand fully erect, with a pronounced hump to his spine and his knees always slightly bent. The attendant had been a servant to Naram's family since he was ten years of age, when he had been enslaved due to his father's indebtedness. Slight of frame and sunken-chested, he had never aspired to freedom, and was willing to remain a slave, even after Naram had offered him freedman status. The attendant had only asked to have his slaveknot shaved off.

"I still live, and pains are less today, so yes, thank you." He pivoted on his good leg and led the way to the *edubba*'s courtyard.

En-me left the attendant in the relative coolness of the home and re-entered the heat of the outdoors, looking about for his lover. He quickly spotted him sitting on his raised chair, a pensive look on his face. Enmerkar brightened immediately on seeing En-me and rose at once, walking toward him with his staff held up in the air, though still limping.

"I'm making myself walk more without the stick; I know you're right about it making my bad leg stronger. Muda told me the same thing when he was making me exercise after the accident." He kissed En-me and squeezed his lover's shoulder with his free hand. "Even I think I sit too much."

The men walked back to the home and entered, where they were greeted by Uttu, Naram's wife and Enmerkar's adoptive mother. A portly woman of late middle age, her face etched with the wrinkles she had gained from grieving the loss of both of her children on the same day during a widespread plague some eighteen years before, she was instrumental in admitting Enmerkar to her family. She insisted on the condition that the adopted boy use her late son's name. The arrangement had been advantageous to Enlil-Bani and Lith-el as well.

"Can I bring you some broth or wine before dinner, son?"

"Wine, mother, if you would join us." Enmerkar spoke for both men, as he knew what En-me would prefer. Hot broth seemed to make the *a-zu's* nose run even more than usual, so he avoided it.

"I'd love the company. Naram's deep in concentration over some scribal issue. He's been no company half the day." Her mild complaint was stated without rancor; she was grateful for the offer to join the men, uncommon even in her own home. "I'll return shortly."

The men settled into adjoining chairs in a room near the front of the home, obviously intended for casual visiting, as it had several chairs and small tables. The chair Enmerkar chose had a thick bolster added to the seat.

En-me spoke up as soon as Uttu had left, saying, "I know you invited me for dinner to discuss something else, but I'm curious about the two girls I saw leaving the *edubba* a short while ago. I thought female scribes were always attached to a temple. Why would they be studying here?"

"There's a story." Enmerkar laid his hand on En-me's arm, explaining, "Their father's General Ashgi; he's retired but still has influence with the council and the younger officers of the army. He had the twins late in life, and his wife died when they were born. He declared immediately that he knew nothing about girls, and made it plain he wanted little to do with them, so they were sent to an elderly aunt of his wife, along with a slave as wet nurse. When he arranged with Naram for them to study as scribes, he declared, 'Boys become men; men become soldiers; soldiers have more boys. What will I do with girls?' He thinks maybe they'll both marry career soldiers if they become scribes for the army."

"What do the girls think of that?"

"Don't know. They're good students, but keep to themselves. Hardly speak except to ask questions about their assignments."

"Does he have sons?"

"Yes, by his first wife. Let me think." He glance upward searching his memory, then announced, "Yes! Ibbi and Sigsig." Pleased that he had remembered, he added, "The girls will likely finish their studies here within two years; they're already fourteen summers in age. The sons are much older than the twins; in the army of course."

Just then Uttu entered the room, trailed by a young female slave who carried a tray with a pitcher of plum-and-raisin wine and three ox horn cups with flat wooden bottoms. A small dish of nut- stuffed dates completed the contents, and the tray was placed between the men, after which the slave moved a chair to where Uttu and the men could all easily reach the refreshments before she withdrew following a nod from Uttu.

"Many thanks, Lady," En-me said after taking a sip. "The wine smells delicious, and will help my throat after the walk from the palace." He turned his head away slightly and sniffed as quietly as he could manage.

"You're always welcome, En-me. I should let you know that raising the head of my bed has worked wonders for my sleeping. How did you know to do that?"

"I've done the same thing with my bed in the palace. If I didn't, I'd wake up gasping for breath. I'm happy it helped you."

Enmerkar spoke next, saying, "The thing I wanted to ask you about is whether Tikal has made any progress with finding out who killed the guard who was walking with my father. It has been several weeks since then and I've heard nothing, yet the civil patrols still come by many times a day, never at the same time I'm told."

"No, nothing's been reported to me. The only thing new is that his son, Neti, has started to accompany Tikal as he conducts business for the palace. He's about eighteen, and was trained in the temple *edubba* as well as being a soldier. I suspect Tikal intends to groom him to be the next Chief Counselor. That's what I would do."

"That makes sense," Uttu contributed. "Naram told me that Neti has been attending the Elder Council meetings for almost a year now. He started when he turned seventeen." She turned to Enmerkar and asked, "He's not much younger than you, is he?"

"No, that's right. But I haven't met him; maybe I will soon." He addressed En-me and asked, "What's he like?"

En-me looked about as if searching for the answer, before responding, "I've only seen him a few times, but he's confident about his opinions and rather assertive. He pays close attention, never seems to get off track. He may be in apprentice mode right now, but he's not shy."

"There was some activity last week," En-me continued. "I think Tikal's getting frustrated at having no results in the search for the archer, so he had his own stewards search all the attendants' quarters, free and slave alike." He pointed at his own chest and added, "Even mine. I don't think

I told you. He's looking for a bow that would shoot a short arrow like the one that killed the guard."

———— • ● • ————

The setting sun cast long shadows across Isin as Enlil-Bani descended in the center of the broad zigurrat steps with two guards in front and trailed by two more. Everyone on the stairs walked with great care; with no barrier walls a misstep would likely be fatal if one were to fall.

"Stand aside," one of the guards barked to a young man who was ascending, head down, also in the middle section. With stubbly hair on his head and a soiled headband across his forehead, he wore only a short gray work skirt. His hands and arms were full; a common grit-rough clay pitcher was held in one hand with a discolored copper basin with a lid in the other. He clutched a dingy cushion under one arm and a dark roll of burlap under the other; the latter was threatening to slide down his sweaty side.

The youngster looked up from his careful mounting of the stairs and recognized the king and his attendants above him; he immediately lowered his gaze.

"Please forgive me, *Ensi*. I'll put these things down over here," he wheezed. In fact, he was happy to be able to rest briefly and re-situate his burdens.

Enlil-bani raised his hand to stay the guards behind him and said loudly enough to halt the ones in front, "I want to speak to this man."

"Aren't you Ningal's servant? Why aren't you with him?"

Keeping his eyes lowered, the man took great care to lower the broad-based pitcher to the stair just above him, meanwhile corralling the burlap roll at his feet. Now having a free hand, he sat his other items on the upper stair.

"*Ensi*, I've already brought Ningal to the top of the zigurrat; he's waiting for me there. I needed to bring more oil for my lamp, and he wanted me to bring his cushion at the same time." He gestured to the items with one hand as he wiped his face with a sweat-stained cloth he pulled from the waistband of his skirt.

"Doesn't Ningal object to your lamp? He told me he keeps his vision primed to see the lights of the heavens by never allowing himself to be out in daylight."

"That's true, Exalted One. He's wearing a blindfold even now, as he waits for me. I use a lamp under a canopy strung between the two temple walls so I can see to write on the tablets what he tells me he sees. He climbs to the roof of Inana's temple, and tells me what to write." He pointed to the copper basin and added, "I have lighted charcoals in here to light my torch." He lifted the lid, protecting his fingers with the cloth he had used to wipe his face and blew softly into the interior. He added, "We have a position for my use that doesn't interfere with the pigeon coops the temples have."

The king smiled as he imagined the scene described by the young man, then said to the guard closest to him on the upper stairs, "We've delayed this scribe already. Pick up the cloth and the pillow and help him carry these things up to the top."

All four guards frowned at the prospect of leaving the king un-attended, and the lead guard started to protest, but Enlil-Bani silenced him with a wave of his hand, saying, "We'll wait here until he returns. The guard and the scribe gathered the items quickly, and the scribe grinned broadly and said, "Shalamu, my *Ensi*."

CHAPTER FOUR

TURNING TOWARD THE SUNLIGHT

Little remains unchanged for long, neither people nor circumstances. It is the wise person who can predict what will ensue from a transformation.

Zambiya's caravan approached Isin in the latter part of the afternoon, everyone having pushed hard these last days on trail, anxious to rejoin family or to confer with trade associates. Now late summer, the air itself was searing against bare skin, and the sun was still well above the city walls, illuminating the top of the ziggurat and its twin temples. It shone on both the northwest and southwest sides; as is common throughout Sumeria and Akkad, Isin was laid out so that the corners of every major building and the city walls themselves pointed in the cardinal directions. Isin had been planned centuries before. With the Buranun River running first along the northwest side and then making a gradual turn back toward the south, it made it difficult to attack it from either of those sides.

"You'll stay in the palace until we figure out what to do," Zambiya said to Muda as they entered the city market square and saw the palace across from them to the left, with the zigurrat rising to the right of it. The other guards had been sent to the barracks entrance of the palace to report their return. "Let's find Enlil-Bani and tell him why you've come back."

The palace stood apart from other residential buildings. Elevated on a foundation of four tiers of bricks, a broad set of steps separated the entry doors from the square; the top level formed a broad stage for ceremonies.

"Muda feel… belly sick… see this place." He slowed his pace and looked around the square as if expecting to be challenged.

"I can understand that, Muda. The first time I saw you was when Saman and Esme were whipping you." Zambiya pointed to the flogging wall set up far to their right, standing apart from the vendors' stalls. "Then you and Enlil-Bani stood in this square most of the Akitu celebration waiting to be executed; it would make my stomach churn, too. Things are different now, and you're a freed man. Let's proceed." But having been reminded of the significance of the city center, he stopped to see if he could discern any changes.

There could be no change in the two main structures of the city. The center wall of the immense ziggurat sat at right angles to the front of the palace with the main steps that mounted it in the center. These structures defined the civic and religious boundaries of the square and market area.

The palace had substantial high walls, and was decorated at the front entrance with geometric designs, colored with alternating green, blue and gold fire-baked bricks. Two life-sized sculptured guardian lions stood on solid dark brown bases, half the height of a man, placed at the top of the stairway ascending to the first landing, with yet another stairway before reaching the level on which the palace was situated. Its twin doors stood impressively high, taller by half again than the tallest Isin male. Made of thick imported cedar planks, they were adorned with thin, polished bronze plates depicting scenes of priests and royal figures offering gifts to the gods.

"Come on, Muda, let's go in and report." They strode across the square until they were approaching the lowest set of steps when Zambiya said, "That's new, sort of. The old door plates have been shined. They look good."

Muda returned to a high state of vigilance as they approached the doors, for there were two guards with ox hide shields standing watch at the sides of the doorway. They were armed with swords and bronze-tipped spears. Four archers added to the vigil, scanning the area of the courtyard facing the palace from a vantage point on a balcony above the door. Zambiya had told him that two more guards would be inside with sickle swords; as anticipated, battle axes rested near each one at the sides of the portal.

Zambiya identified himself and Muda to the interior guards, having been recognized by those outside. Now confident of his bearings, he strode into the first long hallway, which led to the public entrance at the rear of the throne room. This was designed to defend the throne room from direct attack from the outside. The only illumination in the hall was from two torches, one at each end of the hall. On days when the king was on the throne for official business, the torches between those at the ends were lit as well.

Zambiya had been a palace guard during the reign of Erra-Imitti until that king's sudden death and knew the corridors quite well, so he had no difficulty making his way directly to the royal apartments. All seemed quiet within the palace walls, and he and Muda encountered only one minor steward before arriving at the entrance to the residential chambers of Enlil-Bani. The two guards there, however, recognized neither travel-stained Zambiya nor his Gutian companion.

"Halt where you are!" the larger of the two guards ordered as they were approached. Both guards readied their reliable socket axes and moved together from the edges of the curtained portal to bar the way. "How did you get here? Why weren't you stopped outside?" the second man demanded.

"Shalamu, friend." Zambiya held up both his hands to shoulder height, palms forward. "The *Ensi* is my stepfather, and I have been gone for over six full moons. I don't recognize you either. I'm here to report on my mission to the land of the Gutians and beyond. Enlil-Bani knows this man with me, who was expected to remain there."

Both guards looked skeptical, and the larger one asked, "Who can vouch for you?"

Zambiya hadn't expected to be challenged, but he remembered his married status, and replied, "Ezina, my wife, is here. She's bearing my child. And certainly Tikal knows us both; so does Zid-tara. I was a guard here in the palace until I left on caravan." He hesitated a bit before adding, "I don't remember either of you."

The smaller of the guards answered this time, after the guards had exchanged a look. "I don't know if the gods favor you, if you're Ezina's husband." He turned to his fellow and said, "I'll go ask Ezina if she will come here. I'm not going to bother Zid-tara." He turned back to Zambiya and said, "She's not been in a good mood today, but having you come back may improve it. If you're who you say." He thought again and opined, "If you're a fake, we'll all be in trouble, but you more than me."

The guard passed behind the drape that separated the hall from the royal chambers, his footsteps fading into the interior. The other stood easier, but still alert, now standing in the middle of the passage. "If you were supposed to take this Gutian back to his land, why is he here?"

Zambiya knew this question would arise, but didn't think it was a lowly guard's concern, so he just replied, "If he wants to tell you, it's his choice." He stepped back into the hall a pace and lowered his hands, which he had been holding up to signal that he wasn't a threat. "My suggestion, though, is that you get used to seeing him. He may become a guard, like you."

The guard snorted a short chuckle, saying, "A Gutian palace guard! Might as well dress up a whore in a uniform and give her a spear; just as useless."

Muda had remained silent through the entire exchange with the guards, but now his chin jutted forward. Frowning, he put his hands on his hips and responded, "Gutians are warriors, good fighters." This was his first display of animation since he had encountered Zambiya on the trek from the north. Pointing toward his own chest he declared, "Enlil-Bani decide if Muda be guard, not you. Muda do what Enlil-Bani say."

The guard was surprised, and made a rapid survey of Muda's size and build. He raised one palm toward Muda, saying, "I didn't know you could understand me. You hadn't said anything. I was just joking, but truly, the only Gutians I know of are slaves, and most of them are women, so I didn't think you could be a guard." He thought for a moment, looking puzzled, then mused aloud, asking, "Where would you sleep? Where would you eat? You'd be the only Gutian in the guard quarters, and no one would work with you."

Zambiya interrupted at this point and said, "He'd eat and sleep where Enlil-Bani directed, wouldn't he?"

The guard started to respond, but his fellow emerged from behind the curtain and said, "Ezina will be here shortly to see for herself. She said Enlil-Bani's in one of the ceremonial dressing rooms with Tikal. They've been there much of the day."

The curtain behind the two guards parted and the guards both stood aside. Ezina looked through the portal, her arms crossed over her breasts. Her eyes were puffy and her mouth was turned down at the corners, with prominent creases indenting her brow. She wore a yellow and red headband to hold her curly long black hair in place, crooked on her head and obviously just put on. She was covered only by a long yellow skirt over her belly and a diaphanous linen blouse on top. Barefoot, she stood with her feet spread under her frame. She was showing her eight months of pregnancy, her belly swollen and her always ample breasts raising the fabric of her upper garment.

"Zambiya, you're finally back." She then said to the guards, "Yes, it's him." Then she looked at Muda, puzzling, and shook her head slightly before adding, "Let them in." Her voice displayed little energy, and she breathed with effort, not seeming to be able to utter a long sentence without stopping for air.

She turned on her heel and retreated down the passageway toward a facing hall, ambling with short steps, saying as she went, "You need to wash and change your clothes." She breathed twice again, then added, "The slave, too, but not in our rooms." Another pause, then, "I'll have him taken to the slave quarters."

"Stop, Ezina!" Zambiya ordered her, using a tone that left her no choice. "What's wrong with you? I've been gone over five moons, and you act like I've been late for supper. And Muda's not a slave, he's a friend. So he won't be going to any slave quarters, he'll be coming with me for now. We do need to clean up after the trail, but this is not a proper welcome for your husband!"

Ezina turned around, looking both chastened and annoyed. She opened her mouth to speak, but saw Muda behind Zambiya and the guards behind them, all staring at her, and thought better of her first response. "We'll talk more when we have privacy." She put her hands on her sides and bent forward a little, drawing in a shallow breath and wrinkling her nose. "You both smell like donkeys."

She turned back around and led the way to the facing hall, then turned right and walked a few more steps before stopping to breathe again, then shouted, "Sud! Come here. Now!"

"Guard!" Enlil-Bani was still hugging Zambiya close to his chest, and shouted over his step-son's shoulder to the guards outside the doorway.

"Yes, my *Ensi*. Command me." A young guard stepped into the room, with another close behind him.

Stepping back from Zambiya, the king placed his hand flat on Muda's chest in greeting, then turned to the closest guard and said, "Find En-me, and tell him to go get Enmerkar; tell him his brother is home. And tell Tikal to have my daughter and her husband sent for, also. They're all to join us for dinner. Tell him it will be soon."

The three men, Enlil-Bani, Zambiya and Muda, were soon alone in the king's lounging room, an ornately decorated chamber with a shallow pool in the middle, now drained and dry, decorated with stylized fish with blue lapis eyes on the floor. Due to its use for dressing the king for religious occasions the room was better lit than most.

A circle of chairs surrounded the pool; hanging racks had been placed inside the pool for holding ceremonial costumes, each with its own meaning in the religious life of the city. Though he was not superstitious, after Enlil-Bani learned that it was in this room that Erra-imitti had fallen into the pool and choked to death, he ordered the pool emptied and used the room only as a dressing area.

Zambiya and Muda were brought here after the king learned that they had returned while he was in the process of changing to more relaxing garb.

Zambiya was jolted by the memory of having helped Tikal remove Erra-Imitti's lifeless body from the pool, but quickly banished the images from his consciousness.

The king stepped to the door and directed the remaining guard to arrange for hot spiced ox-broth to be brought, even though a meal was planned for later. Unwilling to leave Enlil-Bani alone with no guard at all, the man left the room just long enough to shout to a companion at the end of the connecting hallway to come to him, and relayed the order he had been given.

Recognizing that this was an unsuitable space in which to have a visit, Enlil-Bani headed out the doorway and told the guard to lead them to Erra-imitti's former bedroom, now a sitting room. There the men sat and recounted their experiences of the last several months, focusing on the trade arrangements that had been made along the northern reaches of the Idiglat river, plus Muda's tragic situation.

———————— • ● • ————————

"I feel now like I did when I was being trained for battle as a young man, running in place to build endurance. Lots of effort, little visible progress. There are endless meetings and ceremonies which I must attend. Plus the judgments of fault that the Isin Council hasn't decided; those are endless. I was more comfortable as a gardener; I knew what I was doing then." Enlil-Bani leaned back in his chair as he finished his complaint to Muda and Zambiya. He sighed once, then his visage lightened and he stretched before exclaiming, "It feels good just to be able to tell you. I don't think Tikal understands how I feel. Much of what I'm learning just seems pointless, but that's because I'm not yet able to discern the important things from the trivial."

Yawning and stretching his back against the cushions, he suddenly smiled and said, ruefully, "It's better than being hung!"

He paused a moment, noticing that both of the others looked distracted, shifting in their seats and less intent on what he was saying to them. "I'm being careless. I'm so pleased that you've returned safely that I haven't paid attention to your need for rest, and for you to spend time with your wife, Zambiya. Muda, what do you want to do here in Isin?"

"Father," Zambiya said, "I'd like to go back to my apartment until dinner, when Enmerkar and Nani join us. Why don't you and Muda talk and we'll meet at dinner?"

"Please ask Ezina to join us then," offered Enlil-Bani. "She's not been in good spirits during your absence."

"I will. Perhaps she feels better now."

Zambiya left, leaving Muda and Enlil-Bani alone in the room, but with two guards still posted outside the chamber.

"Muda not want bother Enlil-Bani, now *Ensi*. Muda go to market square, try find work. Find room with family. Not know how Gutian be if not slave. Enlil-Bani know if other Gutians not slaves?"

"I don't think I do, friend. People of Isin will always be suspicious of you, so it'll be hard for you to fit in. Earlier I had a thought that could make your life better, though. You always declared that you're a warrior, and I know you fought hard to protect Lith-el. I saw those four you fought. You almost lost your life doing that, so I'd like you to be my bodyguard. That will relieve one of the palace guards, and keep you near to protect me. Would you like that?"

"Muda be warrior again, protect Enlil-Bani? Stay by you, keep safe? Muda be happy Gutian, be Isin man. Muda do what Enlil-Bani want. Yes!"

"I'll have Tikal and Zid-tara do what is necessary to make this work. As I told you and Zambiya, Tikal thinks someone is planning to kill me, and he almost succeeded." Enlil-Bani stood up and called out, "Guard. Ask Zid-tara to come to my bedroom right away."

CHAPTER FIVE

BRIAR SHOOTS EMERGE

Many superior men and women never have the opportunity to demonstrate their talents, having been born without the favor of the gods, or shackled to a life of drudgery. The priests say the gods determine our fates.

Ezina sat up on the edge of her bed in the midafternoon, feeling her belly with swollen fingers; her skin was taut and stretched. Sitting up made her feel an urgent need to empty her bladder. Her back ached; her nap had been intermittent, having not found any position that allowed her full relaxation.

"Sud, get in here. Get me up." Ezina's tone blended whining with impatience in equal measure, giving full testimony to her misery. The certain knowledge of her eventual delivery presented no diminution of her present outlook.

Sud, a short and sturdy plain-faced slave of thirty summers' age, entered through the opening from the hallway, having anticipated her mistress's call. Sud was bought for the palace at the age of ten, and previously worked in the palace kitchen. She was assigned to serve Ezina when the former priestess joined the royal household as Zambiya's bride. No less weary than her mistress, she said nothing, but offered her shoulders for gripping while she helped Ezina to rise, her own hands lifting and pulling behind Ezina's elbows.

After relieving herself Ezina sat back on the edge of her bed to recover from the effort of standing erect after voiding. "Did Zambiya tell you when he will return? I haven't seen him since the midday meal."

"No, lady. He left with that Gutian without saying anything; why would he tell me?"

As the only two females living in the royal suite, Ezina and Sud had an uneasy bond between them, with their statuses clearly defined, but with the need for feminine companionship underpinning their reliance on each other. Ezina was not close to anyone else in the palace, having moved there from the temple of *Egal-m*ah on the day of her marriage to Zambiya, just before he left on caravan.

Ezina became pregnant during a sexual affair that Ninmah, another priestess, had initiated with Zambiya some months before and invited Ezina to join. If Ezina had not been allowed to leave the temple and marry, they would all have been denounced and burned alive, as priestesses were expected to remain chaste as was befitting a servant to goddess Ninisina. Zambiya had been able to arrange for the marriage to save the three of them only by dint of his step-father becoming king.

Despite Enlil-Bani being her father-in-law, Ezina had not even met him before she moved to the royal quarters, and he had little to do with her. At first it was due to Ezina's morning sickness, then to Enlil-Bani's rehearsals and appearances in his dual roles as king and religious figure, coached by Tikal and the high priest, Banda.

"Now that Zambiya's back, I'll arrange to have my evening meal with him and *Ensi*. That'll be a welcome change from just you." Ezina examined her swollen ankles by raising her feet off the mat that covered the floor, frowning, and then added, "I could probably have dined with Nintud and Dagan, but they're even older than you."

Sud said, "The guards say that Dagan's still suffering from his affliction, and En-me hasn't been able to stop the pains or the welts, just relieve them some. They seldom eat with the *Ensi*. Maybe that will change, but who can tell? The gods so chose."

"When Zambiya comes back, I'll tell him I want to join him and the others. You can eat here," Ezina said, then as if a veil had lifted from her eyes, she proposed, "Or you could eat with the kitchen staff, like you did before."

"Thanks, Lady. You're kind. Hardly seen them for months."

"Well, I'm going to dress for the meal. First, comb my hair and find a pretty headband, then I'll choose a dress that makes me look less like a sow." She suddenly grunted and felt her belly again, saying, "Ow! This one kicks like a whipped onager [a wild ass]; probably a boy. Pour me another goblet of wine; maybe that'll settle him down."

———— • ————

Aga, the only son of Erra-imitti, the former king of Isin, stood in the central passageway of his assigned quarters in Larsa. He was sent to Larsa as emissary to keep him from interfering with Enlil-Bani's transition to the status of king. It was a small set of rooms on the outer wall of the periphery of the palace, separated from the royal suite by a series of intervening halls, also away from the throne room by a lengthy and circuitous route. Discolored copper holders for oil-burning torches jutted out of from one side of the wall about every eight paces and at head height above the floor, but only one torch in every two was lit, so there was scant illumination. The oil in these torches was of a cheap variety, tingeing the air with an unavoidable acrid aroma. Both of Aga's Isin slaves were with him, dressed in plain dull linen work skirts that covered them from waist to below the knees. Two Larsan palace guards waited at the end of the passage entering a central hall that would lead to a great ceremonial space, the palace throne room.

Aga's frustration was keen as he had just been summoned to attend the third function of the Larsan court this day. From the moment he arrived king Nur-Adad insisted that Aga attend all official functions, even minor ones.

Keeping his voice low, Aga ordered his attendants, "Let's go see what they're doing now. Probably another trial."

His slaves trailed behind him, alert to any whim Aga expressed. They made their way to Larsa's throne room, a large space with vaulted ceilings and with many oil torches on the walls, all ablaze. An ornately carved dark oak chair inlaid with white shells and polished stones occupied the place of central focus. Like throne rooms throughout Mesopotamia, the walls and floor were constructed from clay bricks with brick columns supporting the ceiling; three tiers of brick raised the throne itself above the level of the floor as well as creating steps on all four sides of the dais. Five rows of benches faced the throne, separated from the throne by a full fifteen paces.

"Enter, Aga of Isin. Sit over there this time," Nur-Adad announced from his throne on the dais, pointing to a spot on the far edge of the row of benches and away from the few other observers, clearly intended to show his disdain for the Isin.

Aga, not quite eighteen but familiar with the innuendos of court affairs owing to his upbringing as Erra-Imitti's only son and intended heir, bowed in the direction of the throne, but at a slight angle away from it. He responded, "As you please, *Ensi* of Larsa." Aga took his seat, but rather than direct his attention to Nur-Adad, he busied himself arranging his clothing, straightening the embroidered crimson belt that encircled his waist, pulling his headband further down on his forehead and adjusting a strap attached to his sandal. Once he had completed these refinements, he sat back on the bench and crossed his arms over his chest. His slaves stood against the rear wall in a section reserved for slaves, near the door.

Nur-Adad, a husky man with the physique of a wrestler, sipped from a goblet while noting Aga's attention to his clothing, but said nothing about that display. Instead, he motioned for one of the four guards who attended his safety and said, "Have the landowner who's complaining come forward."

<hr />

Nur-Adad returned to his royal suite, where he was immediately joined in the dressing area by Asgi, his Chief Counselor. Asgi was an aged man with a withered left hand which he kept close against his waist and covered with a cloth the size of a child's loincloth. His skirt was embroidered with an ornate design, a series of black and yellow crosses all along the fringe, which came down to his ankles; he was bare to the waist, his skin slack and pallid with his hair and beard trimmed short.

Asgi spoke to Nur-Adad as soon as he entered the room, saying, "I know this last trial was not worth your attention, *Ensi*, but we agreed when Aga arrived that he must have been sent here as a spy, and we cannot allow him too much time to explore."

Nur-Adad waited until his personal attendant had removed the ceremonial shawl from his shoulders and then faced Asgi and responded, his voice strong and decisive.

"I know what we decided and why, but this ploy of having him attend me in trivial events in court is a waste of my time. That common gardener now on the throne of Isin couldn't have sent a more inept spy, if that's what he is. And Tikal is too bright to have sent this petulant stripling; he would have had several more servants, so we couldn't watch them all. As it is, he's only had one visitor since he's been here, that half-a-man Chaldean who left with the caravan from Ur several days ago." The king motioned to his attendant as he settled onto a backless chair; the servant immediately brought a short toothed comb and commenced to comb Nur-Adad's long hair, arranging it so that it clung closer to his head and behind his ears, then moved on to comb his beard as well.

Asgi bowed to his king, his tremulous voice adopting an acquiescent tone.

"I agree, *Ensi*. I've thought about a better solution. Rather than keeping him on a short leash like a balky donkey, you could offer him an excursion. My sources in Isin tell me that Aga used to go hunting in the wild areas over toward the *Idiglat*. I'll arrange for him to go hunting with the emissaries from Uruk and Bad-tibira. They're all young men with too much time and too little to do. They won't form alliances because they don't trust each other. Sending three will keep them contending like male geese in a pen. Best of all, there's no opportunity for spying on us when they're off in the scrub lands looking for antelopes." He laughed briefly, adding, "Maybe a lion will take care of him; we can't be blamed for such an act of the gods."

Nur-Adad smiled at the last comment, and said, "Tell them each individually that I suspect the others aren't competent with a bow, and this is a chance to prove themselves. I like your plan, Asgi. In fact, have them seated together at dinner tonight after you've told them about the outing. Watching them should be amusing. And arrange it soon."

That night in Nisaba's home in Isin the Chaldean put on a dark tunic and pulled a black covering over his head and face that only showed his eyes; then he lit a small hand torch from a sconce on the wall. Quietly parting the curtains that separated his room from the hall, he slipped barefoot into the dark interior corridor that connected the sleeping rooms and also separated them from the public areas. He moved along the wall sideways, instantly noting the guard who was snoring and motionless just outside the sleeping area.

He slithered along the wall, silently entering each dimly lit bedroom and standing quietly until he confirmed that he knew in which room each of the three females of the family slept. He inhaled deeply with a thrill of anticipation when he realized that the youngest girl, Ninegala, was in the room across from his own. The mother, Nisaba, was in the room closest to the common spaces, with Sherida, her eldest daughter, in the room across the hall from her.

He had insisted as soon as he arrived in Nisaba's home that he was not a slave, and shouldn't be housed in the servants' quarters, as he was on an important mission from Aga, her son. After appraising the man's diminutive stature Nisaba reluctantly agreed to give him Aga's previous bedroom.

Since he arrived in Nisaba's home, he had made a point of remaining in the common area at night until the women had retired, affording them a sense of privacy and giving himself a time of uninterrupted thinking. Of late, he had been recalling the progress that was being made on the addition at the palace. That project occupied many of his internal deliberations, proposing and discarding ways to breech the palace by that entry.

He lingered a while in the portal to Ninegala's bedroom, watching her and listening to her breathing as she slept.

By the time he had crept back to his own room, his male member was as rigid as a dagger handle. He was always aroused whenever he was successful in sneaking into a woman's bedroom, as he had accomplished many times before, but seeing Ninegala asleep in her bed was special. He knew he couldn't return to sleeping unless he relieved the tension in his loins, and as his hand moved between his thighs, he only regretted that he had to pleasure himself alone, with Ninegala so close.

CHAPTER SIX
BRIARS AND NETTLES

It is said that the gods play favorites, but perhaps some people are just ignored. Further, when people pray it is often for something opposite to what other people are praying. The priests of Isin and Larsa both beseech the same gods for opposite outcomes. How do the gods decide?

"It's agreed, then," said Enlil-Bani. He and Tikal sat at the head of the long table in the banquet room of the palace; Muda and Zambiya sat across from each other down the sides.

"Yes, *Ensi*," responded Tikal. "We'll use the room next to your bedroom for Muda to sleep in at night. For twenty days he will train with the guards each morning, then he will be your bodyguard. Whenever you leave the palace he will be with you. And he will decide what guards will be on your outside detail. They may grumble since he's a Gutian, but soldiers grumble; that's their nature."

Now mid-morning, Tikal had earlier advised the king that there were no plans for further ceremonial rehearsals, saying, 'You've already been through enough appearances and tributes to know what's expected. If there are unusual expectations in the future, I'll tell you.'

"Muda happy do this." The former slave's red hair and blue eyes contrasted with the others present due to his Gutian origins. Idly scratching the hair on his chest and shoulders, Muda stood up from his seat and spoke directly to Tikal, saying, "One more. Muda need know better Isin. *Edubba*

59

where Bani-mur live not like where Suba and Nani live. Need know where *Ensi* go, so no more attack like when Lith-el killed. Need soon… look at places before."

"I'll add you to the patrol schedule, and I'll create a special insignia for you to wear, so the guards and the citizens give you respect. Good." He looked at Enlil-Bani and added, "I'll use this same training time to have my son Neti learn the districts of Isin. I'm hoping he'll make himself useful and follow me in serving you." Tikal stood up and addressed Enlil-Bani with a half smile, saying, "I don't think I've told you this before, but several moons ago, I convinced Erra-imitti that we should buy Muda and send him to an army outpost. Instead, you bought him. Perhaps this is how the gods keep us humble." He bowed to his king and motioned for Muda to accompany him, and they both exited.

"Until Muda's ready to guard you, Father, I'll be pleased to do it when you leave the palace. Have you any current wish to do so?" Zambiya took a sip of a pungent spiced ox broth, now tepid. Frowning slightly, he sat the copper cup down on the silver tray that held a flagon of broth; it was hot when the meeting started. Enlil-Bani rose and Zambiya stood as well. The king walked around the table and placed a hand on Zambiya's shoulder, declaring, "It always pleases me when you call me 'Father.' Our days of tension and disappointment with each other have now fallen and withered, like overripe fruit."

"That's so, Father. When others are present, though, I will always call you *Ensi*."

"I'd be very happy for your company, but I'm not leaving the palace today before my evening walk up to the temples, since I expect to see your brother for lunch. Oh! When Tikal offered to have a guard assigned to Muda to show him Isin's neighborhoods, I thought to myself that you know them too, since you served as a city guard when you first started working at the palace."

As the men left the banquet hall, Enlil-Bani offered, "I hope Ezina feels better now that you've returned. She's been much like a blossom that was stuck shut, unable to open and show her innate beauty."

"I'm going to try to help with that. She told me that she only left the palace a few times while I was on caravan, to attend important ceremonies. I'd be very down if I never saw the sun; maybe that's affected her as well."

The king mused out loud to Zambiya as they proceeded down the passageway, saying, "I think Tikal's losing patience with me; he believes I should re-marry as a political matter to gain an ally. I wish he'd drop the matter, though I understand his concerns. I'm too preoccupied as *Ensi* to be thinking about getting a wife, or being a husband, as far as that goes."

———————— •—●—• ————————

True to his word, starting early the next day to avoid the intensity of the sun and heat, Zambiya escorted Ezina on a leisurely walk out of the palace. She wore her best veil, a cream-colored linen cloth with crimson border with small gold beads dangling from the corners.

Bare chested, Zambiya wore a white skirt with a fringe of black and yellow decorations reaching to mid-calf; a dark leather armband held a short dirk in a scabbard on his left forearm and a silver bracelet circled his right upper arm. Nothing indicated his elevated rank in the palace guard.

Ezina used one hand to hold onto his upper arm for support, as her lower back ached and her legs were swollen. Nevertheless, they made a slow circuit of several permanent shops, making a point of stopping to chat briefly with Suba, Nani's husband, at the stall he and his father maintained to sell their pottery.

Several paces away were open stalls, just mats on the ground mostly attended by women from the countryside, usually wearing light shawls shading their heads and shoulders, but often wearing nothing above the waist except a veil. A perpetual din prevailed as vendors called out to nearby patrons, their sounds mixing with the added contributions of goats, ducks, chickens and geese, plus donkeys and the barking of feral dogs on the prowl for scraps. The dogs roamed the outskirts of the square at this time of day.

There were vendors for baskets and woven goods, dyed yarns and dried fish, fresh eggs, and tethered birds intended for food. Mostly women, the shoppers were often attended by boys too young to be employed in the fields, which surrounded Isin on three sides, Buranun forming the fourth boundary.

After re-acquainting themselves with the market offerings, Zambiya and Ezina sat together under a faded green palm frond awning in front of a baker's stall, sharing a date-filled pastry. Using straws cut from the riverside reeds that the vendor provided to avoid the barley husks floating on the surface, they drank frothy warm beer that tasted salty and smelled vaguely of mold.

Delighted with the attention being paid to her, Ezina enjoyed her husband's presence and reveled in the stimulating sights and sounds of the market. Even the combination of odors added to her experience, having remained inside the palace for several moons. With the fragrance of baked breads and pastries so close to her, she could ignore the stench of animal dung.

She failed to notice the numerous surreptitious glances Zambiya made toward the top of the zigurrat, as he yearned to see Ninmah once again.

Neither of them saw the Chaldean crouched in the shade of the zigurrat at the first level above the community square. He paid no attention to the market activities, but watched the final touches being made to the new palace veranda overlooking the kitchen courtyard. A heavy woven canopy with the heft of canvas, striped with dark brown and light yellow bands, was being attached to the wall over the doorway with brass bolts, although the weight was supported by light pinewood posts on all four corners.

The Chaldean allowed himself a half smile of anticipation, then rose to standing and joined the early communicants who were descending the zigurrat from the two temples above. He vowed to himself that he would wait a full fifteen days of observing the activities to answer his questions: Who would use the veranda? Was there to be a routine schedule? Following hard on that resolve was a regret that he would have to wait that long before he could have Ninegala and leave for Larsa.

Early morning several days later, Ninmah, a priestess and revered singer of the sacred hymns to goddess Ninisina, stood just inside the entrance hallway to Egal-Mah, the goddess's home and temple atop the zigurrat. It was light enough for her to discern the throng of field workers as they streamed forth from the city gate to the south, creating a din of discordant sounds. She leaned against the painted wood frame of the doorway, a slight frown on her face as she waited.

Hearing the sound of footsteps ascending the steep stairs across from her, her lips parted to allow a smile, greeting Zambiya as he completed the ascent from the city square.

The aroma of cedar incense and scented lotion emanated from her, as usual. Zambiya was transported in memory to his past liaisons with her, many months in the past, before his caravan trip to the north.

Ninmah's black hair was arranged loosely, framing her face and falling to below the tops of her shoulders. Her dark eyes shined in the morning light, and the shape of her full lips and completely symmetrical nose still seemed to him the most beautiful face he had ever seen. Her nose was narrow and her eyebrows perfectly shaped. He had always admired her unblemished skin which was like a tawny marble. She wore a loose white tunic that covered only one shoulder and ended at mid-calf, belted around her slender waist with a crimson rope that ended with pointed silver dangles. She wore a necklace and matching earrings made of hematite beads, but at the end of the earrings and in the middle of the necklace were polished pendants of amber, the one on the necklace the size of a small bird's egg, with a tiny flower encased in it. The pendant hung from her neck to a point just above the cleft between her ample breasts, the amber contrasting with her skin in a manner that guaranteed that any male would look there.

Zambiya had given these to her after he had returned from his first caravan and after becoming a palace guard. He recognized them at once, and knew that Ninmah wore them to signal that she wanted to see him, too.

"I hoped with all my heart that you would be willing to see me. Our parting left me with an ache that I have carried all this time, fearing that you hated me," he said.

Ninmah held up her hand to stop him from saying more, and pulled him into the passageway that led to the interior chambers of the temple and the sanctuary of the goddess. From the darkness, they watched silently as Ningal and his scribe passed, carefully making their descent from the uppermost stairwell of the zigurrat.

She held her hands crossed over her bosom, saying, "I was in such pain from your decision to marry Ezina." A tear fell down her cheek, and she swiped it away impatiently. "I said horrible things to you, I was so angry about her getting pregnant, and you left within days, so I had no way to take them back." She touched Zambiya on his forearm, a gentle stroking motion, and continued, "You never left my thoughts, nor my heart; still, I knew there was no other way to save our lives but for you to marry her."

She looked past him and formed her face in an unusual expression, combining a frown with her chin jutted forward, as if only civility required her to ask, "How is she?"

Zambiya had anticipated this question and knew there were answers that were as if wrapped in sharp blades, while others were cushioned. "Miserable, I'd say. Her ankles are swollen, like her belly, and she can't sleep easily." He hesitated before continuing, "She doesn't know I'm here, of course. So I won't give her any well-wishes from you. She is all too aware that I had always come here to see you, not her."

Mollified, Ninmah replied, "I liked Ezina, but she did tend to be pouty. Honestly, she never settled in to being a priestess. She always said she liked being married before her husband died." She turned back to him and looked directly at Zambiya's crotch before saying with a slight smile, "She likes being married to you, I'm sure." She took a deep breath before she continued with the speech she had rehearsed before agreeing to see him. "I think about you and even dream about being with you, but that is ended. You're married to Ezina, and can't be married to me, so we can't be anything more to each other." She stopped him from responding by placing two fingers flat against his lips, then continued, "It would be torture for me, and the gods would punish us both if we were to continue a dalliance outside your marriage. It would be wrong."

Zambiya had expected her announcement, and was prepared with a response. He shook his head slowly before answering, saying, "Much as I'd like to continue to share pleasures with you, I agree we can't be more than friends. I still want to see you though, just to talk and be in your presence. The gods won't mind that."

Ninmah started to weep, softly at first, then turned her back to Zambiya so he could not see her face, which she was already covering with both hands as she gave in to quiet sobs. Zambiya pulled her close to his chest, his arms encircling her shoulders and arms. "Please, goddess, say that we can meet as friends."

Ninmah pulled away from him and strode purposefully into the hallway of the temple, wiping at her cheeks with one hand and gesturing with a backward swipe of her hand to keep him from following her, and repeated just the one word of resignation, "Friends."

———————— • ● • ————————

Neti and Muda met for the first time when they reported to an early morning patrol for the first of several forays into the various districts of Isin. The palace guards maintained several shifts and schedules for the purpose of displaying and maintaining civil order. Muda now wore a helmet of polished bronze and leather with black ornamental horns, signifying his elevated guard status and at the same time covering his red hair. Like other guards, he wore a white cape that covered his body from shoulder to mid-calf, open in front, displaying a bronze short sword with a leather-wrapped handle.

Dressed in simple garb without weapons, Neti wore just a knee length tunic over a light red skirt, but he wore the un-adorned white conical cap of a palace official. Like a miniature version of Tikal in build, squat in stature, he had the muscular forearms of a scribe. Despite his youth, he was doing his best to grow a beard, which was gathered and fed through a small silver bead with a center of rough leather, so it wouldn't slip out. The itching already caused him to question his decision not to be clean shaven.

It happened that Nabi was the leader of this particular patrol, which had only three other ordinary guards, and he knew both Muda and Neti. He suggested they walk behind him but in front of the other guards, so they could ask him questions.

Neti was extremely curious about Muda, even though Tikal had given him some information along with a description, which was as brief as, "He's a Gutian."

Nabi planned to start the patrol by walking directly to Isin's farthest wall from the palace, then give further detail about the neighborhoods they passed while returning. Heading out Muda and Neti walked together.

Neti opened the conversation by volunteering, "As you know, I'm Tikal's son. He's training me to be either an emissary to another city or, if I'm worthy, to be an advisor to the *Ensi*. He'd like me to take his place in the palace eventually, but I've much to learn before then, of course."

"Muda from Gutia land, other side other big river. You call *Idiglat*. Was slave when come Isin. Muda warrior, captured in battle. *Ensi* buy Muda when he work … worked temple … groundsman.”

"It's not usual for field supervisors to have slaves. How did that happen, anyway? I hope you don't mind me asking you about this; I've never had any real talks with former slaves, and actually, no Gutians either. I think we will see each other quite a lot in the palace.”

"Is all right ask Muda.” He thought about what to share and what to withhold and finally said, “Muda sold from farm to Isin man. He tell Muda be like woman for him. Muda warrior, not like. Hit with stool, ran away, hid. Guards find Muda, whip for punish.” Muda pulled his cape aside and showed Neti the multiple divot pocks in his flesh. Neti cringed at the sight, his brow furrowing.

"Enlil-Bani buy Muda next day. Him… his … son, Enmerkar… was have name Bani-mur then. Leg broke, need help to move, to get leg strong, later go to *edubba* from Enlil-Bani and Lith-el house.” Muda thought as he took several more steps before inserting, “Lith-el… was Enlil-Bani's wife. Muda take Enmerkar in cart to *edubba*, bring back after Muda work in field.” He paused a moment, looking at Neti with concern, and asked, “You know Enmerkar?”

"Not yet. I've lived with soldiers, with guards, with the minor palace administrators, and even with the temple priests. Once Father had me work on a river barge between harvests.” He thought for a while then shared, “At times I think I know a lot, then I realize all of it's on the surface, like knowing the river only when it's calm. The river's not the same in flood, nor in drought. I have to remind myself about that.”

Impressed by the young man's reported insight into his life, Muda responded, “Muda think same. Enlil-Bani buy… bought Muda, promise to free him, let go home in one year. Muda have wife, son in Gutia land.” He waited a brief time, considering that Neti must know how Enlil-Bani had become the *Ensi*. “Enlil-Bani keep bargain. When he … be *Ensi*, free Muda, let go home with Zambiya with caravan to Gutia.” A cloud passed over Muda's countenance with the memory, but he continued on, saying, “No family in Gutia. Wife have new man, son have other father now, father of Muda dead.”

"How long were you gone, Muda?”

"Five year." He hesitated, then corrected with, "Years. Wife sure Muda dead. Muda not blame wife. Blame gods."

Neti reflected before commenting, and chose to leave the content of Muda's life alone, but to suggest instead a refinement to the Gutian's speech mannerisms.

"Muda, you name yourself often when you speak. Most people don't do that; they say, 'I' instead. It would be faster for you to do that, too. I wouldn't mention it, but you correct yourself when you speak, so it sounds to me that you are trying to improve your speech."

"Mu…" He smiled at Neti and chuckled, then started over saying with emphasis, "I…I…I need practice doing. Neti tell when Mu… I forget." He smiled more broadly this time.

Neti laughed out loud, and considered adding 'me' to the lesson, but quickly rejected the thought and just said, "You'll get it soon enough."

———————— • ● • ————————

Half of a moon's full cycle later Enmerkar woke early from a troubled sleep, becoming aware that his arms were encircling his chest tightly and that the familiar ache behind his eye was forming. He forced himself to focus on the dream that had wakened him, more confident about the feeling of those dreams that had seemed like divinations in the past. Noting the details he marveled at the clarity of some features contrasted with the vagueness of others. He was aware that he only observed the dream events without participating in them and then allowed himself to become immersed in the ominous nature of this dream as the scene progressed.

The locale was clearly Isin with its twin-templed zigurrat, late in the night. Enmerkar seemed to be hovering over a snake, notable for its small size, watching as it gained entry under a corner of the barricaded city gate, unseen by the guards atop the wall. It made its way by side-winding across the grit and ruts through the alleys and broader lanes, always staying near the walls of the buildings, eventually skirting the edge of the market square before making directly for the palace platform. At first there was nothing to distinguish the snake, but as it turned along the edge of the plaza steps, two bronze colored spikes with black center lines became prominent on top of its head. It turned once and seemed to look toward Enmerkar, holding its gaze, its tongue searching the air, then slithered away. Instead of trying to circumvent the night guards and enter under the palace doors, the snake wound along the ground and disappeared when it rounded the steps that faced the side of the zigurrat. At that point Enmerkar wakened shivering, his mouth dry.

No doubt clouded Enmerkar's mind that this dream should be brought to his father's attention. He dressed hurriedly and limped out to the front courtyard, noting that the sun's rays were already starting to illuminate the top of the zigurrat, visible for miles around Isin. He started to return inside when he was joined by the elderly door attendant, who looked at him with a puzzled gaze.

"Shalamu, Lord. What roused you?" He rubbed his eyes with both hands as he waited for a response.

"I'm merely restless, and I need to go to the palace. As soon as the students start arriving, let me know. And please tell Naram I'd like to see him as soon as he's up."

"That should be soon if he slept well, young master," he replied. "Like me, his old body keeps him wondering what will hurt next."

"Not all a matter of age, in my case."

"I'll let you know when the students start arriving."

Enmerkar nodded agreement and turned toward his sleeping room, needing the steadying presence of the walls to help his balance in the dim hallway, wishing that he had brought his staff with him. He knew to expect a delay before he could be gathered by litter bearers from the palace, but impatience impelled him to divert his attention to some other activity.

He shifted his awareness to the stiffness in his 'good' left knee, and he gratefully sat back on his bed to wait for Naram. He kneaded his thighs to reduce the stiffness in his knee joints as he waited, willing his legs to do his bidding with a minimum of pain.

CHAPTER SEVEN

A SERPENT IN THE FIELD

What can a person do when their life suddenly changes, even for the better? Wisdom suggests seeking counsel from others with experience, then making a choice between likely alternatives. Failure to choose is itself a choice.

Zambiya was awake and dressed as he had not gone to bed. There had been talk early the previous day that there might be an attempted incursion of the palace and he was prepared, his unsheathed sword leaning against the doorway frame. He knew several guards roamed the palace halls, and had confidence that they would call him if any threat was detected.

He idly felt the stubble of beard on his chin as he lounged in a padded divan chair. He started and stood when he heard Ezina make a loud grunt. He turned toward their bed from his place by the doorway and saw that she was awake, trying to sit up. Although only the two night sconces illuminated their chamber, he sensed her distress and crossed the room to her when she groaned and saw her put both her hands over her abdomen.

"I'm having a cramp in my belly," she declared, grimacing. Breathing shallowly, her respirations came in little starts and stops. She clenched her hands into fists, willing the pain to stop, then made a loud, "Oooohh!" She sat up and swung her legs off the side of the bed and shouted, "Sud! Sud! Come here!"

"What hurts, Ezina? Are you cramping?" Zambiya sat next to her on the bed and tried to calm her, putting his arm over her shoulder.

"I need Sud," she shuddered, leaning her head against his chest. Then pointing toward her thighs she said, "Look, my water broke. This baby's coming…nowoooooh!" she moaned again, the sound increasing in volume, and reaching her arms out to grasp her lower abdomen with both hands and shifting her weight back and forth, seeking a position that might make her comfortable.

Sud entered the room wearing just an ankle length shift and a shawl over her shoulders. She grasped the situation quickly and knelt in front of Ezina, grasping her shoulders and saying, "Finally you will have this child, Mistress, and feel much better." She looked up to Zambiya and said to him, "Please, Master, light all these torches and have En-me send for a mid-wife and a priestess. I'll see to the bedding and Ezina. No need to hurry. It's her first child and I'm told the first is never fast."

Nevertheless, Zambiya hurried to light the four large sconces in the room, and rushed out past the doorway drapes. When Ezina let out another louder groan he resolved to remain ignorant of the mystery of childbirth, a province of women alone.

Ezina tried to stand, imploring, "I don't want to have a baby, Sud. Make this stop."

Sud turned away so that Ezina couldn't see her smile, and stated with confidence, "I'm going to get fresh bedding and another nightdress for you. Don't get up!" she ordered.

Sud left the room, chuckling to herself. She had heard of other new mothers insisting that they didn't want children at this point in childbirth. She quickly changed her own clothes and then got a set of bed coverings to put on the bed, making a mental note to have one of the household slaves dispose of the entire bed case.

———————— • ● • ————————

Two days after his last visit to Ninegala's room, and well before dawn, the Chaldean rose and dressed in dark loose clothing. His face was covered and his knife was secured in its sheath, attached to his lower right leg. Nisaba's home was dark. Barefoot, he carried his sandals under one arm as he crossed the hallway from his room to the bedroom of Ninegala; with one hand he shielded the light of the torch he carried so as to not disturb the servant at the end of the hall.

He didn't hesitate when he reached the portal, quickly pushing the drape to one side and angling into the room, his back to the hallway. With a silent bending of his knees, he placed his sandals on the floor and then replaced an unlit wall torch with the lighted one he had brought. It was of no consequence to him that the oil of the torch he removed was spreading across the reed mat that covered the floor, though the scent of the oil briefly reminded him of wet donkey. His hands now empty, he slipped his dagger from its sheath and silently approached Ninegala's bed.

The young girl was sleeping on her side and facing the wall which her bed was butted against, barely visible in the subdued light. Her right hand was under her cheek on the overstuffed bolster she used, her back to the Chaldean. 'Perfect,' he thought to himself, and he moved to the girl and put his hand over her mouth, waiting only a moment until her eyes fluttered open before he whispered into her ear, "Do what I tell you and you will live. Make even a single sound, I'll slit your throat." He showed her his knife in the dim light. "Do you understand?"

Her eyes were wide with terror and she started crying, trying hard to make no sound; her breathing was a shallow panting and she indicated ascent by moving her head up and down under his hand.

"No noise!" he ordered in a rasping whisper. "Kneel on the floor and stretch your arms out on the bed." With his dagger held at the side of her neck, he released her head and smiled as she hurried to obey. She covered her mouth with one hand to keep from making any but the smallest weeping whimper, barely able to restrain a scream as she felt her nightshift raised to her waist.

※　●　※

The Chaldean arrived at the city square when the sky was still dark. He skirted the edges of the open area by using the permanent market stalls and then the steps of the zigurrat as cover for his progress. He crossed the open area past the steps by moving slowly, bent over, watching the two night guards at the palace door to make sure he had not been detected. Even though the sentries had been warned to be watchful, the Chaldean's dark clothing and small form kept him hidden from sight with little illumination from the sliver of a setting moon.

Once he rounded the steps of the zigurrat, he moved along the wall that separated the kitchen courtyard from an open space. This broad corridor led to the guard quarters and passed by the refuse fire used by the palace staff. Gaining entry via this route had been part of his plan once he realized the palace could be entered through the door to the newly created upper terrace. Excited by the prospect of accomplishing his mission, he acquired the long pole that was used by the fire attendant to distribute the cinders. It had a flat rake end which he jammed into the ground and leaned the pole onto the top of the wall, testing it to be sure it was secure. As quietly as he could manage, he started climbing toward the top of the wall, hand over hand on the pole, foot over foot on the rough bricks.

The Chaldean was unaware of the two men descending the steps of the zigurrat. Ningal the priest, having determined that he was done with his observations for the night, was intent on comparing the tablets made this night with another set from the previous week. His blindfold was around his neck, since it was still dark.

Ningal abruptly made a sweeping motion with his hand and bent his knees. Putting his hand on his companion's shoulder he pointed to the palace wall. Keeping his voice low he said to his scribe, "Be quiet. Look there at that part of the palace wall. Do you see a child there? It looks like he's climbing the wall."

"I can only see him when he moves, like just now," the scribe whispered. "He's reaching for the top of the wall."

"Leave me here with these tablets, and I'll wait for you. Go tell the guards at the entrance that someone's trying to get into the palace."

'Why's a child out here anyway?' he mused to himself.

———— • ● • ————

Ninegala regained consciousness to find herself lying on the floor next to her bed in complete darkness although the sun was just rising. Confusion gripped her, and it took her a few moments to register that her private parts were painful and wet. Feeling the moistness between her legs jolted her memory and dread flooded her. Unable to see, she worked her way upright, first using the bed for support and then as her guide to orient herself. She slowly crawled toward the doorway but almost sprawled on her face when her hand reached the oil from the empty sconce. When she reached the door she used its frame to stand up and step into the hall, which was also still dark. She leaned against the frame and held onto the drape for additional support, but she lost strength and slumped onto her knees, holding onto her abdomen. She took several deep breaths before screaming, "Mother! Mother! Help me."

By the time Nisaba reached her, torch in hand, Ninegala was collapsed and lay shivering on her side, wailing with pain and terror. Sherida soon joined them, also carrying a torch. Nisaba feared that her daughter had been raped from the blood she saw on her night dress, since she knew Ninegala's fourth moon blood was not due yet. Although she was trying her best to comfort her, she was also beset with the thought that this daughter's prospects for marriage had suddenly become far less hopeful if she was correct and this night's events ever became known.

Nisaba finally registered the fact that she and her daughters were supposed to be guarded from intrusion, and she shouted, "Engu!! Where are you?"

With no immediate response and while cradling her sobbing daughter's head in her lap, stroking her hair, Nisaba ordered Sherida, "Go wake that sluggard right now. I'll have him flayed." Then, as an afterthought, "Where is that runt Aga sent?"

Sherida held her torch in both her trembling hands, as they were slippery from sweat, and she moved hurriedly toward the end of the sleeping quarter hallway. She could see the feet of the watchman past the portal drapes and stepped through the opening. "Engu," she said loudly and started to shake him by the shoulder, but reflexively pulled her hand away when she felt blood and saw the great gash in the man's throat, his staring eyes lifeless. She inhaled to shout to her mother, but was overcome by the odor of so much blood; seized by a fit of vomiting that continued to gripe her insides, she leaned against the wall while trying to wipe blood off her hand. She began sobbing even as the heaving prevailed, but managed to hysterically call out, "He's dead, Mother!"

Zambiya hurried into the main hall of the royal chambers where Enlil-Bani was sleeping.

"Call for En-me," he ordered the first guard he encountered. There were two more stationed outside Enlil-Bani's bedroom suite.

At the same time, two guards ran into the hall from Tikal's household within the palace. The Chief Counselor had been alerted by the front door guards about what Ningal's scribe had reported. One of the guards said loudly, "An intruder's been seen climbing the courtyard wall, but it's just a child. Nevertheless, Tikal wants this area secured until the child is found. He might be a scout."

Zambiya ran into Enlil-Bani's room, declaring urgently, "Father. Muda. You need to wake up." Muda had not been asleep and joined them in the bedroom instantly, carrying a sickle sword in one hand and a short spear in the other.

Enlil-Bani sprang off the bed where he had been dozing against a bolster propped on the wall; he was fully dressed in a knee-length tunic, with his sandals laced to his knees. His personal obsidian knife was in its scabbard at his waist. Shortly after his elevation to the throne, he had been offered an ornately carved ornamental bronze knife, but stubbornly declared that he was content with this one.

"Has there been an entry, son?"

"Don't know yet. It was reported that a child may have entered the palace after climbing up the courtyard wall. Could be a scout with plans to open a door for a larger team. Tikal's already deployed archers to the roof to watch for an attack. We'll start looking right away."

"Is it even light yet?"

"Doubt it." Zambiya suddenly recalled why he had even come here, and announced, "Oh, Ezina's in labor. We should call En-me and summon a mid-wife."

"He's in his quarters, I'm sure. When we were alerted that there might be an attempt on my life he refused to leave the palace." The king never alluded to the fact that the warning had come from Enmerkar.

Enlil-Bani took control of the situation and said, "Now that you're here, son, I'll send a guard to get En-me. We'll have a mid-wife come from the temple." He left and entered the hall, dispatching one of the guards to fetch En-me.

———————————— • ———— • ————

Pairs of men examined the halls and rooms throughout the palace. Nabi and another guard separated to search the kitchen area and the courtyard but found nothing. Finished there, Nabi and his companion made their way toward the central area behind the throne room that separated the royal suite from the other living quarters. In the lead with his sickle sword, Nabi gripped the handle in both his hands; the other man following behind with a short spear in one hand and a torch held aloft in the other.

The Chaldean had been delayed by bridging the separation between the courtyard wall and the veranda railing. He was just descending the stairway that led into the interior of the palace when Nabi and the other guard passed by on the ground level. Startled to find anyone at all at this time of the night, the short man was re-considering his plan to penetrate the interior on this night when the second guard spoke.

"Nabi, we should check up these stairs to see if the child is on that new veranda they built. It won't take long, and ..."

Knowing he was trapped, the Chaldean went on the offensive. Running down the stairs, he lunged at the guard holding the torch. Aiming his dagger at the hand with the spear in it, he hoped to go next for the man's throat. Instead he connected with the man's forearm but the knife passed cleanly between the bones. The guard gasped and inhaled sharply, but despite his surprise, he struck at the Chaldean with the torch, dousing him with oil along one arm and setting him ablaze.

"Nabi," he shouted. "He's here! The boy's here!"

The Chaldean was trying to strike with his dagger and beat at his clothing with his other hand at the same time. The flames overcame his intent on remaining silent and he began screaming. By this time Nabi appeared; instantly reading the situation, he struck the Chaldean's arm at the wrist with his sword, severing the hand with its dagger, then knocked him to the ground.

Nabi chuckled mirthlessly as he grabbed the stump of the Chaldean's arm and held it over the flames to stop the bleeding. He used his foot to smother the last of the flames, which was already burning out from lack of fuel. The Chaldean's incomprehensible screams were annoying him, so he kicked him in the jaw, rendering him senseless.

Nabi asked his mate, "Did he cut you?"

The guard held up his arm, which was still bleeding, but said, "I'll live. Surprised me, though. Where d'you think he's from?"

"Don't care." He took the torch from the guard and said, "Wrap your arm now." When the injured guard jerked the Chaldean's black skirt free to use as a bandage for his own arm, the Chaldeans genitals were revealed. Nabi suddenly exclaimed, "Great An! That's no child!" He held the torch closer for a better look at the prostrate man on the floor, then kicked him in the ribs to see if he was awake, but got no response.

"Go get that taken care of and send a couple men to gather up this piece of dog shit. He'll answer some questions before he's hung."

· ● ·

Still unconscious, the Chaldean lay on his back on a litter in the throne room. The stump of his arm slowly dripped blood and he made grasping motions with his remaining hand. He occasionally moved his head back and forth. Nude below the waist, he now wore only a rawhide strap encircling his abdomen. His scorched shirt caused the dominant odor in the room, like a guttering torch. Except for a gap in the almost-closed circle of observers that allowed Enlil-Bani to see, he was almost surrounded by men at a distance of about two paces.

Seated on his throne, still wearing his informal attire, Enlil-Bani was attended by Tikal along with his son, Neti. Also in attendance were Zambiya, Muda, Nabi and En-me the *a-zu*.

The latter examined the charred flesh of the wounded arm, his stomach objecting to the odor, which up close reminded him of any other seared meat. He was not expected to attend the birth of Zambiya's child so he had chosen to be in the throne room, knowing that Enmerkar would be arriving soon.

There were also three guards, two of whom had carried the litter into the throne room and the third who had carried the torch to light the way. These latter retreated from the circle of high-ranking men, but since they had not been sent away by Tikal they remained standing in the background behind Nabi, curious about the intruder. Neither of them wanted to call attention to the fact that they were still present, so they stayed silent, fascinated by the small man's form with its adult genitals.

Finally Tikal spoke to the almost silent group, saying, "I see now why Ningal sent word that a child was trying to enter the palace. I'd have thought the same thing in the dark." He added idly to no one in particular, "Ningal must have the eyes of a cat." He held up the Chaldean's dagger, which had been brought with him on the litter, along with the detached hand. He called one of the litter bearers forward and pointed at the hand, ordering "and get rid of that." The guard hastened to obey, picking the hand up by the thumb and striding purposefully toward the door behind the throne, fully intending to seize a little attention by displaying the hand as a trophy.

Neti spoke up right after, saying, "The scribe that brought Ningal's message said this thing had climbed a pole onto the courtyard wall. That needs attention so it can't happen again. Do you want me to see to that, father?"

"Of course. Deal with it by mid-day."

Enmerkar passed Neti as the young man left to carry out his father's order. Walking with purpose though limping he made his way forward from the public entrance. He was summoned as soon as the Chaldean had been found in the palace. The threat seemed to be just the one person, as no other attempt to breech the palace had occurred. He unobtrusively stroked En-me's upper arm as he walked around him, making close observations of the Chaldean. He asked whoever might have the answer, "Where are his weapons?"

Nabi responded, "There was just that one." He pointed to the weapon in Tikal's hand, and then added, "I have to say it's quite sharp."

Enmerkar started to speak, but remembered his conversation with Enlil-Bani about the danger of acknowledging his gift of prescience, so he said nothing directly, but frowned at recalling the serpent in his dream, especially the two notable spearhead barbs above its eyes.

Instead, he resumed walking around the form on the litter, then asked, again to no one in particular, "What is that for?" He pointed at the leather strap around the lower mid-section of the Chaldean, which held no clothing and wouldn't have been used to support a skirt.

Zambiya stepped forward from the group and pulled on the strap, finding that it was sturdy and snug, worn low on the man's torso. "I think I know."

He grabbed the handless arm at the elbow and used it to pull the Chaldean onto his side, revealing a very slender sheath suspended between the buttocks. He removed the weapon it held, revealing a dirk with a short handle and a double-edged bronze blade. Zambiya pulled out his own knife and cut the strap and handed it with its weapon to Tikal. "He was ready to kill, that's certain. When he wakes, I'll find out who sent him." Then with a familiar slap on Enmerkar's shoulder he smiled and said, "Good observation, brother."

Enlil-Bani had been silent until now, but made a decision that broke with past precedent and declared, "I don't want him killed. Not yet. I also don't want him escaping." He spoke directly to Nabi, ordering, "Get a strong cage from the stables, hopefully a new one like we'd use for lambs, and put him in it. Keep him in the guard room, and bring him back here when he wakes." He raised his voice for emphasis and, pointing in an encompassing circular motion to the guards, commanded, "No torture; no beatings. I'll see to his punishment when I'm ready." Then to Tikal, "Where's he been living 'til now? Did everyone think he was just a boy?"

"That is what I will find out, my *Ensi*." He transferred the two weapons he was holding to one hand and with a motion to Nabi and the remaining two guards, he sent them from the throne room to obey the directives of the king.

Zambiya raised his hand toward Tikal and said, "I'd like that small knife when you're done."

• ● •

The midwife approached Zambiya and Ezina's suite accompanied by a eunuch and found that a priestess from the temple of Ninisina had already arrived. The eunuch was relieved of his weapon by the guard who accompanied the pair to the living quarters. The eunuch, a burly man with soft features and a shaved head, carried two cushions under one arm. Shaped like flattened triangular ramps, they sloped up for the knees then back down for the ankles and feet. Stuffed hard and stained, it was obvious that attempts had been made to clean them; they still reeked of blood and birth fluid from past uses, a smell vaguely reminiscent of the sea at low tide.

A woman of late middle age with downturned mouth and heavy-lidded eyes, the midwife carried a beaded instrument bag over one shoulder plus two new covers for the cushions in one hand, knowing the pregnant woman was daughter-in-law to the king.

The priestess entered the combination sitting and ante-room first and was greeted by Ezina's slave Sud, who left her mistress when she heard people approach.

"Shalamu, Revered One," Sud said. The midwife entered right behind the priestess, but the eunuch stayed right outside the door, waiting for permission to enter.

"Shalamu," said the priestess. "Where is the lady who desires the blessings of the Great Goddess?"

"She awaits you and the midwife in here." She lowered her voice and warned the priestess and midwife, "She is very frightened. Her name is Ezina." She then announced at a normal volume, "I will bring you any supplies you want."

"I will do the mother's blessing now, the baby blessing when it is born." The priestess was barely twenty years of age with a body shape as featureless as a wooden pole; she had only recently advanced from novitiate status. This was her first attendance at a childbirth, so her mental preparations had focused on the ritual, none on the birth. She intended to remain present after the ceremonies in case mother or child did not survive.

She found Ezina lying supine on the bed, crying, moaning, holding her abdomen in her hands and rocking from side to side. Ezina looked toward the doorway when the two women entered with Sud, and raised up part way, propping herself on her elbows.

"This hurts. Can you make it stop?" Ezina implored to both. Her breath came in short gasps, straining from bouts of contractions.

The midwife replied, saying without emotion, "I will attend you as soon as you have been blessed."

After a sharp intake of breath the priestess exclaimed, "I know you! Ezina? You were a novitiate at the same time I was. How did this happen?"

Ezina had lain back on the bed holding her head in her hands, her eyes shut tight, shaking her head and moaning. Sud answered for Ezina, saying,

"It happened the usual way, Revered One." Sud's tone was dismissive despite the difference in their stations.

Then she said with urgency, "Can you begin the blessing ceremony now, so the midwife can help my lady?"

The birth rites now held new meaning for the priestess and she quickly surveyed the bedchamber, mentally noting the corners of the room to determine where to start.

She shifted a deep ochre-colored linen purse tied around her waist up her nearly hipless slender frame and pulled out a small draw-stringed leather pouch. It held two effigies. The first was a palm-sized clay form of a woman, facially without distinct features but with a body denoting large full breasts and an abdomen hanging over the genital area, the legs ending at the area of the knees. The second figure was much smaller, clearly that of a baby with indistinct sexual parts, exaggerated lips and closed eyes. Markings on the head seemed to suggest rather than describe hair. Both were fashioned from a dark clay, dis-similar to the clay used to make ordinary bricks.

"Water," the priestess called to Sud, who moved at once to bring a water pitcher. Sud poured some into the leather pouch when it was held out to her by the priestess, and watched as the effigies were added to the bag, the drawstring then pulled tight.

The priestess addressed the midwife then, saying, "I can do the blessings while you attend Ezina." She stood still a moment, mentally rehearsing the sequence of the ritual, representing the four corners of the world revealed by the stars, then commenced.

"Aruru," she intoned. "Attend us, we beseech you. Be benevolent...."

CHAPTER EIGHT
AMENDING THE GARDEN

The gods have revealed that all the dead must cross the river of the underworld, but none has revealed from where new spirits on the earth come. Are we all created anew at birth? What is the fate of those who do not survive their birth? The gods do not share their secrets.

Nisaba arrived at the palace shortly after the sun had risen, accompanied by one very nervous old male servant. Her hair was mostly covered with a quickly chosen multi-colored scarf, but many strands of her hair had escaped the cloth and protruded like a nest of snakes. Her dress was a shapeless long smock missing its belt, and her sandals were the first she encountered.

Ninegala had declared that she was never going back into her own room, and she and Sherida had moved to their mother's bedroom to console each other as best they could. Nisaba's other household servants remained at her home, and were following her instructions to move the servant's body to the courtyard, then to clean the murder scene.

As the former Queen of Isin, Nisaba asked the sentries on duty at the main entrance to admit her and to arrange an audience with Tikal on an urgent matter, and further declared that she would wait inside until she was received. The sentry inquired further about her business, but she would only disclose that the subject was both private and urgent, though she added further that there was a dangerous person at large. She had determined that she would tell only Tikal and Enlil-Bani about the rape of her daughter, and in private, but would publically proclaim the murder of her servant so that the king would have his guards apprehend the vicious little man. She was pre-occupied with trying to figure out how to protect Ninegala's reputation as a chaste girl. It was only after she declared that the dangerous man was very short that a sentry hastened inside to call for the Guard on Duty.

All the interior guards were well aware of the Chaldean's presence, but they had been strictly admonished by Neti and Tikal to keep the fact of an intrusion completely secret.

———— • ● • ————

Ezina was reclining on the floor of her bedroom, her knees on the thickest parts of the two ramp-like pillows. As instructed by the mid-wife, Sud knelt behind her mistress, cradling her head and shoulders, and giving support in those times when Ezina was able to lean back and rest between contractions.

Ezina's lack of activity for the last many months had made her incapable of extended exertion. She was already exhausted by the middle of the morning from contractions which presented themselves to her with astonishing regularity. Sud did what she could to calm her mistress, but she was impatient with Ezina's cries and moans. Sud, a virgin herself, had never had a child. Nevertheless, she wanted at least to reduce the volume of Ezina's laments. During a lull between contractions, and after tenderly pulling her mistress' damp hair away from her forehead, she told her owner, "Mistress, you must remember that you are the wife of Zambiya and the daughter-in-law of the *Ensi*. You must present yourself as a model of bravery and resolve, better than a mere commoner like me. Try to direct your energy into the effort to push your child from your body. Do that with the very next cramp."

If Ezina had had the strength and could have reached her, she would have slapped her slave, but she considered what she had said, and tried to comply. With her next contraction, she gritted her teeth and only allowed muffled sounds out of her mouth, and found that it seemed to help with the misery.

The priestess had retreated to the comfort of the bed, newly cleaned and made up, waiting for the birth to occur so she could perform her next blessing, this time exhorting Damu, goddess Ninisina's son, to make the child healthy and strong. She divided her time between silently rehearsing her ritual and watching the actuality of birth, acknowledging to herself that she was ecstatic that she would never go through this misery herself.

The midwife was crouched on a low stool made of palm frond stems with a seat of woven leather straps, her feet inside Ezina's legs. She was chanting to herself in a low voice, entreating her own favorite gods to be kind to this mother and the child. Meanwhile, both her hands stroked Ezina's abdomen with pressure in a downward motion, occasionally stopping to pull the lips of the birth portal aside, trying to widen the path the infant must take. She could see the crown of the baby's head stretching the flesh of Ezina's nether lips. Ezina was panting, looking to the side toward the floor. The midwife lifted a hand up to Ezina's chin and raised her head to get her attention. She looked into her eyes and commanded, "Next time, Ezina. Pay attention! Next time you feel the need to push, bear down with all your might and don't make a sound. Use all your force to make your baby get out. This is where the baby belongs, not inside you. Next time!"

Ezina's arms had been crossed across her breasts, and she looked intently at the midwife. She closed her eyes and focused on the muscles that had created such misery for her, and shortly felt a contraction commence, growing more insistent. She moved her hands to the top of her abdomen and held her breath, shallow though it was, and when the urge and the pain seemed to be the greatest, she pushed down with her hands and squeezed out with her muscles as hard as she could. The midwife smiled approvingly and stretched the birth portal as wide as she could manage.

Too much for the strain, Ezina's flesh tore open at the edge of the canal by the anus, although little blood resulted due to the pressure on the tissues. Finally, the baby's head started to emerge, and the midwife said with urgency, "It's coming! Keep pushing, over and over. Push!"

Ezina gritted her teeth and held her breath, willing her very being to expel this child from her body, her face getting red and her hands clenched into fists.

The head and face were now free of the birth canal, and the midwife swallowed a gasp when she saw the infant's features, for the baby's upper lip was split nearly to the right nostril. 'Hope it's a boy,' she thought to herself, but said to Ezina only, "Your baby's almost free, Lady." She turned her gaze to the priestess and announced, "This'd be a good time to involve the gods in blessing this child."

By the time the priestess had finished her blessing ritual, a matter of several more contractions, the birth was complete, resulting in what appeared to be a robust and otherwise unremarkable boy with considerable straight hair and an elongated head. The eunuch was sent out to have a guard dispatched to summon Zambiya.

Sud and the midwife helped Ezina get onto the bed and propped her on her side leaning against a large ochre-colored bolster. Sud had anticipated what would likely please her mistress, and presented Ezina with a cup of honeyed plum wine while the baby was cleaned up and made presentable for the parents to see and hold. After several grateful swallows of the drink, and for the first time in their many months together, Ezina touched Sud's cheek and said, "May the gods bless you. Thank you."

• ● •

The Chaldean sat trembling in a corner of the cage, a sturdy contraption designed for transporting unruly rams. Made of supple green palm frond ribs lashed together with leather bindings, it contained two ordure-stained mats of common woven reeds covering the bottom of the crate. He held the stump of his arm up near his opposite shoulder to reduce the aching, but glared out at the porters who were transporting the cage along a passageway toward the throne room, accompanied by four guards. Still naked from the waist down, his dark brown upper garment was now nearly black with dried blood, some from the stump and some from raw flesh that had separated from the charred skin along his other arm. Anything that touched the burn was agonizing, and he cursed the bearers whenever they changed direction in the halls.

"Put the cage down right here in front," Neti ordered the porters. He had been directed by Tikal to arrange for the prisoner to be brought from the guard quarters, where he had been held.

"I have to piss," complained the Chaldean with misery in his voice.

There were now six guards in the room, including Nabi. Neti directed a porter to fetch a bitumen-coated night soil basket from the slave quarters.

84

Another was sent to the royal quarters to let Enlil-Bani know that the prisoner was present in the throne room for questioning, but he returned immediately followed by the king. Nisaba followed Enlil-Bani and Tikal, and of course, Muda. Zambiya was with Ezina and their new son.

As ordered by Enlil-Bani, Nisaba remained in the hallway outside the throne room, where she could see the Chaldean but not be seen. After conferring with Tikal, Enlil-Bani had granted Nisaba a private audience in which she divulged to him the rape of her daughter.

The porter who had gone for the basket to collect the urine returned at the same time that the others arrived, and he was directed to let the Chaldean relieve himself. One of the porters held the cage door up while the porter with the basket crouched down and pushed the basket in toward the small man. He warned him in a low voice, "Aim true, or I'll gouge out your eye." The Chaldean merely nodded and, despite the pain in his burned arm, managed to void without mishap. The porter removed the basket and left the room.

Before Enlil-Bani sat on the throne, he strode back to the passageway and asked Nisaba, "Is that the man you described to me?"

Nisaba was glaring at the Chaldean in his cage, and replied, "Yes, *Ensi*, he's the one. Please let me kill him. Please!"

"People would wonder why, Nisaba, and then what happened to your daughter would be known to everyone. I know you don't want that, so no, you can't kill him. But you can witness his death if I'm satisfied that he killed your servant."

Enlil-Bani had a nearby guard escort Nisaba to the king's dressing room to wait, intending to have her accompanied to her home by Tikal and Neti to inspect the room the Chaldean had occupied there. He then entered the throne room and walked slowly all the way around the cage and then took his place on the throne, making it clear that this was official business.

Without delay, Enlil-Bani asked the Chaldean directly, "Who sent you to kill me? You have the choice of telling me now or after you have more parts of your body removed by my barber, slowly. Or else I can have your other hand burned off, not cut off. Who?"

The Chaldean had no illusion that he was going to be allowed to live, and couldn't conceive of any strategy that would ensure his escape, so he swallowed hard and answered with anguish in his voice, "*Ensi* of Isin, Aga paid me to kill you. It was arranged by one of his servants, a relative from Ur. I received ten silver coils to seal the bargain, and was to get another ninety coils when I succeeded. I left the ten with my wife in Ur." He said all this in hope that he would be dispatched soon, as the pain of his injuries was nearly unbearable. His whole body was shivering with pain and fear, and his complexion was transforming to the color of the clay floor.

"How many others have you murdered, half-man?" inquired Neti.

Before the man could answer, Enlil-Bani interrupted and said, "No matter. He's a killer. More important is whether Nisaba or her daughters knew about his mission. Tell me now," he demanded of the Chaldean.

"No, *Ensi*, unless Aga had told them, and one of them would have brought it up with me if that was true." He groaned loudly when his stump suddenly felt a stabbing pain. "Nisaba kept asking me when I would be done and leave."

"Give him a blanket and get him some food," the king said to Neti. "Take him out of here." With a sweep of his arm toward the guards, he repeated his previous order, "No beatings. No torture." With that, Enlil-Bani rose from the throne and, with a look of disgust at the prisoner, left the throne room, motioning for Tikal to follow him.

With Muda leading the way back to the royal chambers, Tikal said to his king, "I'll go with Nisaba. I want to search his room."

"Wait, Tikal. Is it true that he gained entry to the palace from the new veranda?"

"It's true. He must have been observing it being built."

"His entry was my fault for having it built, like leaving a dike open so a field is always wet. See that it is barred from the inside."

Tikal had almost reached the doorway to leave when Enlil-Bani added, "Have Nisaba's household wait outside while you search the rooms. All of them. Take Nabi and Muda."

At first Tikal was puzzled by this order, then understood that someone in Nisaba's family might yet be involved and said, "Yes, *Ensi*, I will."

"Can he nurse?" Zambiya demanded of the midwife, pointing at his son's mouth. The baby was being cradled awkwardly in Sud's arms, having already been bathed, but not yet fed.

"I'm sure he can, and he wants to. Let's give him to his mother and let him try."

Ezina was dozing, but not fully asleep despite her depleted energies. Vaguely aware of the conversation despite the low volume in which it was held, she raised up from her bed, but started and groaned from the tenderness of her body. She decided to ignore the discomfort and said with more enthusiasm than she felt, "Give him to me; put him at my breast." She held her arms out to accept her baby after first baring one breast. It was at this time that she first saw her son and realized the deformation of his mouth. She instantly started crying, but nevertheless cuddled the boy to her breast where he commenced to nurse, using his gums and tongue as well as his malformed lips to suckle. Ezina said to the priestess, who was standing at some distance from the family and close to the door, "What horrid god would do this to my child? Asag-mouth!"

"Lady Ezina, I've not seen many births, but I've seen many children who were born with Asag-mouth before. The boys get along all right, but girls are often disposed of in the river, since it's hard to find them husbands, and some people think the family may be cursed. It's not as bad with boys. I'm sorry, Ezina. I know I did the ceremony right. Really, I did."

By this time the midwife had gathered all of her assortment of supplies and handed them to the eunuch to carry. The priestess joined them, but paused to say, "I will say two blessing rites a day for the next ten days to beg the gods to help your boy, Ezina. I was glad I could be here with you."

After the birthing team had left, Ezina managed a half smile as she stroked the back of her boy's head while he nursed, and said to Zambiya, "What should we name him, husband?"

"I didn't know if we would have a boy or a girl, so I hadn't settled on a name yet. But I've thought about it." He permitted himself a wry reminiscence and stroked the long raised scar under his upper garment, a linen smock. "If you don't already have a name, I want to name him after my mother's father, Indur. He was very generous to me and gave me the experience to get into the palace guards by sending me on a trading caravan. Does 'Indur' sound good to you?"

She looked at the baby at her breast and said, "Indur. Indur." Then to Zambiya, "Indur. It's good. Isn't it good, Sud?"

Standing just by the door to her adjoining room, Sud was astonished to be included in the discussion, but she stammered, "Very…very good. Indur."

———— • • • ————

It neared mid-day when Nisaba crossed the market square. Dust rose from the feet of everyone who moved across the shimmering surface and barely a hint of shadow showed on the ground. She was accompanied by Tikal, Neti, Nabi and Muda, who had been released by Enlil-Bani to join the others for the search of Nisaba's home. Two additional palace guards brought up the rear.

The group drew some curiosity from the remaining shoppers and vendors in the square, mostly from Muda's auburn hair, but also due to a single matron being escorted by palace officials.

The neighborhood was that of wealthy landowners and civic leaders. Every home had a front courtyard surrounded by a clay brick wall the height of a tall man. Nisaba's home sat back from a sturdy hardwood gate with a strong barrier bar; it was seated into a pocket chamber inset on both sides of the entry. One of Nisaba's servants, a freedman with one deformed arm, left the shade of the doorway as soon as he saw his mistress and opened the gate.

Tikal took charge as soon as everyone had entered the front courtyard, telling the servant, "Call everyone out of the house. Do it from the doorway; I don't want you going inside. Everyone's to wait here." The servant recognized Tikal from when the family and their slaves lived in the palace, so the servant started to comply.

"It's too hot out here," Nisaba protested. "Can't we just stay together in the anteroom?"

Tikal considered the request made by the last king's widow and softened his approach. She had always treated him with respect during their years of living in the palace when he served Erra-Imitti. "Yes, Nisaba, of course. I'll go with you to get your daughters. I've not seen them for several months now, not since Enlil-Bani took the throne. I imagine they've both grown."

Mollified, Nisaba allowed herself to display a wry smile and said, "Yes, they have. You won't recognize Sherida; she's become a woman."

The thought caused her to recall her youngest girl's defilement and her empty stomach turned over with such force that she suddenly vomited a small puddle of bile and mucus onto her door stoop. The servant ambled over to an upright cabinet at the corner of the house and returned immediately with a cloth to clean off the stoop. Just then her household staff arrived, followed closely by her daughters, Sherida and Ninegala. The younger girl, clearly distraught, was being supported by her sister. Those in the house remained there, looking out the door.

"Back into the house, everyone," commanded Tikal as he entered, "and stay in the front room."

"You," he ordered the closest female servant, "tend to your mistress." The woman hurried up to Nisaba, pushing past those who were in the way, and led her inside to a wide wooden settee with plainspun cushions. With deference, because she recognized him, she said to Tikal, "May I bring our lady some water, or some broth?"

"Fix her some honeyed wine for her stomach. Don't be long." Tikal said to Neti, Nabi, and Muda, "Each of you select a slave to go with you and start examining the bedrooms. Neti, start with the one the half-man used. I'll join you after this lady is served." He waited until the female attendant returned with a large silver tray holding a pitcher of wine and another of water with a large cup and a ceramic bowl of honey with a spoon in it. The cup was already prepared as Tikal had directed, and he shortly left, leaving one guard in the anteroom to keep everyone there, taking the other with him.

Nisaba leaned back against a pillow, closing her eyes. Tears had been coursing down her cheeks for a time, and both her daughters were kneeling at her feet, each of them holding one of her hands and trying to console her. She straightened up when the servant offered the cup of wine and said to her, "Thank you, Ninti." She stood up and moved to the center of the couch and beckoned her daughters to sit on each side of her. She had ceased weeping and said to her girls, "We will get through this. That horrid runt has already been caught, and he will die, be sure of it."

After a few swallows from the cup, she offered it to Ninegala's left hand and asked, "Have you girls eaten anything?"

Sherida answered, "No, mother." She started to sob, "Engu's still in the courtyard covered with Nina's sheet, and there are ants all over it." Her lamentations started to rise in volume, but Nisaba squeezed her hand hard and said, "Take charge of yourself, right now! You weren't the one..." Nisaba hesitated, then chose the right words to finish, "who was murdered." She looked her daughter in the eyes, commanding her attention by pressing her hand even harder. Setting her lips in a straight line, she hissed in a whisper, "You're the oldest. Bear up."

Enlil-Bani held Zambiya's sleeping newborn son in his arms; he felt deeply that the child was truly his grandson, despite the lack of direct lineage, since Zambiya had been his step-son from two years of age. It was now late on this day, and he had been on high alert status for much of it, so he was feeling the strain on his energies despite a couple hours of sleep as he waited for Tikal and the others to return from Nisaba's home. Nevertheless, he wanted to share this momentous event in the life of his family. He had already arranged to send word to Nani and Enmerkar that they had a nephew now.

"I think your mother would be so proud to have your boy named after her father," he said to Zambiya. "She loved him and he doted on her; said she was like her mother in a new body." The king was undisturbed by the boy's mouth, as he had seen many like it in his life.

Ezina volunteered, "There was no one in my family, even my parents or their kin, that I would want to so honor, *Ensi*. I'm happy to agree with Zambiya's choice in this matter." She had recovered some of her energy after sleeping many hours and was sitting up in bed with a woven reed tray next to her on a heavy wooden table; it held a cup of wine and another of water, plus wheat cakes, candied fruit and a dish of strong-smelling soft cheese with a spatula. Sud had seen to her needs as soon as she declared that she was famished. Ezina sent Sud back to her room to rest; it was as if giving birth had given Ezina a new perspective on her slave.

A guard entered just then, saying, "*Ensi*, your son and daughter are here, with En-me and your daughter's husband."

"Admit them," the king ordered. Only moments later the same guard returned to say, "Pardon, *Ensi*. Tikal waits for you in your chambers."

"Send word that I'll join him there in a while. I've not seen my daughter for many days."

• ● •

Neti's search of the room the Chaldean had occupied was fruitless. He found the abandoned clothing the man had brought with him to Isin, even the boy's costume that had been his disguise while reconnoitering the palace environs, but nothing else that would indicate any kind of conspiracy. Tikal then directed his son and Nabi to concentrate on the other bedrooms, with special attention to Nisaba's room. There, too, nothing suspicious was found, nor was there in Sherida's.

Muda inspected the scene of the servant's murder while the others were occupied with Sherida's room. The floor and bench had already been cleaned by Nisaba's servants after they removed the corpse to the rear courtyard, along with the blood-ruined floor covering they had used to drag the body there. The night sentry had been a favorite among the servants and slaves, and there was a general lamenting during their labors. They struggled to make the sitting room where the killing had occurred look normal.

Muda addressed the slave who accompanied him, a boy of about fourteen years. "How long you live here?"

"Four years, Lord. I was bought at auction for the royal family when they were in the palace, but I worked at the farm until the old *Ensi* died."

"Where is bedroom of youngest girl?"

"Ninegala slept in the room across from the half-man."

"You know more what happened, more than murder?"

"No, but Nina was terribly upset, and her mother and sister absolutely kept the rest of us away from her after the murder."

"All right. Bring a torch and show me room; you stay by door while Mu... while I look." Muda went with the slave to Ninegala's bedroom, having first told Tikal and the other men that he would need no help with the youngest girl's room. Tikal took Nabi and Neti to the courtyard to examine the body.

Muda instantly noted the smell of the rancid spilled sesame oil on the woven rug just inside the doorway after he entered the room, the empty torch still lying on it. He moved to one side of the room so that he could

91

scan the location of the furniture and any other features that would be of interest. He told the slave to bring another lamp from one of the other rooms, and then used it to replace the one on the floor in its wall holder, then he moved along the wall to the right of the portal holding his torch up. He found another torch holder between the room's only window opening and the bed and put the torch into it, freeing his hands.

The long table next to the bed held an ordinary cup and pitcher, plus a small pile of ankle bracelets next to a shallow cup with several rings in it. A black wooden box lined with yellow linen held hair ties and headbands, while a silver 'tree' was adorned with necklaces, mostly of carnelian and lapis lazuli beads. The table itself had a shelf built into it below the top, a handspan above the floor. On it were a beaded bag and two nightgowns.

What held Muda's attention was the lack of bedding. The bed had been stripped down to the flat mattress. Looking to his left past the doorway he saw an ornate carved cabinet almost as tall as the room, with several shelves and cubbys holding sandals, dresses, belts, and loincloths. Three long pegs of dark hardwood were sunk into the left side, held in place with bitumen that had dripped down the side, visible under the many scarfs and belts that hung from them.

Muda crossed over to the cabinet and searched through the shelves and compartments. These held mostly cloth garments. On a middle shelf in a flat sided basket was a pile of graybrown flax fibers the color of a common rabbit, scotched and hackled, with a spindle lying on top holding several rounds of completed linen thread wound on the shaft.

It was not until he looked to the right side of the cabinet that he saw the quiver with several arrows, between the cabinet and the wall. Determined to discover the bow if it was present, he ran his hands over the top of the high cabinet and found it. It was no longer than from the floor to his breast bone, with its string fitted onto only one end. The handle section in the middle was wrapped with leather laces, very taut, with no decorations.

Muda carried the quiver and bow in one hand out to where Tikal and the palace staff stood in the courtyard, watching where two of Nisaba's slaves had dug a grave in the deep dry silt of the earth, far across the courtyard from the home near the rear wall. The grave was done and the slaves were dragging the body toward it, stopping their progress now and then to flick ants off their arms and hands, sweating and muttering.

Tikal saw Muda's booty and exclaimed, "Where were those, Muda?"

"Room of youngest daughter. Bow on top of, uh, um, shelf thing, arrows by wall." As he searched for elusive Akkadian words he had a habit of raising his right hand up into the air, as if they could be encountered there. At this moment, he had the quiver in that hand, and he waved it in the air briefly before continuing. He removed one arrow from the quiver with the hand that held the bow and asked Tikal, "Arrow look like one that killed guard?" He hadn't been in Isin during the attempt on Enlil-Bani's life, and hadn't ever seen the arrow.

Tikal examined the arrow, with particular attention to the sharpness of the bronze arrowhead. "I haven't looked at it for weeks, but I think so." Then, recognizing the pink fletching feathers, he exclaimed, "Ah, yes. The very same."

Leading the group back into Nisaba's home, Tikal returned to the anteroom where the household members were being kept, and immediately confronted Ninegala by thrusting the arrow toward her. "Explain this, girl."

Ninegala blanched and first looked toward her mother, but then straightened up and looked back at Tikal, her open palms held toward him and stammering, "I, uh, I don't know anything about it, Lord. Where did it come from?"

Without answering her, Tikal grabbed the girl's right wrist and first looked at her fingers as he responded, "Your room." Then peering at her face, "Your room!" he repeated more loudly. He motioned Neti and Muda both to come closer, and said, "Look at her thumb and forefinger, those cal;ouses." They both nodded in assent, observing pronounced callouses on the inner part of the thumb and a corresponding one on the forefinger, the latter running from close to the tip to the middle joint.

By this time, Nisaba was on her feet, also looking at her daughter's hand.

"What does that arrow have to do with us, Tikal? Why are you hectoring Ninegala? She's had a very difficult time today, with Engu being killed near her bedroom. And you should know that her left hand is her favored one." Both Ninegala and Sherida started crying as soon as the servant's name was uttered.

Tikal still had no intention of disclosing the fact that an attempt had been made on Enlil-Bani's life, so he was circumspect in his response. "A palace guard was killed weeks ago with an arrow just like this one. I don't know why Ninegala would have done it, but she has callouses that look like she's used to using a bow, and the arrow was short, like a young woman would use."

Nisaba covered her mouth with both her hands and looked hard at both her daughters before she recovered and said to Tikal and the others, "Those callouses on her hands are from twirling the spindle for spinning thread from flax. I know she has a basket of flax in her room, and the spindle as well. That's how linen's made; everyone knows that. I made her learn the art so she would have a skill she could use as a wife, but more important to me was that my daughters know that they are very favored by the gods to not have to spend their lives doing ordinary crafts." She lowered her voice to barely above a whisper, to keep her history confidential from her household staff. "I wasn't born high, you'll remember." Looking then at Neti, she continued quietly, "When Prince Erra-Imitti met me I was selling my father's woolen goods at the market and serving beer and cakes at night."

She raised her voice to normal again and directed her protest to Tikal again, saying, "Ninegala could go with you and get the spinning supplies right now, Lord." She turned to her daughter and said pointedly, "Couldn't you?"

Ninegala covered her face with her hands and declared, "I can't go there, Mother. I can't!" She turned to her sister and started sobbing in her arms.

Muda spoke up then and supported Nisaba's declaration that the supplies did, indeed, exist, but went further by pointing out, "Those not marks of archer, Tikal. Archer holds bowstring with all fingers, not thumb with finger. Callouses be on ends of all fingers. More, uh, uh, con...trol, Muda think is word." Muda moved his hand up but quickly withdrew it. Then he looked at Neti and said with a smile, "I mean 'I.'"

At this point, Nabi spoke up and said to Tikal, "That's right, Lord. I've been an archer, and he's right." He held out his left hand and pointed out, "See, I still have callouses, because I practice several days each month."

Tikal was unwilling to absolve the entire household on the basis that Ninegala was blameless, so he and the others conducted an examination of everyone's hands, but found no one suspicious. He was forced to conclude in his own mind that Aga, Erra-Imitti's son, had acted on his own initiative in sending an assassin, and was already planning to get him back to Isin for execution.

Tikal readied his temporary retinue for their return to the palace, but called Ninegala aside. When they were alone he said, "I know this was a truly horrible night and I'm sorry for accusing you of something you didn't do. I hope you get over this night very soon."

He then made a point of speaking privately with Nisaba, saying, "I think it would be wise for you and your daughters to move to your farm for a couple seasons. Ninegala may be able to recover from this horrible event much sooner in a different place. Agree?"

"I do. It'd be good for all of us, I'm sure. We can return in the winter, maybe, so we can start looking for a husband for Sherida." She started to thank Tikal for his concern, but then thought to ask, "What was your concern with the bow? I never saw the half-man with it, ever. I would've told you so. And I don't know how it got into Ninegala's room."

"A palace guard was killed by a short arrow like those, and after you told us the short man had been here, we needed to look. I'll let you know when you can see him killed, as *Ensi* promised you."

Nisaba clenched her fists and gritted her teeth at the thought of the Chaldean, but thanked Tikal before he left with the others.

CHAPTER NINE

PRAISE THE SICKLE

How blessed it is to be favored of the gods, for the people have the use of the tools the gods bequeathed, and our marvelous hands, while the animals we use and those we eat have none. So we plow, we plant, we tend, and we reap, all with tools. Blessed are the gods.

Late the next day the Chaldean was taken from the guard quarters, where he had been held in his cage in a weapons store room. By this time he was already feverish from infection in his throbbing severed arm, and he limped due to his confinement in the cage. Hoping the guards would kill him quickly with their spears, he tried to fight them with his good arm, but they had strict orders to deliver him alive and 'well' so he was simply clubbed to the ground, then hoisted back to his feet, none too tenderly. He was prodded with spears along the passageways until he arrived in the kitchen courtyard, where he had climbed the outside wall. He sported only minor punctures from the spears.

His execution was to be a private event, not public. Enlil-Bani and Tikal were present, along with Zambiya and Muda, of course. A long discourse between Tikal and the king had determined the manner by which the Chaldean would be dispatched.

With Nisaba in attendance, along with Nabi, Neti followed his father's orders and had the man trussed with his arms bound to his sides, his ankles bound together and his thighs tied up against his chest, as compact as possible.

He started to scream at the guards and the others, so he was cuffed in the mouth, then gagged. Squirming, he was placed into a common cloth sack, tied at the top, which was then hung from a thick mulberry limb. His muffled shouts continued unabated as Nabi fired every one of the short arrows from the quiver into the sack, which nevertheless showed signs of movement and anguished grunts until Nabi fired two standard military arrows into the middle of the sack and its contents. The witnesses all adjusted their breathing into shallow gulps at the unmistakable smell of fresh blood and urine as they dripped together from the bottom of the bag. Now all sounds and movement ceased.

Zambiya approached Nabi as he was unstringing his bow and handed him the small dirk the Chaldean had carried.

He clapped Nabi's shoulder and said, "Use it well."

It had already been decided by Tikal and Enlil-Bani that Aga would be recalled from Larsa, but not for one-and-a-half moon cycles, so that he would have no suspicion that he was implicated in the attempt on the king's life.

All of the arrows that protruded were broken off, and using the same litter from the previous day, the guards transported the sack, now covered with a leather drape, out of Isin and the length of the city wall down the river bank to a deserted and nearly reedless section, where it was thrown into the water. The Chaldean's body floated in the languid current at first, but soon disappeared below the surface.

"I don't know what it means, Father." Enmerkar and Enlil-Bani were seated alone on the new veranda above the kitchen courtyard for the palace. It was mid-morning, and the canopy was providing welcome shade from the sun. They were both drinking an ordinary broth, similar to one Lith-el would have provided for their morning meal. Nani had given Zid-tara instructions on how her mother had prepared it, so that Enlil-Bani could be provided with familiar foods and drinks on occasion, especially when he shared food with a family member.

"Tell me again how the dream went, right from the beginning."

Enmerkar took a deep drink, then repeated the essence of the dream. His headache was already subsiding, but he recounted the dream as best he could. "As usual, I'm not participating in the events, I'm just watching.

I'm at the gate of Isin." He clapped his hands together and exclaimed, "I've just recalled that several of my dreams started this way. I hadn't noticed it before." Then he resumed, "My back's to the gate, and I'm propped on both my sticks, when I look out and see locusts, not in a cloud like you've told me about when they swarm, but marching toward the city, eating as they come, but not everything. There doesn't seem to be any pattern. If they decide to eat, the plant is gone, but they'll leave some plants alone. Many go around the gate, but some go through. A lot, actually. Then the scene changes, and I'm in the square outside the palace; I'm looking at the market and its stalls are really busy with shoppers. The locusts arrive at the square and take wing, settling on some of the people. When the locusts settle on someone's head, that person disappears, along with the locust."

Enmerkar took a deep breath, then a deep drink, then let out a deep sigh. "I know this is a warning of some kind, but I don't know what. Do you understand it?"

"No, but I don't seem to be the one threatened, since I'm not in the dream, nor any of my family. I hope that's true."

The two men's attention was caught by the appearance of a black rat, which seemed to be hobbling across an open space down in the courtyard, when it was suddenly snatched into the air by a winged raptor, which carried it over the wall.

"I've noted more dead rats in the streets, lately. They don't stay long, of course, because the dogs and pigs eat them." Enmerkar's observation was lost on Enlil-Bani, who was still considering his son's dream.

"I don't know if it will help, but I'll make extra offerings to both the goddesses this evening."

———— • ● • ————

The barge was an official rivercraft of Isin, designed for transport of important personages and goods both up and down the *Buranun*. The hull was hardwood brought from far to the north, with the shallow sides made of bitumen-coated pine from the forests to the east of the *Idiglat*. The side pieces had been re-coated with bitumen recently, and the acrid stench was still noticeable. As long as three houses, and a house width across, a cabin in the middle afforded relief from the sun to the passengers. The walls and roof were constructed like market stalls, with light pine boughs for the ribs and loosely woven palm fronds to provide shade and allow air to circulate. Steering and progress of the craft upriver was accomplished by use of a single sail and pushing long poles by the four crew members.

This time the barge was floating down river and passed Larsa on its left. The crew had made this trip on many similar occasions, and due to well-practiced maneuvers beached the prow onto the bank at a launch site many yards below the city, its common oxhide cover protecting the valuable wooden hull from the gritty mud.

The boat arrived at Larsa deliberately in the mid-morning, a month and a half after the Chaldean had been executed. The air blew listlessly in humid flurries, under a sky that was hazier than Isin's due to the closer proximity of the swamps and delta to the south. Much like Isin's, the track outside the city's ornate main gate was packed down from constant use by workers and merchants, carts and livestock.

The senior member of the group was Ashgi, a retired general who had been sent to replace Aga as the emissary for Isin. Nabi was in charge of the attending cadre, two members of Isin's army gathered from an outpost along the Buranun many miles north, two attendant slaves from Ashgi's household, plus a drover who led two donkey-like onagers carrying Ashgi's personal belongings to this diplomatic post. Most of the traffic entering and leaving Larsa's main gate had dispersed by the time General Ashgi's entourage arrived in the front of the entrance. The soldiers from Isin carried shields and short spears, while Nabi carried only a bronze sword, its curved blade secured in its stiff ox-hide scabbard suspended from a waist belt and extending behind him. All three wore polished copper breastplates with two carved ivory gazelles mounted on them, their heads facing away from each other; these signified that they were representatives of Isin. General Ashgi donned his military uniform before disembarking with a bronze and leather scabbard holding a short sword at his waist. He carried a spear-like emblem pole, with the same insignia of pairs of gazelles replacing the weapon end.

Four Larsan sentries at the gate intercepted the Isin delegation as soon as they approached; they had been observed from the city wall while moving down the river and, also, a sentinel had run from the launch area before the raft made shore.

The sentries held long spears pointed toward the Isin men's chests;

Nabi had moved to the front of his group. His men stood erect, but kept their weapons in a non-threatening position, the butt end of their spears on the ground, with Nabi's hands palm open and pointed downward, away from his sword handle.

Nabi spoke first, with a mild, "Shalamu, guardians of Larsa. We come from Isin to bring our new emissary to Larsa." He pointed to him and said, "This is General Ashgi. Our previous ambassador is being recalled home to Isin. His mother and sisters need him there as he is the only male in the family. His name is Aga, and he was the son of the former *Ensi* of Isin, Erra-imitti."

Although the sun was already well on its way in its journey across the sky, the wall of the city created an indistinct shadow for some twenty yards to the west, the direction the main gate faced. It was designed in that manner to make an invading force face into the rising sun in case of a morning attack. Siege warfare was common, and military onslaughts against a city were more likely to be successful when the troops were fresh and the day's heat was less.

A Larsan guard with two copper bands identifying his rank on his upper arm muscles stated with a tone of authority, "I will have you escorted to the palace, but only without your weapons."

"I would do the same, friend." Nabi motioned to the soldiers, who relinquished their spears to one of the sentries; Nabi removed his sword in its scabbard and did the same. General Ashgi made no move to comply, and Nabi stated with an equally rigid tone, "Not him." The Larsan considered but a moment before assenting with a nod.

Nabi made a point of looking intently at the guard who held the weapons and saying, "I expect you to stay with us. We want our weapons returned as soon as we leave Larsa. Understood?"

The lead Larsan sentry grunted and nodded, and the guard with the weapons led the Isins toward the palace, pausing to kick the corpse of a dead rat out of the path. The group was followed by two more of the Larsan sentries, their spears still at the ready.

It was a circuitous route, first through a neighborhood kitchen area where nearly a dozen veiled women quickly stepped out of the path and stilled their conversations, interrupting the preparation and baking of bread in round-topped communal ovens. From there General Ashgi and his men were escorted along a lane barely wide enough for a chariot to pass, through a section of modest one-story homes, the roadway making abrupt and angular changes of direction. It was clear that the city had been planned with defense against a marauding army in mind.

Much like Isin, the palace and the zigurrat formed two sides of a large central market and ceremonial area, and just like Isin, the market was loud with vendors hawking their wares, donkeys and onagers adding their complaints to those of ducks and other fowl. Feral dogs stood or paced along the edges of the area like sentries, alert to the possibility of any unguarded food. The combined aromas and stenches of foodstuffs and dung was almost nostalgic to Nabi. The appearance of the strangers caused a hush that spread across the whole of the market stands and stalls, and the attention of the palace exterior spearmen and archers became acute.

The Larsan with the visitors' weapons approached the guardians of the ceremonial doors of the palace; Ashgi's contingent remained at the lower level of the raised veranda on which the palace stood. Glad to put his burden of weapons down, although carefully, the guard announced the reason for the Isins' presence.

True to their roles, the visitors from Isin did their best to appear nonchalant and non-threatening while nevertheless making the most of this opportunity to observe the layout and defensive barriers of Larsa, their most frequent enemy. General Ashgi in particular was occupied with memorizing those features a professional soldier considered important.

Quite soon, a group appeared from the palace through the ceremonial double doors, massive oak and decorated with copper plates. In the lead was Nur-Adad's Chief Counselor, Asgi, followed by Aga and his two slaves, and then a squad of Larsa's palace guards. Aga's slaves carried a litter containing Aga's official and personal gear; a cattle hide covered the possessions, its legs tied together under the frame. The slave who carried the rear part of the litter knelt on the ground to rest as soon as the litter was put down, obviously ill.

Asgi wore an ankle length skirt, covered with white heron feathers; his withered left hand was covered with a crimson cloth, with silver beads along its fringe. His hair was closely cropped, along with his beard, and he wore a gold breast ornament that hung to the end of his breastbone. The weight of the ornament accentuated his stooped manner, and he leaned forward slightly. Nevertheless, he assumed an energetic manner and hurried forward down the steps to greet Isin's new ambassador, walking directly to the man.

"Well, General Ashgi, I am Chief Counselor Asgi. How will we be able to tell each other apart?" He smiled and laughed at his own joke, and placed his right hand on the General's chest in greeting.

General Ashgi smiled and responded in kind, placing his hand on the Counselor's chest, saying, "We'll just have to wait and see which of us Nur-Adad asks for advice." They both laughed, and General Ashgi was invited to leave the heat of the market and to enter the palace, along with his retainers.

Left outside the palace were Aga and his slaves, along with Nabi's guard contingent and the drover with his onagers, waiting to find out where General Ashgi's possessions were to be unloaded.

"Shalamu, Aga. Your mother will be pleased to have you return to your family." Nabi made a sufficient bow to indicate respect for the previous prince.

"No happier than I'll be to return, guard. Let's get on our way; I can't wait to leave this place." He turned to his slaves and said, "No loitering! Pick it up."

Nabi motioned for the Larsan to pick up the Isin weapons for the trip back to the waiting barge.

Tikal and Enlil-Bani sat together on the veranda early in the morning, drinking beer and eating a plain breakfast of fried cake, dates, and pears.

"I'd like to bring up an old matter, *Ensi*," Tikal commenced, then sipped at his straw from the baked earthenware pitcher they shared. "You know I've wanted you to think about marrying again, but I won't go over my reasons another time." Enlil-Bani started to protest, his countenance displaying the irritation he felt, but Tikal held up both palms and quickly added, "That is not what I want to say."

The king crossed his arms over his chest, then said, "This isn't what I want, Tikal. I have no interest in a marriage that would serve only to acquire some ally in case we need help during an attack; I had a good marriage with Lith-el, and I don't expect to find a mate who will please me."

"That's clear, *Ensi*. Really, I understand you. I've had a good woman for my wife for many years and if she were to die, I'd be a long time in mourning before I would care to be married again. Perhaps never."

"That's good to hear, Tikal. I was getting peevish thinking you were going to raise the matter again."

"Instead of discussing the matter right now, I was hoping we'd agree to put off any further thought of marrying until the next *Akitu* celebration; that's several moons in the future. Perhaps what is best for Isin, and for you, will become much clearer by then, and I won't be irritating you by bringing it up again."

"Tikal, I believe you are mostly responsible for my even being alive, since you could have chosen anyone else to succeed Erra-imitti when he died. So I'm very grateful to you. Maybe I will change later, and that's a reasonable time in which to find out." The king placed his hand flat on Tikal's chest and said simply, "We agree on that, at least."

Tikal started to rise, planning to leave the king to finish his repast, but Enlil-Bani put his hand on the Chief Counselor's shoulder, telling him, "Stay a moment, Tikal. I've another matter on my mind. An old one we discussed at some length, moons ago." He looked off into the middle distance, assembling his thoughts, then declared, "I told you after Saman and Esme were killed that I wasn't happy with myself for having been so brutal. I believe that's the right word: brutal. You told me at the time that I could be merciful on another occasion, and I accepted that."

The king put both his hands on his thighs and looked at the deck by his feet before saying, "I could have been merciful with the Chaldean. I wasn't. What does it say about me that I had him killed slowly?"

Tikal sighed, thinking about this man with so much power and yet with scruples. "*Ensi*, I agreed with killing him that way at the time, and I still do. If he'd only tried to kill you, and not succeeded, I would agree. He could just have been strangled, quietly, and his body disposed of." He stood to face the king, then knelt on one knee in front of him before adding, "It wasn't sufficient! It just was not! Every guard that was searching the palace knew an assassin was inside with your murder in his heart. Dealing with him had to send a strong message that such a thought would lead to a terrible end." He let this settle in before offering another reason. "It was also for Nisaba and her daughter, even though the daughter wasn't there. They had to understand how finally it had ended."

Enlil-Bani leaned forward on his bench, almost bowing, and said, "You're right, Tikal, and wise, too. I was only thinking of the threat to me as a person; I hadn't considered it as a threat to the throne." He hoisted the beer pitcher in a gesture of salute.

———————•●•———————

Nani served dinner to her husband Suba at their courtyard table, a substantial aromatic lamb stew made with carrots, onions, turnips, and cabbage, flavored with garlic and cumin, the latter imported for the king's table, but shared with her by Enlil-Bani. The sun was about to slide below the level of the city wall, which would start the moderate cooling of the evening. She would serve Azuru now and after Suba was finished, she herself would eat.

Bibi, now a full grown cat, was tormenting a mouse in the deep shade of the far wall, throwing it up in the air and then pouncing on it; it had stopped squeaking as shock and resignation overcame its will to live. Suba turned his body so he wouldn't witness the gradual demise of the rodent. He knew that this was how Bibi earned her keep, but watching the cruelty made him queasy.

Now over 8 months pregnant, Nani was acutely aware of Azuru's declining health, and feared for her. So while Suba enjoyed his meal, complete with a few small date-and-honey filled cakes, Nani prepared a tray of food to take to her great-aunt inside the home, so Azuru wouldn't have to endure the late summer heat.

"Nani," Suba called. "I want to tell you about a plan my father is working on. It will mean a change for us, so I want to tell you the details soon."

"I will come back very soon, dear man. Even though Auntie never eats much, she does enjoy her meals." She walked from the household brick oven with its domed top and gritty prep area, carrying the bowl for her aged great-aunt. "And don't think I'm not aware of your feelings about Bibi. But she caught that mouse in our pantry, and good riddance." She picked up the plain vine-woven basket she had made for the household and placed a couple of barley flatbreads for dipping in a small dish alongside the bowl of stew for Azuru, and carried them into the house, using one elbow to move the doorway drape aside as she entered sideways, her swollen abdomen just clearing the entryway. She stood for a moment to allow her sight to adjust to the dim light inside, then proceeded to Azuru's room, automatically checking on the level of oil in the wall torch in the hallway. She allowed herself to enjoy the feel of the cool interior floor on her bare feet, but wanted to serve Azuru and quickly return to Suba, who clearly wanted to share his father's plan with her. She hesitated before entering, to be sure her relative was awake.

"Auntie, are you feeling well enough to have some stew? I think it's good."

There was a pause before she heard Azuru respond, saying, "Dear child, I'm very cold, and my stomach hurts. I don't think I should eat just yet."

"May I come in?"

"Of course, dear." Nani elbowed aside the drape that covered the doorway and entered the room, lit only by the diminishing sunshine from the horizontal window opening just below the ceiling.

Azuru was on her bed, across the room from the doorway, lying on her side with her knees drawn up, hugging a small yellow bolster against her midsection and breathing with effort. Her eyes were closed, but she had affected what she hoped would pass for a smile.

"Oh, Auntie. Do you hurt?" Nani knelt next to Azuru and placed the tray on the mat that covered the dirt floor; she felt Azuru's forehead to assess her state.

"Not hurting, exactly, dear. My stomach's unsettled and I seem to have these bumps under both my arms." She raised one arm to reveal a lump the size of an egg under her armpit. Nani felt the lump, which felt warm, then noticed another lump on Azuru's neck, that also felt warm. The crone's breath caused Nani to cringe and lean back.

"I'll bring you just some of the broth, Auntie, and I'll send Suba to bring En-me if he can come."

"Don't bother with me, child. I've not felt good for so long, and I'm ready to die. We all eventually feel this way, and now I'm old. It's time, I think." She looked into Nani's eyes and said, "I was young, once. I had a good man for husband, and we shared Inana's blessings many times. I'd like to have a priestess from Inana's temple visit me. I'd like to have her give thanks for the blessings of my youth." She pointed across the room to a light, cheap wooden chest, and said, "There's a pouch in there with silver discs, quite a few. Give two of them to the priestess. The rest are for you and Suba, to save for your children. Please tell them about me, dear."

With that, Azuru closed her eyes and took a deep but labored breath, then resumed her panting shallow breaths. Nani abandoned the tray and left the room to go to Suba. She had to feel her way along the wall, as copious tears obstructed her vision.

* * *

Dagan and Nintud stood outside their home, both of them smiling despite being weary from the walk from the palace. Dagan was finally feeling much improved after his lengthy bout with the itchy sores on his legs and pain throughout his intestines, with bloody stool and a dry cough. All had now subsided, and with the exception of a noticeable distention of his abdomen, he now resembled his former self to a considerable degree. His energy had greatly returned after his period of convalescence with superior nutrition at the palace, insisted on by Enlil-Bani, as they had been friends for much of their lives.

"We should tell Suba and Nani that we are home," Nintud said pointing at their neighbor's door. The couple had moved to their house when Enlil-Bani and Lith-el had lived here, before Lith-el's murder.

Dagan thought about the suggestion briefly, but replied, "If we do, they'll want to invite us in for food, just to be polite, and we ate at the palace. You must be as tired as I am. This is the longest I've walked for weeks; you as well. Let's just go in and get a good night's sleep, and let them know tomorrow. We'll need to go out tomorrow to bring in food, too. Next day I'll go tell the priest I can return to the fields."

Nintud reached up to stroke Dagan's cheek and said, "I'm sure you're right." She started to unlatch her door when Suba came out of his door, his shoulder bag swinging against his side as he used one arm to close the door, the other hand grasping a staff.

"Dagan!" he exclaimed with shock in his voice. "And Nintud. You're home; how good it is to see you both." Suba was a little taller than most Sumerians, with a slender body and muscular forearms from his potter's vocation. He propped his staff against the wall and placed his free hand on Dagan's chest. "You look well, friend."

"Shalamu, Suba." It was Nintud who responded. "We have just come home, and plan to retire early. But why are you leaving now, at dusk? Is Nani well?"

"She is, but Azuru is not. Not at all. I'm going to Inana's temple compound to ask a priestess to visit her. I'll let Nani know you're home, but go ahead and get settled in." He re-entered his home briefly, and by the time he returned, Dagan and Nintud had gone inside their home. He walked with a hurried but measured stride toward the temple complex at the base of the zigurrat, slowing down only one time to avoid a pack of dogs who were snarling and fighting over a rat.

• ● •

Ezina held baby Indur to her breast, rocking to-and-fro, crooning to him with a gentle smile on her face. The pleasure she felt in nursing him was completely unexpected, visceral and primal. Now close to two moon cycles old, the boy was thriving under her and Sud's care. Sud was growing more solicitous for the babe by the day, and her attachment was beginning to grate on Ezina; the child was hardly ever allowed to sleep except in her slave's arms.

Zambiya entered their bedroom and immediately smiled at the scene of his wife and son. His initial dismay at the infant's disfigurement had completely dissipated, but he was all too aware of the challenges their child would face.

"Ezina, dear one, how are you feeling now? Are you ready to introduce our son to the outdoors? When you're ready, we can take him to father's veranda, in the shade, and let him see the world."

"Husband," she smiled as she said the word, "it would give me just as much pleasure to spend some time in the air, if it isn't too hot. You decide when you want to take us there."

"Tomorrow, then." He sat on the edge of the bed and stroked Ezina's hair, which had already been arranged in a fashionable set of curls on both sides of her face, framing her high forehead. He leaned forward and kissed her lips lightly; he had always felt her lips to have a sensuous quality, and he was filled with gratitude that they were now getting along so well, especially after her unplanned and almost disastrous pregnancy. Since the birth of Indur, her spirits were much more elevated.

"I've been talking with En-me, and also with father. Just this morning

I had a talk with Banda, the High Priest of Egal-mah. I think we should give our son as much of a chance to do well in this world as possible, so I want to arrange to have an orant made for him and placed in the temple. It will cost us to have the orant created, and more to dedicate it, but I believe it will be worth it. Banda certainly encouraged us to do so."

Internally, Ezina had an immediate revulsion to the idea, but didn't respond right away, saying at first, "There is certainly merit to engage the gods to help Indur. Do you know what payments will be required?" This response seemed bland enough to her, and gave her time to assess what was causing her to reject the proposal, clearly designed to benefit her son.

"I won't know what the cost of the orant will be until I talk with Suba. He is an artist with his craft, and I think he would do it. Banda said that the temple would require the hind-quarter of a sheep, and every three years a new orant would need to be made and dedicated that looked like Indur, until he's fifteen years old and an adult."

Ezina looked down and contemplated her son, resting peacefully at her breast and searching her face with his deep brown eyes. She imagined the sacred chapel of the goddess in the temple atop the zigurrat; she was very familiar with the chapel and the array of orants placed in perpetual worship of her, as she had been a novitiate priestess until just before her marriage. She started to picture an orant of her infant son in that space, when the image suddenly included Zambiya's first love, Ninmah, filling the torches that illuminated the goddess and her worshippers. Her reluctance was as clear to her as an amber jewel with a spider inside.

Her stomach churned inside, but she could not bring herself to deny any advantage to her son. She turned her gaze from her son to her husband and asked him directly, "Zambiya, do you love me? I mean truly love me?" She peered at him intensely, hoping to be able to gauge his response and its authenticity.

He responded with feeling, lightly stroking her cheek with the back of his fingers, declaring, "Truly, dear, I love you more than I ever expected to. We may not have started out right, but we are good for each other and good together. Our son will be lucky to have such devoted parents. I hope you'll always feel my love."

Ezina felt embraced by the obvious sincerity of Zambiya's declaration, and she started to weep. She dabbed at her eyes and cheeks with the top of the light sheet that covered her, and lightly stroked his chest, saying, "I think you should proceed with getting Indur's orant ready. I want to have time to prepare the mother's vow for the ceremony."

The stars above the Buranun were luminous, even with a half-moon still visible low in the western sky. Still a full day away from the bankside dock downstream from Isin, the barge polemen in the stern had just changed shifts. Grueling work and slow, they pushed against the current. Despite the river's own coolness, the air was still oppressively hot.

Most of the passengers stayed in the cabin along with the crew who were not on duty. Aga's slave who had started the journey ill had declined further, alternating between being feverish and shaking with chills. His companion provided him with water, but sincerely hoped he would avoid the illness himself. The ill man clasped his abdomen and let out a loud wail.

"Help me outside," he demanded, rising with effort and lurching toward the portal at the side of the cabin. His fellow slave helped to support him, and they made their way along the side of the structure toward the rear of the vessel. They had barely reached the side when the man began retching into the water, a foul-smelling watery substance. He knelt along the low side of the craft, leaning on it for support. His companion reached into the water with a cloth to hold against the man's head, but breathed shallowly with his own head turned to the side, recoiling against the odor of the other's breath.

Nabi hoped this would be the opportunity he was seeking, and he rose from the bench he had been sitting on. He approached Aga, who was shifting uneasily on his part of the same bench, and said, "Lord, you may want help with getting your possessions ashore when we arrive. Your slave is sick and won't be able to do his job."

"He'll do what I tell him, guard. He's not that sick."

"Pardon, but I've seen this before. He may want to work, but he's either vomiting or shitting over the side right now, I'd bet a pitcher of beer."

"Maybe so. I'll go brace him up, or threaten to sell him to a tannery. That'll get him functioning." Aga rose and headed out the doorway, followed by Nabi.

Even in the dim light, Aga could see his slave leaning over the side of the barge, emptying his innards and scooping water into his mouth to rinse it with one hand. Aga started to retreat back into the cabin, but Nabi said, "What's that near the bank?" He pushed past Aga, motioning, and walked briskly toward the bow, away from all those other passengers who were outside the cabin.

"Where?"

Nabi ignored Aga's question until he reached the front of the vessel, directly in front of the cabin, when he pointed vaguely toward the near bank, and declared, "Right there. See?" From this position, he was out of view of all the other passengers and crew.

Aga joined Nabi, and inquired again, "Where?"

"It's right at the edge, there," Nabi insisted. He indicated a section of the bank where the reeds were the darkest, and stepped to the side and behind Aga. As Aga searched the darkness, Nabi pulled from the hidden sheath at his waist the short dagger the Chaldean had carried and thrust it upward into Aga's skull just above the neck. Aga collapsed instantly, and Nabi eased his body over the railing and under the center of the barge, the knife still in his neck.

Nabi returned to the stern of the barge after disposing of the sheath, and approached Aga's two slaves, who were about to return to the cabin.

"I haven't seen Aga for a while. I wanted to ask him if he will want any help with the gear tomorrow."

"I think he was in the cabin when we went out." Gesturing to his fellow, the well man said, "He's too sick to be any use, so I'll tell Aga that when I see him." He lowered his voice and confided, "He'll still expect him to work, though."

"Let me know what he wants. My guards can give a hand." With that, Nabi re-entered the cabin and took up a place on the bench, falling asleep shortly thereafter.

———— • ● • ————

"No one knows where he went, Lady. No one saw him leave the barge when we arrived."

Nabi spoke very respectfully to Lady Nisaba, Aga's mother, when Aga's clothes, adornments and weapons were delivered to the family's farm a few miles to the south of Isin. The slaves who had been serving Aga had been allowed to go to the slave quarters immediately, as both were now gravely ill.

"Are you certain he was on the barge when he left Larsa? He wouldn't have gone anywhere else, I'm certain." The creases on Nisaba's forehead were now permanent, and she left no doubt that she was worried that her family was under threat from some unknown source. Having spent the last several days at the farm as Tikal had suggested, she and her daughters had been very gradually returning to some semblance of normality, until today.

She continued to question Nabi, who had offered to bring Aga's goods to the farm. Under instruction from Tikal, he was under no illusion but that he would be questioned closely by Nisaba about her son's whereabouts.

"I personally talked with him the night before we arrived at the city. He spoke about going into Isin to buy presents for each of you before coming home, but I didn't see him after that. I was helping to make sure his things were guarded, especially with his slaves being so sick."

"Do you think he's still there?" Her tone was incredulous, since it had been a full day and overnight since the barge had arrived, and there had been no sign of her son in all that time. "What could he be doing?"

"No idea. He's a young man, and he certainly wouldn't tell me, high born as he is, Lady." Nabi maintained an attitude of unconcerned civility, looking directly at Nisaba.

"Well, I'm his mother and we need him here, not drinking with some slattern while we worry about him."

She gave up on the questions and turned away to go inside the front courtyard of her home, but remembered that her son's gear was still packed onto the backs of the onagers, waiting to be unloaded. She made an impatient but silent gesture toward the house, and an attendant quickly appeared.

"See that these things are taken to Aga's room, and give these guards something to eat and drink before they return to Isin."

"You're very kind, Lady. The gods will reward you, I'm sure." Nabi bowed toward the widow and then looked directly into her eyes, saying, "Perhaps we will see one another again when you're in the city, Lady. I'd like that."

Nisaba almost failed to notice the obvious flirtation, it had been so long since she had enjoyed the attentions of a man, since Erra-Imitti, her deceased husband, had been a philanderer for years before his death.

Despite her concern for her son's absence, she allowed herself a moment of pleasure in the encounter, and said, "Perhaps, guard. Maybe during a festival." She looked away, but not before capturing an appreciative glimpse of Nabi's athletic physique and rugged face.

Suddenly everyone's notice was drawn by a shriek sounding from the slave quarters; then the second slave to become ill emerged shouting for the overseer of the staff.

"What's wrong?" Nisaba yelled to the slave.

The man turned to see his owner, and responded, "Ilum's dead, Lady." Having made his announcement he surrendered to his grief and fear, and knelt on the ground, wailing.

En-me reported to Tikal and Enlil-Bani in the king's private quarters late in the day, having returned from a meeting with other healers within Isin. Even though the cause of his deep concern was a matter of common knowledge throughout the city, he kept his voice low to keep the conversation from the attendant guards, who were close by in the hallway.

"It is clearly another visitation of *mutanu;* the swollen lumps in the armpits and neck make it obvious. It's been more than a dozen years since the last one, according to the older healers, those who lived through it. In the past the priests of both temples held ceremonies, but no one wants to attend public rituals, even to beseech the gods. I'm afraid *Namtaru* has just started with us, and all the *a-zus* and the *ashipus* fear the same. It's both in the city and the countryside, as Nabi reported several days ago."

Tikal pondered the import of En-me's opinion, and pointed out, "The season for autumn planting is hard upon us, and the gods will still expect us to plant the crops. We need it and they do as well. The workers must report to the fields, both the hearty and the mildly sick. How can we get them to overcome their fears and plant the fields?"

Enlil-Bani had already considered the issue, and recognized the necessity of getting the crops planted, and what it would take to do so, having been responsible for the crops of *Egal-mah* before he became king.

"Call Banda to attend me, early tomorrow. We will need the participation of both temples to assure success, so the High Priestess from *E-sig-mese-du* will be needed as well."

Tikal responded immediately, "Banda is ill. But I'll have a priest here in his place."

———— • ● • ————

Nabi was standing bare-chested in the relative coolness of the deep shade of the zigurrat somewhat before midday and had a clear view of the market square. Not officially on duty since he had returned from city patrol, he nonetheless maintained a watchful awareness of the vendors and their patrons from his position, practically invisible to anyone in the sunshine of the market. He had a visceral appreciation for the aromas of the market, as he had worked there with his mother selling plaited and woven reed baskets as a child.

He made note of a gaunt, elderly beggar standing at the corner of a beer seller's canopy with two listless, naked children in tow, neither more than three years old. The beggar held a tattered basket in one arm close to his chest, and entreated anyone who passed by, whining, "Food, please. My daughter's husband's dead and she's sick." If anyone paused, even slightly, he would add, "No food for two days."

Nabi had brought some barley packets to trade for the flat cakes with date toppings he liked, and intended to walk over to that stall shortly. Accustomed to the normal two meals per day, he was not quite hungry, so he chose this opportunity to draw a fine-grained stone from his shoulder bag and began to sharpen the arrows from the half full quiver secured at his waist, one by one. His unstrung bow leaned against the gritty bricks of the immense structure of the zigurrat. He turned his full attention to the task; for thoroughness, each arrow was removed and its point sharpened, then returned to its original position.

When he finished, he returned the sharpening stone to his bag and took out one of the barley packets, intending to give it to the beggar. However, as he emerged from the shadow of the zigurrat to walk toward the market, he saw that a pair of strangers, both wearing unusual headgear and carrying short swords at their waists, were standing in front of the beggar.

While one man held one of the children by the neck, who by now was crying pitifully, the other was extracting what little the beggar had been able to garner by his entreaties, a couple of small bags of grain and a pomegranate.

Nabi walked up behind the men, his bow in one hand, and demanded, "Give them back!"

The two turned to look at Nabi, and one spoke to his companion in a foreign tongue. The man who had been holding fast to the child's neck tossed the child away from him as he reached for his sword, but without hesitation, Nabi struck him in the throat with one end of the bow, and turned his attention to the man who held the beggar's loot.

"Now!" Nabi spat the word, the end of his bow just an inch from the man's eye. The man stepped back but complied, mumbling something indiscernible, and stepped sideways to assist his companion, who was still choking and drooling, his eyes filled with tears, kneeling in the dust.

Keeping a watchful eye on the pair, Nabi jerked the shoulder bag of the man who was still standing off of his shoulder. He dumped the contents on the ground and distributed them with his foot until he found three grain packets and two silver discs. He placed these in the beggar's basket, along with his own packet he had intended to donate.

Pointing with his bow in the direction of Isin's great central gate, Nabi ordered the would-be robbers, "Leave now. Don't return." They complied without even retrieving the shoulder bag.

———— • ● • ————

Enlil-Bani stood on the top step of the palace platform, flanked by Tikal, two high-ranking priests, an assortment of priestesses, fourteen wealthy landowners and their overseers, plus the principle groundsmen (lead field supervisors) of the temples and the palace. All except the priestesses were dressed in clothing appropriate for working in the grain fields and canal tributaries. Enlil-Bani was actually enjoying this brief foray into his former life. He held his own hoe up near his breastbone, clearly visible to those in the front of the populace. Distributed throughout the crowd were almost all of the palace guards and many soldiers from the army, armed but prepared to work.

Enlil-Bani had excused those actively suffering from the pestilence by sending guards as messengers to each of the neighborhoods. Those present in the market/civic square were most of the able-bodied male residents of Isin, the largest number of whom were regular field hands, but also included skilled craftsmen like Suba and his father, brick makers, temple specialists and priests, and the fourteen wealthy private landowners. Work in the fields was so universally expected that most of those present carried a hoe somewhere on their person. The crowd was subdued, though the sounds of grumbling was constant. It was Tikal who addressed the men in the square. "Shalamu," he shouted.

"Shalamu, people of Isin." With his first greeting, the dignitaries on the platform all held up one hand to signal the need for quiet. He shouted his first remark with enough volume to be heard to the end ranks of the crowd, and the hush was immediate.

"This is what the gods expect of all of us." He indicated the religious men and women on the platform, who nodded in assent. "We must plant the crops in order to eat. The gods demand to be fed as well. Even our *Ensi* is prepared to lead us to the fields and work, but all cannot be done in one day and each of us will need a period of rest." He waited to proceed so that all could understand the balance of his instructions. "We will sort ourselves into two sets of workers." He waited again, then pointed to the center of the crowd and moved his arm up and down in a cleaving motion and directed, "Move apart along this line."

The guards and soldiers had been prepared for this direction, and they cleared a path in the middle of the citizens. When this was finished Tikal spoke again.

"All of you," he shouted, sweeping his arm to the left, "return tomorrow prepared to work. Bring your tools. Go home or back to your normal work for the rest of the day." He waited again until the din of hundreds of men moving away had subsided. Then he continued, "Let us join with the *Ensi*, who will work both today and again tomorrow, and do our duty to the gods and to our families."

With this, Enlil-Bani strode down the steps of the palace platform accompanied by Muda and six other guards and walked purposefully toward the city gate. He was followed by priests, attendants and, by prior arrangement, half the landowners. Tikal was to stay at the palace on this day, with instructions to relay any developments to Enlil-Bani who would be working in the closest palace grain field. En-me accompanied Enlil-Bani; most of the other healers in the city were attached to a group of workers, to monitor whether someone became ill.

CHAPTER TEN

A PREMATURE REAPING

Loss always leads to grief, even when the loss is expected. Sudden loss is experienced as betrayal, like hail falling on ripe grain; then grief turns to anger and we seek someone or something to blame.

Pestilence spread across the land, some pockets of devastation worse than others, with no discernible pattern. No city was spared entirely, and both Isin and Larsa experienced the loss of many citizens, even taking whole families at a time. When that occurred, the victims would be buried together inside their home, and the house collapsed over them as a warning not to build there. That proscription seldom lasted much longer than the length of the plague itself, as home sites within a city were scarce.

At first some outlying villages seemed to be spared, but only until conscription started. Half the young men of a settlement would be ordered to report to a city for a fixed number of days of field labor, housed with families for their meals and lodging, and spending each day clearing and leveling the fields and planting the crops, plus improving the canals and tributaries. They returned to their home places with an allotment of grain as compensation, but later some became afflicted with *Namtaru's* curse. Most of these died, sometimes with others in their family or close acquaintances. After a while, it was challenging for a city's soldiers to find conscripts when they arrived in a village. It became a common practice for the soldiers, in that case, to gather several young women in the village common area and threaten to take them to Isin unless sufficient men arrived to surrender for duty.

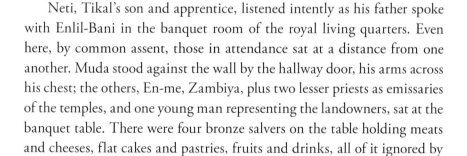

Azuru was one of the first to die. Since she was both elderly and frail, there was no sense of blame when En-me's ministrations were insufficient to save her, and her passing was expected. Dagan and Nintud helped Nani and Suba make arrangements with the priests to have Azuru buried in the commoner's cemetery outside the walls; Dagan and his wife suffered in the privacy of their home while they assisted their neighbors, having had to make similar arrangements for their own daughter many months before. Suba employed a local youth to send word of her demise to her family in a nearby village.

By now there was an unspoken agreement by city dwellers to maintain distance between people in the market and at the neighborhood bakeries and wells.

Nani and Suba maintained cordial relations with Dagan and Nintud. Nani had been present when the older couple's daughter died; that was the result of a priest falling on her when he jumped off the zigurrat.

Neti, Tikal's son and apprentice, listened intently as his father spoke with Enlil-Bani in the banquet room of the royal living quarters. Even here, by common assent, those in attendance sat at a distance from one another. Muda stood against the wall by the hallway door, his arms across his chest; the others, En-me, Zambiya, plus two lesser priests as emissaries of the temples, and one young man representing the landowners, sat at the banquet table. There were four bronze salvers on the table holding meats and cheeses, flat cakes and pastries, fruits and drinks, all of it ignored by those in attendance.

Tikal remained standing until all of the participants were present and seated; then he walked to the colorful mural on a side wall of the room, which depicted the goddess Ninisina and her son Neti. Both of these healer gods were shown in the process of blessing the king, who was wearing royal garb and carrying the symbol of the ruler of Isin, an ornately decorated double-bladed bronze axe.

Pointing to it, he asserted, "We can hope this is a true representation of your blessed status, Enlil-Bani. I'm genuinely saddened to have to report that even Banda has died; his priests are all in mourning, as he was much loved by them. And Ningal is beside himself, too; his apprentice, the one who was a scribe and learning about the heavens from Ningal, was afflicted and died very quickly. There seem to be no kinds of our citizens who are immune from *mutanu's* effect, although there've been some few who've survived. But even those are greatly weakened, as I'm sure you've heard. Vendors die; priests die; guards die; four of my stewards died, though one is better and improving. I've heard from my sources at the river that all the cities are suffering. I don't know what to make of it, but many rats are dying as well. That's good."

"Can anyone predict how long this will last?" Enlil-Bani asked the question in general, not expecting an answer. En-me responded, nevertheless.

"My older colleagues say it could last until the weather turns cold. They expect many more to die; two of my friends are ill and three *ashipus* are dead already. Tikal is certainly correct; almost no one afflicted is spared."

Muda spoke up then, saying, "Two guards dead. More from kitchen ill, Zid-tara tell Mu… me."

"Worse yet," Tikal said solemnly, "is that General Ashgi died in Larsa. Nur-Adad is sending his body back to Isin for the ceremonies and burial. His own advisor, Asgi, died the same day. The messenger told me those two had almost become friends, since they both loved the game of 'Chase the Hares'." After a moment of reflection he continued. "Nur-Adad is sending a new emissary to your court, *Ensi*. He's re-calling Tuma, whose wife and son both died. The new one's named Lipit. I hear he's very formal."

En-me started at the announcement of the General's death, but waited until Tikal had finished to ask, "Has anyone told his daughters that General Ashgi's dead? They're students in Naram's *edubba*."

"I'd forgotten he had children," Tikal answered. "His sons are both posted at border garrisons, and I've sent word to them, but I don't think the girls know." He frowned at his oversight.

"I'll go to the *edubba* today and tell them," En-me said. "They'll need some permanent guardian now that their father is dead. I think they live with a sister of the General."

"Has Naram lost any students?" asked Enlil-Bani with obvious concern. "Does my son seem well?"

En-me answered immediately, saying, "Enmerkar's well, but also suffering from the loss of two of his youngest students. The rest seem to be well for now, but they are scheduling the lessons for different groups on different days."

The enormity of the tragic loss of so many citizens, both young and old, male and female, high-born and low, cast a cloud of uncertainty over those present, and there was silence for a while, until one of the priests spoke up and said, "The gods will reward Isin for having an *Ensi* who made certain the crops were planted and tended. The people will still have reason to give thanks when this is over."

Enlil-Bani wanted to end on this note and waved his hand in dismissal, thus declaring the meeting over.

•●•

Nani went into labor several days after Azuru died. The birth was assisted by Nintud and a mid-wife who had been recommended both by En-me and also Ninmah, who had sent word to Zambiya with great secrecy, as she didn't want Ezina to know. In Ninmah's note, enclosed in a cylinder seal for privacy and inscribed by a female scribe attached to the temple of Ninisina, she said, 'I know your sister is due to give birth. I will perform blessings in the Goddess's sanctuary for her health and that of your niece or nephew. Send word when her child is born, or visit me.'

Zambiya couldn't read, of course, so he took the message to Enlil-Bani in the privacy of his quarters. The king was now reading well enough to make out its meaning. As soon as he heard the message, Zambiya went into the hallway and crushed the clay message and its cylinder seal onto the brick floor with his foot, certain that he didn't want Ezina to suspect he was in contact with Ninmah.

Muda and Neti were friends despite the difference in their ages and backgrounds; they had a mutual respect for their shared dedication to the king and his family, so it was arranged that when the call went out for a midwife to attend Nani, it would be known to the palace.

During the labor, Zambiya waited with Suba in the family courtyard; no male was desired to be present for the mystery of birth.

Despite this being her first pregnancy, Nani had an easy labor and gave birth to a daughter, Gibil, a name she and Suba both liked, meaning 'deified fire.' The baby was small with an amazing amount of curly hair, but what both of her parents noted with satisfaction and shared delight was that she seemed to be alert and searching with her eyes, even when she nursed.

Gibil was born in the middle of the afternoon in this dark part of the year, and during a dark time in the life of Isin, but Suba set out from his home while it was still light to give the good news to his parents, who had stayed in their home to avoid the rampant affliction. Zambiya, at the same time, returned to the palace to share the news with Enlil-Bani and to have word sent to Enmerkar.

———————————•●•———————————

The land of *Ki-en-gir* was decreased by thousands; many hundreds in every city and attendant village were stricken, and most died. The most common event for weeks was burials; the sounds of keening and wailing, weeping and cursing punctuated the very air, daytime and night. The priests and priestesses were unrelenting in conducting services to beseech the gods and goddesses to heal those who suffered, and to spare those who were not afflicted. In every city, the dogs and feral pigs grew fat on the corpses of dead rats.

———————————•●•———————————

Zambiya was barely able to sleep from exhaustion. He had spent the last eight days supervising the work force of slaves and free men who were re-surfacing the sides of the zigurrat. Since the crops had been planted, and even with the death of so many from the plague, Tikal and the High Priests of both temples had agreed to correct the swelling sides of that mountain of earth and brick that supported the twin temples of the goddesses. Trapped water from the seasonal rains inevitably caused the sides to bulge over time; the weepholes built into the structure were insufficient to obviate the eventual need to construct another layer. It was hoped that by this improvement, Inana and Ninisina would respond favorably to the plight of the people.

Having just thrown off the light covering from his chest, he was surprised to hear Ezina, lying next to him in their bed, groan and complain, "I'm so cold, husband. Come next to me."

"I don't feel cold, dear wife. I'll hold you and you'll warm up right away, I'm sure."

He moved over next to her and slid one arm into the space between her neck and shoulders; after sensuously stroking her hair with the other arm he reached over her and pulled her next to him. It was then that he felt a warm wetness on his legs.

"Have you been sweating, dear? You're damp on your legs."

"No, I'm cold. Feel my hands, you'll see." Ezina took his hand in hers to demonstrate what she was experiencing, but realized that her night dress was wet below the waist and sat up, feeling her thighs in amazement. "Why am I wet, Zambiya?"

She sat up, and her husband followed suit; Zambiya got off the bed and went to the only lit torch on the far side of the room and used it to light another near the bed.

The two stared in disbelief at the sight of their bedding and became aware of the sickly-sweet, salt-rust odor of blood. Bile rose in Ezina's throat and she threw off her light blanket; raising the bottom of her dress she was horrified to see blood flowing from her genitals.

"Sud! Sud!" she screamed. She clenched her thighs together and swung her legs off the bed, starting to stand up, while Zambiya rushed to her to help. He reached her just in time to keep her from collapsing to the floor. He picked her up and laid her down on his side of the bed, using his side of the blanket to try to staunch the flow with only temporary success.

Sud entered the room from her sleeping space, rubbing her eyes with one hand and scratching her back with the other, sleepily asking, "What, Lady? If you're not quiet you'll wake Indur."

She looked at her mistress and gasped, a quick inbreath. "What've you done? What's happened?" Without waiting for a response, she ran back into her room and shortly returned with a fresh nightdress and several plainspun cloths intended for use as baby diapers. With difficulty, she ignored Indur's crying, which was increasing in volume as he was so unused to being alone.

As soon as Sud was attending to Ezina, Zambiya went into Sud's room and picked up his son, then hurried out to the hallway and yelled to the night guard from the adjoining hallway, "Get En-me. Right now, hurry."

"It's not the time for your moonflow, Lady," Sud pointed out, her voice a tossed salad of irritation, distress, and concern; all was compounded by the sound of Indur's continuing cries, despite Zambiya's distracted attempts to console him. Ezina lay on her back, her ankles off the end of the bed, trying to concentrate on keeping her thighs tight together. Meanwhile Sud did her best to ease the soaked nightgown off her mistress without getting blood on her face or hair, finally deciding to sit her up and roll the fabric up from the bottom, then using the dry diaper material to wrap the ruined garment, then pulled it over her head. As soon as Ezina was naked, Sud pulled the clean nightgown over her head and down over her breasts and back, but stopped at the waist, then settled her back down on the bed with a rolled diaper pushed tight into her genitals.

It was at this moment that En-me arrived, barefoot and with his hair in disarray, his professional shoulder bag in his hands. He had been fearful that a member of the family had been stricken with the wide-spread malady afflicting so much of the city, but immediately recognized the issue as serious blood loss. He blanched at his unconscious calculation of how much blood was on the bed and floor.

"Zambiya, please take Indur out in the hallway and walk him up and down 'til he's quiet. Have the guard call for the wet nurse, too." En-me waited until Zambiya had left with the still crying child, then took both of Ezina's hands in his. He sniffed lengthily and loudly, then said to Sud, "I don't think there's time to call for a midwife before we deal with this blood flow, so I want your help. Take away the cloth and tell me what you see."

He squeezed Ezina's hands, noting how cold they felt, and said to her, "Ezina, I will do what I can, and you must trust me. Do you want me to call anyone from *Egal-mah* to conduct special prayers?"

"Yes, En-me, you're thoughtful," she said weakly, her gaze wandering but trying to focus. "It's not fair, but I don't think I'm going to see Indur grow up. Can you ask for Ninmah to see me, please?"

"Right away, certainly." He turned his attention to Sud and asked, "What do you see?"

"I can't believe she still has blood to bleed, lord. It's running out slowly, but still coming." She looked at her mistress and started crying, but put a freshly rolled cloth in place again.

En-me shook Sud by the shoulder with one hand and said, "Not now! You can cry later. Right now send to Egal-mah for the priestess named... Ezina, who do you want called?"

"Ninmah." Ezina started panting, and said, "I think she must hurry, Sud. Hurry."

Sud took a deep breath and rushed out of the room, saying to Zambiya as she passed, "Tell the wet nurse when she gets here that Indur needs to be changed." Indur was crying with pitiful sobs by this time.

• ● •

Chief Counselor Tikal and his son Neti joined Enlil-Bani in his chambers, where they were sharing a late day meal together with En-me and Enmerkar. Muda stood with his back leaning on the wall next to the doorway, relaxed but alert.

Zid-tara, the palace Chief Steward and kitchen supervisor, had managed to present a sumptuous repast despite the loss of four workers from his kitchen staff. The table held two kinds of beer, one flavored with anise, and there were three cheeses to supplement the meats, rabbit and lamb. Some naturally leavened breads had been baked in molds shaped like fish, and shared a silver platter with fried barley cakes. The room was filled with the aroma of ox broth, laced with peppers and very hot.

"I'm happy to see the cold weather return to Isin," Zid-tara proclaimed as he personally served the men. "I'm told this should end the onslaught of *mutanu*, which can't happen too soon for me. I'm having to train some household slaves to cook and arrange the plates, and I'll have to buy more slaves because some of my staff died. I'm glad to have Sud back, even though she keeps having crying fits. She misses Ezina and the baby, and mourns them both. You'd think the baby died too, but she took care of the boy most of the time when the wet nurse wasn't there. She always had good sense, and initiative too."

"I'd wondered where Sud went. She was truly distressed by Ezina's death," Enlil-Bani said. He reached for one of the flat cakes to eat with the broth, adding a portion of soft cheese to it with a flat wooden spatula. His brow was furrowed with concern as he added, "Zambiya has been little use since then, naturally. I was no better after Lith-el was killed, though I had to learn what it meant to be *Ensi* even while I grieved."

Tikal volunteered, "You've endured much, *Ensi*. I hope Zambiya can recover his balance, but I know he has the child to consider as well. Nevertheless, I'd like to include him in considering why there's been a reduction in our trade from Meluhha. It's been reduced to a trickle, and we've not heard why." He re-filled his cup of broth and skewered a piece of lamb to add to his plate, then added, "I even believe Nur-Adad when he had his emissary, Lipit, report that he had the same concern. Ordinarily I would suspect him of some scheme, but Larsa's been struck even harder by *mutanu* than we have."

The king had been concerned with the trade issue and commented, "I'll ask him to attend the two of us soon," then, wanting to include Neti, "and you as well." He motioned to Zid-tara to refill his cup with broth.

Then En-me asked Tikal, "I've forgotten why we trade with a city so far away, far past the swamps and the sea I've heard. I know we send barges and boats of grain to them, but what do we get in return?"

Neti interjected with the answer. He had been a silent observer until now, waiting for a chance to contribute and display his knowledge, but not interfere with business between the king and the two palace chiefs. "They're our source of lapis lazuli, those blue stones that our craftsmen form into pendants and other jewelry, as well as other stones like agate. No one is better at sculpting than our people, no matter what the Larsans say. Though there's a *meluhhan* village of sorts out a distance from Isin whose people make good beads. Both of our temples have artisans creating trade items, mostly to the north for wood and stone, lots of other goods." Tikal smiled and nodded toward him in acknowledgement.

Enmerkar stood up from the bench he had been sitting on and precipitously said, "Please, everyone, I have to return to the *edubba*. Both Naram and his wife are doing poorly, but not from *Namtaru's* curse, I think. They're very warm, and the servants were told by En-me to give them lots of hot drinks." He wiped away tears with the back of his hand and exited, his limp more pronounced than usual.

En-me agreed by a nod of his head, and added, "They're both struggling to breathe, and can't seem to take a deep breath. Naram has been very firm that he wants to die when his wife does, and it's looking like that's going to happen." He stood up as well, and said to Enlil-Bani, "*Ensi*, if you'll allow, I'll go with Enmerkar and check on them again."

The king assented, and declared as the two were leaving, "If this is the will of the gods, I hope their passing is easy."

En-me stopped before leaving the room to state, "It's not likely to be, I'm afraid."

———————————— • ● • ————————————

A few days later, Zambiya carried his sleeping son across the market square, striding with purpose toward the section of the city where his sister Nani lived. With the exception of the beer taverns, the vendor stalls were deserted, as it was late in the afternoon and a light mist was falling from the sky, as gloomy as Zambiya's mood. He had waited until Indur had finished suckling at the breast of the wet nurse, then rocked him and crooned a wordless lullaby embedded in his memory from his own infancy, until Indur fell asleep.

He nestled his son close over one shoulder, using his staff to keep up the cadence, hoping the rhythm of his progress would contribute to keeping Indur asleep. The child was wrapped in a dark red linen blanket, which was augmented by a light, gray woolen throw for warmth. Nights in this winter season were cold, and Indur had a tendency to congestion in the mornings, so his caregivers took care to keep him warm.

Zambiya stayed in the middle of the lanes as he walked; some of the common houses were made of clay bricks of lesser quality that sloughed off their outer layers of clay onto the ground during heavy rains, making the path slick. He was careful to plant the staff into the earth for added stability, making his ambulation like rocking, for his son's sake.

He arrived at the home of Suba and Nani when the sun, hidden though it was, remained just above the city wall in its descent into evening. He knocked on the door, then stepped back into the lane so that he was easily visible from the window opening to the right of the portal, even though he was expected. There was little delay before Suba opened the door to admit him.

Zambiya entered and placed his staff into a tall, basket-like palm strut frame with woven sides along with those of the household members, then carefully shifted Indur to his other shoulder.

"Shalamu, Suba," he said. "I am truly in your and Nani's debt for your willingness to care for Indur while I am gone. The gods may curse me for leaving my son, but I'm not going to be the father I want to be for a while." He patted Indur's back lightly, then asked, "Is Nani in back or in the courtyard?"

Suba smiled at Zambiya, his brother-in-law, and reached up to pat Indur's head, and answered by explaining, "She's next door. Dagan's ill again, and Nani took some broth for him, about all he can eat now. Enlil-Bani made him one of the supervisors on the construction of the flood wall, since that isn't finished yet. I expect Nani back very soon. Why don't we sit here and wait for her?" He indicated the earthen brick bench with its multiple pillows along the wall that separated the home from the lane, and sat down. "May I hold Indur, Zambiya? I will need to get used to him and he with me."

"May the gods bless you, Suba. Many another man would not have wanted to add a child to the family so close after the birth of their own child, I'm well aware. I'm very grateful to you both for doing this for me, and for him. He needs someone to mother him, not just feed him, and I can't think of better foster parents than you two." He relinquished Indur to Suba's arms, and noted with satisfaction when Suba lightly brushed the infant's lips with his own before cradling him in both arms.

Nani walked into the room from the lane soon after, and gave her brother a light caress on his head, which was now shaved clean, along with his face. Zambiya made an effort to smile in response, with marginal results that appeared more like a grimace. His forehead was furrowed like a newly plowed field, and the lines seemed as if they might be permanently etched. "Is Gibil still asleep, husband?" she asked.

"I've not heard her, and she has a loud cry, as you know. I'm sure she's asleep. Bibi's in there too; she was dozing in full tuck position when I left." He added for Zambiya's benefit, "The cat's good at keeping pests out." Turning back to his wife, Suba asked, "How is Dagan? I'm sad to see him suffering again. This must be so hard on Nintud."

"She's suffering as much as he is, I think. These bouts of griping cramps are taking all the strength out of him, and she's worn out, too. En-me says he may not survive this time, but I hope he's wrong."

Zambiya noted their conversation and added, "Dagan was a really strong man just a few years ago. One time when he was leading a crew I was on, I got my back up and challenged him. He rewarded me by throwing me into the irrigation ditch we were cleaning out." He allowed himself a wry smile at the memory, then stood up and repeated his gratitude to Nani for her willingness to care for his son.

"I've made arrangements with our father to have a share of grain allocated to you during my absence, plus more. My needs on the journey to *Meluhha* will all be met, so this will be some recompense to you both." He thought a moment, then added, "I trust you to raise him like your own son. Help him to be strong, and wiser than I was. Tell him about me and about his mother."

Zambiya stroked Indur's head, then abruptly rose and retrieved his staff and left the home, saying bitterly as he departed, "The gods so chose."

$$\cdot \; \bullet \; \cdot$$

Sud entered the royal dining room, her muscular arms easily managing the tray of foodstuffs for the evening meal, and carried it to the long carved and inlaid table, setting it down close to Tikal and Neti, who were sitting opposite each other, flanked by Zambiya and Enlil-Bani. The men were all seated on benches; the king had moved from the head of the table and was facing Tikal.

Sud wore a shawl of finely woven wool over her shoulders; dyed light brown and edged with a fringe that sported black chevrons, it was a gift from Ezina in gratitude for Sud's help during Indur's birth. The front barely concealed her breasts.

After quickly filled the cups with hot broth, she distributed the platters of meats and cheeses, and then arranged the assortment of breads and an array of dried fruits: apples, peaches and figs. Finally she presented a plate of fried locusts that had been coated with honey and rolled in sesame seeds.

Before she could leave the room, Zambiya caught her forearm and said, "Sud, I want you to know that Indur is with my sister and her family. He's done well due to your care, and I want you to know that I'm aware of it, and thankful. I'm trying hard to not let my grief keep me from noticing the kindnesses I've been shown, and I've appreciated yours."

Sud, ordinarily so stoical, burst into tears and blubbered, "I miss him so, and Ezina too." She pulled away, covering her mouth to stifle her sobs and retreated to the hallway to recover, leaning against the wall outside the doorway.

Enlil-Bani took a long drink of the ox broth, then observed, "We have important things to decide today, but I intend to speak to Zid-tara about Sud. The last two servers got the broth to us only warm, and didn't know what went where. From now on I want Sud to be my server."

Tikal spoke up in agreement, adding, "Before Sud was assigned to Ezina, she was always a better worker than most, and I know Zid-tara was glad to get her back."

Zambiya gathered food for his dish with so little thought that Neti observed, "Did you intend to put apples on your mutton, Zambiya? I've never tried that."

Zambiya responded with a wry smile and an embarrassed, "Me either."

Tikal decided to guide the necessary parts of the discussion, and said to Zambiya, "You were wise to ask your sister to care for your son while you are on this mission to *Meluhha*. It will take several months, and we can't wait until winter ends." He turned to Neti and said, "I know this will come as a surprise. I intend for you to go with the caravan, with Zambiya's agreement."

Neti's hand stopped in midair on its way to his mouth with a sliver of pork, his mouth open. At first he looked frozen, but slowly lowered his hand and carefully returned the meat to his plate, looking first at Enlil-Bani and then at his father.

"I thought that Muda would be Zambiya's second on this mission," Neti said. After a moment he added, "I've hardly ever been outside the walls of Isin without a cadre of soldiers, and never very far." Looking across the table at Zambiya, he raised his voice a little and said, "Please agree, Zambiya. I'd love to go." He looked at Tikal and said, "Thank you, father, for even thinking of it."

Despite his in-turned mien, Zambiya noted the enthusiasm in Neti's voice and recalled how much training Tikal had exposed the young man to, and said, "You'll be very welcome by me, though I'm as surprised as you are by your father's offer."

"Muda is still Enlil-Bani's personal guard, and he looks foreign, so he would be a distraction in *Meluhha*, especially in trade negotiations. You're well prepared for that role," Tikal said to his son. "This is the kind of experience you will need to serve our *Ensi* in the future."

Enlil-Bani reached for the plate with the locusts and helped himself to several, and then turned to Tikal and said, "I want to try to increase cooperation and peaceful relations with Larsa, and this venture may help us do that. Don't answer right now, Tikal, but think about this. Both of our cities want a steady supply of lapis, and carnelian as well, and neither is getting it. If we are able to secure a favorable trade agreement, Nur-Adad is likely to demand tribute to allow the stones to pass Larsa to us. I propose that we arrange with him at the outset that we both get the same amount of stones from *Meluhha*. That will give him an incentive to maintain our current truce, and even lead to better relations on other issues. It's like digging a canal that waters two fields equally, so neither farmer needs to cut the supply of the other to get an advantage."

Tikal pushed his plate to one side and moved his broth toward the middle of the table, leaving a large clear space in front of him. He used this to project an invisible map from his mind; with his left index finger he traced a route from the upper left, meandering to the right, then with a slow circular jog, ending at a spot on the table on the table where he had positioned his right thumb. A drawn out, "Yes," came from lips, and a slow smile formed. "I need to stop trying to figure out how to keep Nur-Adad from getting the advantage of us, *Ensi*. We are all depleted from the *mutanu*, Larsa as well, so peace is in everyone's favor. He's likely to agree with your plan."

He reached out for his cup again and then retrieved his plate before adding, "When I was much younger I thought Isin could arrange with some trader to bypass Larsa and Ur and use an overland route to *Meluhha*. I got tired of being laughed at. They told me, one after another, that it was a great idea." He waved his hand in the air as if he were wiping something away. "Except for the mountains, then the deserts, plus crossing the *Idiglat* both directions."

Zambiya had forced himself to concentrate on the discussion, recognizing the importance of the trading prospects, then inserted, "I don't want to wait very long to leave, but the palace guard is depleted by at least five men right now and I want at least eight to make up the squad who will make up caravan security. Four could be soldiers then, not guards. In particular, I want Ansar as my second in charge."

Tikal responded by offering Neti as one of the eight, and agreed to select another three seasoned fighters from the ranks of the palace crew, but then asked, "Not Nabi? He traveled with you on your last caravan."

"I don't want to have to make conversation for a while, and Nabi would expect me to talk about Ezina and Indur. Natural enough, but not what I want."

"It's settled, then. You chose the other guards; I'll find the soldiers from the army."

"One more point, and an important one. I know no one who can speak to a *meluhhan* in his language. We'll want an interpreter we can trust to speak truly, faithful to our interests. I'm going to go to their village and try to recruit one; if we do that now, we won't be stuck with some lackey from Larsa who looks like a slave but is really Nur-Adad's cousin."

Tikal smiled with admiration and declared, "Excellent, Zambiya." He then inserted a further thought, based on his experience. "Try to choose a young man with every reason to want to return to Isin from a successful journey."

———————— • ● • ————————

Zambiya arranged to meet with Ninmah two days later, using a priestess from *Egal-mah* to offer the invitation, and making sure that it was understood that they would meet in the market square, not at Ninisina's temple. He selected a table in the shady interior of the largest public food and beer establishment and had the proprietor reserve it for him. He waited in the shade of the awning until Ninmah arrived.

Although Zambiya didn't expect to leave Isin for another ten days, he was dressed for travel, a shawl over his shoulders and his palace insignia prominent on his chest and forearms. His sickle sword in its scabbard hung from a sturdy oxhide belt circling his waist; a short sword with a leather lanyard was on his other side. He inhaled sharply as soon as he saw

Ninmah crossing the square from her temple's administrative complex at the base of the zigurrat.

She approached him with an air of confidence, her movements graceful and her manner of dress designed to impress. She wore a garment as white as an egret that covered one shoulder, with several bands of feather-shaped fabric rows ending just above her ankles. A corded belt with silver dangles all around adorned her slender waist, emphasizing her shapely bosom and hips. She was again wearing the amber pendant he had given her many months ago, and she wore gold bracelets on both wrists. Her hair was adorned with a narrow gold headband with lapis lazuli cabochons at the forehead. The bottom of her dress swayed as she walked, with the ankle straps of her sandals sporting tiny silver bells that tinkled as she made each step. A temple guard followed her, a short distance behind. At a gesture from Ninmah, he stopped.

"Shalamu, goddess," Zambiya greeted her. "I'm very pleased that you agreed to meet with me."

"How could I not agree to meet with a friend?" she responded, emphasizing the word 'friend.'

Zambiya sighed, recognizing the edge of bitterness in Ninmah's voice. "We have been so much more than friends, and when I was married to Ezina, I didn't want to offend the gods by betraying her." His voice caught, and he motioned toward the rear of the public house, saying, "Let us sit together and share a portion of beer."

Ninmah gestured to her guard to come into the shade of the establishment, then followed Zambiya to the small table he had reserved. The server, a middle-aged man with a distinct limp and ravaged facial skin, brought an open topped gourd beer container and two reed straws. He bowed toward the priestess, but then inquired of Zambiya, "Any food?"

"No," Zambiya declared, then held up his hand to stay the waiter, having re-thought the question and asked Ninmah, "Unless you'd like something."

"Later, perhaps. Not now." She waved the man away, and as soon as he had left them said, "I heard about Ezina, of course. You may not believe it, but I'm truly sorry about her death. We were very close when she was a priestess. Who's caring for your son?"

"My sister's caring for him, along with her own daughter. The children are close in age." He sipped at the beer, and Ninmah did the same. Then Zambiya decided to launch into the reason for his desire to see Ninmah, saying, "Ezina and I were very good together, I believe, even though we never intended to marry; I think we loved each other. That is why I only visited you once after I returned from the north. You can't help but know that I love you as well, and always have, since we met."

"I do know; that's why I was so hurt when you said we should be friends. I also know that I'm the problem. I love being a priestess, and I'm considered special because of my singing." She fingered the pendant at her breast, looking pensive, and patted the hair by her ears into place. "I'll never give up my post in the temple, Zambiya, but I love you, too." She hesitated and sipped again from the gourd, then offered, "Can we be lovers again, as we used to be? Remembering, I'm a virgin and must remain so."

Zambiya felt a quiver in his chest and an ache in his loins at the thought of being with Ninmah again, yearning to reach out and caress her, but said, "I wanted to see you before I leave; I have a mission for Enlil-Bani that will cause me to be gone for several moons, many in fact." He took the initiative and reached across the table to hold one of her hands in both of his, adding, "When I return, I'd like to see you again." He lowered his voice to add, "All of you, goddess."

Ninmah felt her throat tighten as tears began to flow, but she shook her head to regain control and said, "Be sure you come back, Zambiya. I long to hold you close to me."

The server was approaching the table, but Zambiya raised his hand to stop him, then said to Ninmah, "Could we share one of their pastries again? This is where I bought those we shared all that time ago."

"I'd like that. It will bring back some very pleasant memories, I'm sure."

The server was invited over by Zambiya, and the two former lovers ceased discussion until he had returned and presented the pastry, a leavened cake with honeyed fruit paste, topped with another cake and cut in half.

Once the server had left them, Zambiya told Ninmah about the orant Suba was making for placement in Ninisina's temple atop the zigurrat, to create ongoing good will toward his son, Indur; he asked if she would be certain that the orant was given a favorable place in the temple when it was completed. She agreed to do so, then she asked, "When do you leave Isin? And you didn't say where you are going on this mission."

"I leave in several days, headed to the sea and then on to *Meluhha* to arrange a trading partnership. That will be new for me. I'm not a trader, but there will be some in the caravan I'll be leading."

Ninmah moved her small bench so that she could hide her movements, and then reached under the table with one hand and stroked the inside of Zambiya's thigh, quietly saying, "Perhaps we could continue our discussion about the orant in a more private setting, perhaps in the palace. Before you leave."

Zambiya's male member responded instantly, and he responded throatily, "I'm sure we could. Yes. I'll escort you." He slowly removed her hand from his thigh and said, "I'll need to stay here a while before I get up, goddess."

<hr />

As usual, Muda took up his vigil near the hallway door, armed with a short spear and a new oval shaped shield. The shield was of his own design, a handspan wider than his shoulders in width, the narrow part covering him only from his throat to the bottom of his breastbone. Two thicknesses of polished beaten copper were attached to the front of a standard oxhide cover on a poplar frame, with bronze spikes affixed to both narrow ends. He held it by means of padded forearm and hand braces, angled across him from shoulder to hip.

Tikal and Neti were already present and flanked Enlil-Bani in the informal palace greeting room; Nabi and four guards provided additional security. The room itself had been re-purposed from Aga's former bedroom, but still retained the stylized painting on the longest wall. It showed Inana and her female entourage, with the goddess dressed in battle gear with helmet and armored breast plates. In an effort to make the former occupant's mother feel more welcome, tamarisk and cedar incense had been lighted several minutes before Nisaba was expected.

True to her nature, Nisaba arrived promptly, accompanied by both of her daughters. All three were dressed elegantly, with matching ankle length fine linen dresses, but with adornments that emphasized their different tastes and body types. Nisaba looked every bit the matron that she was, with an inverted pyramidal shaped silver and lapis necklace starting just below her double chins and covering the upper part of her ample bosom, with similar dangle earrings reaching nearly to her shoulders. Despite her corpulent physique, she walked more gracefully than one would expect as she approached the king's position alone, leaving her daughters by the doorway, and bowed. She stopped at a point where she could see Tikal clearly, but directly in front of Enlil-Bani.

"Shalamu and welcome, Nisaba. I hope the gods have been good to you of late, after the distressing events in the past. I'm glad you were spared the ravages of *Namtaru*." Tikal spoke as the official who would conduct the entreaty from Nisaba to the king, a matter of protocol Nisaba expected. She acknowledged the king with a bow, but directed her speech to Tikal.

"I am here to beseech the *Ensi* to allow me and my girls to return to Isin to live. I had not wanted to return while *mutanu* was claiming so many in the city, but apparently *Namtaru* is satisfied with the many souls who've passed through *Ganzer*." She adjusted her light shawl before motioning Sherida to come forward.

The older of the two girls approached her mother and stood to the right of her and inclined her head respectfully to the king. She had an ample bosom, and her necklace, made of several strings of silver beads ascending in size from a grain of millet at the outer edges to that of a peach pit, rested on the fabric of her dress. Her thick hair was held in place with four silver combs. She remained silent, but was visibly alert to the proceedings.

Tikal again addressed Nisaba, asking, "And how is Aga? Did he tell you why he was so late coming home from Larsa? I thought that was disrespectful of him, you must know." His voice emanated concern for Aga's mother, not betraying his knowledge of Aga's fate.

The furrows in Nisaba's forehead became more pronounced as she took a deep breath before responding with a strained tone in her voice. "I've not yet seen him, lord. I don't know what has become of him, but my daughters can't wait to marry until he returns." She took a cloth from a subtly constructed pocket in her dress and quickly dabbed at her eyes before continuing, "I miss him terribly, and I know something's wrong. I just wish I knew."

Tikal turned his attention to Sherida and asked, "Young lady, do you have a potential groom in mind yet? Surely there are already prospective suitors."

Sherida glanced at her mother for permission to respond, which Nisaba granted with a nod of her head. "Where we live on the farm, Lord, there is no one my mother would consider even suitable, let alone desirable. No, Lord, there is no one."

"Well, there are lots of men in Isin without wives now, but women without husbands, too." Tikal's customary mindset as a problem solver started to engage, and he almost automatically made an assessment of Sherida as a wife for one of the many men he knew who were without a spouse. Nevertheless, he re-focused his attention and looked over at Ninegala.

"I know you're the youngest, so you may not have given any thought to getting married yet." Ninegala remained in her place, and she shook her head slowly, looking quite grim. Although she was dressed like her mother and sister, her adornments were much plainer, a silver articulated chain encircled her slender waist with the ends hanging down to her knees, emphasizing her long legs. A matched bracelet on her right wrist completed her jewelry.

Ninegala looked at her mother, but without advancing toward her said, "No, Lord Tikal, I have no intention of marrying. I might dedicate myself to Ninisina's temple."

Nisaba whirled to look at her youngest and a scowl formed on her face, but she quickly gained her composure and said to Tikal, "These are matters that are still being considered, Lord. For now, I want 'Rida to have opportunities for a good match." For the first time she looked at Enlil-Bani and said, "Please, *Ensi*, my girls have their whole lives before them. Allow us to live in Isin."

Tikal started to admonish the woman for addressing the king directly, but was stopped by Enlil-Bani. "Tikal, the lady asks little of us. I will grant her request." The king then spoke directly to Nisaba, offering, "Lady, would you be agreeable to considering a widower as a possible suitor?"

Nisaba was taken aback at the question, as she had not considered that possibility for her eldest, who had only shared fantasies about what kind of young man would be available. The question raised the possibility in her mind of a rich older man, one who might well want a young wife. Her vexation at Ninegala was shed like a broken sandal, and she responded with enthusiasm, "You mean for my daughter, of course, not me." She looked at the king for ascent, who nodded and smiled, and then said, "I certainly would, *Ensi*, and," turning to look at Sherida with determination in her voice, "she would, too."

Sherida felt alarm grip her, a clenching from her breastbone to her bowels, but she knew better than to express her anxiety here, now, so she nodded and gripped her arms tight across her bosom. She began forming a prayer to her household god, and her palms started perspiring.

CHAPTER ELEVEN

STAKING A NEW FIELD

There seems to be a pattern in the world the gods created, that the building up follows the breaking down. To plant a field the clods must be beaten apart; a serpent must shed its skin to grow. Growth seems to follow loss.

Kulla, the king's barber, was finishing the shaving of Enlil-Bani's head, feeling for any errant stubble and removing it with an obsidian blade. His normally garrulous manner was much subdued, but he responded to the king's inquiry with a sigh, saying, "I was very blessed, *Ensi*, that Mas survived the *mutanu* and is recovering well; he was stricken early into Namtaru's visit to Isin, so I stayed in our home to help my wife in caring for him. Many neighbors died, and even our *ashipu* died. Even now Mas is working in the market half the day, he's that much better. You must know that we had no income for many days, with so many passing over *Id-kura* and others afraid to be caught outside by Namtaru." He took care to wipe the king's head and neck with a dedicated cloth with flower scented lotion on it before adding with resignation in his voice, "I don't think that helped, honestly. My parents never left our home, but they both died." His voice caught in his throat, but he swallowed hard and started gathering his tools and cloths.

Enlil-Bani felt his pate and smiled; Kulla had been his barber for several years, and now he could enjoy having his head shaved three times per month and his scalp pampered with lotion. This was one of the few kingly perquisites he allowed himself. He still shaved his own face.

"You should tell your customers the new Chief Priest of *Egal-mah*, Enmul, will shortly begin directing a major re-surfacing of the holy zigurrat. The priests and priestesses from both temples held a day-long conference and they believe Ninisina and Inana together can protect Isin from Namtaru."

The king reported to Kulla the decision the religious community had reached without personally having any confidence in the reasoning, especially as the pestilence was in clear retreat now. Tikal and he were more concerned with keeping the populace engaged in some project at a time when fewer citizens were needed to keep the canals and tributaries in good repair, thus contributing to order and stability.

Enlil-Bani lowered his voice and confided in his longtime barber, "Kulla, I still wonder what I am doing in this palace as *Ensi*. When I was a simple groundsman, I just worried about the ditches and grains and how the root crops were doing. My own children and Lith-el were the only people I was responsible for."

"Many citizens think it's your personal leadership and foresight that allowed Isin to get crops in the field while the misery spread, so they'll believe what the priests say."

By this time, Kulla had gathered all of his supplies and was prepared to leave. The king placed his hand on Kulla's shoulder and said, "Give Mas my good wishes, and tell him I hope to see him with you next time." He hesitated a moment and added, "We were blessed to have such fine men as sons."

<hr />

"This way, goddess."

Zambiya led Ninmah by the hand through the narrow passageway that was used by kitchen workers to enable them to expeditiously transport meals to the royal quarters and serve them hot. The ceiling was low and only one torch had been lit by him before escorting her from the temple administration building and dormitory. It was well past the time when staff would be at their duties.

They had gained entry to the palace via a hidden and well-secured service gate in the courtyard wall, designed to allow the removal of kitchen waste and palace detritus, very close to where such were dried and burned. Zambiya knew every corner of the palace, having spent many months as a guard to the previous king's family, prior to his step-father's ascent to the throne.

It was critical to both of them that no one be aware of their liaison; Ninmah was nowhere near the age when a priestess could legally wed, and celibacy was demanded of her. Both were covered by long dark cloaks, and had removed their sandals to reduce the sounds of their progress to the suite of rooms that Zambiya now occupied alone.

There was no one on guard in this section since Ezina had died and the infant Indur had gone to Nani and Suba's home. Sud had returned to the quarters of the other kitchen slaves.

As soon as Ninmah was safely in the interior of the bedroom, Zambiya shrugged off his cloak and helped remove the one the priestess wore. He placed both cloaks and their sandals on a bench near the doorway. A wall torch illuminated the outer vestibule; scant light in the bedroom was provided by one small torch. Little remained of Ezina's possessions, and there was nothing left to reveal that a baby had been present just a few days ago. Zambiya had removed everything not intended for the caravan he would be commencing two days hence.

Ninmah stood in the middle of the room and turned in a circle, employing all her senses. She satisfied herself that there were no sounds from the passageways, then walked to the opening that had previously led to Sud's room. Almost absent light, she could see that it now contained only a single bed, a small light table and a free-standing poplar shelf unit that was empty. She noted that a pleasant incense had been lit in the bedroom some time recently and smiled, and then saw there was a table with food laid out near the bed, pastries stuffed with dates and soft cheese. Two silver cups sat next to a matching silver wine flask.

"Was this Ezina's bed?" she asked.

"Yes." He hesitated before continuing, sensitive to a tone in her question that required explanation beyond the mere acknowledgment. "I've not had time to have it removed."

Ninmah made no comment. Instead she walked directly to the table next to the bed and poured wine into the cups, close to full. They kissed for some time before Ninmah pulled away and offered him one of the cups, and then drank from hers.

She then broke off a piece of pastry and placed it in her mouth, holding it lightly between her teeth before approaching Zambiya and pulling his lips to hers. She bit into the pastry so that a portion entered his mouth, then kissed him with lips and tongue, savoring the feel of his arms, already encircling her body. Zambiya drained his cup and started to lead the priestess to the bed, but Ninmah backed away. She placed her hand on his bare chest and said, "Not here. And remember, I must remain a virgin, but you know how to give me Inana's blessings anyway."

Ninmah was wearing a one-piece sleeveless red ochre linen dress that was held onto her body by a single string, tied just above her bosom. She untied the string and let the dress fall to the floor, allowing Zambiya to appreciate every curve of her body and also to inhale the scent of her perfume, emanating from between her breasts and under her arms. She stepped over her abandoned dress and approached him with deliberation; with tantalizing slowness, she removed his clothing, amounting to no more than a mid-length skirt tied around his muscular body. She took another draught from her wine cup, then offered him what remained, which he finished.

After lightly stroking Zambiya's face, her hand traced the middle of his body down across his chest and abdomen until she reached his erect member. Then she moved away from him and took the lighted torch from its holder on the wall and walked toward the small adjoining room, saying, "Come."

"Because I'd like the company, Chief Steward."

Zid-tara had expressed mild puzzlement at Enlil-Bani's insistence that Sud both serve him and share his meals with him whenever no royal function was planned.

The two were sitting together in the royal dining room after his midday repast. The attendants had already cleared away the food and dishes from the long table, and Sud had been told to return to the banquet room after she was done with her cleanup duties.

"I won't be poisoned by food from your kitchen, Zid-tara, so I don't need a 'taster'; having someone with no official status to visit with will be relaxing for me." The king stretched his legs out in front of him and took a deep breath, then resumed, saying, "But I don't want it to be a command, and I especially don't want anyone to think that I'm courting her. She's pleasant and attends to my food with thoughtfulness, so I could just enjoy a woman's presence without any other expectations on her part or mine. Do you understand? Do you think she'll understand?"

The Chief Steward stood up and walked around the table as he thought, rubbing his shaved pate, trying to adjust his habit of assuming that anything a king wanted was automatically a command. What Enlil-Bani was requesting was so laden with human need and humility that Zid-tara was unnerved by having been consulted, rather than commanded. Enlil-Bani had been king for several months, but the contrast with the previous king's demeanor continued to have an exotic feeling to it, reminding him of one of those strange spices from the north that gave good broth a taste like wild weeds had been thrown into it. It took a conscious effort for him to dispel that feeling, and attend to the actual request.

"I'm of two minds, *Ensi*," he opined. "I think it will be hard to keep my people from speculating about why Sud is spending her meals with you if you don't intend to sleep with her, and I think she'll wonder, too. I would." Then he added, "Maybe not, though. She's plain as a brick." He walked slowly back to the king and sat again, showing both his palms to the king as a sign of acceptance, then continued, saying, "But if you make it a request to her, and she understands it for what it is, something you'd like but don't require, I'll see that the idle chatter is held down, like a pot with a lid." He then added, "You always have Muda in the room, anyway."

"That's right."

Sud returned through the hallway entrance and bowed, first to the king, then to Zid-tara. Her stocky build was accentuated by the plain beige sleeveless shift she wore; it ended at mid-calf, revealing her bare feet. She held her hands together over her midriff, and inquired, "What do you require?"

Zid-tara communicated the basic request for Enlil-Bani, giving his permission in the telling, leaving Sud with a stunned and quizzical look. She searched the king's face trying to glean any hidden tone or motive.

She opened her mouth to start a question, then closed it again, and edged her way to the doorway, but stopped as she had not been dismissed.

Enlil-Bani could see the hesitation, so he said, "Zambiya has told me how much help you were to Ezina and their baby, Indur. Ezina spoke well of you before she died, and you've been a good steward when you had occasion to serve me." He held up his hands as though he were holding a large basket and said, "You know I used to be married, and having a woman to serve my food and then just talk would be a comfort to me. I want nothing more from you than your company, your comments. Would you try it for ten days' of meals and then give me an answer?"

Even though she was a slave, expecting to do as she was told, Sud felt a sense of certainty that the king's request was just that and nothing more. She sighed and visibly relaxed, then smiled at the two men and said, "My *Ensi* honors me by asking. I need no time for deciding. I will return when it is time to serve next time." She bowed again, then left.

"I'm glad, *Ensi*. But let me be clear. If she becomes a burden or displeases you, you must tell me. As good a worker as she's been, I'll sell her to a Mitanni trader."

Despite his general weakness, Dagan had returned to work in the fields, now that the flood wall was complete. He was supervising the maintenance of the irrigation ditches owned by the temple of Ninisina. He had never sought to be a groundsman, supervising the work of others, but he had often been cast in that role due to his friendship with Enlil-Bani, at that time an official groundsman, plus his long experience and complete reliability.

When he was absent in the daytime, Nintud regularly visited with Nani in her home next door, helping her with the two infants. She was very welcome, and the two women felt blessed by each other's easy sharing. The difference in their ages gave ground to mutual respect for their individual talents.

Nintud was grinding meal in the courtyard of Nani's home when Alim, the groundsman, came to Nintud's door, crying out her name. Without any response to shouts and pounding there, Alim tried at Nani and Suba's, waking both the infants from a midmorning nap.

"Nani!" Alim shouted; he had been one of Enlil-Bani's field workers and was acquainted with her. "Please come to the door. We need to find Nintud." He waited briefly, and was just about to pound on the door again when Nani opened it, having seen him from the elevated window next to her door.

"Alim, for An's sake, hush up." She kept her voice low but urgent, even though it was clear that the children were now awake and fussing at ascending volume. "You've wakened the babies, and I just got them to sleep. What's wrong?" Her exasperation was obvious.

"Is Nintud here? She's not answering." His voice was low but insistent.

Donning her veil, Nani stepped into the lane to continue speaking with him, at which time she saw four more men, who were still in front of Dagan and Nintud's home. When she recognized Dagan's motionless form in the arms of the workers, she gasped and leaned onto the doorframe, gripped her door with one hand, covering her mouth with the other.

"What's wrong with Dagan? Has he been hurt?"

Alim could barely raise his voice to answer, but managed to explain. "Dagan's dead, Nani. He was bitten on the throat by a cobra. It was hiding in the stubble of a field next to the canal we were mucking out." He recollected his thoughts and asked again, "Is Nintud here? I have to tell her. And I've got to tell Enlil-Bani."

Nani straightened herself upright and squared her shoulders, making decisions even as she shook tears away from her eyes. "One moment, Alim; wait for me here." She walked to the men gathered outside Nintud's door and opened it, motioning them to follow her inside. She led them to the couple's bedroom and indicated that they should place Dagan on the bed, giving him a gentle caress on his head before leading the men back outside.

She returned to her own house and led Alim and the others into her home's front entry, motioning the four to sit on the bench by the wall and for Alim to follow her. The babies were now howling in a rear bedroom, as much from the insistent sobs of the other one as to their own distress. Close to weeping herself, she nevertheless followed her maternal instinct and hurried down the hallway to the nursery and picked up Gibil, her daughter, and held her over her shoulder, patting her back. She had been trailed by Alim, and she said to him, "Hold Indur for me, please?"

"Of course, Nani." He moved to the child and mimicked her placement of the babe on his shoulder, alternating stroking the child's back with a patting motion that proved soothing to the boy. The babies gradually reduced their fretting, giving Alim the chance to inquire, "Nani, where's Nintud?"

"She's in the yard." Hesitating long enough for both of the babies to quiet further, she motioned for Alim to follow her to the pantry area that led to the courtyard and wait inside for her. She stepped through the doorway, taking care to keep the heavy curtain from rubbing against her baby.

"Nintud, my friend, can you come here, please?"

The middle-aged matron sat back on her thighs from her position on the ground, where she had been grinding mixed barley and flax grains together; she straightened her back carefully before looking toward her friend's voice and stood up.

"What is it, dear? I was about to come inside anyway. I thought I heard the babies. Won't they sleep?"

"Please cover the grain and come inside. I'll finish the grinding later."

Nintud scooped the grains together into a pile and covered it first with the tightly woven kneeling mat, then with a flat bottomed basket upside down over the mat.

Once both the women had entered the home it took Nintud but an instant to recognize Alim and the import of him being here at this time on a fieldwork day.

"Where's Dagan?" The immediacy of her concern showed in her tone, reflecting worry that had become chronic due to his recurrent affliction.

Alim was shocked to find Nani handing him Gibil, asleep now, to hold in his other arm, and saying to Nintud, "We've put him in bed at home, dear. Alim's going to stay here while we go see him." As she led Nintud through the home to her front door, she called back, "Thanks, Alim. I'll be back in a while. Offer the men some beer."

Alim looked from one shoulder to the other, a sleeping or drowsy baby on each, at first puzzled by the suggestion to provide beer to his companions, but then he realized that Nani had taken the responsibility for dealing with the newly widowed woman away from him, and silently gave thanks.

———— • ● • ————

Zambiya, Neti and Ansar stood together outside the city walls; each had taken primary responsibility for one critical phase of the caravan, and each was surveying their assembled men and beasts. There had been a light rain in the night, always a blessing when it settled the ubiquitous dust of the track they would be traversing.

The designated commander of the project, Zambiya had experience with prior treks to distant lands, which neither of the other leaders could claim. Neti was responsible for the negotiations once they reached *Meluhha*, as befitted his training by his father and those officials and traders chosen by Tikal to increase his knowledge and skills as an administrator. Ansar had been replaced in his former duties to conduct Isin's patrols; his assignment now was to keep the caravan's soldiers and guards well-disciplined and prepared for raids. None of the men was married, and everyone had volunteered for the caravan's rigors, looking forward to an adventure.

Zambiya had consulted with Tikal, who wanted four of his stewards to be added to the company for the first few days. These men were to travel along the track leading to Larsa and return, one at a time, to report on the condition of the fields and villages considered to be part of Isin's territory. Once the caravan had arrived at Larsa, Neti would participate with Zambiya in making the caravan a joint venture to benefit both cities, an unusual arrangement considering that the two cities had long been adversaries. Nevertheless, both *Ensis* wanted desperately to establish a robust trading relationship with *Meluhha's* trade in lapis and other prized imports.

Satisfied that the troop was in order, Zambiya stepped away from the other leaders where he had been standing, wrapped in a yellow wool shawl against the coolness of the early morning and the river mists. He searched his group for sight of the *meluhhan* youth he'd recruited from the bead-maker village, a light-skinned man of angular build with his hair arranged in a bun at the back of his head. Named Rangu, he was betrothed to a village girl, the daughter of the headman.

An older drover was standing nearby holding the harness of a ruddy young onager with a light stomach, whispering quietly into the creature's long dark ear. Zambiya took off his shawl and secured it onto the back of the mule-like animal with two of the available lashings, then asked the drover, "What did you say to her?"

The man smiled, showing many gaps in his teeth and replied, "Lord,

I told her to behave today or I would break her legs and leave her for the lions to eat."

"Did she believe you?"

"Of course; I tell her that every day. That's why she's such a good worker." He laughed heartily at his own joke, stroking the beast's neck affectionately.

Zambiya had opened his mouth to give the order to commence walking when he was surprised to see Ninmah. She exited the gate accompanied by a male priest and followed by two temple guards. Both religious officials wore matching stoles over stark white linen clothes, a pleated tunic for the priest and similar dress for Ninmah; the stoles sported alternating bands of pink flamingo feathers separating embroidered black chalices with scarlet flames in the middle. The priest had a high crowned hat with four crimson felt bands, descending in size as they ascended the headgear. While the priest carried a short spear in one hand, Ninmah held a silver bowl in hers, filled with scented flax oil and with a light colored wooden dipper with multiple rough spurs at the end resting in the bowl.

Zambiya made his way through the assembled animals and leaders and approached the religious emissaries, saying, "Shalamu, priest and priestess." He looked first at the priest as he spoke, but then fixed his attention on Ninmah, who smiled and bowed her head slightly toward him.

The priest responded to Zambiya, saying, "Shalamu, Zambiya. Enmul has sent us to bless your company and your mission. We will not delay you for long, but it will be good to secure the blessings of Ninisina and Damu before you leave."

"We always hope for the blessing of the gods, so you are most welcome. What do you need from us?"

The priest looked at Ninmah, who handed the bowl to one of the guards, who had moved to join her. The priest instructed, "Have your men hold fast to their donkeys and onagers, as the blessing includes a song to the goddess and her son." He waited while the company complied with the warning, then continued, "You are fortunate indeed. Priestess Ninmah has been recognized for her devotion to the goddess and for her mastery of the sacred songs, and is now the Lead Singer of the Elite Corps. This is her first ceremony in her new role."

Zambiya looked directly in Ninmah's eyes and said, "I've had the good fortune to witness her ecstatic voice in the past." Ninmah colored slightly, her eyes growing wider, but Zambiya quickly added, "At other great celebrations, of course."

He turned to look at his troop and said, "It looks like we're ready. Please commence."

The priest raised the spear over his head and began a low chant as he meandered around and through the caravan. Ninmah followed him with the guard next to her, holding the bowl steady while she used the dipper to flick the oil in small quantities over the creatures and men. While doing this, she started singing a familiar entreaty to the goddess, praying for good fortune and a successful venture. Her voice was, indeed, superb, and she alternated between lilting lyrics and ecstatic ululation. The latter seemed to startle the draft animals at first, but Ninmah started with low volume and gradually increased until near the end, when she and the priest had returned to the area closer to the city gate, when she waved her right arm in a symbolic arc to encompass the entire company and offered a full-throated ululation that lasted a long time with descending volume, then stopped. She recovered the bowl from the guard during the silence that followed the ceremony, then without further pause, the priest and priestess returned to the city. With the priest leading the way back to the temple compound and the guards following behind, no one could see Ninmah's tears falling into the sacred oil.

Zambiya had watched Ninmah until she disappeared past the city walls, but without delay, he turned to the company, seeking Neti and Ansar. Having located them and satisfied himself that all was ready, he adjusted first his headband and then his sickle sword and announced loudly, "Onward!" and strode to the front of the troop.

Nabi stood outside the gate to Nisaba's home, aware from a recent city patrol that her family was again residing in Isin. It was midmorning and he wore his best uniform covered by a light cloak, with only a short sword as a weapon. He shouted to attract the attention of someone in the home, then waited patiently, as he knew he was not expected.

After a short time the slave with a withered arm appeared from the side of the house, a two-story home with a front portico over the main structure, plastered a pale pink.

"Shalamu, guard. What do you want?"

"Shalamu, friend. I would like to speak with Nisaba, your mistress. I want to offer an invitation to her. Please tell her that."

The attendant disappeared back around the side of the house, and Nabi leaned against the dark brown plastered wall next to the wood of the gate apparatus, watching a young feral pig ambling away from him toward a crossing lane while sniffing the air. He listened for the return of the attendant, and felt the weight of his shoulder bag under the cloak with satisfaction. A frugal man, he had many days of accrued credits to his account with the palace; he was carrying many grain bags to pay for the day he had in mind. He started to idly hum a marching tune as he watched the pig turn the corner of the lane.

Nisaba appeared at her front door looking in his direction quizzically, but then recognized him as the guard who had been in charge when Aga's property was returned to her. That memory caused her a moment of distress, but she had come to accept that her son would not be returning, though why was still a mystery to her.

The matron was wearing a heavy shawl over a high quality green linen dress with a cream colored fringe with dark brown embroidered exes on the edge. The shawl covered her back and her large bosom, and she was wearing sandals over leg warmers. Her graying hair was combed and pulled back from her ears to show off the dangling gold hoops in her lobes.

She approached Nabi and said, "Shalamu, guard. My slave said you had come with an invitation. Is it from the palace?"

"No, lady. I hope you won't feel that I'm brazen. I'd like to escort you and your daughters to the market square for a midday repast. A troupe of acrobats and exotic singers and dancers have arrived from Sippar and the northern cities on their way down to Ur. They're permitted to present just one performance and then must be on their way to Shurrupak by nightfall." Nabi finished his recitation, which he had rehearsed for some time, observing Nisaba closely for any expression of disdain, as he felt the difference in their station acutely. Then he added, "I knew your family had returned to Isin very recently, and moving household locations is always stressful, Lady. I remember it from my own childhood. I prayed to the wise goddess Sag-buru that you would be ready for some diversion. I am."

Nisaba found herself conflicted between the prospect of a complete change of scene and added entertainment she'd not heard of, and the knowledge that this guard was well below her station. Further complicating her feelings was the recognition that she was surprisingly attracted to this muscled and assertive guard in a way she had thought long dormant in her, if not dead. Aware of primal sensations in her body, she was close to blushing. Instead she turned away and took two slow deep breaths, looking toward her home as if searching for some key information, then returned to face Nabi.

"I'd..." She cleared her throat before starting again at a higher volume and stepped closer to the gate. "I'd like to see the performance, guard." Then, smiling, she said, "But I can't keep calling you that. What's your name?"

"I'm Nabi, lady. You should tell your daughters to call me that, too. There is no great hurry to return to the square, and we will have time to eat before the show starts."

Nisaba thought but a moment before saying, "I'm only going to bring Rida; Nina's still very sad about Aga being gone, and that he didn't say farewell to us." This was a lie, of course. Ninegala was in a chronically somber and spiteful mood, and Nisaba was doubly welcoming an opportunity to have some time away from her. The matron was also hoping Sherida would be noticed by a suitable young man while she was watching the performance. To this point the only landowners that Nisaba might have consider suitable were old widowers, except for the two lifelong bachelors who favored other men.

She un-latched the gate and invited Nabi into her home, calling for one of her attendants to bring Nabi beer to drink while he waited in the anteroom.

All too willing to enjoy a diversion and time away from her sister, Sherida was very curious about why this palace guard had invited them, and even more curious about why her mother had accepted. Nevertheless, she made a great effort to adorn herself and even use a perfume she had bought recently.

Nabi was neither surprised nor offended when it was clear that Nisaba and Sherida would be attended by two armed retainers from the household.

He had become part of the palace guards after Erra-Imitti's death, so he didn't know the former queen and princess. Conversation between them touched around the edges of what was shared information, polite and superficial. Sherida was oblivious to the tentative reconnaissance comments between the middle-aged widow and the somewhat younger guard.

CHAPTER TWELVE

ROOTS AND FRUITS

The gods give some the gift of boldness, a trait that favors accomplishment, but it can also lead to envy in those more cautious; envy breeds vengefulness.

The caravan moved at a steady pace along the beaten track, now two days into their journey and approaching Larsa, still about a day and a half away from their present location. Early winter under a hazy sky, the sun shone pale and indistinct, and no rain had fallen for some days. The track had veered away from the river, skirting fields and irrigation channels to avoid damaging them. Every canal and ditch was the product of hundreds of men's labors, and keeping them in repair and flowing was a never ending process.

The sun slanted toward the low horizon in the west, with the promise of a chilly evening suggested by an increase in gusty breezes from the south.

Zambiya walked in front of the troop, as usual. He kept one hand on the handle of his sickle sword to keep it from swinging about and chafing his waist from the belt it hung from, over a light mid-thigh tunic. There was room on the track for three or more men or a couple of draft animals walking abreast, and Ansar was just behind and to the left of Zambiya. The clatter and squeaks made by the creature's hoofs plus the armaments of the guards and soldiers faded from everyone's consciousness, constant and with little variation. Talk was at a minimum as the day's labors had begun to wear on the leaders of the animals and the guards as well.

Ansar hastened his pace to come abreast of Zambiya, pointing and saying, "Lord, have you noticed the birds out there?"

"Yes, been watching'em a while now. What do you think is causing all the uproar?"

The track appeared to be headed directly toward the scene they were observing; many large birds launched themselves off the ground but settled back toward the earth a short time later. The trekkers were too far from the birds to see the cause.

"Do you think we need to be concerned about it, Lord? It doesn't seem like it's a threat to us, but I'd sure like to know why there're so many there." Ansar shifted the grip on his spear though he left his shield hanging over his back as he normally carried it when hiking.

"If it were one dead animal, they'd be in a much smaller area," Zambiya surmised. "They're covering quite an area. Nothing living's that big."

Cocking his head to one side, he aimed his left ear toward the area where the birds were congregated. He walked on a few more paces, then stopped abruptly and raised his hand from off his sword handle, signifying that the caravan should stop. He turned around and faced the troop and shouted, "Everyone be still! Listen!"

The sounds of the group diminished; by putting their hands behind their ears, he and Ansar were able to discern the insistent bleating of sheep in the distance. Then they could make out barking and howling as dogs added to the squawking of the birds and the cries of the sheep.

"What can it be, Ansar?" Now everyone was aware of the remote clamor, and puzzlement was the shared emotion.

Tikal's inspection steward came up to the two leaders and volunteered, "I used to live in an area like this one. There's a village up ahead, and it's the last one that's ours. I'll start back to Isin after our first meal tomorrow to give Tikal my report, so I'll go ahead and check with the head man, see what's going on. With your permission, Lord." The man bowed slightly toward him and Ansar.

Impressed by the man's initiative, Zambiya agreed with a nod and said, "Tell the head man we won't stay at his village so he's not concerned about us. We can make progress past the village before we set up camp. I'd like to be closer to *Buranun* before we start the cook fires anyway, so we won't have to carry water very far."

The steward shifted his bag further toward the middle of his back and trotted down the track in the direction of the clamor, loosely carrying his hiking staff parallel to the ground.

Zambiya signaled the troop to resume their steady progress, but quickened his own pace, curious to learn what was happening. Ansar followed close by.

The caravan covered the equivalent of several fields in distance and had just re-organized after being forced to ford a dry but steeply rutted seasonal tributary, ascending at an angle up the steep sandy slope. The steward came sprinting back toward the troop, minus his bag but carrying his staff. He started shouting as soon as he saw Zambiya and Ansar, who'd already gone past the stream bed.

"What's he saying, Ansar? It sounds like, 'They're all dead.' That can't be right; we're too far from the border for a raid this far from the *Idiglat*."

"I heard the same. Doesn't make sense."

Zambiya motioned to his troop to stand fast, then he and Ansar trotted toward the steward at a rapid pace, aware of the increase in the din emanating from the village that was masking the man's shouts. Upon seeing the two leaders of the caravan approaching him, the steward slowed his run to catch his breath, resuming the jogging pace until they were next to him.

"The whole village," he reported gasping, "is dead. The carrion birds are gorging, so I couldn't tell what killed the people." Beside himself, he lost his composure, his face contorted, reporting, "The first body I saw was just a boy, looked to be about ten." With that, he sunk to the ground on his knees, then resumed, trying to control his voice, saying, "There was no flesh on his face. The buzzards, or maybe they were vultures, I don't know, were gone further into the village. I tried to scare the crows away from him, but they kept coming back." He looked back in the direction of the village and waved his hand toward it as if to banish the memory.

"Did you see any sign of weapons?" Zambiya asked, putting his hand on the man's shoulder comfortingly. "Arrows?"

"No, Lord. I saw several more bodies, men and women, even children. All covered by birds. I couldn't tell for sure, but it looked like they'd tried to run." He dropped to one knee to take several deep breaths and wiped his eyes and nose, trying valiantly to not give in to outright crying, then added, "There're a few dogs fighting with the crows, some're dead."

"Thanks for scouting. Go with Ansar now." Turning to his second in command, he said, "Tell the company to come ahead, but keep watch front and rear. We'll try to find out what happened and deal with the bodies. The gods will expect us to bury the dead, and I don't intend to offend the gods."

While Ansar and the steward returned to the assembled caravan, Zambiya walked toward the village, scanning the view in front of him and to the sides, vigilant to any hint of threat. He scanned the track on both sides, noting the exceptionally dry look to the stunted brush. It seemed to him as though the seasonal rains had skipped over this area, withholding the water vitally needed for crops and livestock.

He was now close enough to see the body of the boy the steward had described. Any flesh not covered by clothing had been consumed by birds; the head and neck along with his hands, arms, feet and lower legs had been reduced to bones. Now only smaller scavengers vied for remaining morsels; even the crows had moved on. The youth's body was not on the track itself, but off to the right. The buildings of the village were still a distance removed from where Zambiya stood, trying to make sense of the scene.

Scanning the area in his immediate location, Zambiya saw that the boy had been holding a hoe, now separated from his skeletal hand, and there were several gouge marks in the ground, as if the child had struck at the earth several times before he fell.

Several squawks behind him and off to his right caught his attention before he moved on. Several yards away, mostly hidden by grayish brown spiked bushes, a group of four vultures with dark feathers except on their necks and downy heads contended loudly with a larger set of crows, launching into the air then plunging zealously toward the grisly repast with their downward-curving powerful beaks and strong grasping feet. Zambiya could tell from the spread of the fluttering that there was more than one victim being plucked to bone, and he left the track to investigate, his sword handle held in readiness.

He found four corpses, all males according to dress, together in death and faced in the same direction, only yards from a roughly assembled wooden sledge. By means of a sturdy plaited leather rope, it had been pulled away from a depression in the surrounding dry earth. Warily, Zambiya approached the concave hole; it was empty now, but the bottom and sides bore signs of scrabbling activity in addition to several shed snake skins and he stroked his chin in puzzlement. A strange, unpleasant smell like rotted fur grew stronger the closer he approached the depression.

He left the area of the sledge and passed the boy's body and continued on toward the village, confirming the report of the steward. Mostly near doorways of the mud brick buildings he encountered more bodies, not distinguishable as to age, although their home-spun drab clothing identified them as to gender.

Entering the village itself, he understood the constant sound of the sheep; they were in two separate wattle-and-daub pens made of interwoven sticks and reed stalks with clay daubing built up around the bottoms, hip height to a man. This stratagem had apparently protected them, but their feed troughs were bare and the beige hand-formed, unfired clay water basins were nearly empty. The creatures bleated incessantly, and huddled together as far from the track side of the pens as possible.

The sight of so many dead people made Zambiya concerned enough to draw his sickle sword from its case as he continuing into the village common area with its rustic well and communal oven. He scanned the roofs of the buildings; despite the absence of any sign that the people of the village had been killed by arrows, he was wary anyway, concerned for an invading foe.

He could hear the approach of his caravan, and was about to return to greet them when he saw a man starting to stand up on the roof of one of the homes, calling out to him.

"Be careful! They're probably not all gone," the man croaked loudly through lips that revealed several missing teeth. He stood up, steadying himself by holding the upper part of a ladder propped against the wall. Two children clung to his legs, neither more than three years of age. He wore only a worn out work skirt and was bare chested; the children were naked, their ribs and hip bones evident just under their skin, their abdomens protruding.

"What happened here?" asked Zambiya. "Are more people alive like you?"

Without warning, the man vomited over the edge of the roof, and knelt back down to compose himself before answering. He made no move to descend. The conversation was necessarily conducted at high volume due to the bird and sheep cacophony.

"I don't know, Lord. I carried my children up here as soon as I saw the vicious things enter the village. I yelled to warn everyone but they ran out of their homes just when the snakes got here..."

"Snakes?" Zambiya interrupted.

Quickly scanning the area around himself, he demanded of the villager, "How many? How could all these people be killed by snakes?" He first waved his hand in a broad circle, then pointed at various bodies, still covered by birds. "How could they die so fast? I've seen people who were bitten by snakes, and they don't die right away."

The man settled back down on his haunches, holding the ladder with one hand while hugging his children to him, and surveyed the scene below. He then declared vehemently, "I watched my people die from up here, Lord. Many snakes, many bites on every single one. But some ran toward the fields." He motioned with one arm in the direction in which the track continued and brightened slightly, hopefully. "They'll be back if they survived. I saw my oldest son running toward the river."

The caravan approached the village in a compressed group, Neti and Ansar in front, both carrying unsheathed swords. Zambiya turned away from the villager and ordered Ansar, "Have your men start killing birds." To Neti he said loudly, "Have our beasts kept in a tight bunch, but have a couple men give some of our food and water to those sheep. If we can reduce the noise, we'll be able to think and it will keep our animals calm."

He pulled Tikal's steward out of the crowded bunch and said to him, "Take one lead man and light torches from the houses. Start searching the houses; be careful! All this was apparently the work of snakes. Kill any you find, and try to find them all. There've got to be more people who didn't get bitten, and they'll need to live here." He considered the task, then the type of men in his crew, and said to the steward, "Tell the lead man, 'Take nothing!' If you have to, search him after, and remind him how thieves are dealt with." Zambiya pointed at his right hand with his left and made a chopping motion at the wrist.

Ansar returned to Zambiya as soon as he had assigned three of his guards to killing the vultures; the scavengers were willing to abandon the fray rather than fight, as they were satiated already. Nearly a dozen of them settled onto the upper roofs of the tallest houses, waiting, hunched over with eyes that bespoke of lifelong hunger and patience.

"I've got one guard who needs archery practice, Zambiya. I'm going to have him kill the vultures on the roofs and then retrieve the arrows." Normally a dour man, Ansar looked positively enthusiastic at the prospect of killing the scavengers which he had seen eating the bodies.

"As soon as we can, we'll gather the bodies into the first dry cistern we find and burn them then bury them all. We can't let them just rot or invite the birds to come back." Zambiya stopped and pointed out two of the men who had missed any other assignment. That pair had taken the initiative to use their whips, at which they were expert, and were methodically killing the crows crowded onto the bodies that the vultures had abandoned. Zambiya smiled with wry satisfaction as the noise continued to subside. He then said to Ansar, "Gather up the birds as well, for the burning of the bodies. There are other scavengers out there, on four legs, not wings."

Ansar sheathed his sword and raised his hands over his head in a long and satisfying stretch of his whole body, then motioned expansively to the village scene and said to Zambiya, his voice quavering, "This is the worst thing I've ever seen."

———— • ● • ————

"This is the best time to go to market, Tikal." Mid-morning in early winter, the permanent stalls bustled with customers, mostly veiled women and their daughters, accompanied by some male relative to maintain the decorum demanded by the culture. A contingent of temporary vendors from outside the walls were settled on faded gray-green woven palm frond mats, their individual wares spread out in front of them: duck eggs, new woven reed baskets, dyed woolen sashes, gleaned and gathered root vegetables, leather sandals, ropes made of plaited reed fibers. "Sometimes I'd go with Lith-el when she shopped, especially if she needed help carrying; that was before the boys were grown. We'd even have an early meal, save her the need to cook that night." Enlil-Bani sighed at the memory and the pain it evoked, irrevocable loss.

Tikal walked next to the king as they meandered around the temporary vendors' mats. There were four guards, of course, plus a steward carrying a leather bag with barley packets for barter, even some silver in a smaller bag. Enlil-Bani had insisted from the time of his first foray out of the palace that they refuse anything they didn't pay for. 'These are all poor people. They get paid or they don't eat.'

The small entourage walked around a temporary pen set up containing two nanny goats, udders full, with black faces and smelling like a damp woolen blanket. The woman who offered milk to potential customers sat cross-legged on her mat with a gourd ready to receive the fresh milk. She smelled as gamey as her goats, and her lack of teeth made her entreaties difficult to understand.

"Why are we here today, *Ensi*?" Tikal noted the effect Enlil-Bani's memory had on him, and wanted to lift his mood. Pointing, he noted brightly, "There's Mas, shaving someone's head."

"Yes, I see him. We had a good talk when he was there yesterday. He's as good at shaving as his father now." The king smiled and reached up, lifting a white woolen cap with its three, crimson and quilted, pointed decorations off his head and stroking his pate, still as smooth as an egg. Then he answered Tikal's question, saying, "I want to buy gifts for my grandchildren, young as they are. It must be some strain on Nani to care for two babies, even though Nintud moved in with them after Dagan's death." The loss of Dagan, his best friend for over twenty years, pained him deeply. Even though he could honestly get some comfort from the fact that his friend no longer suffered the recurrent bouts of misery from his ailment, he mourned his passing and took offerings to both the temples to ease Dagan's passage into the underworld.

"How did that happen, *Ensi*?" Tikal was only vaguely aware of personal issues that didn't affect the palace, but had expected the king to insist that Nintud move back into the quarters where she and Dagan had lived before.

"They're good friends even though Nintud is older; after Azuru died it helped to have her close by, and she's a great help. She cooks, as well as looking after the babies while Nani weaves."

The king and his Chief Counselor moved away from the guards and around a woman sitting on a mat with a small collection of unusually colored chickens, nearly white in front and rear, with mottled russet and black over their backs, with at least a dozen growing chicks held in a makeshift pen separated from the hens. The hens maintained a constant level of clucking, pecking at the bare mat. The woman looked up and waved her arm in a gesture of invitation to encourage the men to look at her poultry, but desisted as soon as she recognized the clothing of the royal pair. The guards, meanwhile, made a valiant effort to stay close so they could actually do some guarding.

"I should've asked earlier," Tikal noted, indicating the guards. "Where's Muda today? He almost never leaves your side on outside trips."

"He's gone over to Nani's; I gave him permission. He hasn't said so to me, at least not yet, but I think he hopes to court Nintud. She and Dagan were always very kind and accepting of Muda, even when he was a slave. Zid-tara let him take a kettle of antelope stew." The king stopped in front of a vendor who had small carved animals offered, made from light pine: several pigs, some goats, two donkeys attached to wheeled carts by leather thongs. The creatures were the size of a woman's hand and painted with juices to make them more life-like, all gray and made shiny with linseed oil.

Enlil-Bani motioned to the steward to join him and Tikal, which also gave the guards the opportunity to position themselves strategically. The king picked up the two donkeys with their carts, looking them over and feeling the edges for splinters. "How many packets, son?"

The boy who was attending the mat, perhaps six years old, was struck mute by being addressed by the king, and looked fearfully at the surrounding guards. He stammered, "Uh. Uh. Muh," and started crying, attempting to stand up. It was clear when he reached for a forked stick that he had one clubbed foot.

"Stay seated, son," said the king. At this point a bare breasted young woman wearing an old skirt made up of alternating yellow and brown strips of linen and carrying a baby on one hip approached the mat.

"You may have those, *Ensi*." She cast her eyes down but offered, "My sister's son's not used to royalty, he's scared."

Tikal interjected at this point, saying, "We'll pay the usual price, lady. How much?"

Afraid to try to gouge the royal pair, she replied, "Two packets each, Lord. Believe me, only that."

Tikal waved to bring the steward closer and said, "Pay her."

As this transfer of goods and packets was being concluded, the king said to Tikal, "Let's go visit Suba at his pottery stall and show him the toys."

Tikal waited until after the visit when he and the king were walking back toward the palace before he again gradually raised the issue that most concerned him.

"*Ensi*, tell me. When do you want to take the toys to Nani?"

"After the market closes for the day, but first I want to take them up to Ninisina's temple for blessing. Then I want to visit with Nani and Suba and say 'Shalamu' to Nintud. I'll bring Muda with me that time. That'll please him! I'd like to see how Nintud acts toward him, too."

"I hesitate to bring this up again, *Ensi*, and I do so only because Isin needs stability, especially in succession. My friends among the landowners continually ask me when you'll marry again. I don't know what to say. What I tell them is that you're still in mourning for your wife, and you're not interested in having a wife yet."

"Still not, Tikal," Enlil-Bani declared with a frown, just one wrinkle less than a glare, toward his Chief Counselor.

Tikal raised both his hands, palms forward toward the king as they continued walking, and bowed his head, saying, "If you could give me some hope that you'll be thinking about it, *Ensi*, I can put some of the speculation to rest. There are those who think we have a princess from another city in mind who's demanding a stiff bride price, so the rumors are swirling like a dust sprite on the track. Others think you're too sick to think of a woman's body with pleasure, so you'll die soon and leave us with no *Ensi*. I know those aren't true; you've quickly become a true leader of Isin. Nevertheless, I'd like to strangle the rumors at their source. Can you give me any help, *Ensi*?"

"I've given it some thought, Chief Counselor, despite my reluctance to marry so soon." Enlil-Bani stopped at the steps to the palace, before mounting them, turned to Tikal and said, "I know this is a surprise, but you've convinced me that we have to have a plan, so I've been thinking already. When I think I've thought it through, I'll ask for your help to arrange it." The king had already relented in his irritation at Tikal for raising the issue again, and smiled, saying, "My plan does depend on someone else, of course. I don't know of anyone who's married himself, no matter how satisfied he is with his own company." He became somber again and added, "No one can replace Lith-el. I miss her every day." Starting up the steps to the level of the palace, he grasped Tikal by both shoulders and said, "You serve Isin and me very well, and no doubt saved my life on that day when Erra-imitti died."

———————— • ● • ————————

Winter was drawing to a close and the Buranun River was watched closely for signs of the spring flood; shallow cisterns were dug deeper and new fired bricks were layered along the sides to keep water from dissipating into the ground. Tikal and his stewards worked with the administrator priests of the temples to organize crews of commoners to strengthen the free-standing outer wall that protected Isin's city walls, increasing its height as this year's flood was predicted both by the diviners of the heavens and those who read the innards of animals to be high. Improving irrigation canals and ditches only stopped during planting and harvest, so a routine process of inspection and response engaged the middle level supervisors of the owners of the fields: private landowners, the palace, and the temples. Without surplus grain for trade, Isin would suffer greatly from reduced prestige. This was a significant impetus for Zambiya's and Neti's caravan.

"Dear one, those two girls have me worried." Enmerkar removed his hand from his lover's thigh and pointed them out to En-me; the six students in that group sat on common gray flat cushions filled with barley husks, occupied with copying from a dry template onto their own wet clay tablets. Even seen from a distance across the courtyard, both girls seemed to be listless and prone to lose focus. Despite the cooler weather, the reddish clay nevertheless tended to dry out if left without activity for long, engendering frustrated sighs. Dressed alike as usual in long light blue belted tunics over white skirts, the girls frequently looked at one another but didn't speak. The four boys, sitting a little apart from the girls, ignored them completely.

The thirteen-year-old orphaned twins of General Ashgi, neither seemed to be making progress with their scribal studies of late. The report months ago that the General had died failed to affect them that Enmerkar could observe, but he attributed that to the commonly held rumor that the General had ignored them from the time of their birth.

"You're a healer, and a great one at that, my love. Do they seem well to you? Do you detect anything wrong with them?"

En-me and Enmerkar were seated in the shade of a large bare plum tree, sharing a pitcher of freshly salted barley beer that sat between them on a weathered palm wood table. An intricately decorated pottery bowl filled with dried chick peas, the bowl a gift from Suba, sat within easy reach. The sun dropped through moderately warm hazy air toward the western horizon.

Now that his professional opinion had been asked, En-me made more of an effort to observe the youngsters; they had interested him since he first encountered them. His first impression led him nowhere until one girl looked up from her tablet and in his general direction. Her sunken cheeks and dark-rimmed eyes made him start, and he turned to Enmerkar and asked, "Could you ask her to come over here?"

"What do you see?"

"They're from a wealthy family, but that girl looks like starving children I've seen. Don't they get fed here each day?"

"Of course," Enmerkar replied with a hint of irritation at the suggestion of neglect. "They eat the same food as the others... maybe more," he mused, trying to recall whether he had personally made note of their meals. "You know, since both Naram and Uttu are getting frail, the servants are doing light meals at midday and I don't watch them."

Enmerkar got up abruptly and limped toward the house without using his staff, disappearing into the building. He re-appeared a short time later with a portly kitchen slave in tow. The woman looked first at En-me, who stood, and then at Enmerkar, who sat back down.

"Was there something wrong with the beer or the peas, Lord?" She looked somewhat fearful of the answer, wiping her hands on the stained skirt covering her ample hips.

"No, don't be worried. We're concerned about the girls over there." En-me pointed vaguely in their direction; since there were only the two female student scribes, there was no mistaking who was being referenced.

Looking suspiciously at them, she asked, "What about them? Have they complained about me?" She braced for criticism, searching for some defense against an unspecified accusation.

"No, no. Nothing like that." En-me lowered his voice, trying to sound more engaging, and said, "Do they eat as much as the boys? Do they eat the same food?"

The slave looked back and forth between En-me and Enmerkar and visibly relaxed, her shoulders dropped and she scratched her head, her eyes darting from one side to the other, recalling this day's mealtime with the students.

"They're very quiet, Lord. They mostly talk only to each other. They eat what I give'em. Never ask for more but don't leave anything." She searched the faces of the two questioners for signs of disapproval.

"That's all. You can go back." Enmerkar dismissed the slave with a wave of his hand; she hastened to return to the kitchen.

Both En-me and Enmerkar looked in the direction of the girls without staring directly at them, then En-me said, "I'm going to follow up by asking Tikal to inquire about who is caring for them at home.

"Shouldn't be necessary to involve Tikal," Enmerkar declared. "I'll question the slave who brings them and collects them at the end of each day. He'll know what's happening at their home."

Neti, Zambiya, and Ansar huddled together near the cook fire, after the journeyers in their caravan were settled for the evening and sentries were posted and shifts settled. The sun had set and the stars were alone in the sky; not even a sliver of moon was visible.

"We lost time, I know, but we had to take care of the situation. Couldn't just leave them." Ansar passed a gourd half-full of beer to Neti, who had expressed the comment, then he stood up and stretched. "I think we did the right thing. My father'll decide whether to send people to re-settle that village."

Zambiya rested easily, squatting on his heels, and nodded in assent, saying, "That's right. Only ten adults survived the snakes, plus those two little children. They'll barely be able to feed themselves with what remains, and there aren't enough of them to plant crops. We used much of the furniture to burn the bodies, and lots of oil as well. They can herd the sheep to Isin and that'll give them enough to keep them through the winter. Maybe some will want to return here if Tikal decides to keep the village going."

"At least he'll have the advantage of having his steward to give a full report, not full of personal desires one way or another."

Ansar turned away from the other two leaders, holding his night wrap around his chest and said, "I'm going to check on my sentries and make sure the animals are secure, then I'm going to settle onto my blanket and get some sleep. We're all well past tired; it was horrible to have to move bodies of people who were alive only a while ago." He hesitated before adding with quavering voice, "Two of the women were pregnant, and so many children." He covered his mouth to quell a sob, then declared throatily, "Horrible."

• ● •

Nani and Nintud sat on one of the two benches in the courtyard of their home enjoying the spring-like air and the night sky. Many days after Enlil-Bani's visit to present the babies' gifts, they had been carefully stored until the infants were older. The babies, Gibil and Indur, were sleeping, while Suba was in the entryway working on a design he hoped to create in a pottery vase; he was drawing it on a scrap of linen with a charred end of a split palm frond faggot. A single oil torch was his light source.

"Nani," Nintud said to her in a low voice, though she was looking away, "I'm having thoughts and feelings that confuse me, and truly worry me. I think one of the mischievous gods is toying with me, and I don't know what to do. Can I tell you and not have you laugh, or think I'm a bad person?"

"My dear friend, I would never think you were bad. Never! You can tell me anything, Nintud." Nani reached over and placed her hand on Nintud's arm, leaving it there in a sign of reassurance.

Nintud sighed, still looking away, but then turned back and placed her hand over that of her young friend. "I almost don't know what to say. I could be wrong in what I think is happening, but I know what I feel, even when I'm not sure what the feelings mean." She sighed again, then allowed her words to spill out all at once, again looking from Nani.

"I've never thought about another man than Dagan, really, and we were married when I was barely fifteen summers old, so I've spent most of my life with him, bore him our only child, shared his life and his illnesses and Nanse's death and in all that time never even thought about a time like now, when Dagan's dead and I'm looking to spending the rest of my life alone." She paused to take a breath, but launched into another set of thoughts, her voice lower yet.

"Nani, how can I have yearnings to be with Muda, a Gutian? I've known him a long time now and never thought of him as anything more than Dagan's co-worker. First he was Enlil-Bani's slave, and then his guard, and now he comes here to visit with you and the babies and sometimes Suba and when he's here…." At this point Nintud started to weep, but continued while daubing at her eyes, "and after he's gone back to the palace, when I'm trying to go to sleep I think about him, and not just as Dagan's friend, but as a man." At this point Nintud gave in to her deep need to cry, sobbing into Nani's bare shoulder.

At first Nani was unable to do anything but join her friend in crying, patting her arm, but quickly composed herself. Holding Nintud close, she told her softly, "What do you think is wrong with how you feel, dear Lady? Dagan had been ill over and over for a couple years now, and you're not much older than Muda, I think. It's obvious to me that he has feelings for you, too. He's very discrete, but I see him look at you with admiration. Is it that he's a Gutian? What's that matter?"

Nintud looked at Nani and started to speak, then blushed and looked toward the pantry door to the home. She practically whispered, "Last night I dreamed I was visited by Muda in my bed and I woke having Inana's pleasures. Twice! That can't be right, Nani. What would Dagan think of me? What must you think of me, and…oh! You mustn't ever tell Suba, or anyone." Her voice rose urgently. "Promise me!"

"Of course, dear Lady. I do promise." The two sat together in silence for a while, then Nani added firmly, "We can't help what happens in our dreams, you know. The gods do that."

———————————— • ● • ————————————

Tikal and En-me, accompanied by Nabi and four palace guards, stood in the front courtyard of General Ashgi's sister's home. They waited to be announced to her by the slave who had greeted them. Late midmorning on a quickly warming day, the shadows were stark in profile with clean lines separating light from dark on the wall of the home; an overhanging roof shaded the front door. The palace officials stood in the shade of the roof; the guards waited in the sun.

"My lady will see you now." The sound of the voice came from inside the home through the doorway.

A large man with the soft physique of a eunuch, the slave led Tikal and En-me inside through a large windowless waiting room and then to an interior sitting room with narrow, ceiling-high, east-facing window openings. With no lighted torches, the light in the room was dim. The doorways revealed that the walls were four bricks thick, more like a border fortress than a home. Motes floated in the light entering the windows. An open narrow doorway looked out at an angle onto an exterior courtyard; mature, dark green bramble bushes with formidable thorns lined the ground in front of the courtyard walls, which sported corroded bronze spikes embedded all along the top, angled outward.

"What do you want of me, Tikal?"

The voice, weak and tremulous, came from a chair placed between the windows. A very thin woman with sunken eyes and cheeks sat holding a bronze cup with two handles. A dark brown woolen shawl covered her shoulders and a throw was tucked around her legs.

"Do I know you, Lady?" he questioned.

After a brief fit of coughing, the woman responded, "I knew your mother quite well." The crone paused to clear her throat, a rasping sound. "We entered palace society at the same time, as young women." She pointed at Tikal with one hand, which she raised with effort. "I knew when you were born, and visited her on that occasion." Pausing again, she declared, "I know who you are. What do you want of me?" She suffered through another coughing spell, waving her hand at him to keep him from answering. The eunuch offered to pour fresh water into the cup she held on her lap but she declined it with a petulant wave.

"We are here about your nieces, Lady. They don't seem to have the energy common to young people and their work at the *edubba* is suffering. We're concerned about them. This man with me," gesturing toward En-me, "is healer to our *Ensi*."

En-me stepped forward and inquired, "Do you have an *a-zu* or *ashipu*, Lady?"

"Dead. Like my brother, dead. Namtaru claimed them both." Another fit of coughing ensued, splashing water from her cup onto her lap. She flicked the beaded drops onto the floor and ignored the wetness that was soaking into the pale yellow linen throw. "I don't know why I've been spared. I can't even care for myself." She leaned forward, trying to take a deep breath, but fell back into her chair. Then, without warning she straightened and shouted weakly toward the door to the courtyard, "Hush up out there! Stop it!" She looked back toward En-me and said, "The girls, they keep to themselves. I don't bother them and they don't bother me." En-me approached her slowly, asking, "Lady, could I examine your hands and listen to your breathing? Your cough sounds serious."

"Go ahead, but I hope to die soon. Been ready for years."

En-me put his ear near the woman's lips and listened to the dry rattles in her throat; at the same time he lightly pinched together the skin on the back of her hand. He frowned as he observed the skin pucker then ever so slowly recede back over her bones.

The *a-zu* knelt in front of General Ashgi's sister and stated simply, "Lady, you're not drinking enough. You don't take care of yourself or your nieces either. You may be willing to die, but those girls aren't."

"All I've ever asked of them is quiet," she protested. "Children are so noisy, and I can't stand noise. Everyone I knew is dead," she added.

"Do you have other servants to help you?"

"A woman serves me, a slave given to me by my brother years ago. No help anymore — older than I am. Can't see well so she can't cook like she used to. The wretch is supposed to feed the girls, too." She suddenly looked up at the eunuch and demanded, "Where's the woman?"

The slave had been standing nearby listening, but finally he stood between Tikal and, with his back to the old woman, lowered his voice and confided, "My lady has trouble remembering, Lord. Her slave died during the last assault of *mutanu*. I do everything I can but there's no one left." He made a downward motion with his hands, as if he was acknowledging defeat and continued, saying with a sigh, "The servant who used to escort them to and from the *edubba* left with the General's youngest son so sometimes they go on their own. I go if my lady is sleeping. I feed the girls, but cooking's not my job and I don't know how to do it. The General put me in charge of the household and the other slaves when there were other slaves. Both his sons are at remote border posts, not here in Isin. The oldest arranged with the temple to provide for us." He motioned toward the courtyard doorway and said, "I'll care for my lady 'til she dies, Lord, but couldn't the girls live somewhere else? She hears things that aren't real, and yells at the girls to be quiet; she's been yelling at them since they were babies. They shouldn't have to stay here."

Tikal turned to En-me, his brow furrowed and his eyes looking intense. "They're not a team of onagers pulling a sledge, but everyone just says, 'The girls.'" He held his palms out toward En-me and said, "Do you know their names?"

"I had to ask Enmerkar that same question. Yes, they're named Ninlil and Ninmul, but I couldn't tell you which is which. I've never seen them apart." He looked chagrined at the admission, then turned to the slave and asked, "How do you know who's who?"

"I can tell, but the General had them both marked as babies," he said. "Ninmul has a crescent mark on the back of her left hand and Ninlil has the same on the right." He held out his arm and showed his slave tattoo. "Like a slave mark."

En-me shuddered to think of the infants being marked and didn't wait to hear more, saying to the crone, "Lady, we'll see to it that the girls don't bother you any longer. They're going to move to the *edubba* to work on their studies." He turned and walked back to Tikal, saying quietly, "I've spoken to Enmerkar about this and he's agreed it'll be better for them."

Her memory failed her once more, and the old woman declared, "I'll let the General know when I see him." She took a small sip of water, but wrinkled her nose and spat it out, demanding of the eunuch, "Get me broth, hot broth. This tastes foul!" She pushed the cup away from her onto the floor, where the water spread onto the finely woven rug and immediately soaked in to the clay floor below.

"Of course, Lady." The eunuch picked up the cup but didn't leave. He turned to Tikal and said quietly, "Lord, when can the girls be moved? Soon?" he implored.

Looking toward En-me for confirmation, Tikal said, "They won't be coming back." The *a-zu* nodded in agreement, and Tikal continued, "Take care of this lady as best you can. I'll be responsible to send word to General Ashgi's sons, so they know where their sisters are." He thought a moment, one hand raised up and his eyes closed, then speaking to the slave added, "I'll send some stewards to collect their things. Have them ready mid-afternoon."

"Of course, Lord." The eunuch looked from Tikal and then back to En-me and asked hoarsely, "Could you tell them I'll miss them? I will!"

As the two men re-joined the guards at the front of the home, they could hear the old woman shouting, "Stop that right now!" After a slight pause, "Now! Now!"

"You know they're spies for Nur-Adad." Neti stated his declaration with a firmness that was out of keeping with his ordinary mild manner, even though expressed in a quiet voice. Zambiya and Ansar nodded in agreement.

The three men stood along the riverbank near the docks that served Larsa at mid-afternoon, waiting to complete the arrangements necessary to engage the services of large barges and crews. The decision to travel from Isin to Larsa on foot had been made with the knowledge that the King of Larsa would likely want to send his own set of animals and keepers to transport the lapis, carnelian, flints, and any additional goods. All six of Larsa's animals were onagers, and the keepers were responsible for two each. Brought for trade, both Larsa and Isin were sending troves of finely decorated bronze implements, bags of emmer wheat, linens and finished jewelry. While the primary goal was to return with large quantities of raw lapis lazuli for their cities' craftsmen to transform into beads and cabochons, traders were always looking for novel imports.

The men stood away from the crowd of animals and lead men, guards and soldiers, surveying the collection and calculating.

Finally, Zambiya proposed, "With the men and creatures, plus the two carts we bought here, I think three barges will be sufficient. Thoughts?" He looked at his companions, waiting for their responses.

"Should be enough," ventured Ansar. "I'll assign my guards accordingly if you agree, Neti."

Neti made a show of looking from the area at the docks where the barges were gathered and back at the enlarged caravan, then slowly nodded in assent. "Where should we put the Larsans, do you think?"

Although the question had been asked of both, Zambiya answered at once with finality. "On the middle barge, with three of our soldiers."

Ansar smiled in agreement, and said, "I know just which ones." He then turned to Neti and said, "I agree with you. The Larsans are spies as well as traders and animal drivers. We need to tell all our people to keep their mouths as tight as a snake's butt."

• ● •

"There's no real place for them here, and we'll need space for a female slave to care for them as well." Talking with the mistress of the house, Enmerkar felt exasperated; even though he had proposed bringing General Ashgi's twin daughters to live at the *edubba*, the practicalities were overwhelming him. "What should we do, Uttu? This is more your home than mine, and Naram's never said what he thinks."

Uttu felt frail and dispirited, but was nevertheless alert and as generous of spirit as ever. Leaning in the doorway to the rear courtyard in the early morning, she searched to observe Ninlil and Ninmul at their study stations and saw them bent over their tablets. They were concentrating in the shade of a pear tree that was just beginning to show swollen light green leaf bundles, in a group with four older students.

"Naram will do anything to encourage students; you know that. And although you'll never bring it up, you know we aren't going to live much longer. His struggle to breathe makes me want to cry."

Enmerkar put his arm around Uttu's shoulders and hugged her; even under her woolen shawl, he could feel the lack of flesh over her bones.

"I thank the great gods for you two. I've been blessed by your love and his great teaching. I wish he'd been able to complete his catalog of all the gods of heaven." He hesitated and looked out at the twins before going on saying, "They can have my room until we have a better solution; I can do quite well sleeping on that large bench in the study."

"We have a better solution already, dear." The crone sniffed back her wave of grief, and made a dismissive motion with her hand toward the floor before continuing. "Our daughter's room's been empty since she died." She impatiently wiped away a tear starting to run down her cheek before adding, "I always told you it was for storage, but I couldn't bear to go into it so it's been there all these years. It's actually quite large, and when we've found a slave to attend them they can all stay in the same room."

"Are you sure, mother? Won't it make you sad?" He called her mother to lighten her mood, having recognized from the time he'd been adopted by her and her husband that she craved hearing the term.

A look of defiance came over Uttu and she stated firmly, "This will show the gods who took my children that they've not won anything!" She stood away from the wall that had provided her with support and left, calling out to her principal household slave.

As if they had been called, both of the twins started and ceased their labors, looking first around the courtyard then at each other. Slowly they settled back to copying the symbols, sub-vocalizing the sounds.

CHAPTER THIRTEEN

A BOUNTY OF STONES

The mind rebels at things too novel and strange to absorb, until they become familiar; infants spit out their first pap from a mother's finger but later learn to crave it.

Zambiya surveyed the port of Dilmun with amazement. His frame of reference was the docks along the cities served by Buranun; some ships there had sails, but mostly there were barges. Here, dozens of ships with tall masts and an even larger number of wide barges stood side by side along the long wharves built to serve the trade business on which the island thrived. Many small coracles, round boats with sides as deep as a man's waist, plied the calm waters of the port, propelled by men using long poles and paddles. Several of the masts sported narrow, long flags with designs that flapped about in the steady breeze.

"Look at that!" Neti pointed with breathless amazement at a group of men struggling to right a wheeled cart that had toppled and was lying on its side; piled too high with sacks of grain, one wheel had sunk into a deep muddy rut and spilled its load. The donkey that had been pulling the conveyance was lying on its side, braying and kicking, held fast in its harness. The cacophony of shouts and cries from the men added to the furor.

Neti's astonishment was not about the spectacle, but the men themselves. All had deep black skin, shining with sweat; their hair was kinky and their skirts were brightly colored in patterns of deep orange,

172

maroon, and blue. Their foreheads sported bands of cloth that encircled their heads and trailed down their backs.

A swarthy man dressed in a flowing sandy-yellow robe with a turban-like olive colored headdress rushed up to the workers and, with a light leather switch, organized and marshalled the dark-skinned men, and the noise diminished except for the donkey, which continued to protest. The man in the robe directed the others in completely emptying the cart and then righting it. Once the donkey was on its feet, its protestations stopped. One of the black men, seemingly the driver, bent over and inspected the creature's legs carefully, feeling up and down, all the while speaking to the animal in a calming tone in an incomprehensible language.

"Where could they be from?" asked Neti, staring.

"Look away, Lord," cautioned the captain of their barge, taking up a stance between Neti and the group of laborers. The captain had a perpetual scowl on his face, and spoke to everyone in a gruff tone. "They're from the main land off the coast of this island, not native to here, and they're quick to take offense. Lots of 'em'r here, and we don't want trouble."

"Thanks, Captain," said Zambiya. "Are we expecting to do any trading here ourselves? The Larsans may have orders to convert some of their wares for more exotic goods from here to take to *Meluhha*."

"Far as I know, I'm the only one with plans to trade here. Need fresh water and some food. While I do that, there's a small market on the outskirts of this commercial area with stranger wares than you're used to in Isin." The captain started to walk off, but came back and warned, "Go in a group, stay in a group, not less than five of you. Don't let any of you be threatening. And they're used to bargaining. Most everyone speaks our language enough to make a trade for what they sell, especially the women and boys who're selling sex." The captain looked out over the boats and barges, then added in a quieter tone, "Don't do that; one of my sailors never came back from that area a couple trips ago."

Neti and Ansar had been listening to the conversation, both wondering who else might join them for a trip to the market. Rangu, as usual, stood slightly away from the group, but pointed to himself and announced, "I'd like to go. Might see some kinsmen."

Then Neti, who was still fascinated by the dark-skinned men, asked, "Captain, uh, mmm, are there women here like those men?"

The captain turned away to look at the area where the cart had been moved to and was being loaded again, then looked back at Neti and replied, "Oh yes. And I'll tell you something about them. The reason their men are so jealous and guard them so carefully is that their women are different from our women." He stepped closer to Neti and the others and said in a conspiratorial tone, "Their sex parts are sideways; the wider they spread their legs, the tighter it gets. But don't try to find out, youngster. They'd cut your throat." The captain turned away, chuckling to himself.

———————●—●————————

"I don't know what's confusing, dear." Tikal's wife Kusu, a pretty and exceptionally slender woman for a native Isin, ran her hand over her husband's shoulder and down his arm as they sat together in their suite adjacent to the throne room. "He's much like you, probably why the gods replaced that rutting pig, Erra-imitti, with him. I never thought much of the way the gods treated us until they did that."

"What do you mean, like me? We're not similar in any way I can think of."

"You're concerned with everyone's benefit, and he seems to be the same. But what I was thinking is that he's loyal to his wife, just like you." She adjusted her position on the padded bench on which they sat so that she faced him more directly, then said, "You've never strayed, looking for the easy woman, not even slaves, and I know you could've." She moved her hand down his arm to his fingers, then over to his thigh; she pulled his skirt up a little with her fingers, then bunched it into her palm and kept pulling up more until Tikal's knee was bare, then reached under his skirt with her other hand, gently stroking his inner thigh and getting closer to his privates. "I'd have known," she declared quietly as Tikal reached for her.

———————●—●————————

Enlil-Bani stood up to welcome Ninegala and her mother as they entered the informal dining area of the palace. The invitation to share the evening meal with the king had been transmitted to them the preceding day by Nabi; it was now common knowledge among the guards that Nabi and Nisaba were spending time together in a tentative kind of courtship.

The disparity in their stations caused some quiet speculation, but nothing that would be mentioned to Nabi himself.

The room was comfortably arranged with dark red cushioning on six short benches around the ornately carved light oak table, inlaid with ebony and ivory strips in a geometric pattern. There were enough torches lit to illuminate the room, deep in the interior of the palace and separated from the sleeping area by a narrow hallway. While guards stood vigil in the hall, they had been instructed to remain away from the room. Muda stood outside the door to the room to insure privacy.

"Shalamu, Nisaba. Shalamu, Ninegala. I hope the gods are keeping you well."

The king gestured toward the table and benches in invitation without waiting for a response to his formal greeting and inquiry, then he added, "Why don't you sit together? We can have dinner before we get to my reason for asking you to visit with me."

Hearing sounds in the hall, Muda hurried through the portal to see what was occurring, but returned immediately to announce, speaking clearly but slowly, "Sud and the slaves are bringing food, *Ensi*." The Gutian allowed himself an inner congratulations for having spoken properly, then guided the attendants as they laid out the food and drinks while standing between them and the king.

"Sud," said the king drawing her attention. "I'll not be needing you for this meal, and the kitchen staff can clear this away when we are done. You're done for the evening. Tell Zid-tara I said so." Sud bowed to the king, but waited until the other attendants were finished before withdrawing with them. After respectfully passing the king's message to Zid-tara, she returned to her area of the slave quarters, giving silent thanks to the king and the gods.

One elderly slave remained in the dining room to serve the king and his guests; the meal the king had ordered featured roasted wild duck with an onion, garlic and minced beet sauce, spiced with cumin. Three kinds of cheese accompanied the barley cakes, with two varieties of those, one fried and the other baked. Beer flavored with garlic and mint was served in addition to ordinary beer. As a special treat, a honeyed pomegranate wine started the repast.

Nisaba maintained a superficial conversation with the king throughout the meal, sparing Ninegala from having to participate to any degree. For her part, Ninegala ate slowly, drank but little, and spent much time in silent contemplation of her food. Her ordeal with the Chaldean continued to wring energy from her body and her affect, and she was only minimally responsive, even to direct questions.

"Are you sure you've had all you want?" asked the king of his guests.

"Yes, *Ensi*, and thank you," said Nisaba.

Ninegala was listlessly pushing some remnants of her main course around in her bowl with a doubled barley cake until her mother gave her a forceful nudge on her arm. For the first time since they had entered, she looked at the king and said, "I have, *Ensi*. All I want."

"Leave the drinks," the king directed the slave, who acknowledged the order with a bow and commenced to clear the plates and serving dishes, using two large reed baskets. He filled one basket, took it into the hall and set it on the floor, then returned to the dining room and finished clearing. No one spoke until he had left.

"I hear that you've been returned to Isin for some time now, so I wanted to find out how things are going with finding a husband for Sherida."

Nisaba spent much of her waking life with this subject on her mind, so she was very willing to discuss it, really with anyone she thought might help.

"That girl is going to turn my hair gray before my time, *Ensi*. She has prospects, but I hear nothing but complaints." She mimicked, "'He's too old. He's too fat. He smells of rotting fish. He's not rich enough. I'm his daughter's age.' I'm exhausted coming up with new possible suitors."

"I can sympathize with your efforts, but I have no prospects to suggest to you for Sherida." Now was the crux of the matter for Enlil-Bani, and he fairly squirmed at the need to broach it, but he had promised Tikal that he would do so, since it was his solution to the need to have a queen on the throne of Isin. "I'd like to talk with you and Ninegala about marriage."

Both women inhaled sharply, and simultaneously put their arms over their respective bosoms. Mother and daughter looked at each other with deep frowns, while Ninegala's mouth stood open, but was silent at first. Then with a deep frown Ninegala asked the king, "You want to marry my mother? Why, in the name of all the great gods? You hardly know her!" The girl was now displaying a level of spirit and animation that even surprised her mother.

The king stood and motioned downward with both hands, palms forward to the women, and carefully explained, "You mistake my intent. I have nothing but respect for your mother, but I've no wish to marry her. I doubt that she would accept me as a husband, and that's not what I want."

Although this declaration had been made to both women, he faced directly to Ninegala and continued. "Isin needs a Queen. Tikal insists that our people actively think the gods are displeased with me because I've not married, and even suspect that's why Namtaru sent the great sickness that took so many. I don't think it's true, because I visit the goddesses every evening, and I've tried to listen for any dissent from them." He resumed his seat, and continued in what he hoped was a reasonable and convincing tone, speaking directly to Ninegala. "I want to marry you." Ignoring the shocked expression on the young girl's face, he crossed his arms over his lap and leaned forward toward her after glancing at her mother. He then solemnly declared, "But I'll not take you to my bed, Ninegala, ever." He waited for them to absorb this, then said to Ninegala, "I know you were grievously harmed by the Chaldean, and I'm truly, personally sorry for your pain."

Nisaba started to speak, but the king held up a hand to halt her, saying, "I know you both must have serious doubts, and maybe questions as well. Please let me explain my thoughts." He looked up toward the ceiling of the room, catching a memory and sorting out what he wanted to say. "My wife was the one love of my life, and I've no interest in replacing her. So if you agree to marry me, it will be a ceremonial arrangement. Completely! We'd attend functions together, but you would have your own room and your own attendants. If you'd like, we could have our meals together." The king had rehearsed how he hoped to convince Ninegala, and pressed another incentive. "Your mother and sister could visit with you whenever you'd like and you could go out to visit them." He waited again for the arrangement he was suggesting to become clear to them. "Finally, and this is just as important to you as it is to me: if it should ever come to pass that you find someone who you'd like to marry in the traditional way, I'll divorce you." Nisaba started to speak again, but a wave from Enlil-Bani stopped her. "I will say that you're barren, since we had no children." He turned toward Ninegala's mother and sat back on his bench, saying, "Now, lady, do you have a question? More than one? I would, if I were in your place."

Ninegala stood up and defiantly put her hand over Nisaba's mouth, saying, "No, she doesn't! I'm the one you proposed to. The decision's mine." Taking her hand away from her mother's face, she instead grasped her shoulders, bringing her face very close to Nisaba's and said to her, "Mother, the gods must have been listening to my prayers." With vehemence she asserted, "I hate our house! I've hated it since that night. I never wanted to return from the farm, but Sherida needs to find a husband, so I kept silent even though my stomach was churning." She turned to the king with a curiosity that had been absent from her life for months, as if she had given herself permission to put the memory in the distant past. All at once she began paying attention to the details of her present experience, no longer lost in the horror of the rape. She noticed his eyes first, then a serious expression on his mouth that changed to a wry smile, then the history of work and injuries revealed by his knotted knuckles and misshaped fingers.

"*Ensi*, Lord, I thank you for this generous offer, and I accept with gratitude." Turning in a circle she took in the details of the room and casually said to her mother, "I don't remember this room. I was born in this palace, but I don't remember this room."

Clearly not recovered from the king's proposition, plus her daughter's newfound assertiveness after months of lethargy, and then Ninegala's acceptance without even consulting her, she focused on something known to her and said, "I think we used it for storage." The former Queen of Isin started to rise and address the king, but felt drained of energy by this momentous shift in circumstances and slumped back onto the bench. She finally recovered enough to say to the king, with returning enthusiasm, "There's much to do for a royal wedding!"

The king surveyed the two women, thinking quickly about all that had been said, then called for Muda, who entered immediately from his post in the hallway.

"Yes, *Ensi*, what would you like?"

"Muda, send a guard to find Zid-tara and have him come see me." Smiling at the young woman, the king said, **"**Ninegala will be staying here tonight. She'll need an attendant for the next few days, so there won't be any rumors about her virtue. The room she and her sister shared when they lived in the palace before is empty, so she can stay there tonight, with the attendant." Muda left to do the King's bidding.

———————— • ● • ————————

Despite the rising heat of the humid day, En-me strode toward the *edubba* with determination, ignoring the nagging twinges in his shins from his unaccustomed pace. He turned into the last lane in this neighborhood of middle class dwellings, barely noting the spinning dirt serpent sucking up dust as it rose into the air just in front of Enmerkar's home. Spurning custom, he reached through the wooden grate at the top of the gate and lifted the latch without calling out for an attendant and walked directly to the door, shouting, "Shalamu! It's En-me. Please admit me."

He waited impatiently until the door was opened by the still-surviving old hunchbacked slave, who craned his neck up to look at the *a-zu*, who asked him, "What can you want in such a hurry, Lord? Shall I get Master Enmerkar for you?" Then, added with barely masked irritation, "The gate's open." The decrepit servant brushed past En-me, shuffling with a show of urgency to close and latch it.

"I'm sorry, truly. I forgot to close it. I'll go find your young master if he's in the courtyard." Decorum was lost on En-me and he hurried to the courtyard, where he found Enmerkar seated in his usual supervisory chair in the dappled shade of a large old pomegranate tree whose leaves were only half emerged. On his way through the house, En-me had picked up a light leather-seated stool, which he carried to where his lover was instructing an older student.

"These marks, as usual, are too shallow; tell him that they won't dry distinctly. Tell the others, too, and show them how you do it. You've always made the number symbols as plain as the balls on a ram and they need to do the same. Make them practice until you're satisfied that you couldn't do it better." Enmerkar, who was now the acknowledged head of the scribal school, dismissed the youth with a wave and a smile, which served double duty to encourage the student and greet En-me. The latter couldn't help but notice that regardless of the smile, twin depressions flanked the bridge of Enmerkar's nose and his brow was furrowed like a plowed field.

"Shalamu, my dear one. How did you know to come so early this morning? I'm surprised he lasted the night."

En-me was only a little taken aback with the news, assuming the report was about Naram, the owner of the *edubba*.

"I didn't know, sweet man. I came about something else. But can I help him? Why wasn't I called last night? You know I'd have come."

"He forbade it, said he'd curse us all from the nether world if we did anything to delay his death. Even ordered the same to Uttu, who's at his bedside now even though she's barely able to sit upright her breathing's so bad. Won't permit his slaves or servants to feed him, nothing, not even water."

"I'll be back shortly, dear. I've got news that may help you with those twins, but let's see if I can make Naram more comfortable until he passes over." He returned to the home, searching in his combination shoulder bag and medicine kit as he made his way to the old man's bedroom. He had to let his eyes adjust once he'd entered, as the transition from bright daylight to a nearly windowless building required time, and the change in temperature caused him to clear his throat and swallow phlegm. There were some few torches to help him see. He quickly found the container he wanted, a light black hollow end of a gazelle's horn with a wooden stopper attached to it with a leather thong. He had it in his hand as he placed his bag on the floor outside Naram's room and entered.

"Shalamu, Naram. May I approach?"

The nearly skeletal man on the bed was clearly fading, his energy clearly exhausted, and his eyes in the darkened room were without luster; he invited the *a-zu* with labored breathing, saying, "You may, En-me.... but you may not give me.... anything to keep me.... here. No treatment.... I mean it. Agree?"

"I absolutely agree, friend. I hope to leave this world the same way if the gods let me live so long. I've only brought you a salve for your lips. If you don't drink, your lips chap and get raw. This will help with that, if you'll let me."

Managing a grimace to serve as a smile, Naram said, "I thank you. I'm so dry my tongue.... bangs against my teeth and lips. Can you leave some ....with Uttu?" He seemed unaware that one corner of his mouth was split open but failed to bleed.

"Of course." En-me un-stoppered the horn container and gently applied the creamy preparation to the old man's lips. "Uttu, I'll leave some in the kitchen."

En-me looked over toward Naram's wife to be sure she understood, but slowly exhaled when he realized the crone was slumped backward in her chair, her head at an extreme angle and her sightless eyes open, her mouth agape.

"Naram, I'll tell her later. I don't want to waken her."

"Good. Thanks, En...." He took a last few shallow breaths, then they stopped. En-me waited to hear another inhalation, but none came.

"The gods so chose," En-me whispered to himself as he left the room to return to the courtyard.

Enmerkar listened to En-me's description of the death of Uttu and Naram with profound grief. At first, briefly, he held himself taut with resolve, inwardly reminding his consciousness that this was expected and even welcomed. Sitting upright, he called his three student subordinates to join him and shared the news with them, and directed that the day's lessons continue, though he would be inside until the end of the day. He did declare before they left, "Naram's always been the *ummia* of this *edubba*. Now I am." Once the three youngsters had returned to their stations, he accepted En-me's arm to help him rise and enter his home.

"Please let me help you with the arrangements for your adoptive parents. I really liked them both." En-me led Enmerkar to the pantry and dining area where the slaves were congregated, already expecting to hear of their masters' deaths.

Enmerkar's statement was direct. "Naram and his wife are both dead. Please prepare their bodies for burial with the respect they deserve. They'll be buried in the yard with their dead son and daughter, of course. They arranged long ago that the *edubba* and all they owned are now mine, including you slaves." He waited briefly, then added, "Whenever such an event happens, slaves become fearful that they'll be sold. That won't happen. This is your home, and you've treated it and me with respect. We'll go on with our lives together without more change than is necessary." He waited again, searching the faces of the staff, who all seemed far more sad than fearful. "Let us carry on together. The gods so chose."

En-me couldn't help but notice that Enmerkar leaned more heavily on him as they made their way to the new *ummia's* bedroom. Propping him up on the earth tone bolsters he favored on his bed, he held both of Enmerkar's hands and told him, "You've been the best substitute for their dead son that they could have wanted, my love. I hope you've no regrets."

"Only that they became so desperately infirm as they aged. But I don't favor dying young, either." He withdrew his hands from En-me's and covered his eyes with the crook of his arm over them. Without enthusiasm he inquired, "I remember now. You wanted to give me some news when you first arrived. What was it?"

"Yes, I did have something to tell you. I think there's a good prospect for buying a slave to serve and monitor the twins."

"I hope so. None of the slaves here would be suitable, only three are females; they're pretty old and they all have their own tasks. Tell me."

"A commoner who's seen over thirty summers; never been a slave. Was married a long time, no children, was a regular communicant at Ninisina's temple hoping to be cured of being barren, then went into debt without her husband's permission trying to buy favor from the goddess. The husband divorced her for barrenness, but mostly for disobedience, and she's going to be sold at auction tomorrow to discharge her obligations. The husband refused to pay them. Wears a veil, of course, but anyway she looked kind of frumpy when I saw her at the market, not a temptress. I think she won't attract many offers, and she'll probably be happy to have two girls to care for."

After letting out a sigh that bespoke of deep care and sorrow, Enmerkar entreated his lover, "Could you handle that for me? I really can't do that right now."

En-me leaned over and kissed Enmerkar lightly on the lips and said, "Of course, dear one. Right now I'll make sure the staff are caring for Uttu and Naram properly, and the graves are being dug. I'll be sending a priest and a priestess to do the blessings, so I'll tell the staff to expect them."

— ● —

Nisaba and Tikal's wife, Kusu, had struck up a re-acquaintance with the advent of a royal wedding. When Erra-imitti was the king, the two matrons had an uneasy relationship, with the disparity in their status a constant factor demanding deference by Kusu. Now that the power differential was indistinct, Nisaba welcomed the participation of the Chief Counselor's wife, and each was satisfied to call the other 'friend.' Nisaba had sent an invitation for the two of them to share a midmorning meal and then go to the market to shop. Decorations and food would be required for an immense celebration as well as a solemn religious ceremony that would involve the entire population. Certainly the bulk of the arrangements would be done by factotums and emissaries of the palace and both temples, but the specific desires of the bride could not be ignored.

"I'm just so happy to have her enthusiastic about something after this long period of bleak spirits. The murder of our servant really affected her." Nisaba couldn't ignore the possibility that Tikal had told his wife about the rape as well, but she would never acknowledge that it had occurred.

"You should be pleased that Ninegala is such a sensitive girl, even though it caused her so much pain. She'll be a good mother. I always liked your girls." The wife of the Chief Counselor enjoyed knowing the intimate details of palace affairs, and never let on to anyone that she knew anything.

The matrons were on a mission this day to find five veils to be wedding gifts from Nisaba, veils that announced Ninegala's high status. They needed to be richly adorned but not so heavy that they wouldn't stay on her face, or hurt while being worn. Both women knew the requirements, and Nisaba was determined to encourage a deeper relationship with her counterpart by accepting at least three suggestions from her.

"This one's gorgeous!" declared Tikal's wife, picking up a veil and motioning for Nisaba to join her. Its loosely knit cloth portion was suspended from double stranded silver chains, with tiny silver beads dangling from the bottom of the fabric and deep olive colored threads decorated the cloth.

They were standing inside one of the shaded booths in a row of textile vendors, being watched carefully by a buxom young woman of foreign extraction by the look of her garb, which was made up of three layers of diaphanous, multicolored skirts, with her breasts only covered occasionally by the light silvery scarf that hung over her neck and down her bosom. Her stretched earlobes sported spools made of deep black ebony, and she had multiple rings on her fingers.

"Does my lady want to see another like that?" asked the clerk. "My uncle makes them. He's crippled, injured in battle, so I have to ask a good price," she cajoled.

Nisaba started to respond with irritation at the clear attempt to add to the cost, but held her tone in check, not wanting to give a bad impression to her companion. Instead, she answered diffidently, asking, "Do you have one with lapis beads?"

"My lady has wonderful taste. Let me look."

She moved quickly to lift a set of baskets that was hidden under the coarse wool cloth that covered the display table, trying hard to keep an eye on the patrons without seeming suspicious. Knowing exactly what was in her assortment of wares and where they were, she managed to extricate the bottom basket from a stack and set it out on the table for display. She draped several veils across her arm next to each other, revealing a surprising variety of adornment available. "Ah! There it is," she exclaimed, pulling out one veil with two matching lapis pendants at the cheek area and more diminutive beads of the same hue descending from the cloth. She put the other veils she had displayed on her arm back into the basket and held up the lapis decorated veil in front of but not touching her face. "See how pretty, ladies?"

"Do you like them?" inquired Kusu of Nisaba after guiding her away from the vendor so they could talk in private.

"They're both lovely. But she's going to make me pay the price of a young slave for each one, I think." Nisaba was torn between paying more than she wanted to and not letting her companion know that price was a concern.

"I think they're both splendid," her companion said, "and Ninegala has just the right skin tone for wearing them. So I'm going to give them to her as a wedding gift. No argument." She waved her hand toward Nisaba to stop any demurrer. "I want to!" She was thinking to herself that it couldn't be a bad thing to have the mother of the queen as a friend, and even the queen herself. "Stay here, Nisaba. I'll make the purchase." Walking away, she called out to the vendor and pointed at her imperiously, "I'm not a donkey to be given straw instead of hay, so we'll only pay a reasonable price."

———————————— • ● • ————————————

Muda and Nintud sat in the courtyard of Nani and Suba's home. The two occupied opposite ends of a brick bench, across the yard from the house and cooking area. Nani and Suba sat together on a bench next to the table, several paces away from the other two, each holding a baby on their lap, acting as chaperones for protocol's sake. As a widow in the company of an unattached man, Nintud was wearing a plain, light veil, proper attire despite their long association with one another. The evening was cooling down as the sun had gone below the city wall but was not below the horizon beyond the river. The river had gone into flood and receded since Zambiya and the others had left, and Muda had tried to visit at least every other day during that time.

"Muda wants…" He shook his head slightly, stopped himself and began again. "I want to ask you to marry me, Nintud, even though I'm not an Isin person." He cleared his throat before adding, "I've always …admired you, and I respect you too much to… insist on what I want if it's not what you want. I would never have said anything to you if Dagan were still alive." He started to say more, but Nintud put her hand on his lips to stop him.

"Are you fond of me, at least?"

Looking confused, Muda searched his mind for the meaning of the word, and found nothing. "What does 'fond' mean, Nintud? I know what 'love' means. I loved my wife in Gutia, but that was long ago." He didn't know whether he'd already been rejected, so he pressed forward by saying, "If 'fond' means 'love' I can…con… con-fess? that I've wanted you as my wife for a year. Before Dagan died." He looked away before continuing in a lower voice, "Ashamed. Didn't want to tell… myself. Dagan…was a good man. Very good man, deserved you for wife."

Nintud smiled under her veil, then removed it and spoke very clearly, saying, "'Fond' means not love yet, but close to love. Do you love me, Muda?"

Turning back to look at her directly, and seeing that her veil was on the bench between them, Muda ventured to take one of Nintud's hand in both of his and declared with passion, "Yes, lovely lady, of course I love you. I can't help loving you." Wondering if he'd gone too far, he felt he had to ask, "Could you love me, Nintud? Will you marry me?"

Nintud wanted to share this moment, so she stood up and announced loudly enough for Nani and Suba to hear, "Yes, Muda, I'll marry you as soon as you want."

The two were married the day before the New Year ceremony and moved into the palace, sharing a suite close to Enlil-Bani's quarters.

———— • • • ————

The winds maintained a steady drive from the northwest, pushing

Zambiya's three barges along the coast, helped by the sails that had been fashioned at the port of Dilmun. The captain never allowed his crafts to get out of sight of the southern shore, until at one point the whole watery passage, actually quite broad in comparison to the Buranun's banks, veered toward the north at which time the northern shore was visible. Then he directed the sailors to guide the barges toward that bank and to cruise along that side. The water was nearly the same temperature as the air, and for several days the weather was comfortable.

Not until the transition to the open sea occurred did the swells and chop cause the men of Isin to spend long periods along the rails, chumming the waters with undigested food. The Larsans and Isins alike vowed to never repeat this voyage if they survived the misery, though it lasted but a couple days.

It was several days later before Neti could forgive the Captain's chuckling at the land lover's plight. "I suspect he's steering the boats to make the motion worse," he'd complained to Ansar at the height of their distress. Ansar only nodded, then rushed for the rail to continue dry retching.

Midmorning on a hot day, a full month after they had left Larsa, the captain shouted to Zambiya, pointing toward shore, "There it is! First port's right there." Rangu, who sat on a grain sack watching the shoreline avidly, took a deep breath and smiled, anticipating setting foot again on his land of birth. From his shoulder bag of soft dark leather, he extracted a long piece of cloth that was indigo along one side and dark yellow on the other, which he coiled and tucked around his forehead and crown in a distinctive headdress. He muttered a thanks to his own gods, and walked to the rail.

———————— • ◆ • ————————

After two months of marriage Nintud was astonished to find that she was pregnant; she explained to Nani that she had thought she was barren after not conceiving after her first pregnancy. Nani laughed out loud when Nintud shared the news with her and said, "The gods so chose, dear lady. That's a blessing!"

CHAPTER FOURTEEN

A GARDEN OF EXOTICS

*The gods must love variety above all, for they made the
earth to hold different stones and metals, clay and sand
and bitumen, men and women of different hues and size.
The people mold and form and shape everything, and all
becomes part of the rich display that beautifies our world.*

"Because it's how it works here, Lord." The captain was weary of explaining
to Neti and Zambiya why they had to pay two whole discs of silver to the
officials at the mouth of the river in order to proceed up the water course.
That had been five days before and the question had come up from one
of them every day since. "That banner," he said, pointing three times for
emphasis to a black flag with a crude yellow figure of a unicorn sewed
onto it that was flapping briskly at the top of the mast of the lead barge,
"told all the minor officers along the way that we're permitted to proceed."

"Couldn't we go further than Manjadar?" Neti asked. "Rangu says
there's another large city further up river, closer to the source of the raw
stones we've come for. 'Harpa,' I think he called it. It'd be an advantage to
us to trade there." Even more exasperated than Zambiya at the requirement
for tribute extracted by the men who confronted them when they started
up the river; Neti considered them little more than pirates. He was also
appalled by their strange dress and ornaments.

Zambiya answered for the Captain. "We'd all like to make this trading
venture a success, but I've decided. That would add more than twice the

distance and too much time. I want us back to the Buranun before the rains hit this land." Ever the realist, he was becoming reconciled to the payment of tribute as a needed expense. He clapped the youngster on the shoulder and assured him, "We'll still do well, Neti. The stones we saw in that first bazaar we visited were very reasonable, and we'll do even better up there."

"Rangu, join us." Zambiya called to the *meluhhan* bead maker, who was seated as far forward on this, the lead barge, as he could go, clearly enjoying the scenery and the scent of its familiar reeds and brush and occasional trees along the banks, unlike those along the river at Isin. Past the nearby vegetation and past the fields of barley he seemed entranced to see again orchards of pomegranate and the vibrant green of bananas as well as date palms.

Responding immediately to his name being called, he adjusted his turban-like headdress as he approached the leader of the venture.

"Yes, Lord. What is it?" He made his way around the covered burlap sacks of grain and packs of linen cloth that were their primary trade goods for the trip; an aging coracle sat upside down over the middle of the stack of merchandise.

As soon as Rangu had joined Zambiya, the Captain spat over the side and took his leave, automatically checking the wind and the flow of the water ahead for obstacles, happy to put the conversation about tribute behind him.

"I've been interested in the sights along the way ever since we entered five days ago, but some things seem more important for us to know than others. I'll start with that banner." Zambiya pointed to the cloth at the top of the mast and asked, "A unicorn? Do they actually live here? I saw bowls and pots and such decorated with them at that last bazaar, but I've never actually seen one."

Often taciturn in manner, Rangu allowed himself a short laugh and smile and said, "Neither have I, Lord. I don't believe they exist, but when we get to Manjadar you'll see them everywhere: on flags and walls, plaques over doorways, painted on dishes and the sides of boats. But no such creatures. They're an important symbol of our gods, though, especially the protectors." He looked away from Zambiya and gazed up-river again before adding, "You'll see. Very important to us." He turned his attention to observing the skill with which the crew maneuvered out of the path of a downed tree floating down the river toward them; a sparkling white egret perched on a root just above the water, looking downstream as if it were steering. The tranquil scene suddenly turned dramatic, as the bird was snatched into the toothsome maw of a crocodile, which dove beneath the surface of the water with its prize. Rangu shuddered, and said, "Did you see that?"

"Yes," said Zambiya. "What was that creature? It looked like it could have been longer than an ox and plow together."

"Could have been; I've seen skeletons of them, and one was that long. This is pretty far south, though; unusual." Rangu closed his eyes and shuddered, and then almost ritually dry-washed his face with his hands.

Zambiya absently rubbed the faded scar on his chest, a reminder of his first caravan trip, and frowned, then remembered his other question for Rangu.

"I'm sure you told me when we first spoke at your village, but I don't recall how you became so good at our language as well as your own. That's a blessing for both of us, especially if you want to become a trader and emissary for Isin." Zambiya noted that Rangu was now focused on the distant river bank upstream with some intensity, and followed his gaze as they conversed.

Rangu answered as he turned his gaze momentarily to watch the tree as it passed behind the boats. Scanning the bank again, he answered, "I'd only seen ten summers when my family moved to K*i-en-gir*. My father was certain the family would do well there, making beads for the temples for trade. There are lots of bead makers here in *Meluhha*, too many in fact, and my whole family polishes and drills the long beads in a way that's better for the stones we import. The temple bead makers at Isin work in more common stones and do it well, but ours are different and more highly valued." He paused, for long conversations were not comfortable for him.

He continued his explanation saying, "My father demanded that I learn your language and took me with him to Isin's market every week. I seem to have a skill for learning languages as well as drilling beads. I don't..." He broke off and pointed toward the bank, deep into the shadows of a stand of tall reeds. "There they are!" he said, pointing.

"What are you looking at?" Zambiya asked.

Neti had noted the excited tone in Rangu's voice and hurried toward where the two were standing near the left side rail.

"Buffalo!" Rangu declared gleefully. "I heard them snorting, but couldn't see 'em. Haven't seen one since we left here." Rangu seemed to completely ignore the rest of the scene along the bank; several small boys took turns climbing onto the backs of five large creatures standing neck-deep in the river's flow and then jumping off; the cattle themselves seemed oblivious to being used as platforms for the cavorting children. The largest buffalo stood facing the middle of the river; the deepest brown in color, its large head was all that was out of the water. With its flat horns curved out and back, it was wide as a cart's wheel. As the men watched, it sounded a bellow, husky and resonant.

"Are they wild?" asked Neti, amazed at what seemed to him to be a huge body judging by the size of the head and horns.

"No, of course not. They're very valuable. Hard to see from here, but I think I can see the ring in the big one's nose. It's probably tethered there by the owner." Rangu could not restrain his smile; he took a deep breath and sighed as he sat back down on an uncovered stack of grain sacks with a satisfied air.

— • ● • —

Preparations for the royal marriage of Enlil-Bani and Ninegala engaged all the official strata of Isin, as well as the members of both families.

Nisaba had many relatives living outside Isin in distant villages, mostly to the north along the river, all land-owning farmers or owners of domestic herds of cattle, sheep, or goats. Once the date was specified, she engaged Enmerkar's *edubba* to prepare invitations on clay cylinders to send to those she wished to invite; these were sealed inside clay cases, also inscribed to indicate the contents of the case with her own identifying script, even though she couldn't read the symbols herself. The invitations had already been delivered by couriers, who were also prepared to recite the invitation by heart to those who had no access to a scribe. Most invitees had responded and she expected many kin to arrive to participate in the festivities; she made arrangements with her many friends in Isin to accommodate them.

She and Nabi sat in the shade of a new, bright green, palm frond canopy in the market square, so newly woven that there were few spaces between the fronds to require avoiding the piercing sunshine. This was one of their now-frequent daytime meetings, sharing a spiced beer. Enough noise came from the mid-morning bartering in the nearby vendor area that their conversation could not be overheard, but was not so intrusive that they missed the nuances of their communications.

"I can see it in your eyes — you're troubled, Lady. What is it?" Nabi never used Nisaba's name when they were in public.

"Same thing, Nabi, now it's worse. 'Rida declares she'll die a spinster, and she's started muttering curses against her sister for having, in her words, 'snared an *Ensi*.'" Nisaba voiced the last phrase in a whiny, reproving tone. "I'm almost losing hope of finding her a husband, truth to the gods. Her spiteful attitude makes my stomach hurt."

"I know it's a worry. As a palace guard, the kinds of men I know would be useless as husbands." He discretely stroked the back of Nisaba's hand with the back of his own, and added, "If she were married, you'd have much more … privacy, I'm sure." He looked at her meaningfully to see if her eyes would reveal whether his thoughts were clear to her; she looked into his eyes, then dropped her gaze.

"We could share … dinner together, couldn't we?" she replied. She sighed, then looked around to see if anyone was nearby, then quietly added, "Or more, if the gods would allow."

Nabi warmed to the solving of this particular problem by contributing, "Sherida needs to widen her view of potential mates, I think. All your people and friends," he probed, "are any of the wedding guests prospects? A wealthy farmer, or a first son? Or maybe would know of some? If the priests find favorable reports in the clues the gods give us, the marriage is just a few days from now."

"I've only considered men here in Isin, I don't know why. That's an idea that may help her and," she added with lowered voice in a sultry timbre, "would please me, too." She raised her eyes and looked over Nabi's head to search the canopy as if there might be a resolution there, actually searching through her memory for those she had invited.

"I know!" she declared loudly, startling the nearby patrons as well as Nabi. "Oh!" She stood up, arranging her peach colored tunic and feather-fringed white skirt over her matron's body. "Walk me straight to Enmerkar's, Nabi. I've got to send another invitation to my aunt down by

Shuruppak right away, before she leaves." She sucked up a large swallow of beer through her straw, too much as some escaped down her chin, which she wiped off impatiently, drying her hand along the tunic at the small of her back. "Her stepson would be perfect for 'Rida. I've only seen him once, but he'll be wealthy in a few years, and he's not an old man and he's not related to her." She mused a while longer, biting her lip, then speculated further as she and Nabi left the beer parlor, "He's a bit short, but that's his only flaw." She scowled, imagining Sherida's possible objection being added to the previous ones.

By this time Nabi was already standing; he arranged his waist belt with its matching short swords and the two hastened to make their way to the *edubba* to add a new cylinder and seal to the assignment for the scribes.

Manjadar's docks along the river's edge were more than adequate for the ships and barges that were in port, with many berths unoccupied; the wharves seemed to have been built for a much more active level of business than was now evident. As the Captain yelled orders to his crew, he noted a spot at the end of one long quay that was seemingly perfect for his needs: close to the road leading to the city, few other boats were tethered there, and no crews visible on those that were. He barked directions to make for that spot.

Nearing midday, the sun beat down on the massive walls of the trading city, visible in the distance atop a hill, with the upper bricks a color similar to a donkey's hide, though some of the lower parts had been painted at some time in the past. The city was connected to the port by a rutted and poorly maintained road that led past stalls and barns, several of which were empty and abandoned. Those that were tended seemed to be devoted to the commerce of everyday necessities: prepared foods, cooking pots, clothing, dyed fabric, rope, bedding and cheap pottery.

Viewing the road from the pier, Zambiya said to Neti, "This looks like the market square of Isin laid out in a meandering line. I wonder if there's another inside the walls." He helped Rangu up and off the gangplank from the barge. The *Meluhhan* had been struggling to keep his balance on the narrow wooden walkway as he carried a bulky leather satchel over one shoulder. As soon as he was on the wharf, and with help from Zambiya, Rangu set the satchel down and sighed with relief.

"What's in your bag, Rangu?"

Just then the wind shifted from up-river and came from behind Manjadar, carrying the usual smoke from cooking fires, but something more.

"By the great gods," declared Neti covering his nose with a cloth he had snatched from his shoulder bag, "That smells worse than a pig's fart."

Rangu turned to Neti and declared through clenched jaws, and with uncharacteristic venom, "Make it your friend, Neti. What you say is like a 'pig's fart' is a favorite sauce here, and it'll be served wherever you eat." He turned away before scowling.

Not wishing to contend with one of the expedition's designated leaders, Rangu turned to Zambiya and answered the question he had asked. "My father wants me to take some tools he's improved to my uncle, my mother's brother. They make holding the long beads steadier as we drill holes."

He turned back to Neti again, saying with a somewhat more genial tone, "There are lots of different sauces used in our cooking, but most of my people like the flavor of kri. That's what we call it. You might find you like it after trying it. I'll try to find a stall that serves a mild one."

Always mindful of how this caravan was supposed to broaden his experience, thus making him a better Chief Counselor in the future, Neti held up his hands palm forward in a placating manner and said, "I was just surprised, Rangu." He returned the cloth he'd been holding across his nose to the shoulder bag and explained, "I didn't mean any offense. I'll try it, certainly." He thought a moment than added, "I like strong flavors, so if it tastes as strong as it smells, there's a fair chance I'll like it." Still practicing to be the diplomat his father intended, he observed to Rangu, "I didn't see a zigurrat at the port at the river's mouth, and I don't see one from here. Where are the temples?"

Just as keen to maintain his place as the interpreter of *Meluhhan* culture, Rangu responded with an almost jovial tone, "Our people have family gods, of course, so there's a chapel in most homes. But the great gods, like the sun, the unicorn, the great bull, even the snake, we mostly see them everywhere, so we don't need a special temple to be reminded of them."

Neti hesitated before responding, squelching an instinct to belittle such a patently absurd set of beliefs. Then he declared, "I still don't think there's such a thing as a unicorn, but just because I haven't seen one doesn't mean they don't exist. One of the traders down south described a huge animal that used its long nose to pick up tree trunks, swore it was real. He sounded sincere, but I can't imagine it."

"I can only imagine it myself, Neti, and I've heard about them all my life."

"One last question, then. Do you have priests?"

"Of course we do, but they're also kings and mayors and successful traders. They keep us in touch with the gods during festivals and at special events, like weddings and death parades before the burials."

Neti looked back toward the city with its massive walls and lack of a high temple, and marveled, "Thanks, Rangu. You've probably kept me from making some horrible mistake due to ignorance."

Their conversation ended when Zambiya called to Ansar, who was still standing on the barge with his military contingent gathered near him. "Keep your men alert." Turning to the Captain, who was standing near the gangplank, he instructed, "Captain, you can decide if any of your crew can leave the boat, but after they've come on shore, I want you to stand off the wharf a way, just for safety. ... And none of the locals come on board. I mean it."

The last admonition was added after Zambiya took note of a group of four women hurrying over toward this quay from another. Gaily dressed, they sported flamboyant hairdos piled high on their heads, festooned with flowing ribbons and long clay beads, yellow and red, hanging next to their ears. While they wore only scanty revealing clothing - no veils - every one of them had a variety of bangles of many colors, red and maroon, white and purple on both their arms and ankles; they walked with an accompanying clanking, dinging announcement of their presence, like a herd of goats with their bells.

At first Rangu, the betrothed *Meluhhan*, stared open mouthed at his countrywomen but quickly composed himself and said to Zambiya, "There are many such women in the river ports." He hastened to add, "I'm told. I hear they favor servicing sailors, so they won't have jealousies to contend with. Should I send them away?"

Zambiya considered the offer, but looked to the Captain to see his reaction, but it was non-committal. Already, two crewmen had been designated to be the first ashore; the larger of those two shoved his way ahead of his crewmate and mounted the gangplank, striding with determination toward the bevy of women. The other sailor hurried to catch up, and within a short time pairings had been arranged and the two couples left the port area headed up the hill. The two rejected women waited a short distance from the barge, expecting more sailors to disembark. When that failed to occur, they looked appraisingly at the more important looking men already on the dock.

Rangu only glanced at Zambiya before approaching the women. Keeping his distance he said something to them in a low but menacing tone. They glanced at one another and then at the others on the dock before retreating, but not before one of them made a verbal retort and spat on the ground toward Rangu before hurrying away.

"My family lives within the walls," Rangu said to Zambiya. "I'd like to start by visiting them and introducing all of you." He gestured toward the bulky bag and said, "And I'd like to leave that with them right away." He shielded his eyes and glanced toward the sun briefly, noting also that due to the river haze there were no shadows being cast. He continued, "We should eat before we arrive, since they won't be expecting us. I'll be able to find a food vendor by the aroma, Neti." He smiled thinly but promised, "I'll also make sure they're serving goat meat, not donkey."

With that, he accepted the help offered by Zambiya and Neti to hoist his sack and hold it while he adjusted the tumpline strap across his forehead, and then steadied the burdensome sack and led the way toward the city of his birth.

———————— • ● • ————————

Ninmul and Ninlil, the late General Ashgi's twin daughters, sat in the shade of a freshly leafed out pomegranate tree in the *edubba*'s courtyard prior to the evening meal. Late afternoon, the shadows stretched and elongated across the courtyard with a riverine breeze adding a dollop of moisture to the warm air. The girls continued duplicating and memorizing the scripts of the day's lessons, comparing each other's work. They were distracted by a pair of birds the size of wrens high in the branches over their heads, black across the front and white behind. The birds busied themselves by studiously constructing their nest and talking to each other.

Now that they lived at the *edubba*, the household staff was confronted with the difficulty of telling the girls apart, so the twins had agreed to wear distinctive headbands, woven and decorated specifically for them by Nani. She had met with the girls at her home, now that she had two infants to tend and no one else to assist her. They agreed on the designs and colors before she created them; Ninmul wanted a chevron design in red on a black background, while Ninlil chose white with alternating yellow and brown stripes for herself.

"Girls," En-me called from the doorway. "Can you come in?"

The two looked first at one another, then gathered their practice tablets and wooden styluses. In order to prevent the clay from drying out before they could resume, each removed a saturated cloth from a bitumen-coated basket they shared and covered their work with a slightly wrung cloth. Quickly selecting a spot under the tree that seemed to offer the most shade, the tablets were placed there before they walked to the door and went inside.

En-me ushered them into the front sitting area where Enmerkar sat on his elevated chair. Near to him on another chair sat a woman, thinner than many women of Isin, wearing a common white tunic over an unadorned plainspun ankle-length skirt. Her sandals were aged, and the straps that held them on her feet had been tied back together on more than one occasion. She appeared to be some years older than En-me, though not yet middle aged. She wore no adornments of any kind; no bracelets, no hair stays, no necklaces, no rings. Her gaze was lowered, but she looked up when En-me entered with the girls. Her eyes were bloodshot, looking as though they were perpetually damp with tears. She had obviously been crying for an extended period and was poised to resume at the least provocation. She was leaning forward, but sat more upright to take note of the girls. On the floor next to her chair was a dilapidated shoulder bag, practically empty.

Enmerkar needed no distinctive headbands to distinguish the twins, and said to the woman, "This girl's Ninmul," he said pointing. Ninmul inclined her head in a slight bow. "That one's Ninlil. You'll learn which is which pretty soon, I'm sure." Ninlil placed one hand over her chest and mimicked her sister's acknowledgment.

"Yes, Master," the woman said, her voice catching in her throat. She strained to declare to the girls, "Just call me 'slave'. That's what I am now." At that she burst into tears again, leaning forward to sob quietly into her hands, which now covered her face.

"Master, why make us known to a household slave?" Ninmul asked, truly puzzled. Her brow showed her concern with furrows like a plowed field despite her youth, and she reached for her sister's hand without thinking.

"Because of your age. It's necessary to protect your reputations so that you'll have good marriage prospects. Your brothers insisted that since you live here in my home, since I'm an unmarried man, you should have a woman to safeguard your privacy, sort of like a guardian. This woman was married, but has no children. She can help you to, uh, answer female questions as you develop and grow." Enmerkar ignored the crying woman next to him, searching the faces of the twins to discern whether they understood.

It was Ninlil's turn to voice reluctance, if not outright refusal, by declaring, "She can't sleep in our room, Master. She can't!"

"I've seen the room; it's large enough for three. What's wrong?"

The twins looked at each other, furtively at first as if consulting silently, but seemed to arrive at an understanding between them, then Ninlil stepped next to her sister and held her close, one arm around her waist. She took her free hand and held her sister's hand with it.

"Please, Master, send 'Slave' away so we can speak freely with you."

Enmerkar was filled with a haze of perplexity, along with questions without words, but he said to the weeping woman, "Take your bag and go to the kitchen. Introduce yourself and tell them I said you're to be given a quiet place for a while, and some hot broth. We'll sort out the details of your place here later, probably by dinner." He looked meaningfully at the twins as he said the latter, determined that he would remain in control of his home, his students, and his staff, slave or other.

The newly arrived slave had no sooner than left the room when Enmerkar said impatiently, "Well?"

Ninmul held up one finger against Ninlil's lips to signify that she, Ninmul, intended to make the explanations required by the *Ummia* and master of the scribe school and house.

"We know all too clearly what our father intended for us, and our brothers intend the same: to become scribes assigned to the army. They plan for us to gain the attention of soldiers with good prospects, then marry, so then they'll have no further responsibility for us." She looked to Ninlil for some silent confirmation of her declaration, which was given by a nod.

"I knew all that, Ninmul; it was stated plainly when you two first came here. What's different now?" Enmerkar held out his hands in question, looking from one to the other twin.

"In plain words, Master, we lost our mother at birth and our father by his choice. We were housed and fed in our aunt's home, but we've been treated like orphans. The eunuch who ran the household was kind, but not a parent, and our aunt had all the warmth and caring of a bat." Here, she swallowed, hoping she wasn't being too disparaging, but received no responsive signs from Enmerkar, so she continued.

Her next words tumbled out without pause, in a kind of personal manifesto that included her sister, who nodded affirmatively throughout. "We don't want to marry, not anyone. We love each other. We want to become priestesses in the temple of Inana, and serve as scribes there. We want to always be together." She hesitated only briefly before adding, with considerable trepidation, "We sleep in the same bed every night," and paused again before saying, "like you and En-me." She waved her hand in a motion to signify the two adults together. "Just like you and En-me." She swallowed hard, with a throat that was now very dry. "That's why that poor woman can't stay in our room. We're sorry for her, but she can't sleep with us."

Except for the insects buzzing and rasping outside, sounds that seemed magnified by the absence of speech by the people in the room, utter silence prevailed. Ninmul let loose of Ninlil's hand in order to hold her around the waist; her countenance started to contort, as though she might cry.

Enmerkar finally broke the silence by observing, "You're very young to commit to the lives of priestesses." He thought further before asking, "What do you think we should tell your brothers? Unless you've already shared this with them."

Ninmul declared with resigned resolve, as though she had already given this matter much thought, "They won't care — they'll be relieved! They won't have to be concerned about us, trying to insure that we find husbands from among their ranks."

Ninlil added cynically, "If we got into a coracle and poled our way to the southern sea, they'd be just as concerned about us. We're just burdens to them both!" Her hands clenched into fists, but only briefly as she became aware of revealing her defiant attitude.

"Well, I've got to see that that woman has a place to sleep. We'll discuss your brothers and your aspirations for religious life later." He sighed audibly, feeling the pressure of this added complication from what he'd intended as a charitable offer to this pair of orphans. Even the purchase of the slave had been motivated by compassion. "No point in telling your brothers that you love one another completely, is there?"

"No, Master," the two said together. Again without visible consultation, Ninlil and Ninmul knelt in front of their teacher; each took one of Enmerkar's hands and kissed it, then left to resume their scholarly activities in the courtyard.

———————— • ● • ————————

"I remember that girl, Rangu. Talked too much. But maybe she's changed from when all of you left to set up your village near Isin." Rangu's uncle had no hesitation expressing his doubt about the young man's intended bride, but said it without malice; it was just an opinion, expressed to continue the discussion.

"I think she did then, Uncle." Rangu sat next to his uncle in the small circle of men who were sharing the obligatory light refreshment one must offer a guest in one's home. Neti was next to him, then Zambiya. Rangu's aunt and two un-married cousins had served the men and then withdrawn from the public room of the home. The bundle that Rangu had carried there had already been removed to the uncle's workshop, with an agreement that Rangu would return to demonstrate the improved bead drill the next day.

Despite the meal the travelers had shared at a public house they had encountered on their way earlier, protocol demanded that they partake of the patriarch's offering of food. A round flat basket served as a tray set between them, holding crusty tan and black-speckled griddle cakes that surrounded a shallow bowl filled with freshly mashed bananas spiced with lemon juice and cinnamon. Neti had eaten lightly at the public house, with 'kri' still not agreeable to him, but he found the banana preparation delightful.

Zambiya and Neti were anxious to present themselves to the trading officials of *Meluhha*, but out of deference to Rangu and his family's hospitality, sat quietly, cross-legged, smiling at the uncle when he looked at one or the other. Rangu had taught both of them, and Ansar as well, some of the words and phrases of polite discourse for his countrymen. These, of course, had all been exhausted early in their meeting of the family, but the men from Isin were anxious to utter the *Harappan* words for 'Thank you,' and 'May the gods be with you,' when they left the uncle's home.

Neti had just finished his second griddle cake with the bananas; mindful of his primary task to learn from his experiences here, he refrained from reaching for a third, and instead asked Rangu, "Would it be disrespectful to offer your uncle some form of payment or gift for his hospitality? I've enjoyed being here, Rangu."

Rangu smiled at Neti, placated by the question. The morning's exchange about 'kri' had been forgotten by both men.

"A sensitive question. The answer's a little complicated, but not greatly. If you offer him anything under any pretext now, today, he'll be required to feel offended, as if his gift was just part of a barter. Barter requires a judgment as to who got the best of the bargain, so there must be a winner and a loser. That's not good for how people should treat each other." Rangu paused and scooped up some of the banana spread, but held it over the bowl before continuing. "Before we return to Isin, when we say our farewells to him, then you can give him a gift, which you will say is for the benefit of his children. Even though his children are grown, that grants him the respect he is due, and no exchange is implied. He has given you an earlier gift; you later give his children a gift."

Neti considered this nicety of protocol and made a pact with himself to commit it to memory in order to compare the *Meluhhans* with other peoples with whom he might come in contact. A suspicion began to form in is mind, and he turned to Zambiya to inquire, "You weren't born to palace service. Does Rangu's explanation sound unusual to you for the regular citizens of Isin?"

"It sounds perfectly ordinary to me, Neti. My uncle was a trader; his brothers were all traders and still are. Nevertheless, when I saw them dealing with people during their travels, bargaining was kept strictly away from being civil and social. My uncle was a very generous man, but a fierce bargainer in business. Speaking of which," he said turning to Rangu, "we must excuse ourselves from you family's hospitality, with thanks. I want to make some progress with our task here in *Meluhha* today. Please tell your uncle how much we appreciate him and his family."

The uncle guessed from the gestures and tones of the men that they intended to leave soon. He clapped his hands and was very shortly joined by his wife, who bowed to the men and picked up the basket from the middle of the circle and disappeared through a draped doorway.

CHAPTER FIFTEEN

A GRAFT UNION

*Often marriage is a convenience of familiarity, but on
occasion it is a refuge from solitude. People more willingly
share their pleasures than their terrors or regrets.*

In the early morning shadow of the zigurrat, Isin's market square was deserted with the exception of eight novitiate priests wielding brooms, short shovels and baskets, detailed to remove any excrement or trash from the hard-packed ground. The steps and dais leading to the palace had already been scrubbed clean. Both full-size guardian lion statues atop the steps had been draped across the shoulders with new banners: a bright yellow field with a pair of stylized gazelles facing in opposite directions. Every avenue leading into the square was guarded by soldiers to prevent entry until Enmul, Chief Priest of *Egal-mah,* declared the space suitable for the effigies of Ninisina and Inana to be carried from Isin's two temples high above on the zigurrat to the public space. There they would witness and bless the marriage of the king to Ninegala. Enmul's declaration was not anticipated before the square was in full sunlight.

The soldiers at the entrances to the city square had two main purposes: first, to prevent feral dogs or pigs from entering at all; second, to impose order on the citizens who would gather in the latter part of the morning to observe the ceremony and then partake of the communal feast. The priests were determined that the goddesses not be exposed to even a glimpse of an unclean dog or pig.

With his counterpart Chief Priest at *E-sig-mese-du,* Enmul had spent many hours over the past several days in consultation, both with each other and huddled with their respective diviners of the gods' intentions, searching and hoping for favorable signs. Ningal observed the stars, while other priests consulted the signs in newborn lamb entrails; still others lit incense and tried to discern the meaning of the rising smoke. There had not been a royal wedding in Isin for over a generation, and even the oldest priests and priestesses could not remember any details of the protocols. Much time was spent reading the clay tablets in their libraries in both temples, but the prevailing question remained: 'What do the gods want and expect?'

"How could you even think I would be interested in that man, mother?" Sherida and Nisaba approached the square, preceded by a guard who had been sent to avoid any problem with their being admitted to the palace to help Ninegala prepare for the ceremony. They were trailed by two husky slaves, bare to the waist, carrying tied bundles suspended from yokes across their shoulders; their slave knots swayed as they walked. "He's young enough, but his manners are so – crude!" the daughter declared. "He was dressed like a bumpkin, could only talk about sheep and donkeys, and spent his time looking at the other women at our dinner, even ones as old as you." She shuddered visibly despite the heat already mounting, recalling the man who had been seated next to her during Nisaba's feast for her invited guests.

"He's going to own a profitable farm within just a few years," Nisaba retorted. "Besides, you've had an objection to every man who's been proposed. I'm thinking you're a better prospect for being a priestess than a wife."

"There must be some rich, young, single attractive men in Isin, mother. My sister's getting married, and I'm older. And better looking, too! Getting a husband shouldn't be so hard!" She let out an exasperated sigh, but thought briefly about her mother's threat and added, "Priestess? Huh!"

"Well, I don't care about your crankiness today. You're going to pull your manners together and help make your sister look like a goddess. Keep your bile in check. Please!"

The pair reached the square and crossed it without incident; after being admitted to the palace they went straight to Ninegala's suite of rooms.

Standing behind Ninegala, who sat on a green split-cane chair on two beige cushions to raise her position so her head was above the chair back, Sud glanced up from combing the young girl's naturally straight hair when the mother and sister entered. She had been instructed on what was desired, a popular style at the time, parted in the middle and arranged into a pair of buns with short cascading ribbons on either side of her head, held in place with small, five-toothed combs with lapis and garnet jewels set as cabochons in the spine above the teeth. Her ears were kept visible to show off her matching dangle earrings which reached nearly to her shoulders.

"Shalamu, Lady," Sud said, continuing her work. "And you too, 'Rida. Isn't this a day of blessings?"

The set of rooms Ninegala had chosen as her own was the suite vacated by Zambiya when he left on caravan to Manjadar; he had left word that he never intended to occupy them again. Despite his tryst with Ninmah in what had earlier been Sud's bedroom, the memory of Ezina's death was a constant torment to him. Sud had been assigned as servant and companion to Ninegala since the youngster had moved to the palace, and was again settled into her previous room. The bride-to-be knew of the death that had occurred there, but it had no personal meaning for her. Death was not a stranger in Isin, especially since the depredations of the plague.

"Let me see you, Nina," her mother said, making her way around to the front of the chair to see her daughter's face, but mostly the look of the hairdo from the front. Her appraising observation lasted a while, but she seemed satisfied after a slight re-positioning of one comb, announcing, "You've a gift, Sud. This looks excellent. I wish I'd known that when I still lived here in the palace. I'd have gotten you out of the kitchen to be one of my servants."

Sud was unimpressed by the flattery, but responded with an enthusiastic, "That would've been a gift of the gods, Lady." She turned to the older daughter and said, "Sherida, do you like it? You're young, and this is a modern look."

Remembering her mother's admonition, Sherida summoned her most pleasant manner and stated brightly, "I've not seen it done better, even at one of mother's gatherings. Of course, there weren't many young people at those, and most of the women mother's age wouldn't have tried it." She had been holding her arms across her bosom, but made an effort to seem pleased for her sister's good fortune and placed her hands on her hips. Deliberately biting back her jealousy, she smilingly declared, "That really does look good, Nina."

A smile flitted across Ninegala's lips, but another concern occurred to her busy mind, and she queried her mother, asking blandly, "Mother, have you told 'Rida just what *Ensi* wants of me as a bride?" Ignoring Sud's presence, she tried to see both Nisaba and Sherida at the same time to judge their respective responses to the question.

"She wouldn't care, Nina. It doesn't concern her, so I didn't bother." Her mother's response was equally bland, to keep Sherida from becoming interested in the answer.

Sud's ears pricked up, but her ministrations to Ninegala's hair ceased just momentarily, and she carried on despite her puzzlement at the strange question: everyone knew what was expected of any wife, let alone that of a king, which was, of course, to bear children.

Sherida was actually preoccupied at the moment making a survey of the row of ceremonial dresses. It appeared as though her sister was expected to wear these during the very public events. It occurred to her that in the middle of the day in the square, surrounded by hundreds of people, her slender sister would be severely burdened by so many dresses and skirts, so many sets of jewelry. She said, "Mother…" then noticed the row of slippers and sandals propped beneath each combination. "Oh…" she continued, then asked "Why so many sets of clothing?"

"There's more than the wedding itself, of course. How could you not know that? I've told you all this." A heavy sigh came from Nisaba, who then continued, "Pay attention, girl. We'll be attending the royal feast that follows the public feast, and then a performance of singing and dancing by the best performers of both temples in the evening, each event smaller than the last, more and more selective in who gets to attend. After the performances, the High Priests and Priestesses will escort your sister and *Ensi* to the bedchamber." Nisaba paused, looking up toward the ceiling as she recalled her own wedding, and finally announced with fervor, "Great An, how I enjoyed my wedding."

Sherida took all this explanation in, but asked, "When will you and I go home, Mother?"

"You'll go after the performances. I'll come later. I'll prepare your sister for her wedding night."

"Will you be the one to show the Virgin Cloth?"

"Of course. And in due time," she said with a pointed look at Sherida, an edge to her tone, "I'll be showing yours, after you marry." No one betrayed any question about Ninegala's virginity; the matter would be handled.

* ● *

Enlil-Bani expressed a brief laugh, then said to Zid-tara, "You've many more important things to arrange, I'm sure. Send me a steward you trust to help me with dressing. I'm not a prize onager being fitted with a new harness; the gods will still know it's me. Kulla shaved me yesterday and the fine robes and sandals will make me look just splendid to the people." Enlil-Bani watched from his chair in this, the royal wardrobe room, as the last of the stewards left the room after arranging his clothes on their benches and tables.

The Chief Steward had offered to stay until it was time for the king's exit from the palace with his bride, to join the procession into the square for the proxy blessing of Enmul and the High Priestess of Inana's temple. The Goddess effigies would already have been carried down from the temples on the zigurrat and brought to where the palace front door would be visible. "I'm looking forward to your marriage with as much joy as if it were my own, *Ensi*. It will give the people of Isin a sense that your reign is favored by heaven and is permanent. Next, they'll be expecting an heir to the throne. It's as it should be; the gods so chose."

The king turned his head away, but said nonchalantly, "Not in a hurry, I hope. I've not fathered a child for fifteen years, and Ninegala's very young." He looked again at the robe and stole he was to wear for the wedding ritual and, changing the subject, made a point of sounding enthusiastic about the garments, saying, "You and your staff have done a remarkable job designing this costume ... No, I'm told the word is 'vestment.' This narrow stole: so ornate with the jewels and fine sewing over the light robe." He chuckled to himself, and included Zid-tara in the joke, saying, "Didn't need the word 'vestment' when I was plucking bugs off the underside of plants in the temple's truck garden."

"Are you sure you don't want me to stay, *Ensi*? There are always matters that can use my attention, and I want to be in attendance at your wedding, to see it for myself."

"Certain, Chief Steward. I'll relish some time alone to prepare myself for the blessings by the priests; I've been told they'll be lengthy. That's why I'm so thankful for the robe being so light, with only the lowest row being made of the linen feather strand. When I worked in the fields I could be bare-chested, but not today!" He added as Zid-tara left, "Please send in the guard."

The king was joined by an older guard within moments, who was instructed to admit Enmerkar, Nani and Suba as soon as they arrived at the palace. En-me was already in the kitchen area of the palace, tending to a slave who had suffered a severe burn while removing hot coals from the bread oven in the courtyard.

———— • ● • ————

The top of the zigurrat would have been impossible to see from below, as the sun was directly overhead. This had been anticipated by the priests, so the start of the procession of the goddesses' icons from the temples was signaled by the steady, rhythmic clangs of a newly made brass gong at the top, five evenly spaced strikes.

The market square below was filled to the edges of the permanent stalls (now shuttered) with thousands of citizens of Isin. All wore their finest clothes and there was a collective admonition to hush as the combined male and female choruses of the two temples began a traditional hymn of praise to Utu, the sun god, even though he was the protector god of Larsa. Everyone knew the next hymn would be in praise of the moon, for Inana. The people quickly stopped their observations, speculations and gossiping even in mid-sentence, as soon as the hymns commenced; everyone knew the gods were watching; they turned their attention to the steep course of steps built into the sides of the zigurrat. Even shielding their eyes, it was difficult to see the procession descending the steps from the upper levels.

With the two Chief Priests of the temples in the lead, the platforms on which the icons sat were each borne by eight young priests; for the preceding ten days, early morning and late evening, they had practiced the process of keeping each portable stage level and steady despite the severe angle the stairs presented. The two holding the stage at the rear walked close to each other, bent over at the waist and grasping the frame at a level just below their knees, their priestly garments gathered and tied tightly at their waists to prevent them from tripping; the next two on the sides maintained holds at their hips, the next pair even with their chests, and those at the front bore the stage on their shoulders. The practice runs had been made with a replica of the goddesses' effigies, similar in height and weight. It was unthinkable that the goddesses' representation would be subjected to the possibility of falling off the stage and tumbling down the steps or even off the side.

While Ninisina's dais was draped in white linen with purple streamers cascading off the front corners, the rear streamers were piled on the dais until they had reached level ground at the bottom of the stairs. The goddess was carved of pink marble half the size of a human, and like most god and goddess effigies, she had rudimentary features of a human face with large luminous eyes made of goat's-milk-white ivory with ebony irises.

Inana's, the second in the procession, had four small brass braziers at the corners of the platform wafting trails of sage and thyme smoke into the midday air, both sweet and acrid. The smoke wafted past the inert nostrils of four painted wooden owls that stood at each corner of the platform, representing nighttime. Inana's effigy was carved from dark diorite, and her eyes were formed from pink-toned mother-of-pearl, set into sockets carved into the stone and held in place with a coat of bitumen mixed with pine pitch. The irises were made of shiny black obsidian.

Both representations of their respective goddesses were ornately dressed in new garments and adorned with gold and silver settings for amber, lapis, onyx, and jasper.

Nani and Suba were seated on the zigurrat side of the raised area in front of the palace; Nani held her infant daughter Gibil on her lap, while Nintud, just beginning to show her pregnant state, sat next to her holding Zambiya's son, Indur, who was observing the proceedings with solemnity as if he understood all. Enlil-Bani's family members consisted of only Nani's family plus Enmerkar and En-me. Also seated with them were the twin student girls, Ninlil and Ninmul, as their brothers, captains in the army, had been recalled from their outposts to participate as senior attendants to the king. Muda, true to his bodyguard role, would be dressed in resplendent finery in the royal procession from the palace, but his weapons would be quite functional.

The families of the bride and groom were seated across from each other across an open space a few yards in front of the palace doors, shaded under heavy white protective canopies. Dignitaries from Larsa, Uruk and Ur to the South and Dilbat, Nippur and Kish to the North comprised the next group, on Enlil-Bani's side. The canopies were held up by smoothed pine poles as high as the palace's archers' balcony; the poles were held upright in dense cone-shaped clay stands, painted ochre yellow with dark maroon tiles embedded in them.

Nisaba was in her glory; she had many relatives who had come into Isin for the occasion from their properties outside the walls. Sherida sat next to her under the strictest admonitions to behave. "After all, daughter," her mother had said that morning, "today you'll be seen by many men, all ages, and they won't all be artisans and priests. This may be the time when you'll be seen by your husband-to-be." 'Rida shrugged and scowled in response, but that germ of a thought grew, and she paid special attention to her clothes and adornments.

Nisaba leaned over to her daughter as they waited for the ceremony to reach their level and whispered, "I'm so sorry that Aga's not here to attend your sister's wedding; he'd have loved it."

Sherida recoiled instantly, sitting forward with her eyes wide; it took all her self-control to keep her voice low as she looked at Nisaba and retorted with vehemence, "Aga hated Enlil-Bani! He would have done something to embarrass us all. Really, Mother!" She sat back, conscious of having to slow her breathing, unaware of her mother's struggle to reconcile the difference in perspective Sherida had declared.

Seated on her other side, Nabi, who had received permission to sit with the bride's family, although in his guard uniform, couldn't hear the exchange but became aware of Nisaba's stiffening torso, and leaned toward her to ask, "Is anything wrong, Lady? Are you not well?"

He was surprised when Nisaba turned toward him with tears in her eyes and flowing down her cheeks, but she laid her hand on his arm and said only, "This is all so beautiful. Just beautiful."

The hymn to the sun god, Utu, had concluded with a set of three performances featuring just percussion instruments, ascending in volume, starting just with cymbals, then larger gongs, then small drums and climaxing with an extended barrage with the large drums. At the conclusion of the crescendo, all the female priestesses burst forth with a combined ululation of praise, which ended with near complete silence in the square.

By this time the litters bearing the goddesses effigies had arrived at the bottom of the zigurrat steps; as the banners were unfurled at the corners and standing decorations of newly commissioned orants were sat upright on the litters with the goddesses, the Chief Priests signaled for the next part of the ceremony.

This was the cue for Ninmah to step forward from the mass of priestess singers and start a hymn to Ninisina in her clear, trained voice. Dressed like the other priestesses, her eminence as master singer was distinguished by a tiara that sat upon her luminous black hair; it was dazzling gold studded with lapis cabochons. After her first solo verse ended, the rest of the female choruses joined in the hymn as Ninmah resumed her place, all accompanied by lutes, pipes and tinkling bells. As Ninisina was the patron goddess of Isin and this was a familiar hymn, hundreds of the spectators, both men and women, were able to hum the tune in unison with the chorus, evoking a swelling sense of religious as well as civic fervor.

Now the procession with the goddesses had arrived where the marriage ritual would be performed; the new double palace doors with their polished bronze plates were opened wide, held in place by guards in their most impressive uniforms, shining with waxed leather and polished bronze trappings.

Holding hands, Enlil-Bani and Ninegala walked forward slowly between the family spectators, to the accompaniment of a traditional tune sung in alternating stanzas by the male and then the female choruses. The males were accompanied by drums and cymbals; the females by lutes and pipes. The lyrics entreated benevolent treatment and fecundity by the gods, promising dutiful gifts and observances by the betrothed couple. The bride and groom were flanked by the late General Ashgi's sons, signaling the support of the city's army, along with the ranking palace guards.

As soon as the King and his prospective bride had emerged all those who had been seated rose; the couple arrived just three long strides shy of reaching the two Chief Priests who were waiting for the marriage song to end, which was moments later. The King stopped short, waving the attendant entourage away. Before Ninisina's priest could begin intoning the opening monologue of the ritual, more praise and glory for the great gods and especially the two in attendance, Enlil-Bani turned to stand in front of Ninegala and quietly ask her, "Young one, I need to know if you are still willing to enter this marriage under the terms I expressed earlier." Still holding her left hand in his right, he waved at the immense crowd with his other hand and assured her, "I am the *Ensi*, and I can stop this now if you don't want to marry me."

Ninegala squeezed his hand and smiled up at him, saying in a low tone, "You're a puzzling man, *Ensi*. There were many times I thought of killing myself before you made your offer. I've talked with Tikal's wife and my mother, and they have sworn you are true to your word. I'll be honored to be your ceremonial wife, to become friends with your daughter and sons, and be a companion to you. That's what you want, and I can do all that with pleasure." She looked out over the throng, then at the goddesses on their platforms and the priests, and said simply, "Lead on, husband."

CHAPTER SIXTEEN

UNFAMILIAR FRUIT

*All of life is a series of exchanges: health for illness,
one partner for another, sex for advantage, worship for
loyalty, and grain for everything. Do the gods indulge in
these petty bargains?*

The Director of Trade and Exchanges for *Manjadar* waved his staff of office toward a round alabaster bowl, indicating where Neti was to deposit the three silver discs to be paid as tribute for the privilege of trading within the city for a half-of-a-moon's cycle. The rod was the length of a woman's arm overlaid with finely hammered gold foil its entire length, a silver ax blade on the upper end. The Director was short, verging on corpulent, and had a severely pock-marked face, evident despite his long hair and beard. He wore a plain white cotton garment cinched around his waist with a sash of dark maroon; the cloth covered the legs separately and was tied around his ankles. He wore an upper garment that allowed his right hand to be free; the staff was held in his left hand. A heavy silver link chain supported a seal at the level of his breastbone; the seal was made of a stone with carved stylized men along the bottom row. Markings in an unusual script or style surrounded the figure of a unicorn in the center. The carvings were all set off from the alabaster color of the stone by red ochre stain. His right hand sported a large carnelian and silver ring on his thumb.

"Shalamu, men of Isin." His voice caused Zambiya almost to cringe, spoken loudly in a higher register, like a woman, speaking the language of *ki-en-gir* clearly, though slowly.

"We are honored to have such notables in our city; the son of your king, the son of your Chief Advisor, the nephew of one our own eminent artisans." The Director pointed his staff at Zambiya, Neti and Rangu as he recognized each man. "Most cities from your land just send us ordinary traders, coarse men with the manners of goats, and smelling as bad." He chortled to himself, an unpleasant inhaling nasal sound like gas escaping from a wine bladder whose contents had turned.

This was Neti's domain, and he intended to comport himself with distinction, so he stepped forward to extend his upturned hand toward the Director, who responded in the same manner; both placed a hand on the other's chest and bowed slightly.

"And we are honored to have been received so quickly by Your Eminence. Allow me to compliment you on your mastery of our language. Let me assure you and your city that we will conduct our trading with the utmost honesty. We expect to employ only the most cultured of traders in the future, so that your fine sensibilities will not suffer any offense." There was, of course, no such expectation on Neti's part, nor was it expected, merely badinage to demonstrate to each other that they were sophisticated men.

"I will put you in contact with a variety of tradesmen," the Director responded, "not me, personally, but my deputies will do so. You only need tell them what kind of goods you want to acquire, and of what quality, and the trades will be arranged. There is, naturally, a portion paid to my city by both parties to every exchange. Were you made aware?"

Rangu spoke up in his native tongue assuring the Director that all was understood. The Director smiled at him, replying in the same language, "Please give my good wishes to your aunt; you may not know that her husband's first wife was my sister, so my niece, his first daughter, is your cousin."

Rangu smiled in return and said, "I am honored to be related to Your Eminence. I will serve all parties with honesty."

Returning to the language of Isin and Larsa, the Director said, "I will send for the deputies who will assist you in just a little time, so that you can begin meeting with traders." He spread his short arms wide and added, "This evening I would like to invite you to join me for dinner. I'll ask my wife to prepare a meal that will make you want to return here to conduct the trades yourselves. I will also invite my youngest sister, who is an eminent trader in her own right, a bright woman and if I can say so, the equal of any man in the conduct of business." He hesitated a moment before adding, "She's been a widow for over a year now; her husband was an older man, also a trader. He died very suddenly. The gods must have wanted him right then."

Rangu was mindful of the possibilities for violating the protocols of his culture, being of inferior status despite his distant relationship to the Director, but didn't want to leave Zambiya or Neti at a disadvantage without an interpreter being present, so he inquired, "Does my esteemed relative wish me to attend as well? And would his wife desire the same?"

"Of course, young man." Returning to their shared tongue, he added, "Be sure to bring a gift for my daughter; it's expected."

Bowing in response, Rangu said, "Many thanks for your offer of hospitality, and your thoughtful suggestion."

The Director indicated a sumptuous rug on the far side of the room and said, "Sit there. I'll send two…"

A raucous shriek interrupted the Director's invitation, and the visitors all started, looking about for the origin of the sound, while the Director's brow furrowed and his eyelids narrowed.

"Nothing to be concerned…" he started to say.

The sound came again and despite the mud-brick walls, at least two courses thick, it was distinct. It immediately called to Zambiya's mind the execution of his mother's murderers; his shoulders involuntarily hunched.

"Are criminals tortured in this building, Director?" Zambiya tried to keep his tone even and inquisitive, not accusative, but edged himself toward the broad, drapery covered doorway as it seemed to him that the screech had come from that direction and might portend an attack.

"My sincere apologies for the interruption, honored ones." Again, the shrill emanation resounded. The Director suddenly smiled and held his palms upward at shoulder height in an attitude of harmlessness and said with a chuckle, "It's just my sister's bird. Perhaps you'd like to see it; you can meet them both now, before tonight's feast." He led the way into the passageway, beckoning them to follow, and walked deeper into the interior of the building, followed closely by all three men. They passed two doorways on the right of the passage before he motioned them to wait as he pushed aside another heavy unadorned dark drape covering the doorway and entered.

"Sister, can you greet some guests and show them your creature?" He spoke in Isin's language.

The answer was almost instant, as a husky but feminine voice responded in the same tongue, "Now, brother? Ah…..Who're these guests?"

"Dignitaries from Isin, come to conduct initial trading ventures with more hoped for in the future."

"Amabad's eating, so she'll be quiet for a while. Yes, brother, I'll show them the bird in a moment. I need to put on a shawl first."

The Director stepped back into the hall and held up his hand in a gesture of temporary delay; a few moments later, the voice of the woman inside offered, "They may enter now, brother, but quietly. I don't want Amabad disturbed while he eats; Ah … if he gets upset, he yells more than usual."

The Director held the drape aside to allow his guests to enter then followed them into the room.

The woman who greeted them had not seen twenty-five summers. Her dark flowing hair was captured by a slender gold chain encircling her head. She had deep brown eyes and her full lips seemed to be close to smiling as she greeted the men. Her shawl was nothing more than a length of fine cotton that covered her slender, muscular shoulders and barely concealed her upright breasts. Neti in particular was enthralled by the graceful fluidity of her movements as she invited them to accompany her to the adjoining room where several wall torches illuminated the space.

The bird in question moved along a rough perch affixed to a roughly made table; it was busy sorting through an assortment of grain kernels embedded in a piece of cut melon, green in color. Its movements were quick and jerky as it alternately seized a morsel with its loquat-colored hooked beak, and it peered at the intruders before continuing its meal, like a thief in fear of being caught. A brilliant red smooth head contrasted with its body, the light green of a ripe mango from the neck to a sky blue tail nearly as long as its body; lime green wings with a small red patch in the middle rose and relaxed as it moved along the perch next to the melon.

Any doubts as to the origin of the sound that had aroused their interest were dispelled immediately when Amabad spread its wings and let out a squawk that seemed amplified by proximity.

"His mate died several nights ago," volunteered the woman. "I went to feed them in the morning and the female was dead on the bottom of the cage." She pointed at the tall prison mounted on a table in a corner of the room, a lattice rising to a pointed gathering and constructed of sturdy reeds lashed together with leather bindings, close to the size of an oxcart's floor, with a door made of leather.

"Esteemed sister, permit me to present Zambiya, son of the *Ensi* of Isin," the Director indicated with his staff, "and Neti, his Chief Counselor's son, and this young man, son of our most able bead maker, whose name is Rangu." Each man bowed and smiled as he was introduced. "My sister's name is Ila," he declared. She smiled and bowed in return. Though she looked at her visitors with a forwardness that bespoke authority and privilege, her gaze frankly lingered on Neti, scanning him from face to knees.

Neti seized this opportunity to offer a proposal. "Your esteemed brother has told us you are blessed with considerable talent as a trader. Perhaps you would do us the honor of advising us on the quality of the goods we are contemplating—for a fee, of course."

Ila studied Neti's eyes as he spoke; she was easily able to discern his fascination with her beyond the area of commerce and indulged in an appreciative appraisal of her own as she approached him and placed her hand on his forearm. Smiling directly at him, she said, "I'd be very interested in discussing the matter with you. Perhaps after tonight's dinner." Turning to her brother while brushing Neti's bare arm with her own as if by accident, she inquired, "Ah...Don't we have quarters here where these worthies can stay during their time here?" She knew, of course, that they did.

Zambiya registered his own attraction to the sister, a feeling he had not known since Ezina's death, but he could feel the energy flowing between Ila and Neti. Nevertheless, he spoke up at once, saying, "We must return to our boats so that our Captain will know that all is well."

Neti, in an unusually husky voice as he looked into Ila's eyes, offered, "Couldn't you - uh - do that without me, Zambiya? After dinner, of course."

Rangu and Zambiya traded wary looks, but Rangu offered, "I'll be staying with my aunt's family, so I won't be spending the night here. I can return to the boats, tell Ansar and the captain what's happening, then return here for dinner. Will that be suitable?"

"Director," said Zambiya after briefly considering Rangu's suggestion, "You planned on introducing us to some of your subordinates before we were introduced to Ila and," bowing toward the sister with a smile, "your bird." Gesturing to Neti and Rangu to accompany him as he moved toward the hall, he said to the Director, "If they speak our language, perhaps we can meet them now while Rangu returns to the boats."

"Excellent," responded the Director. "They speak your language well."

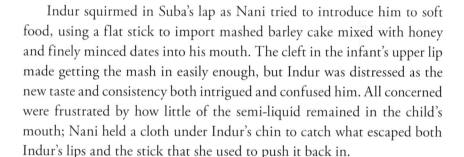

Indur squirmed in Suba's lap as Nani tried to introduce him to soft food, using a flat stick to import mashed barley cake mixed with honey and finely minced dates into his mouth. The cleft in the infant's upper lip made getting the mash in easily enough, but Indur was distressed as the new taste and consistency both intrigued and confused him. All concerned were frustrated by how little of the semi-liquid remained in the child's mouth; Nani held a cloth under Indur's chin to catch what escaped both Indur's lips and the stick that she used to push it back in.

"I'd like to do this more; he can't suckle at the breast til he's an adult, and I can't feed him this way without help." Nani's voice betrayed her frustration, and she frowned as the porridge oozed between the cleft and over the lower lip again.

"You're right, but I can only be here in the evening. I have to be in the shop too early to help in the morning; father is getting more and more frail by the day, and may have to stop altogether." His voice kept an incipient sob hidden within his recognition of his father's declining health, but he continued. "We could buy a slave, I suppose, but…"

Nani interrupted by saying, "No slave. If it's a man, I'd be here all day with him and unless he's ancient, it wouldn't be proper. And probably no help anyway." Her frown deepened.

"No, my dear wife. Of course not. I meant a woman; someone like Nintud. Before she married Muda, she was a real help to you."

Then Indur started choking and the discussion stopped while Suba leaned Zambiya's son forward to help get the substance to run back out of his mouth and onto the cloth Nani held. Indur commenced to wail as soon as he could breathe again, tears squeezing out from his tight-shut eyes. Suba picked him up and held him against his chest, patting his back as the crying subsided.

"Maybe an older woman." Nani reached around her husband's shoulder and cleaned off the child's mouth, then abruptly picked up the dish holding the porridge and stood, surmising, "Might be good. You're right! Nintud was such a help. I'll bring it up with Enmerkar; he has so many contacts due to his student's parents that he may know of a suitable one." She looked back as her husband gently rocked Indur while the twilight shadows deepened on the courtyard where they had been sitting. Another thought intruded into her mind and she added to herself, 'Not too young.'

———————— • • • ————————

Dinner in the Director's home quarters ended and the polite thanks and compliments had been easy to render, as the food was delicious. Neti had especially praised the Director's wife's kri, served with lamb and ginger flavored barley. He made a mental note to apologize to Rangu later for his earlier comments on the sauce.

Rangu had already left in the early twilight to return to his Aunt's home, intending to return early the next morning for the conduct of business. The gift he had brought for Ila was a finely decorated pair of faience bangles, contributed by his Uncle; the work was exceptional and her thanks profuse.

Zambiya and the Director left the room to discuss the schedule for the next day, leaving Neti and Ila seated across from each other while the servants cleared the room of the leavings. Now alone, they continued sipping a thick mango drink garnished with flowers of the 'sleeping' hibiscus draped over the edge of plain earthenware cups, the dark pink petals forming a slender cup-like form with the stigma protruding from the opening; the sexual symbolism was subtle, but not lost on either Neti or gone unobserved by Zambiya.

Neti was searching his mind for topics of small talk, as neither had spoken for several moments; looking around the room, he settled his gaze on a glazed painted bowl the size of a large melon, with representations of various animals all around the outer surface.

Pointing at the bowl, he asked, "What is that creature with the humped back? Is it real or like the unicorn signs I've seen at the gate?"

"Ah, it's real; many of our cattle have such humps on their backs, the bulls more than the cows. Didn't you see any on your passage up river?"

"No. And we came straight to *Manjadar* on the river, didn't go into the countryside at all." He took another drink, at which point the garnish flower fell out of the cup onto his lap. Frowning, he tried resting it back on the rim of the cup without success, but was surprised to see Ila rise from her cushion in one fluid motion and come to his side. He was aware of a pleasing scent like ginger and flowers as she knelt to his right, facing him.

She took the flower and said, "These are delicate in taste, but quite edible." Holding the stem between her thumb and forefinger, she placed the blossom between her lips resting on her tongue, holding it in place several moments before pulling it inside her mouth and swallowing.

Neti felt heat rising in his body, but he willed himself to breathe slowly and attempted to relax; Ila's nearness vanquished his resolve, however.

"I'm done with this drink," he said quickly, hearing his own voice as strangely husky, his mouth dry. Despite what he'd just said, he took another large swallow.

Ila let out an exclamation, at once a triumphant laugh wrapped in a sigh, and said, "I'd like to show you one of the features of our home. Despite all the heavy walls that surround us here, we're not closed in. Come with me and I'll show you." She stood up, again as though lifted from above there was so little obvious effort, and offered her hand.

Neti accepted her offer and rose, placing the cup on the worn carpet to the side of the cushion, aware of how anxious he was to touch her and inhale the fragrance of her skin. "I'd be pleased to see whatever you'd like to show me, Ila." He felt bold by addressing her by name. "But won't your brother and Zambiya be expecting us to join them?" he asked as she led the way from the dining area and toward the inner part of the building.

"Ah, no. The Director plans to suggest a longer term to our trading. We've discussed the possibility of sending one of our traders back to *Ki-en-gir* with you when you return, to suggest goods that've not been part of our trading before. Ah, but let's save that for another time." She placed one hand on Neti's bare chest just above his tunic and added, "I expect to know you better while you're here. Come, let me show you *Manjadar* at night."

— ● —

"It was Muda."

After Nisaba returned home from the palace where she had spent the night, late in the morning Nisaba and Sherida sat alone in the mother's bedroom. Sherida was filled with curiosity about how the priests could have been convinced that Ninegala was a virgin.

"I showed them the bridecloth after a suitable time had gone by. Enlil-Bani and Ninegala had been alone a while, and that was that. Thank the gods."

"What do you mean, it was Muda? I've heard that sometimes there's a dead hare or fowl killed to substitute for the bride's blood, but that would have been hard to arrange in the palace."

Nisaba waved her hand in the air, dismissing the matter as unimportant now, but leaned forward and re-positioned a lock of her daughter's hair before explaining in a low voice, "Muda and I were in a room next to the bedrooms, with the priests and one priestess waiting in the corridor to the royal quarters. I had brought the bridecloth with me when I left the bedroom, so it was not difficult. Muda always attends the *Ensi*, so he was expected to remain until he was dismissed. He cut open a part of his palm and let the blood flow onto the cloth a short time, then held the skin closed with the cloth until the bleeding almost stopped."

"Well, now it's done and she's married." Sherida stood up from the low bench with its many stuffed cushions and bolsters where they had both been sitting, then stepped onto it and sat back down with her legs curled under her, facing her mother directly. "Still," she said with a sigh, "I'm no closer to finding a husband." She kept her voice low, glancing toward the doorway and listening for the sound of any attendant who might be close. Trying to sound nonchalant, she asked, "Mother, did you happen to notice the young army officer seated next to Enmerkar at the banquet? Never seen him before."

Nisaba looked up at the ceiling as she searched her memory of the event, then said brightly, "Oh, yes. Didn't he look handsome in his uniform? I know who he is, but I don't know his name. He's just back from a remote border post along the *Idiglat*. His father died during the plague, when he was our emissary to Larsa. You should remember General Ashgi; he came to the palace sometimes when your father was alive. *Ensi* recalled him and his older brother to Isin. The brother's been ill for some time; he wasn't there last evening." She looked closely at Sherida, who was watching her intently as she listened to the description offered by her mother.

"Isn't he married, mother? I didn't see a woman with him."

"No, neither's married. Oh! I recall. Their twin sisters are student scribes who live at Enmerkar's *edubba*. Maybe that's why he was seated nearby." She thought a moment before adding, "The twins had a different mother."

"He's a general's son; is he rich?"

"Why do you care, girl?" Frowning, Nisaba looked at her daughter, then brightened and said, "If your interest is what I suspect, I'd be thrilled, no, ecstatic, to arrange for him to be invited to dinner here."

Sherida squirmed on her seat, then blushed and covered her face with her hands.

Ila stood very close to Neti as she pointed out the docks from the upper balcony of the building, saying, "Even in my lifetime there is less activity here. My grandfather told me that the lights from the ships and barges at night were so many that it was hard to see the stars near the horizon, even very late. Now, a dozen trading vessels means a busy time for traders." She hesitated before adding, "Many of the foreign traders like doing business with me, though. They imagine that they can make better trades with a woman, so I do better than many older, more experienced traders in *Manjadar*."

Unable to ignore Ila's proximity and the alluring scent that seemed to surround her, Neti nevertheless endeavored to maintain a professional level of conversation.

"What's that complex over there?" He pointed to a set of flat buildings just within the city walls with what appeared to be wider passageways; a series of torches were being lit as the twilight settled in and darkness was nigh.

"That's the artisan quarter. Rangu's family lives in there, along with many other fine craftsmen. Some of the gold and silver workers live in that area, and the metals and jewelry they work are very valuable. It's a rich section, and we keep guards in the public roadways day and night."

She turned to face him more directly, lightly brushing his knee with hers as she did so.

"Ah, why don't we go in, then I won't have to light a torch out here. I'll show you where you can bathe to clean off the dirt of the day." Ila stroked his shoulder with the back of her hand, then turned and led the way toward the stairs leading back to the lower level before she casually remarked, "You must miss your wife."

"Oh, I'm not married." Neti considered how much to volunteer before he divulged, "I'm being groomed by my father to be the next Chief Counselor to our *Ensi*. That's one of the reasons I'm on this journey; he wants me to be comfortable with people from other lands."

"Perhaps you've a favorite slave to keep you warm at night," she said playfully.

"There're men who do that. I'm not one of them. I intend to marry well; it's expected of me." Neti was starting to become uncomfortable with Ila's personal questioning but couldn't keep himself from watching the swaying motion of her hips as she led the way.

A smile played across Ila's face and her eyes narrowed. Torches had already been lit in the hallways as she led Neti past the dining area, then descended another torch lit set of stairs set at a severe angle to the main passage, then to another hallway, cooler and damper than the upper suite.

"I didn't realize there was a lower part of the building," Neti stated, happy to change the subject, though he looked around with some apprehension, listening for potential dangers. Nevertheless, he followed Ila closely as she proceeded toward an opening at the far end of the short, narrow hallway.

"Have you ever been in a bathing room like this?" Ila asked as she led him into the room.

The brick walls were unadorned and ordinary, but to Neti the space was unique. A set of three steps led into a shallow pool already half-filled with water. The size of a large oxcart, the floor sloped toward a square shaped sluice drain, three bricks wide on all sides, closed off by an upright flat stone. Benches of fired brick lined the walls on the far side and on the left. The floor of the pool was also made of fire-hardened bricks the color of a bull's hide, gray tending to brown. Only one torch lit the space, a small one in a sconce at shoulder height on the wall next to the entry portal. The walls were vaulted and disappeared into the darkness above as deep as a moonless sky. Neti could see several more sconces by the door, at varying heights. The sound of water trickling out of the sluice was noticeable in the small space, since there was not a complete seal.

"This is amazing, Ila. Do other buildings have these?"

"Ah, some do, but there's also a large public bath built into a space near the barrier wall, set back from the main gate."

She clapped her hands sharply, and was shortly joined by two female attendants, thick waisted and buxom. Wearing only veils and cinnamon hued skirts that ended at mid-thigh, each bore a deep copper bucket hoisted on her shoulders.

"I'll leave these women to serve you. They don't know your tongue, but they know what to do. Take off your clothing and stand in the pool. They'll take turns pouring water and washing you." She pointed toward a wooden rack with several fabric and light leather sheets hanging from it.

Neti's amazement was clear, and he started to stammer in protest, but Ila said, "Trust me, you'll enjoy it. I'll be back later." She turned and left the bath; Neti could hear a low chuckle as her footsteps receded toward the stairs.

His thoughts raced as he contemplated the women, who were in turn waiting and watching him. Once he had decided to follow Ila's instructions, a thought intruded into his mind. He wondered whether the gods of *ki-en-gir* knew what he was doing at this moment; could they be aware this far away? Were the local gods watching? Did any of the gods care what he did? Would his father have an opinion? Then he dismissed these thoughts and gave in to the experience of being bathed, something he'd not experienced since childhood.

He quickly disrobed. Placing his garments in a pile on his sandals next to the entrance to the bath, he stepped hesitantly into the pool, surprised to find the water already warm and deep enough to nearly reach his knees, above the level of the bottom step. He turned his back on the attendants after his manhood started to stiffen unbidden, raising his arms in a signal to pour the water over him. He expected that cold water would reverse his erection, but one of the women stepped into the pool at his side. The water coursing over his head and down his shoulders and torso was warmer than he was. He blinked and cleared his eyes with his hands, but then felt the woman rubbing him with a wet cloth, downward from the nape of his neck and over his shoulders, methodically swabbing and stroking first his arm then his hand, washing each finger. More water.

She then moved to the other side and repeated gentle attention to the other arm and hand. After more water was applied, Neti became aware that it was scented with an aroma that reminded him of his family's home chapel. The attending woman continued, applying the cloth in a swirling motion across his back, down the shoulder blades and then to the small of his back. More water.

The first attendant stepped out of the pool and was immediately replaced by the second who wrung the cloth out, saturated it in the kettle again, then stroked the muscles of his chest and under his arms, working her way toward his abdomen. She said something in their language to her companion, who giggled quietly. Neti's erection was hard as a sword handle, and his legs began to quiver. He tried to distract himself by looking around, and noticed an object on the far bench, carved from ivory to resemble an erect penis. More water.

Now the first woman joined her companion in the pool, half filled the basin with water from the pool and poured it over his neck, down his torso, and the two of them worked together to rub his legs from thigh to ankle, passing by his genitals.

Neti started with surprise when he heard Ila's voice behind him, asking a question in her own tongue, he surmised from the rise in inflection in her voice. The second attendant responded in their language. He covered his member with his hands and turned around to find her standing just inside the doorway.

She was wearing a sheer sleeveless plum colored garment with loose narrow straps that fell from her neck and covered her breasts, not quite concealing her erect nipples. The straps joined together just below her waist and covered her pubic area, ending below her knees. A thin belt of plaited dark leather circled her waist, tied with one loose knot, but her sides and thighs were uncovered, emphasizing her slender waist and broad hips. She spoke again to the attendants, who responded by moving to the far side of the pool and sitting on the bench.

Ila stepped into the pool and moved decisively to Neti, saying, "Ah, you've a fine body. I expected as much." She made a slow caressing stroke down his arms to the wrists, and then untied the belt holding her dress together and dropped it into the water. Her garment parted in the middle and she shrugged it off her shoulders in a practiced manner, letting it slide into the pool. She then guided his hands up to her breasts. She slid both her hands down his abdomen, slowly, then cupped his sack firmly as she reached up to pull his face to hers and kissed him, her lips parted with invitation and ardor.

CHAPTER SEVENTEEN

SEED AND SICKLE

The gods remind us time after time that all our possessions are temporary, as are our friends, our relations, and even our lives.

"I won't call you 'Slave.'" Nani spoke firmly; she and Suba each held an infant on their laps. "If you don't want to be called by your former married name, that's fine. I understand that, in fact. But you're a person." It was early in the morning and they all sat in the entry room to their home, with En-me seated nearby watching the woman who'd been purchased at auction to serve as companions to the twin scribe students, on his suggestion. A new arrangement had occurred to him after learning that Nani was considering having a slave live with them to help with the children.

The woman sat on a backless stool that had been brought in for the interview. She had shown little enthusiasm for joining a family when the prospect was broached at Enmerkar's *edubba*, and the early questioning about her background evinced little emotional contact beyond a general feeling of abandonment and betrayal, but now she looked from one baby to the other, her maternal hunger rising in her body as a need as strong as if food was presented after a famine. She glanced at Nani and stated, "I don't care what you call me. Please, could I hold one of them?"

An obvious test in everyone's mind, Suba offered Indur, who had started to squirm, and was also drooling from his incomplete lips. The woman eagerly stood up and came forward to lift Indur up under the armpits, then settled back onto her seat and wiped his mouth with the sleeve of her dress. Looking into his eyes, she cooed at him and stroked his head, a smile now playing on her lips, changing her face from dour and plain to almost attractive, a transformation not lost on Nani.

At that moment Bibi the cat entered the room and let out a loud meow, looking around with curiosity, then walked over to rub against the new woman's legs. The slave reached down with one hand to stroke Bibi's fur from head to tail, then said to En-me, "I had a cat before I was divorced." Her smile staying in place, she added, "Aren't they mysterious creatures? My neighbor believed that cats are spies for the gods, so she wouldn't speak in front of mine." She stroked Bibi a second time before returning to attending to Indur. "I think he could use a change," the woman stated as she held Indur up to her shoulder, sniffing his backside. "Could I do it, Lady?" she asked, looking directly at Nani, seeming to understand that Nani was the one who would require convincing and had veto power.

"Come with me and I'll show you where we keep the things for changing them." The woman followed Nani toward the back of the house, where one of the rooms, formerly Nintud's bedroom, was being used both as a nursery and for storing weaving material. Nani stood back and watched from the portal. The woman knelt on the woven floor covering, and after cleaning the boy with old cloths she put a layer of oil on his skin, then a fresh loincloth with absorbent cattail material strategically placed.

Meanwhile Nani was conducting an appraisal of her own, focused on how this woman would fit into her household with one question in mind: would she be a competitor for Suba's attention? Clearly older - wrinkles around her eyes - down-turned mouth - narrow hips – flat bosom. All these criteria she assessed unconsciously, except for age.

The woman finished changing Indur and stood up, tenderly hoisting him and holding him against her bosom.

Her decision made, Nani announced, "We won't have you branded. I know it's common, but that's for permanent slaves. We once had a slave who's now *Ensi's* bodyguard. They had to burn the brand off his arm." She made a sweeping motion around the room and said, "This will be your room now, and your bed. We'll need to make other arrangements for where to keep the baby supplies. And you need a name."

The woman patted Indur on the back, gently, and said with a tentative smile, "When I thought I'd have children, I wanted to call my daughter Aruru. I like that name. Would you call me that?"

"I think she's a birth goddess, yes?"

"That's what I think, too. I'd like that name." The woman seemed to be experiencing an epiphany, moving her attention outside her own misery, and looked into Nani's eyes for the first time since she had arrived. She sighed with what seemed to express satisfaction rather than resignation, then said, "I've wanted to have children since I was a small girl myself. I want to take care of your children as much as you'll allow." She hesitated before adding, "Since we are away from the men I can make you a promise. Many married women wouldn't want to have a female slave. I won't be a problem to you. I'll keep to myself and do what you tell me; I'm even a good cook. But caring for the children will fill me with joy."

"Let's join the men," Nani said, and let the woman precede her; Nani smiled at Indur who was looking at her from over Aruru's shoulder as they went. As they re-entered the foyer to the home, she announced, "This lady's name is Aruru, and she'll be staying."

Enlil-Bani and Ninegala settled into a routine, with neither making demands on the other, but both serving the ceremonial needs of Isin with a strong sense of duty. Except when Kulla the barber was expected, the king ate his breakfasts early, alone in the shade of the canopy on the deck overlooking the kitchen courtyard, enjoying the birds and the dawning sunlight. Without conscious intent, he watched for changes in the trees below him that would signal the change of seasons. No one expected Ninegala to join him at this hour. When his barber arrived to shave him in his bed chamber, he kept his voice quiet due to the adjoining bedrooms. A hallway the length of a large room both joined and separated their sleeping rooms. Even Sud, who had been Enlil-Bani's dinner companion prior to the wedding but who now served Ninegala, voiced no speculation as to where the newlyweds woke in the morning.

The bride had developed an interest in the occasional need for the king to preside over disputes, and often attended these events. One morning toward the end of eating his breakfast on the rooftop veranda Enlil-Bani told Zid-tara to ask Sud to invite Ninegala to the afternoon's scheduled trial. After he had returned to his room the king's young wife called to him from her adjoining room, asking to be admitted.

"Of course, Queen of Isin," he replied. The term never failed to amuse Ninegala, as much because it irritated her sister when he said it publicly as well as that she was so keenly aware of her age.

She entered his chamber, giggling and arranging a cedar colored shawl of dyed wool over her shoulders and bosom, always careful to be properly clothed, even demure. "What is special about this trial, Oh Nearly God?" She had scanned the room before she uttered their shared joke with one another. Enlil-Bani had disclosed how little prepared he felt to be such a central religious figure during the rites that were both sacred and secular, even confiding that Tikal had begun to suggest that he, the king, consider declaring himself to be a god. This was not uncommon among *Ensis* after they had ruled a while.

"I've only been given the 'plucked duck' version of the dispute, but there is more than land at issue. Land arguments would put a hummingbird to sleep, but this sounds more interesting. I don't want you to abandon me due to boredom, Nina. I've grown to like being with you, and you ask questions that make me consider matters more deeply." He looked around and lowered his voice before adding, "I've had a thought that I know would be considered heretical by the priests. I've wondered if you might have lived before, so that you know things beyond your years and experience. As if you'd died and the gods allowed you to come back."

"Oh, *Ensi*, that wouldn't be me." She frowned and looked away, thinking about the novel idea. Then she said, "I could suspect that of Kusu, though. That's a wise lady. I knew her before we moved out of the palace, of course, but we didn't have much contact. She's been very kind to me, even before the marriage, and treats me like an adult. My mother can't seem to see me as anything but a child."

"I knew you were spending some afternoons with her. If you think she's wise, she probably is. Tikal is, too." He thought a moment before offering, "I think your mother is normal, Nina. I still think of my children much the same way, as if they still needed my advice."

"His mother misses Neti more than Tikal, I think. They only have the one child, and she's said more than once she'd like him to return soon."

"That's natural. Especially with just one. Maybe you're filling in the void in her life. Probably a benefit for both of you."

"Certainly more for me."

"Anyway, I'm glad you'll be observing the dispute with me; I'll have Sud let you know when it's time."

———————•———————

There were now regularly two chairs placed next to each other on the dais of the throne room; a carved and inlaid cedar chair had been commissioned to accommodate Ninegala when she attended public matters. At Tikal's insistence the seat of the queen's chair was a handspan lower than the king's throne.

Enlil-Bani and she entered side by side after all the spectators and participants had been seated in the rows of benches. Tikal stood on the floor, forward and to the side of the royal couple. He directed the proceedings, making sure that the spectators rose when the king and his wife entered and remained standing, bowing until the royal pair was seated.

A guard walked toward the first row of benches and pointed at a man standing at the rear of the throne room close to the broad doorway, motioning him forward. Dressed in a discolored skirt and a patched white tunic, the bearded man approached the throne but stayed a discrete distance away and bowed, remaining in that stance until the king spoke. The guard stood at his side, watching him carefully.

"Tell the *Ensi* why you are here, citizen?" Tikal ordered.

The man looked up and stood almost fully upright, with just the hint of remaining in a bowed position, and responded saying, "My neighbor, that man in back in the dark clothing," he said, pointing to another man standing in the rear of the room, "diverted the canal that waters my field. My crops are parched and I must spend all my day carrying water in jugs so the grain won't die." For emphasis, he stretched his back fully upright before resuming his bow. "We were always on good terms before, but this last spring his oldest son, nineteen years old he is, started watching my daughter, who's only eleven. I told his son to stay away from my farm. Later, he and his sons filled in the opening to my part of the channel. I have no sons, only the one daughter, and I cannot change the canal by myself. I beg you to make him fix this."

The king again motioned to the guard, who pointed at the dark-clothed man in the rear. That man came forward but stood at a distance from his neighbor. Behaving much like the first complainant, he remained bowed until Tikal spoke to him, saying, "Answer his charge. Is that what happened?"

"*Ensi*, I would not lie. What he said is true, but not all that happened. My field is farther from *Buranun* than his, and so has always favored his field, but it wasn't a problem until he enlarged the opening to his field. He must have done that during the winter, so I didn't know it had happened. This planting season it was clear that my field would suffer from lack of water if I did nothing, so I tried to fix it myself, with my sons. Four of them, good boys all. But when we changed the course to give us more water, the whole side collapsed across the entry to his field, hundreds of bushels of dirt. It wasn't my fault, so I left it."

"What about your son?" said the first man, trying to re-focus the discussion on his daughter. "The one who said he wanted to marry my only daughter. She's too young to be thinking of marriage." Then he turned and pointed at his neighbor, saying, "He's dull, and has no prospects anyway. That's really why you ruined the canal on my side," he charged, starting to raise his voice and waving his arms.

"Enough!" Enlil-Bani turned and conferred with Ninegala in low tones while the spectators whispered to one another, then he rose and raised his hand. The spectators hushed immediately. "This matter could have been handled by the Elders Council but we're here now." The king pointed at the man in dark clothing and said, "Grain doesn't grow without water. You and your sons are to fix the canal within five days, even if you have to work at night." Turning to Tikal, the king said, "I want it confirmed." The Chief Counselor nodded in assent.

"Further, your son is not to bother his daughter for two whole seasons; you see to it. Go, both of you."

"Oh, but..." The dark-clothed man started to protest, but the guard who had called him forward stepped in front of him and motioned both landowners to the portal at the back of the throne room. They remained silent, but scowled at each other.

The royal couple stood and then exited through a curtained, guarded doorway behind the thrones; the guards cleared the throne room of spectators before extinguishing the torches that lit the space.

"Thank you, wife," said Enlil-Bani as they followed Muda along the hallway toward the royal quarters. "I would probably have focused all my attention on the watering of the fields, without considering the man's daughter. You provided a woman's point of view." They paid no attention to the guards following them, extinguishing every other torch.

Ninegala smiled with satisfaction and lightly stroked his arm before they separated, entering their individual rooms.

• ● •

"I can make my own decisions, brother!"

Ila stood with both hands on her hips, her chin jutted forward with the fire of defiance in her eyes. A complete moon period had passed since she had seduced Neti, and their mutual passion had blossomed into genuine affection, aided by almost nightly amorous liaisons as well as numerous excursions to examine cloth and precious stones as well as decorated copper goods.

The constant arrangements Ila and Neti made to spend time together sparked consternation in both Zambiya and the Director. Both were concerned that the trading in which Neti and Ila engaged would turn to the advantage of one or the other, but neither could detect that it had done so.

"You can, Ila, but this is ill considered. Neti's father won't permit you to marry him. Think about it." The Director and Ila both went silent while a servant removed the dishes from breakfast. He had chosen this time to speak to her because Neti was at the *Manjadar* wharves with Zambiya, helping to determine where the assorted cargoes would best fit on the barges.

The woman's determination to go to Isin with Neti and set up her own trading business there seemed foolhardy to her brother. He thought with time their ardor would cool, but there was scant evidence for that, just the opposite. Zambiya had been pressing his company to leave within ten to fifteen days, as he was concerned about the likelihood of monsoon weather and trading was nearing its conclusion. They needed only to wait for the delivery of some of the promised mineral ores to be delivered within that time span: lapis lazuli and some especially high quality carnelians of the two ends of their color spectrum, nearly yellow and a rusty red.

Ila turned her back to her brother, contemplating, then turned back to face him again.

"Ah, he'll have to, brother," she declared with resignation. "I've missed my moon blood — due at least ten days ago. I know you don't like to talk about woman things, nor even think about them, but Neti's going to be a father." She felt her abdomen before adding, "And no, he doesn't know yet."

"WHAT?" he shouted, then lowered his voice. He stood up and walked past her to the doorway, stepping into the hall to satisfy himself that no one there.

"I thought I was barren," she confided quietly, nearly whining. Ila held her hands out in a resigned fashion, palms down, and added, "I wanted to be a mother when my husband was alive, but there was never any hint of pregnancy. After I'd been with Neti I'd have used one of the potions other wives use. Ah, and to be truthful, if I'd been calculating a better match, I'd have been more attentive to Zambiya. I only recently gave thought to going to Isin to be a trader there."

Still standing in the doorway, his face displayed the conflicting emotions he felt before the Director offered, "Perhaps the gods have blessed you, sister. This is not a tragedy!" He held his arms out to her to welcome her into his embrace, which she gratefully accepted. As they held each other he added, "Let's not leave this to another's decision, Ila. Marry him. Here! Soon! Then it will be done."

"Ah, what if he won't agree? What if Zambiya objects?"

"I still have power here, and you command great respect. I can make sure it will happen." He returned to his seat and smilingly declared, "Even if you go to Isin, I'll be an uncle."

———————— • ● • ————————

"What will my father say?" Neti sat on a large sealed basket filled with cotton cloth, made from a crop not grown in *ki-en-gir*, one of several stacked or loose on the wharf next to their barges. The evening breeze along the river carried the spicy scents of food mixed with the smoke of the cooking fires in *Manjadar*. His shoulders were slumped forward and he held his chin cupped in his hands, his elbows on his thighs.

Across from him sat both Zambiya and Rangu, the latter present to give advice as to the local attitudes toward a foreigner who had impregnated a local woman. He was determined to present information without any hint of advice, if possible.

"Tikal's not here, and you're an adult. It's your life, and the question you've got to answer is simple. What do you want?" Zambiya was no happier being cast in the role of advisor than Rangu, especially to a man only a few years younger than himself. He turned to Rangu and asked directly, "What is likely to happen if he declines to marry Ila? Does he really have a choice, or are we all in danger if he refuses?"

Rangu hesitated, covered his mouth with his hand, thinking hard about his native culture and how an un-married woman would be treated if she became pregnant and didn't marry, and how the man would be perceived. He formulated his answer carefully before speaking, then lowered his hand and directed his reply to Neti, stating it in a matter-of-fact way, withholding any tone of judgment but offering his thoughts.

"You do have a choice. Not a good one, though. You can offer to pay her to raise your child, and you'd have to leave a substantial part of these goods before you could leave. We'd all be paying, actually, since our cargo isn't yours to give. It isn't even ours, in fact. Or you can still agree to pay for the child but stay here and work to do so." Rangu briefly thought about his fiancé at home in Isin, weighing whether to continue, but felt he needed to do so.

"I have no advice," he added. "But I would ask myself the same question I'm going to ask you. Do you know her well enough to want to spend your life with her? What if she weren't pregnant?"

"Thank you, Rangu." Zambiya clapped his hand onto the *Meluhhan*'s shoulder, adding, "I was going to ask that same question, but you said it better than I could." He ventured another observation he had admitted to himself. "She's an uncommonly attractive woman, but would you really want to marry her?"

Neti rose from his seat and walked to the edge of the quay, looking past the barges that had brought him here and then across the river. He inhaled deeply, actually savoring the aroma of *kri* borne on the breeze from the city.

Back in Isin, as he approached his potter's stall one early summer morning, Nani's husband Suba was greeted by his parents' lone servant, a retainer of many years. The air was already warm even though the shadow of the *zigurrat* shielded the grounds of the market area.

"What is it? Why have you come to the market this early?" Suba asked with foreboding.

The man held a cloth in one hand that he was using to wipe his copious tears away. He was bare above the waist. He spoke with effort, his throat straining with grief. "Lord, oh, Great An. Your mother sent me to tell you, oh! ... to... to... come home and bring a priest from *Egal-mah*. Oh! ...Your father won't waken."

Feeling the strength leave his legs, Suba knelt on the warm ground with one hand on his chest and the other on his thigh, trying to cope with the sense of loss he was already feeling, his abdomen so tense he could barely breathe. The servant offered his hand to help him rise, but Suba waved him off.

"How is my mother? When did this happen?" Suba made an effort to attend to the news and also determine how to manage to open his shop for the day. He dismissed his plans for designing a particularly demanding decorated pot that had occupied his thoughts. Shaking his head to make himself focus on the needs of the moment, he sat back on his heels and covered his face with his hands to quell his urge to wail out loud.

"When I left, my lady was sitting on the floor next to your father's bed, holding his hand. We tried to give him some broth, but he ... he ... looked as if he'd choke, so we stopped. Ohhhh!" he keened, again dabbing at his eyes.

As if he had suddenly grown old, Suba struggled to rise to his feet and held his arms around his chest, bent over and breathing shallowly in little spasms, ready to sob at the least relaxation of his will. He made himself stand upright, arranged his bag behind his shoulder and forced a deep breath before directing the servant. "Go back home. Tell my mother I'll be there as soon as I can get a priest." He started toward the administration section of *Egal-mah's* temple at the base of the *zigurrat*, but stopped long enough to call back to the servant, "Pour yourself a measure of beer and another for my mother; tell her I said she's to drink it no matter how she feels. Go now!"

Suba reminded himself that there would be no one to attend to his shop, so he changed direction and asked his neighboring vendor, a basket merchant originally from *Shurruppak*, to tell anyone inquiring about his pottery that he would return within a day or so. Fighting a powerful desire to first go home to be with Nani, he hurried past the early market customers and strode toward the temple quarters.

———●———

Now, ten days later, four barges were berthed together at the port of *Manjadar* in the waning light of afternoon, shadows of the city cooling the air along the river. Ila stood with the captain and Zambiya near the gangplank that connected the wharf to her newly contracted barge, riding low in the water due to the mounded and covered cargo on its deck.

She was dressed in a simple modest buff colored tunic with a stole of bright canary yellow, designating her status as a qualified merchant and inspector. The downstream breeze was stiffening, causing her long black hair to blow up from her shoulders. She held her square steatite seal in one hand, its braided cotton lanyard off of her neck and affixed to her wrist, and was gesturing with the other hand to point out the humpless bull engraved on it along with an inscription.

"Ah, I've the authority to grant transport rights along the river, certified with my seal, but each inspector along the river will be expecting to see for themselves that every parcel is clearly marked." She sighed before continuing, "It's just a fact of life. Crewmen will try to beat our inspectors by burying a bundle of their own goods within the legitimate cargo. At every waystation we have to stop and move the cargo from one side of the barge to the other, or onto the wharf. So, it will take more time to reach the coast, Captain."

Zambiya looked and sounded exasperated as he exclaimed, "So the unicorn flags that let us bypass the stations on the way here don't work on the way back? Why not, in the name of the Great Gods?" His impatience was signaled as he rocked back and forth on his feet.

Ila responded with resignation in her tone as if she were explaining to a child, "We import mostly grain and some textiles, of course. Some exotic foods, too. Ah, there's never enough variety of grain. But we export exotic and rare stones, easily concealed; a sailor with the right connections could conceal a packet of gold nodules, or one of the rarer stones somewhere within other bundles, and bypass the customs cost. So we traders pay for their dishonesty by going through these inspections over and over."

The captain looked skyward and uttered a curse beneath his breath, then took in a deep breath and exhaled lengthily before declaring with resignation, "Three times before we reach the coast. Three times! That's a full day and a half delay, and they aren't equal distances. Great An!" He strode off to the first of his ships tied along the quay, muttering to himself and unconsciously looking for someone to berate.

"And we pay in lost time and running the risk that *Adad* will brew up a storm on our way home, possibly losing everything." Zambiya invoked the god of weather; he was anxious to be well on his way home before the fabled monsoon winds and rains appeared.

Ila put a reassuring hand on his shoulder and said, "Ah, we've likely more than enough time to be in Isin before foul weather strikes. Our gods are perhaps more predictable than yours." She smiled at him and calmly asked, "Where's Neti now? I've not seen him since morning."

"He and Rangu are searching for a suitable gift for Rangu's uncle. As long as we've been here, nothing has occurred to us that would be just right."

"They should've asked me. I know the protocol, but what would be best would be to give a gift his aunt would like. Here, the matrons 'own the biggest whip', as we say. There'll be time tomorrow before we leave; ah, I'll tell him tonight if they've not made a selection."

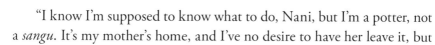

"I know I'm supposed to know what to do, Nani, but I'm a potter, not a *sangu*. It's my mother's home, and I've no desire to have her leave it, but she really can't live alone, even with a servant."

Suba and Nani sat alone in the courtyard of their home, shaded by a sun-faded green canopy attached to the wall by pieces of common bricks, while Aruru tended the two infants. Despite his despondence, evidenced by occasional deep sighs and the deep furrows above his nose, Suba had tended his market stall this day, selling some pots but not feeling up to creating more.

With a priest from Inana's temple in attendance, Suba's father had been buried outside the walls of Isin in a large cemetery; that was both his father's and his mother's desire. Many citizens were buried inside their own homes or yards, but it wasn't universal. When his body was taken from the home for burial, Suba's mother, too frail to accompany them to the graveside, sat in a chair, slumped sideways with her eyes closed, silently rocking and hugging her husband's worn leather sandals to her breast. She had keened and cried for more than a day, and was worn down. In a reversal of roles, Suba had to insist that she eat some of the food Nani sent her and to drink some beer.

"Your parents' home is certainly larger than this one," Nani responded. She slid over on the bench they shared to take advantage of the moving shade and leaned against the wall. "This's my home from birth, but that's not why I don't want to leave. My mother's buried right in there, and Zid-abzu keeps watch over our family. Father's father is buried there, too. I'm at a loss as much as you are. We can't have your mother live here," she stated adamantly, "there's not enough room and she couldn't help with the babies. She hasn't had a child in her home for years; she'd get no rest living with two of them. And they're both teething, too. But I know she can't stay in her home; I agree."

Aruru the slave called out to them from the pantry door, holding their daughter Gibil over her shoulder and patting the crying girl's back. "Lord and lady, there are visitors to see you."

"Who is it?" A scintilla of annoyance showed in Suba's tone.

"Your friends: the Gutian and Nintud. She said to tell you they won't stay long, just want to visit." Aruru turned her head back to listen to the sounds in the home and reported, "Indur's awake now. Shall I bring them out here?"

Nani stood up and, after stroking Suba's hair, walked toward the door while motioning him to stay, saying to Aruru, "I'll bring them out here while you see to Indur. I'll help with him shortly." After entering her home she quickly made her way through the dim corridor to the entry way to greet her friends.

Nintud, their former neighbor, hugged Nani closely, then said, "I hear one of your babies; let me help." She patted her swelling abdomen and added, "I'd better get used to this. I think this one's going to be like his father, big and active." She smiled at Muda before she made her way to the back rooms.

"That lady's name is Aruru." Nani called down the hallway while she ushered Muda to the courtyard. "She's very good with them and a real help," she explained to Muda, "but there're still two."

While Nintud was introducing herself to Aruru she picked up Indur, rocking him as she had done so many times in the past. With newly-developing confidence due to her elevated status as the wife of the king's principal guard, Nintud asked Aruru, "Are you a servant, lady?"

"I'm a slave," she replied, "but they don't treat me like one." She showed her forearm where the slave's brand would normally be. "My lady treats me like a sister; says she never had one." She smiled at Nintud and said, "My lady speaks of you often. You were her mother's friend, too."

"True. There's a longer story there, if she hasn't told you. She will someday." Aware that both the infants were still fussing and putting their hands up to their respective mouths, she added, "Probably some time after these two've cut some teeth."

Carrying the two infants, the women progressed to the courtyard to join the others. By now, the sun had dropped below the city walls and the heat of the sun was noticeably diminished.

Muda walked to Nintud as she exited the home, elbowing the heavy drape across the doorway back into place. "You were … exact … right, my dear. Suba was just telling me that his mother needs care, but Nani doesn't want to leave this house, her home. I didn't say anything about your suggestion; that's yours to explain." He held out his hands to offer to take Indur, who was still fussing. Gibil was nursing at her mother's breast, and therefore quiet. Nintud surrendered Indur to Muda, who offered him a knuckle to suck on, which restored relative quiet to the courtyard. Muda remained standing, then paced back and forth with the baby, close enough to hear his wife, who inserted herself onto the bench between Nani and Suba.

Taking care to look from one to the other occasionally as she spoke, Nintud quickly came to the point of their visit. "I only met your father once, at your wedding, Suba. I'm truly sorry that he's gone, and I know how much you loved him and will miss him. The gods so chose, and we can't question the gods. What I observed was a couple who lived for each other, so your mother is suffering her loss terribly, I'm sure." She turned to Nani and stated with certainty, "You've two babies to care for, so you can't help Suba care for his mother. She lives too far from here for you to manage the trips that would be needed."

During Nintud's speech Aruru stood a discrete distance away, her back to the setting sun, watching silently to see if either child needed anything. Muda continued his regular ambling, with Indur still sucking the Gutian's knuckle while looking intently at his face.

Continuing, Nintud observed to Nani, "When your Gibil was born, I had my own home next door, and I know very well there wasn't any extra room here, so," now turning to Suba, "your mother can't stay here with you. And you've got her," indicating Aruru by inclining her head in the slave's direction.

Suba nodded his head in assent and said, "That's the puzzle we're trying to solve, Nintud. You've stated the situation clearly, but I haven't heard a solution. What suggestion was Muda talking about that he wanted you to explain?"

"It seemed obvious to me," she replied. "My house next door is empty and of no use to me, since I'll be living in the palace as long as Muda is *Ensi's* chief guard. If you make a doorway at the end of the hall of your home and make that a short hall into my house next door, you can bring your mother to live with you there. She'll have the care she needs and can see her granddaughter as she grows."

Suba came close to smiling at the proposal, thinking of the practical advantages and starting already to consider the construction challenges. Nani had other concerns, however, and said, "Nintud, that's a wonderful proposal, and a generous one, to consider selling us your house." Leaning forward to see past Nintud at her husband she asked, "But won't your mother object to moving from her home of so many years? That she shared with your father? I would."

Suba stood up, feeling weary despite his youth, and knelt on one knee in front of Nani. "Dearest wife, you think so clearly about how people feel." He stood up and backed up to see past the canopy and toward Nintud's adjoining courtyard. He conjured in his mind the spaces that would connect the two buildings, his hands framing imaginary renovations in the air. Then, considering Nani's projection of his mother's likely reaction, he sighed heavily before addressing Nintud.

"You've offered a generous solution to our problem, and I thank you for the offer." We can make it work, and will settle the details later. You're very good friends," he said, motioning toward Muda as well. Turning to

Nani he looked into her questioning eyes and declared, "You're right, of course; my mother won't want to leave. So I'm going to tell her she's just visiting here because you can't leave the children. We'll have to have the houses joined right away. She needs care now, so I'll have to arrange for that tomorrow, and for the construction project as well. Shouldn't take long."

• ● •

A far distant storm swelled the silt-laden Indus River, and the four barges rode high against the wharf of Manjadar. Waves slapped the centuries-old beaten bricks creating an undercurrent of sound like dozens of cats lapping milk.

The Isin captain wet a finger in his mouth and held it above his head, divining the direction and briskness of the wind: toward the sea, but at a cross angle. He automatically calculated the required constant adjustment of the sails plus use of the oars to stay mid-stream. "Shit on these foreign gods!" he muttered. Stepping onto the front rail of the lead barge he turned to face the other craft, steadying himself by holding onto one of the lines that held the mast upright. He balanced himself on the rail long enough to cup both hands around his mouth, then bellowed so all of his sailors could hear him, "Pull into the middle then keep in the middle behind me. Watch for logs. Pull away!" he ordered. He grabbed the line again to watch his little fleet pull away from the port of *Manjadar*, one by one.

The oarsmen in the lead barge pushed off from the quay with their oars and into the current, the lone mid-ship sail flapping loose until the captain was satisfied with his position. "Square the sail!" he shouted, watching the other three barges pull free from their berths and follow into the flow as two sailors in this, his barge, tied the ends of the bottom boom to the rails on both sides, maintaining enough slack on each side to allow for altering the angle to catch the wind. The two settled their bottoms onto opposite railings, prepared for a long shift of hauling and releasing the sturdy hemp ropes to keep the boat steady and free from obstacles in the river.

"Ship oars!" the captain demanded as the convoy of barges moved south, borne on the choppy green-tinted water. With two men for each of the two oars on each side, there was a brief flurry of activity as the rear oars were pulled out of the water and secured along the rails. Those sailors moved forward to join the men in front to help as their oars were shipped inward but not secured, remaining in readiness to steer away from any significant snag.

Each barge had a lead sailor in charge. Despite his abrasive manner, the captain was privately confident of his crews. Zambiya rode on the captain's barge with two of the guards as additional passengers; Rangu and Ansar were on the second with two more guards. With nothing to do, they watched the progress of the small fleet and paid attention to the movements of wildlife along the shore and in the air around them. Rangu motioned with his hand for Ansar to look at the far shore, where a sleek brown river otter could be seen sliding off a snag and into the water. The placid scene suddenly turned violent as a long-snouted crocodile snatched the creature from below, breaking the surface with his prize in his maw before disappearing into the stream.

Ila and Neti had arranged to ride together on the last boat with four guards, as the most expensive cargo was carried on that one. Ila intended to use both her position authority and her femininity to charm the inspectors along the river route. Added to the ubiquitous bribes, they hoped to accelerate the pace of their journey.

The captain had directed the lead sailors in the barges behind him to keep little distance between the crafts, traveling in train so that all would be able to see and avoid any obstacles or snags and be attendant to his orders. He jumped down from the front rail and immediately shielded his eyes from the rising sun to the east, scanning the river flow before him.

"Steady on," he shouted to his crew; the lead crewman in the second boat repeated the same to his men, then the same from boat three; finally from the fourth boat, "Holding on."

The wind pushed the convoy south with the flow of the river; gusts made for unsteady walking, so passengers and crew remained in their places most of the time. Everyone had a satchel of coiled moisture-protective leather that held a bedroll as tightly compact as possible; these served as cushions through travel days.

Crewmen who weren't occupied with duties lounged on their satchels or, when they could find a section of the cargo that was soft, rested there. On their respective boats the traders from Isin, along with Ila, kept the cargo under close observation.

Zambiya made his way to the rear of the lead barge and scanned the following craft; as the captain had done earlier, he stepped up onto the railing using a line attached to the mast at one end and a heavy bronze eye secured to the deck at the other. Turning his back to the sun on its upward path, he scanned the decks of the boats behind him, locating each member of his company. Spying Ila and Neti seated forward on the cargo covering on the last barge, he marveled at the turn of events that was leading the young man to return to his home with an attractive and pregnant wife. He compressed his brow, wondering how Tikal and Kusu would respond to this development.

Just at that moment Ila looked up from saying something to Neti and saw Zambiya looking back toward them and gave him a smile and a friendly wave; Neti did the same.

———— • ● • ————

"Really, Mother? Finally?"

Ninegala and Nisaba were seated under the canopy of Enlil-Bani's veranda that overlooked the kitchen courtyard and mini-orchard, sharing a vat of honeyed beer and boiled eggs with baked wheat bread. Sud had served them and then retreated to the doorway, leaning against the frame and awaiting further directions.

"Yes, it's true." Nisaba smiled but emitted a sigh before continuing. "He's an officer with an estate near ours outside the walls; he's one of General Ashgi's sons. *Ensi* brought both of the sons back to Isin not long after the General died in Larsa." She drew another mouthful of beer up her straw and swallowed. "You may know that they have two much younger sisters, twins, students at Enmerkar's *edubba*. Pretty girls, but too quiet for my taste." She thought a moment before adding, "Remind me of you when you were younger."

"Sud. Come over here." Ninegala made a scooping motion with her hand as she called to her slave. Sud responded instantly, covering the short distance with a couple of strides.

"You don't need to stand. Sit here with us and have some of the flatcakes and eggs." Ninegala turned to her mother and said, "Sud was *Ensi's* companion for meals before our marriage, and I trust her to keep her tongue from wagging about us. But also, she hears all the palace gossip; very useful to me."

Sud could sense Nisaba's drawing in at her being included in the conversation as the mother folding her arms over her ample bosom and looked toward her daughter. Silence followed for a few moments until Sud said, "You may not remember me, lady. I served your family when Erra-Imitti was *Ensi*, but I was thinner then." She smiled at the matron before adding, "Eating in the palace kitchen changed that." She indulged in a short laugh as she took a bite of boiled egg.

Nisaba wasn't certain she remembered, but acknowledged Sud's reminder by saying, "I think I recall that, but I had many attendants then." Nisaba was aware of Sud's slave status, but was too polite to mention it.

"So, Sud. My mother tells me that my sister, Sherida, is about to be betrothed to one of General Ashgi's sons. Do you know anything about that?"

Sud glanced from mother to daughter, rapidly sorting the rumors and hearsay she was aware of into the categories of shareable and not shareable. Even though she knew there couldn't be anyone close enough to hear them, she lowered her voice before she confided, "What I've heard, but don't personally know, ... is that one of the sons has no use for a woman; the other one is anxious to marry and settle down at his family estate and take over its management from the overseer. I don't know either by name, though."

Nisaba drew back, sitting up straight and shifted forward, looking poised to stand up; she let her gaze shift over the courtyard walls and up past the market stalls to the distant city walls before declaring, "We certainly need to know which one is which." She looked pointedly at Sud and demanded, "You have to find out and tell us. Someone in the palace must know."

Sud suddenly found herself in a position of importance, and stood up, promising, "I'll find out by the end of this day, Lady. I'll tell my queen when I do."

Ninegala mused, "Sherida can't be marrying one of those men." Her inflection emphasized 'those.' "Why would one of them marry a woman anyway?"

Her mother answered with certainty in her tone, "It would give him an advantage in the ranks of the army; people think a married man is more stable and virtuous." She then scoffed, remembering the philandering of her deceased husband. "Stable and virtuous indeed! Most men are like dogs in perpetual heat, married or not."

Isin's queen ignored the comment and directed Sud by saying, "Find out now if you can. We'll be having the mid-day meal with *Ensi*, but we'll wait here for now. Come back as soon as you can learn which is which and let us know what you've learned."

"Yes, my queen."

"Call me Nina when we're alone, Sud; I've told you before."

Nisaba cringed inwardly, but bit her tongue.

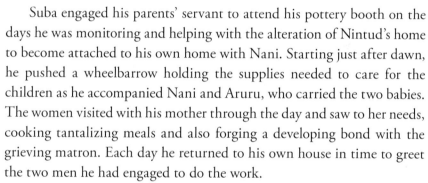

Suba engaged his parents' servant to attend his pottery booth on the days he was monitoring and helping with the alteration of Nintud's home to become attached to his own home with Nani. Starting just after dawn, he pushed a wheelbarrow holding the supplies needed to care for the children as he accompanied Nani and Aruru, who carried the two babies. The women visited with his mother through the day and saw to her needs, cooking tantalizing meals and also forging a developing bond with the grieving matron. Each day he returned to his own house in time to greet the two men he had engaged to do the work.

At the suggestion of Enlil-Bani, he had hired Alim and an apprentice. Alim was now working as a mason in addition to his duties in the palace grain fields. Alim had always been ambitious, and his wife had already presented him with twin children since his marriage two years before. They had been spared the scourge of the plague, although he had suffered the loss of two brothers.

On this, the third and last day of construction, the adjoining walls of the homes had been transformed into a broad but short hallway with new bricks, plus a sconce at each end for illumination. Nintud's house had been neglected during her absence; dusting, sweeping and cobweb removal had required the services of a woman Suba knew from the market.

The junction between the houses required a new brick-and-stick bridge to be constructed to make the structure watertight against seasonal storms, and Alim and Suba were both pleased with this part of the project. An additional course of bricks had to be added to Nintud's former house, which made the two neighboring walls level.

It was now mid-afternoon, and Alim and his worker had left, the work completed. Suba made a last inspection of the conjoined houses, even surveying both courtyards with an eye to either making an access gate between the two or completely demolishing the separating wall. He intended to join Nani and his mother for a light meal before returning home with his mother in tow, as several preparatory comments had been offered to her to suggest that this was the best plan of which anyone could think. He was rehearsing additional arguments he could employ to convince his mother.

"Bibi," he called out the doorway to his courtyard, holding a dish of food in one hand. He had prepared it for Nani's cat, and was holding the heavy drape to one side of the passage as he did so. "Come on; time for food." He made a squeaking noise with his mouth, surveying the outside ground before he spied her scurrying along in the deep shade of the eastside wall. She emerged into the sunlight, hurrying toward him and mewing loudly.

Suddenly a young hawk appeared, soaring low from behind the roof of the house and dove toward Bibi, aiming for her back with its talons spread wide, but only connecting with one set of them. The hawk let out a shrill 'skree' and tried to launch into the air with its prey; Bibi shrieked and twisted as her weight was greater than the hawk could manage. Suba responded by abandoning the dish and springing across the open space, directing a kick at the raptor and succeeded in freeing the cat from the bird, though not before one of the hawk's talons caught the top of the man's ankle, tearing a gash as long as Suba's thumb.

Bibi was sent sprawling across the packed ground with four holes in her hide near her tail. The hawk recovered and despite one damaged wing, successfully became sky borne again.

Suba sat on the ground and held his skin closed with one hand, watching blood ooze between his fingers as he observed the hawk disappear. He beckoned to Bibi with his other hand, saying soothingly in a sing-songy patter, "Come here. That's our girl. Come on." He made a sucking sound with his lips that he'd used before to attract the cat.

Bibi ignored him; instead she turned as far as she could and began trying to lick her hide as she half stood, half sat, quivering. She had to turn so far to reach her wounds that she couldn't maintain in place, scooting in a tight circle as she cleaned the oozing blood.

246

Despite wanting to inspect Bibi's injury, Suba took his headband off and used it to tie his own injury closed tightly, staunching the blood. He stood up, gingerly put his weight on the wounded foot, scooped up Bibi with one hand holding her close to his chest and walking into the house, softly crooning as he stroked her head. Bibi allowed herself to be cuddled, but not before one loud questioning sound.

• ● •

The Isin barges were close to approaching the last duty harbor before leaving the waters of the Indus and entering the open sea. A light rain had fallen in the morning, but now in the latter part of the afternoon, the sun kept up a tantalizing show for brief periods, disappearing behind the clouds long enough to turn the air chilly and then becoming warm again. Everyone was looking forward to docking and finishing business with the inspection officials. The agreed plan was to remain in harbor for the night and get underway early the next day.

The playful appearances of the sun made for a wind that caused the little fleet to stutter forward on the river's flow with less smoothness than was comfortable, and this had occurred much of the day. The unpredictable bouncing of the crafts as they rode made for an underlying level of irritability by both crew and passengers, with the captain the most affected. Standing on the rail in the very front of the lead boat, he directed his sailors to veer from one side of the flow to another depending on what part of the stream appeared to him to be somewhat more favorable. Finally the river widened after rounding a bend, presenting a broad delta with different channels from which to choose, sand bars separating them.

Zambiya stood on the deck at the rear of the lead barge, steadying himself by holding onto a mast support line, watching the following crafts as they maneuvered to remain close to the captain's barge and the sound of his voice as the commands were passed along from one to the other. As well as the little fleet of barges, the river current carried along the swollen remains of a goat and several branches of a flowering tree, seemingly discarded after being chopped from the trunk.

Throughout the course of the journey Neti and Ila had stayed together on the last boat when under way. Zambiya could see them now, sitting together on the protective hide cover over the cargo. They were close enough that he could see Ila's face, animated with what looked like anger, though he couldn't hear her words. He kept his face impassive while he enjoyed the sight of her. He turned away briefly, then turned back to watch them.

"Of course I'm going to live in the palace with you," she declared, raising her voice only a little. "Ah, what do you think, that I'll stay with the *Meluhhans* in their village? Where do you intend to live?"

Neti held up both hands with his palms toward her, in an attitude of supplication.

"I don't know if there will be space in the palace for us. I don't know where it would be, and I don't want us to live with my parents. Really, I imagined you would want to spend a lot of time engaged with the villagers and craftsmen to make your trading business be successful, so I thought I would be visiting you there." He turned his face from her as he mentally searched for a solution that would work for their different interests. "I need to be present in the palace to serve my father and *Ensi*. The *Meluhhan* village is some distance from Isin, but I'm willing to come there often. You're my wife, and I want to spend as much time with you as I can, and our child as well." His face clouded over and he declared with a wry smile, "I actually haven't figured out where I would live, either. I just want you with me; I haven't sorted it out."

Seeing a tree branch floating near where the barge was going to pass, he rose and covered the short distance to the railing to retrieve it. Covered with pink blossoms, he hoped to present it to Ila as an unexpected gift and peace offering, remembering how she had loved having flowers on display during meals. He held onto the rail and reached far out, staring at the prize, but the branch had drifted a bit further away from the barge, and he stretched even further, mentally urging it to move closer to his fingers.

Neti turned his head back toward Ila when she said, "Be careful, don't..."

The branch was abruptly pushed away as a river crocodile as large as a water buffalo sprang upward from the murky gray water just far enough to clamp onto Neti's outstretched arm in its toothy pink maw. With weight sufficient to pull the man off the barge, the croc disappeared below the surface of the river with Neti, who thrashed and beat the creature until he could no longer breathe.

Ila shrieked as she rushed to the rail, frantically searching the water for any sign of Neti, without result. She rushed to the front of the boat and screamed, "Captain! Zambiya! Stop the boats. Stop." She ran back to the rear again, scanning for any sign of her husband.

Having seen Neti disappear, Zambiya shouted to the captain, "Ship oars, Captain. Stop the boats. Neti's been taken by a creature. We have to find him."

"Where?" the captain demanded.

Zambiya pointed to the area of the river where the event had occurred, now far behind the current position of the fleet. "There. Back there," he shouted. "Turn the boats around."

The captain peered back to the part of the river they had passed and, seeing nothing, made a decision. "He's not there. He's gone." He said this loud enough for Zambiya to hear, then bellowed to his mates in the other barges, "Steady on course. Keep up." He turned his back to Zambiya and resumed scanning the river ahead, ignoring one of the flowered branches as it passed under his craft, as well as Ila's screams.

CHAPTER EIGHTEEN

A GRAFT AND A SCAR

When the gods send blight into our lives, some accept the bleak harvest as if it were their due; others protest and then rebel, demanding a full bounty from their labors.

Zambiya and Rangu sat on either side of Ila, close but not touching her. The early summer night wind off the river was damp and offered no comfort. Ila couldn't stand the thought of joining the crew at the tavern near the port. Her companions felt obligated to give her what comfort of presence as they could.

Temporarily cried out, Ila shivered and wrapped the dark brown, thick woolen wrap closer around her shoulders and bosom. She had already purchased a quantity of ochre, purplish red in hue, and had adorned her lower eyelids and the cheeks below them with the pigment in an inverted triangle, to signal her great sorrow.

"Ah, what should I do, Zambiya? Can I just go on to Isin as if nothing has changed? Neti and I ..." She sobbed again and held her breath in to quell another set of keening cries; briefly she buried her face in the wrap, but recovered and continued, saying, "We weren't even sure where we'd live. What can I expect from his father and mother? How will they feel about me and my child, Neti's child? Their grand-child," she added with a hopeful lilt in her tone. "But will they blame me? You know Tikal, Zambiya. What do you think?"

Zambiya started to respond, despite having no real answer for her, but Ila suddenly turned to Rangu, her countryman, and asked, "Should I return to *Manjadar*? Ah, I know much better how my life would go here in *Meluhha*." She slumped forward and expressed a huge sigh, but then sprang to her feet and faced the two men.

"This is not like me! Ah, I'm decisive. I go after what I want, and … but now…" She started sobbing again and slumped onto the deck, rocking back and forth with her legs under her, her arms holding the wrap around her waist. Her companions looked at each other, neither knowing how to comfort her.

Zambiya finally reacted, giving in to his own distress at the loss of Neti. He moved to the huddled young woman and knelt in front of her and pulled her to him. Ila allowed the embrace, so deep was her misery. Rangu sat silently mourning, even welcoming the tears that flowed from his eyes.

After many moments, his own voice quaking with emotion, Zambiya said, "You will know in the morning what you should do. You will know what feels right for you and your child." He waited a while longer before adding, "Tikal and his wife have lost their son and don't know it yet." He hesitated again before going on. "You can give them the chance to know Neti's son, as well as the woman he chose to be his wife; I believe that will help them with their grief." He decided to share a part of his own story with her, saying, "When my wife died, not very long before I came on this journey, I knew I had a son to care for; he's a part of her and of me. You'll have your child, too, and so will Neti's parents if you decide to create a new life for yourself in Isin." He hesitated before disclosing, both to her and to himself, "I hope that will be your decision."

"Aruru, I need you to go to the palace, right now."

Nani called to her slave from the bedroom, where she was carefully placing Suba's foot and leg on a mauve colored bolster she had doubled over to increase the elevation she was arranging for him on their bed. Suba's whole foot was swollen, his wound from the talon oozing a yellow green pus, and he winced when his foot was moved at all. Nani was especially disturbed by the odor of the wound, like the stench of a decaying rat.

The slave discreetly stood outside their bedroom with her back to the room, but held the privacy curtain aside in order to be able to hear clearly;

she held their daughter Gibil up on her bosom with the baby's head over her shoulder, trying to encourage a burp.

"I only know your friends Muda and Nintud at the palace. Should I ask for one of them, Lady?" Aruru asked.

"No. No." Nani tried to hide her exasperation, recognizing that it wasn't the slave causing her such worry. "When you get to the entrance, tell the guards you must see En-me, the *a-zu* for the *Ensi*. Say it," she insisted. "En-me the *a-zu*."

"Yes, Lady. En-me the *a-zu*. I do know him, remember."

"Of course! Tell them you come from the *Ensi's* daughter and to hurry. When you see En-me, tell him that Suba's been hurt and needs an *a-zu* right away. Bring Gibil to me now, and get ready to leave. Hurry! I think Suba's wound is serious, but En-me will know."

Aruru pushed the heavy drape to one side of the doorway and put Gibil into Nani's arms, automatically transferring the spit-up cloth to Nani's shoulder, and just in time.

"Should I bring Suba anything before I leave? Oh, and Indur's asleep, but he needs changing if he wakes up while I'm gone."

"I'll see if he wants anything; please hurry."

Aruru hastened to the nursery room she shared with the two babies, quietly lifting her light beige hooded cloak from its hook. She walked as quickly as she could down the dimly lighted hallway and to the front entry room, where she picked up one of the staffs that served both as a walking stick and a cudgel. She exited the house and eased the door closed behind her.

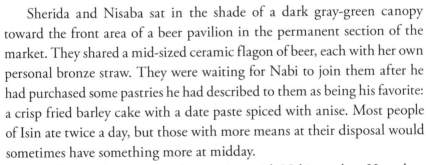

Sherida and Nisaba sat in the shade of a dark gray-green canopy toward the front area of a beer pavilion in the permanent section of the market. They shared a mid-sized ceramic flagon of beer, each with her own personal bronze straw. They were waiting for Nabi to join them after he had purchased some pastries he had described to them as being his favorite: a crisp fried barley cake with a date paste spiced with anise. Most people of Isin ate twice a day, but those with more means at their disposal would sometimes have something more at midday.

"You're spending more and more time with Nabi, mother. How does he manage to spend so much time not being a palace guard?" Sherida sucked on her straw, watching her mother while giving Nisaba a chance to respond.

"Not that it's any of your concern, 'Rida, but *Ensi* has allowed him to spend time just observing and listening to what goes on in the bazaar; you've noticed he's not in uniform." She started to draw on her own straw, but stopped and, waving her hands in the air, exclaimed, "Oh! I wanted to wait until he was gone to ask you how you are getting along with Ibbi, your young officer. I can't tell you how relieved I was when I found out which of the two brothers is interested in you." She lowered her voice before adding, "I don't think Sigsig would suit you even though he's younger."

"I like them both, Mother, but Ibbi's the one who really likes me." Sherida stroked her hair, feeling pleased, but then looked puzzled and asked, "Why wouldn't Sigsig suit me? I was hoping for a younger man, actually."

Nisaba looked up at the canopy as if there were an answer there before saying, "Well, he's younger, but I don't think he's ready to settle down with a wife." She stalled a bit longer by sipping her drink again, then announced, "Oh, here comes Nabi."

The guard edged his way around another trestle table in the beer parlor, carefully balancing a hastily woven tray made of fresh palm fronds that supported the dainties he had purchased for the women. He sidled onto the bench next to Nisaba and immediately set out distributing the treats, declaring, "I hope you both enjoy these as much as I do. The woman who does the cooking there doesn't make them every day." Without waiting for a response, he broke off a piece of the griddle cake and put it in his mouth.

Sherida tried to ignore how closely Nabi had seated himself near her mother by looking past them and toward the rear of the booth, glancing at the few other patrons without staring.

"Good, hum?" Nabi prompted.

"You're right, Nabi," agreed Nisaba. Taking care to keep her motions hidden, the matron discretely lowered the hand she was not using to break off pieces of the pastry. She slid her other hand part way up the inside of Nabi's thigh before looking at him directly, smiling and saying, "Very pleasing; I imagine even Inana would be pleased."

Nabi glanced at Sherida as he started to feel his face flush, but slid back off the bench saying, "I'll get us more beer."

En-me sat next to Suba on the bed; ignoring the putrid smell from the wound, he looked carefully at the flesh and assessed the color of the pus, then carefully felt Suba's foot and his lower leg at the same time. Nani stood in the doorway, tensely waiting for En-me to make his appraisal known.

En-me sniffed inward loudly and swallowed. Then he stood up and clapped Suba on the shoulder and said, "I think we can make this well." Turning to Nani, he asked, "Do you have a lot of cloths you can use for cleaning this? You won't want to use them for anything else, but you can rinse them out in fresh water and use them again on the wound. We have to get this cleaned up, and we don't want it to entirely close too soon. It'd just fester inside and get worse." He lowered his voice, but still muttered, "Much worse."

Nani let out an audible sigh of relief and closed her eyes, leaning back against the doorway.

Suba lifted himself up onto his elbows and said, "We moved a lot of old clothing here when we moved my mother. We'll use that."

Nani entered the room and replaced En-me in his place on the bed. She held Suba's hand in both of hers, watching her husband's face, but reminded the *a-zu*, "When Enmerkar's leg was so badly injured, I helped mother with cleaning the wound. I remember having to gather cobwebs to help stop the bleeding; I think you told us to do that."

"I recall that, Nani. This is different, though." He turned away and sniffed again, then looked at her, explaining, "You see how swollen the wound is. It's keeping him from bleeding much, but it's also keeping the pus inside. His leg and foot will rot if we let it continue." He smiled inwardly, recalling how he had first been Enmerkar's healer, then his lover. He continued, "You know where you keep things, so I'd like you to bring me several cloths and a basket of water, plus two jugs of beer: one for Suba and one for cleaning the wound."

After En-me left to return to the palace, promising to return the next afternoon, Nani and Suba sat together on the bed, Indur on Suba's lap and Gibil nursing at Nani's breast.

"He's a very gentle man," Suba offered.

"I remember that from when my brother was being treated by him and his mentor, Enki-nin." She looked up and around the room and marveled to herself out loud, "I'm surprised I remember his name; it's been a long time now."

Suba looked down at his foot, propped on a bolster and nearly surrounded by a shallow faded green woven basket that had been cut open on one side to allow his leg to move out of it when needed. He flexed his foot toward him, noting with satisfaction that the movement was without much pain. The laceration was covered with a beer-soaked cloth except for one end; flexing his foot had caused a bit of drainage to ooze out and run down toward a rag that held shredded cattails to absorb it.

"I should have asked before, Nani. How is Bibi?"

She smiled and said, "Most housecats don't have an *a-zu* to treat them. She didn't like it, but En-me had me hold her wrapped up with an old towel, and he shaved off the fur around the holes in her hide so she could clean them better; he thought she'd be fine."

As if she had been called, Bibi walked into the room. She looked at Nani and then let out a loud, "Meow!" turned and walked back toward the doorway. She looked back and, when she didn't see Nani respond, she repeated the motion and her outcry. Nani laughed and said to Suba, "She seems pretty good to me. I'm sure Gibil's done, so I'm going to check on your mother first, then feed Bibi."

———— •●• ————

"I'm so pleased that I decided to have you teach me the scribes' skills, even though I'm not an adept." Enlil-Bani sat next to Enmerkar on a long wooden bench holding a tablet frame filled with damp clay in his left hand and a stylus in his right. The king straightened and arched his back, realizing again how tense these instructions made him, but also feeling satisfaction at the progress he had made in these several months. He had to admit to himself that he was now feeling very comfortable with being in charge in his role of *Ensi*; voluntarily submitting to the criticisms of his own son rankled, but was necessary.

"Have you used your training, Father?" Enmerkar flexed the thigh of his bad leg, raising his foot almost to being level with his knee, but looked with interest at the king.

"Yes, in fact." The king smiled, recalling the incident. "The Elder Council asked me to rule on a matter involving a contract between two neighboring farmers regarding a trade: a young male slave for three nanny goats. One farmer declared the slave he was to receive was lame; the other said the goats he had already received gave no milk. Their agreement had been solemnized in writing, and each had a copy of the contract. They'd been arguing about the tablets themselves, each claiming theirs was the original agreement. The Council said they should give up the bargain and reclaim their original properties, but both wanted compensation from the other one. I agreed to hear the matter, but insisted that both farmers bring the tablets as well as the slave and goats in question to the palace." The king added with a smile, "The goats stayed outside, of course."

"How did the tablets differ?"

"A temple scribe and I compared the tablets together in the presence of both men, in front of the palace. The tablets both said 'able bodied' for the slave, who had a limp when he walked; they both said 'young' for the goats, and they weren't young. In fact, they were all past milk producing age. The scribe and I both agreed that neither farmer had produced what the contract required, so the slave returned to his owner as did the goats to theirs. Then I fined the farmers two silver discs each for trying to cheat each other, but more for wasting the time of first the Council, then the palace staff and the temple scribe." The king chuckled recalling the scowls on the faces of the farmers.

"Do you want to move on to reviewing the terms for land boundaries, or is that enough for today, Father?"

Enlil-Bani set his tablet on the bench next to him and twisted his torso from side to side, pulling with his hands on the opposite side's thighs to relieve the strain in his spine before saying, "I think this is enough for today," he said as he stood.

A teen-aged slave came from his post across the room as soon as he saw the king rise; he picked up the king's tablet and covered it with a damp burlap cloth, then stacked it over Enmerkar's, which was already similarly covered. He bowed and took them from the room.

"Is all well at the *edubba*?"

"Quite well, Father. In fact, I've taken on eight new student scribes, even two more girls. Every one of my last group of finished students has found placement with a trader or other merchant, so my *edubba* has a good reputation. En-me says I'm known as both demanding and kind, and I hope that's true." Now he flexed his knee so that it almost reached his chest, slowly lowering it back down, then repeated the motion, feeling his muscles loosen. Then he continued, "You remember I've told you about those twin girls of General Ashgi. Well, I'm now separating them to train the younger students on the things they are individually good at, as well as improving in their own skills. They objected at first, wanted to always work together, but I insisted that they wouldn't be able to do that if they were employed. I don't allow a student to remain in the *edubba* if they can't learn the skills; there are other ways to get on in the world with fewer demands."

"Of course," the king replied. "Like being *Ensi*. But that job doesn't come up often." Both men laughed.

"I don't know why," Enmerkar said, "but that reminds me of a dream I had two nights ago. I didn't feel it needed to be reported because it didn't seem to involve a threat to anyone in our family."

"Was it long, Enmerkar, my son? I need to speak with Tikal during the mid-day time. Another spectacle is being planned for the end of summer and the second harvest season."

"No, it wasn't long, but it felt very ominous. In fact, Tikal was the only one in it I recognized at first, although Zambiya came in at the end."

The king waved off a servant who had entered the room and started to approach, and said, "Tell me what happened."

"As usual, I'm seeing the events, but I'm not present in the dream. I've never had a dream that meant anything about my life in which I was actually present. At any rate, I saw Tikal pacing back and forth on the banks of a river, but not *Buranun*; he was looking across at the waters flowing by, carrying barges and rafts and coracles, lots of them. Then one barge, heavy laden with goods, left the mid-stream group and made its way to the bank where several men jumped out and hauled it onto the shore.

He looked carefully at each sailor, shaking his head at each one, until he saw Zambiya still at the rear of the barge, pointing back at the river and looking very sad. Tikal turned his back on the river, then he clasped his hands across his breast, looked like an *orant*, actually, then he just fell over on his back." Enmerkar held one hand to his own chest and added, "I had such a feeling of sadness when I woke up, the feeling stayed with me through the whole day."

———— • ● • ————

Zambiya and Ila sat near each other in the stern of her barge, facing away from the late afternoon sun and watching the shore in the distance as the little fleet made its way homeward by sail and oar, always in sight of the coast on their right side. Always practical, Ila had dispensed with the ochre on her cheeks, as everyone in the crew knew of her widowhood. Only Rangu and Zambiya knew she was pregnant, since she wasn't showing yet.

"Ah, I must change my mind twice a day," said Ila in a low voice. A close by crewman was coiling rope and lashing it to the low rail for later use. She angled to face Zambiya directly, inquiring, "Do you mind my burdening you with my vacillations? I can't talk with Rangu; he's not yet married and he's part of the village that I'll have to deal with when we reach Isin. I have decisions to make and it helps to speak them aloud as they form in my mind. Really, Zambiya, would you rather not hear my questioning? You don't owe me." She looked into his eyes while wiping sweat off the top of her chest and throat with a retired grey headband, then looked away again and complained aloud, "I'm a young woman and already twice widowed. I must be cursed!" she spat out.

Zambiya was silent for a while, then put his hand on her shoulder and squeezed it slightly, saying, "In Isin we often use an expression that goes, 'The gods so chose,' as an explanation for events we didn't expect. Usually it's about something we didn't expect or want to happen." Becoming aware of how warm and smooth her skin felt, he withdrew his hand and looked away before continuing, "I was thrilled when my wife gave me a son, then my stomach clenched when I saw that his top lip was split; he'd just been born." He looked down at the weathered boards of the deck and added, "I thought I was cursed, too. Then just weeks later Ezina died. No reason. Just died. How do we get through living if the gods are so capricious?"

Ila looked up and asked, "Ah, what is that word? 'Capricious?' What is that?"

"A priest told me that word when Ezina died. He said the gods keep us from getting too certain of our future and too comfortable in our circumstances by suddenly withholding their favors. He believed that it didn't matter what we planned, that all was in the hands of the gods, and sometimes the punishing gods win. When they win, we lose."

Ila cursed under her breath, then said, "Our gods are no different, even though we're told that by giving gifts to the gods, sacrifices of food or cloth or even silver, we improve our fates." She hesitated, then added, "Ah, I think it only helps the priests!"

"What I think is that the gods pretty much ignore us, and many things can go wrong in our lives, but so can very good things." He hesitated before adding, "And I don't think we always know which is which. I'm certain that we don't have complete control over what happens to us, but it doesn't matter. Neither does anyone else." He chuckled and made an effort to lighten the mood, saying, "The priests and priestesses spend all their time pleasing the gods, but they get old and sick and die, too. Accidents happen to them, and our plague god visits them as well."

The sun edged toward the horizon, causing the shadows of the barges ahead to reach almost to the shore, and the wind vacillated in its intensity, causing the sail to flap. Ila noted the fact and pointed at the sail, announcing to Zambiya, "See, even the wind is capricious!"

He thought a moment before saying, "I don't think the captain would agree. He probably can predict that."

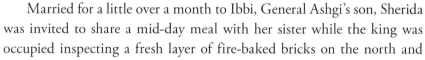

Married for a little over a month to Ibbi, General Ashgi's son, Sherida was invited to share a mid-day meal with her sister while the king was occupied inspecting a fresh layer of fire-baked bricks on the north and east city walls.

Sud finished serving them and then moved away to give them privacy as they conversed, squatting on her heels with her back to the cool doorway frame. Ninegala treated her well, and Sud reciprocated by being diligent in her service and tight-mouthed about her mistress with the other household slaves.

The sisters sat on benches at the corner of a table in the banquet room, facing each other.

"I'm so happy being married, Nina," Sherida confided as she reached for a wheat cake to dip into the steaming oxtail stew in her bowl. "Mother kept arranging for me to meet with old widowed men, or farmers who lived just forever away from Isin, and would have expected me to live out there." She shuddered dramatically, and then took a bite and pointed to her bowl with appreciation, saying, "That's different." Some broth ran down her chin which she salvaged with her other hand, licking it off her finger.

"It is good, isn't it? Zid-tara told me they bought a new slave, a eunuch who's been cooking for a temple up in Kish. I don't know what he did to fall out of favor up there, but I'm glad of it." Ninegala delicately extracted a lump of meat from her bowl using her thumb and middle finger, folded it into a cake, then dipped the cake into the broth, allowing the excess to fall off before placing it in her mouth. She chewed slowly, watching Sherida, thinking about her sister's new status as a wife.

Sherida took a drink of her mint-imbued beer through the silver straw her husband had given her as a gift just the previous day, thus avoiding the bits of barley that floated on the top of her tall cup. Suddenly aware that she was being observed with some intensity, she sat up straighter and said, "What? What is it, Nina?"

Ninegala glanced at Sud before she responded, with her voice lowered and her words precise. "What is it like to be with a man, 'Rida? What do you have to do?" She drew a long breath before asking, "How do you bear it?" She quickly put her food on her plate and covered her face with her hands, weeping quietly.

Sherida sat stock still at first, then the memory of her sister's ordeal flooded into her and she pivoted off her bench and stood behind Ninegala, bending to hug her close around her shoulders, rocking her just slightly.

"Sud," she called. "Your mistress would like a pitcher of strong wine; quickly, girl."

Sud leaped to her feet and strode out of the room, hurrying toward the kitchen where she would need to get Zid-tara to approve the demand.

Sherida resumed her place, sitting on the edge of her bench to face her sister face to face and knee to knee, stroking Ninegala's hair with one hand while holding one of her shoulders with the other. Then, to be sure she had the answer to her newly-raised suspicion before Sud returned, she gently took her sister's hands down and asked, "Nina, haven't you ever lain with *Ensi*? Is there something wrong with him?"

"You can't tell anyone, 'Rida. Not even your husband. Ever!" Ninegala spoke quickly and urgently, her voice low. "He's a good man and a good husband in every other way. He must have really loved his wife. But he promised to never lie with me, right from the first; told me and mother. That was fine with me, better than fine. The thought of that horrid little man and what he did to me still makes my stomach turn over. I don't think I could bear being with Enlil-Bani that way, and I know he won't ever insist." She looked around the room, especially toward the door before adding, "He's been very good to me, and he's truly a wise and caring man and an honorable one."

She looked toward the door, then continued, "But I'm having dreams about him, 'Rida." She blushed, then covered her face again.

"Then I'll tell you, my sister, I don't have to 'bear' being with Ibbi. The first time was painful, I'll admit, but now I want to do it." A smile crept across her lips and she licked them, adding, "I used to overhear the servants talk about 'Inana's blessings' and wonder what that meant. Now I know." She hesitated before adding, "You deserve those same blessings, dear Sister."

At that moment, Sud came into the room with a bronze pitcher of plum wine in one hand and two cups in the other. "Is my mistress distressed about something?"

Sherida responded off-handedly, saying, "She was for a while, but we'll talk some more and I think she'll be fine. Thanks for being so quick, Sud." She waved her hand over the lukewarm stew and wheat cakes and said, "I think we're done with these. Is there some fruit you could bring us after you clear these away?"

Ninegala spoke up at that point, to clarify that this was her desire, saying, "I'd like some of those figs in syrup you brought several days ago; those were special. Take your time, Sud. I'll just visit with my sister while you're gone." Then she added, "I'll save some of this wine for you, too. Bring a cup for yourself; you'll like it."

<hr />

"I know what you're asking, and I don't think it will work." En-me stood off to the side, slowly looked around the courtyard of Suba and Nani's home, then back at Nani, holding Indur in her lap as she sat on the brick bench in the shade of the west wall. She kept the baby amused by pulling and twitching a slender leather strap with four crow feathers tied to it along the ground in front of her, which Bibi pounced on, her claws raking the plumes; Indur delighted in the cat's playing, and he gurgled enthusiastically, drooling.

"I just think it would be so much easier for him if he could keep food in his mouth. He has to be frustrated when it comes back out of his lips before he has a chance to swallow. I know I am." She adjusted where Indur sat against her body. The heat of the late afternoon was causing both of them to perspire where their bodies were in contact. "Now that his front teeth are coming in, it's even harder to put the food in with my finger. Aruru told me she has the same trouble."

She twitched the cat toy again, and Bibi leaped on it, biting at the feather ends.

"I know I've thanked you before for suggesting we take on Aruru as a helper, but she has truly been a blessing. Especially with Suba's mother living with us now," she added.

Suba had carried their daughter Gibil to the back of the courtyard; he was now able to walk again with little discomfort, as his laceration was healing nicely. During the time he had been unable to tend his pottery shop, he had assembled a pen by the rear wall and had purchased four ducklings, hoping for eggs. He had taken special care to provide a light grate made of reeds lashed together with cord to cover the enclosure, one easy to remove by him, to prevent them from being taken by thieving birds, and secured on all sides so that Bibi couldn't get them, either. Gibil was fascinated by the ducklings as they flapped their wings and walked over each other, squawking and contending for the barley meal; she cooed and waved her little arms.

Unwilling to give up so easily, Nani asked, "If you were to try it, how do you think it could be done? And would it hurt him very much? I don't want him to be in pain, En-me. But what would you have to do?"

En-me turned away from her and looked at the ground, trying and rejecting alternative fantasies about how to repair Indur's lip. He looked back at the boy and knelt at the side away from the cat's toy, then slipped one finger between the child's lip and gum, gauging the depth. Indur jerked his head away and blinked, starting to protest, but En-me stood back up and stepped away.

"I'm not saying I agree to do it, Nani." He turned around and walked a short distance away, then turned back and said, "I won't even try before Zambiya has returned and agreed to it; maybe not even then." Without touching Indur again, the healer bent at the waist and again looked closely at the boy's lip. He sniffed a long inhalation and swallowed, stroking his chin and wrinkling his brow. Continuing, he mused aloud, "I've never even heard of an *a-zu* attempting to change a child's lip when it's like this. And I know I've seen worse."

Nani pressed her case, even while bobbing her head up and down in agreement with En-me. "I know it's not up to us to decide. Zambiya would have to want it. I just want to know if it can be done. I feel so badly for Indur every time we feed him." She transferred the toy to her other hand and stroked the boy's head.

"I know it's hard for you; and Indur, certainly." He sniffed again and continued, "But you have to understand that the law is clear. If an *a-zu* harms someone by his treatment, the harm comes to him as well. Isin's great king who turned into a god, Lipit-Ishtar, pronounced the great laws to protect the people. So, if I cause a man to lose an eye, I also lose one. It's not just for fights. 'A tooth for a tooth' applies to healers as well. If my treatment caused harm to Indur, I'd be punished."

The serious look on his face was almost enough to persuade her, but Nani dismissed that likelihood, responding, "Zambiya would have to complain to the Council, or to my father, asking for you to be punished. You know that wouldn't happen."

"I'll think on it some more, Nani, I promise." He saw that Suba was returning toward the house and said, "I'm going to check on Suba's mother. I don't like that new cough she has." He sniffed and swallowed and re-entered the home.

CHAPTER NINETEEN

A WITHERING WIND

The people yearn for peace and stability: the harvest always good, the dates always plentiful, the taxes low and the gods generous. Life can be either abundant or tragic, but the people endure.

The sentry atop Isin's city wall shielded his eyes from the dust-dry wind blowing across the river from the desert beyond. He watched upstream as two men in a shallow coracle poled their round craft toward the reeds on the opposite shore of Buranun across from the city. With the river's flow reduced as summer waned and the second harvest loomed, they faced little resistance from the current, and the larger of the two men held the round boat steady while his companion shipped his pole and cast a net toward the bank, slowly bringing it back in and gathering it along the outside of the little vessel. Scooping the middle against his chest, he opened enough of the seine to allow his catch of small fish to wriggle downward onto the bottom of the boat. He motioned for his partner to pole downstream a way before he cast the net again.

Bored, the sentry looked across at the sparse vegetation past the thick curtain of reeds on the other side of the river, aware of a flight of birds as the coracle passed close by, finally scanning back downstream. Surprised, he saw a fleet of three barges moving out of the white-capped mid-stream, already approaching the city docks, though still at some distance away. He quickly picked up the bronze horn that lay on the wall in front of him and blew it loudly, facing the center of the city, a piercing and insistent wailing sound. His youthful vision allowed him to distinguish the flags of Isin on the masts of the front two crafts, then a strange faded flag on the third.

He was quickly joined by a sentry who had been on the ascending steps to relieve the man on the wall.

"What is it?" the relief guard asked with some alarm as he peered along the course of the river while shielding his eyes from the lowering sun, his hand cupped over his forehead. Following the pointed gesture of his counterpart, he saw the line of barges as they continued veering from mid-stream to begin approaching the docks.

"Tikal told us four days ago that we should expect his son and *Ensi's* stepson to be returning from a trade mission soon, that they were already in Larsa. I think that may be them, and he'll want to know as soon as we can tell him," the first one answered. "I'll report to the palace right now. Stay alert!" he admonished as he ran toward the stairs.

———————— • ◆ • ————————

Tikal, Enlil-Bani and Muda exited the city gate, hurrying toward the docks. Tikal's wife Kusu and Ninegala walked together behind their husbands with the ruling couples accompanied by two squads of the civic patrol. These ten common foot soldiers and their two leaders were also palace guards. Even from a distance as much as five lengths of the city square, they could hear the voice of the captain shouting orders to berth the barges in the order he wanted. The king smiled, certain he could detect Zambiya's voice within the din as well.

"I'm sure it's them, Tikal," he declared. "It's about the time we calculated for the trip, and the sentry said there's two Isin barges. I wonder why there's another, though."

Tikal speculated, "Maybe they needed that many to transport all the trade goods they acquired." Upon further reflection he mused, "But I'd think Nur-Adad would have kept so much that three ships would be more than needed. Too many."

"The sentry said the third ship had a different flag," the king offered, "so maybe it's just traveling with ours and is also docking here. We'll soon see."

Kusu and Ninegala walked hand-in-hand behind their husbands, though Kusu wanted to run forward. A smile played across her lips at the prospect of seeing her only child after months apart; she was humming a familiar lilting chant to maintain her pace with the more sedate progress of the men.

By the time the palace entourage reached the docks, already a procession of many porters carrying tightly-bound bundles streamed toward Isin. First alerted by the sounding of the horn, runners from the docks carried news of the boats arrivals to their sponsors. The porters' various burdens were all heavy, some of dark and stained leather, others of light colored sturdy canvas, all borne on their backs, steadied by their arms and supported by tumpline straps across their foreheads. Sorted according to their different destinations within the city, the groups of porters were directed by a variety of supervisors with one leading and one following behind to prevent pilfering. Most were priests of the temples, but some were tradesmen and artisans; all were anxious for raw goods: precious stones, dyed fabric, copper and even bronze ingots.

"There's Zambiya," the king said to Tikal, and then again, "There," partially turning to Ninegala, pointing. "He's back there on that barge with the odd flag." Enlil-Bani hurried in that direction, ensuring that the entire palace group would accompany him, his white, gold fringed cape billowing in the wind as he moved.

"I've not seen Neti yet," Kusu announced to her husband, concern starting to show in her voice. She stopped humming and asked, "You think he's still on one of the barges?" She hurried forward, but took care not to overtake her husband or the king.

Now the palace assembly reached the stretch of docks that paralleled the river, with berthing stations jutting out into the river's current, angled downstream to give less resistance to the flow. The captain had arranged the Isin barges closest to the city. The cargos were mostly removed from Isin's crafts, but Ila's lay still unloaded and berthed to the rear of the quay. Ansar and two other guards remained on that vessel, along with Zambiya and Ila.

Zambiya stood up on the rail of the barge, balancing easily, and waved to his stepfather, the king, with a visible bow, as the palace group approached the craft, then he jumped down onto the deck and spoke quickly to Ansar before calling Ila to join him from the rear of her barge,

266

behind the cargo. He guided her up the gangplank, since her barge was lower in the water than the level of the dock.

Despite the heat of the afternoon, Ila was dressed in her plainest, most modest clothing: a heavy beige skirt that brushed her ankles and a dark maroon long-sleeve tunic with scalloped edges that reached to below her hips. She had pulled her hair up on top of her head in a two-tiered bun, held in place with a mottled, nearly black tortoise shell comb; a headband of the same material as her tunic further restrained her thick hair. Her lower lids and her cheeks were rimmed with dull red ochre, and she wore a veil of unadorned gray linen that threatened to lift above her chin with gusts of wind.

By now both Tikal and his wife began to be alarmed at the unexplained absence of their son, and Tikal loudly asked Zambiya, now a mere few paces away, "Zambiya, where's Neti? I don't see him. Has he already gone to the palace?"

His wife turned around to look back toward Isin's walls and the entry gate, surmising aloud to Ninegala, still at her side, "How could he have passed us in this short time?"

Zambiya led Ila to his stepfather, protocol demanding that Enlil-Bani be addressed first. These two men placed their palms flat on each other's breast, and Zambiya bowed to the *Ensi*. Even with the solemnity of the explanations that needed to be made, confusion showed briefly on Zambiya's face when he saw Ninegala, but he pressed on.

"Father, Tikal, Lady," he said, including Kusu with a nod directly to her, "This lady here is Neti's wife." He held Ila's elbow, pausing through five heartbeats before continuing. "Her name is Ila, and she's bearing Neti's child." Another five heartbeats. "There is no easy way to tell you this, but due to a terrible accident, Neti drowned in the river in *Meluhha* during our return journey. Whether the work of our gods or theirs, we couldn't save him." He and Ila had spoken about how to spare Neti's parents the anguish of learning the details of the manner of their son's death; all river people knew there were many ways to drown.

Ninegala watched her companion as the tragic news was conveyed. Kusu's hands flew to her mouth, covering her lips and barely stifling a scream. She started to move toward Tikal, but her legs folded under her and she slumped onto her knees onto the grit of the quay. Ninegala immediately knelt by the older woman's side and held her up, as Kusu was starting to fold over onto her side, then held her around her shoulders, saying, "I'm so very sorry, Kusu. Just rest here with me a while."

When Ninegala observed that Kusu's complexion had turned lighter than her linen veil and that she was fainting, the younger woman wrenched a filmy shawl from her own shoulders and placed it under the matron's head. She guided her limp form to lie on the earthen quay, making sure that Kusu's clothing was placed so as to maintain her dignity with all the males present.

Ila instantly discerned that the woman who had collapsed was Neti's mother, and she left Zambiya's side to go to her. She was so distressed that she started to speak in her native language but recovered and said to Ninegala, "Ah, I am so sorry for this lady." She knelt on the other side of Kusu from Ninegala, her breathing shallow and panting, finally saying, "I would do anything to … spare her this sorrow." Unable to fight back her tears, she declared, "Neti always said… no…other children. Just him." She looked hard at Ninegala, dressed in regal finery, and asked, "Ah, are you his sister?" Then another possibility struck her like a blow to the stomach; she stopped crying, shook her tears away, and demanded more loudly, "Are you Neti's wife?"

Ninegala waved her hand at her, dismissing the notion and responded quietly but crisply, "No! Of course not! I'm the wife of the *Ensi*; Neti couldn't have known that Enlil-Bani had married." Still weeping, she added, "I'm Ninegala," and she reached across Kusu's form to lay her hand on Ila's forearm.

Tikal looked back toward Kusu when he heard her scream and saw her faint, but instead of going to her, he looked dazed, then puzzled. He turned in a full circle, looking first around him and then skyward. He walked toward the barge from which Zambiya and Ila had come, as if Neti might still be there. He neared the craft, shaking his head, but then veered off as he saw that there was no one on board except three guards, walking slowly toward the end of the quay.

Enlil-Bani called to him before he progressed very far, saying, "Tikal, my friend. I'm so sorry. Wait here with Kusu." He followed him calling his name, but stopped when he realized that he, the king, was being accompanied by the guards.

Enlil-Bani stopped short and turned around, pointing at each of the lead guards in turn, and demanded, "Stay! Here!" He turned again, briefly placing his hand on Zambiya's shoulder affectionately as he quick-stepped toward Tikal.

By this time Tikal had nearly reached the end of the quay. He peered downstream, then turned his back to the river and started back toward Enlil-Bani and Kusu, looking bewildered.

Suddenly, a grimace of fierce pain altered his face and he stopped walking. He reached for his chest with both hands but dropped over backward like a felled tree, striking his head. Seized by a convulsion, he arched his back and threw his arms down on the bricks, his thumbs covered inside his fingers. By the time Enlil-Bani reached him, his face was contorted with his eyes staring toward the top of his head, his mouth foaming. The king tried to lift his Chief Counselor's body by the shoulders, and despite the twitching of his limbs, managed to sit on the bricks next to him, cradling Tikal's head in his lap and urging him to try to be calm. Within moments the seizure ended and Kusu's husband, Neti's father, went completely limp, voiding his bladder as he died.

—————————— • ● • ——————————

Enmerkar and En-me waited in front of the palace for the king to return from the docks with Zambiya. En-me stood next to one of the life-size lion statues holding his ox-hide medical supply bag by its canvas shoulder sling as it rested at his feet; Enmerkar sat close by on the top step of the platform that comprised the floor level of the palace, his weak leg stretched out in front of him, the other bent and resting on the next step down.

The king had sent a courier and litter bearers to the *edubba* to fetch his son and En-me, with yet another to tell Nani that their brother was coming home from his journey. At this level within the city, there was little evidence of wind, protected as the city was by walls along the river's bank.

Expecting to see Nani, the two men glanced frequently toward the main thoroughfare where it entered the square and market area; the vendors' booths forming one of the sides of the square. Instead, they were both surprised to see Aruru and two guards enter together from the avenue; the guards abandoned her and moved rapidly toward the barracks part of the palace, while Aruru hurried toward Suba's pottery stall, stopping outside.

This late in the day, the market area was nearly deserted, with many permanent stalls already closed for the day and none of the itinerant produce and craft mats occupied. Nevertheless, both beer gardens were open and waiting for evening customers, one at each end of the long established booths.

"My love," said Enmerkar, "could you go ask Aruru why she's here and Nani's not? I'm sure our father sent for her as well as me."

En-me sniffed loudly as he descended the palace steps, saying, "I'm curious myself. I'll return as soon as I know."

They didn't have to wait, as Aruru and Suba came out of Suba's shop and noted En-me striding across the open area toward them. As soon as Suba saw En-me, he stopped to speak to Aruru, pointing out the *a-zu*, and then turned on his heel and hurried toward the avenue leading toward home. Aruru was able to intercept En-me nearly in the center of the bazaar.

"Shalamu, Lord," she said, bowing courteously. "My master begs you to come to his home as soon as possible. Nani sent me to get him." She absently raised one hand to adjust her veil, then remembered again that she was no longer a married woman and wasn't wearing one. She shook her head with irritation at herself, then went on saying, "His mother's breathing is very hard for her, and she's making a sound like gravel shaken back and forth in a wet dish every time she breathes. I'm to hurry back, Lord; two babies and a very sick old woman are more than she can manage alone."

"I'll be there as soon as I can, tell her." He hesitated before explaining, "I'm supposed to be here when Ensi returns with Tikal and the others, in case there's been an injury during the trip, but I'll be there when I can." It occurred to him that Aruru's gaze had remained on Suba longer than necessary as her master left the square, but the notion evaporated in his haste to report. He had no further time to reflect on that observation; he had no sooner reached Enmerkar when two guards appeared in the thoroughfare, jogging toward the palace.

En-m stopped them before they could round the raised steps on their route to the corner of the palace leading to the guard barracks, saying, "Shalamu, but what's happened? Why the rush?" He raised his hand to stop their report while he quickly sniffed and swallowed; he knew his hearing suffered when he sniffed.

"Shalamu, Lord," one of them said, recognizing En-me, "we've been sent to fetch a litter to bring Tikal back to the palace. We need to go, now!" They hurried to resume their jog toward the side of the palace.

"What's wrong with Tikal? How'd he get hurt? Quickly, you know I'm the palace *a-zu*; I need to know."

"Sorry, Lord. Of course you should know. Tikal is dead, though; you can't help him. The gods so chose." He and his companion jogged away to accomplish their mission.

En-me and Enmerkar stared at one another, stunned at the guards' report. When another pair of guards entered the square jogging toward the palace, Enmerkar stood up as quickly as he could manage with the use of his staff and En-me's help. Balancing on his good leg while the other engaged to steady him, he said with a strain in his voice, "You're probably needed, my love."

En-me shouted to the two new guards as they approached, "Are you sent for another litter, guards?"

"Yes, Lord. Tikal's wife is unwell." They hurried on.

Ignoring the two guards at the great doors of the palace just ten paces away, En-me paused long enough to caress Enmerkar's cheek before saying, "Wait for us inside the palace. I'll see what help I can be at the docks." He commenced a fast jog across the square toward the distant docks, hoisting his supply kit along his spine as he ran. Upon reaching the avenue, however, a coughing fit seized him so severely he dropped to one knee. He stopped to catch his breath, but made himself stand and resume walking, though at a slower pace.

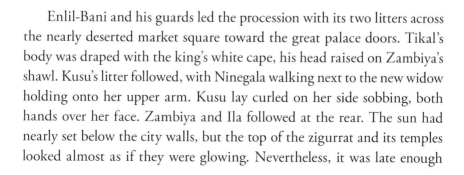

Enlil-Bani and his guards led the procession with its two litters across the nearly deserted market square toward the great palace doors. Tikal's body was draped with the king's white cape, his head raised on Zambiya's shawl. Kusu's litter followed, with Ninegala walking next to the new widow holding onto her upper arm. Kusu lay curled on her side sobbing, both hands over her face. Zambiya and Ila followed at the rear. The sun had nearly set below the city walls, but the top of the ziggurat and its temples looked almost as if they were glowing. Nevertheless, it was late enough in the day that Zid-tara was prepared for a late arrival, and six attendants hurried across the square with lit torches to greet the king.

• ● •

Suba sat on the edge of his mother's cot holding her hand in one of his, while also trying to lift up her pillow, doubled to try to ease her breathing. The sound made him weep with frustration at his inability to ease her suffering. The one window opening led out to the courtyard side, nearly at ceiling height, admitting some light but little air, and the room felt warm and stuffy.

Outside in Nani's courtyard, Nani and Aruru sat in the shade of the west wall in the waning light of early evening, each with a baby perched on her lap. They were agreed in their intent on giving Suba and his mother as much privacy and personal time as possible. No one imagined that the crone could survive much longer, and all wished her dying would be easier and soon. She had firmly expressed her desire to journey to Ganzer to join her husband in the underworld.

"I hear someone at the door, Nani. Could finally be En-me. Shall I see?"

"Thank you, yes. If it's anyone else, call me."

Aruru hoisted Indur up onto her chest with his head looking over her right shoulder, patting his back and crooning softly as she made her way to the front entry; she then called out, "Who's there?"

A slight pause followed while En-me sniffed, then coughed, but he answered, "It's En-me, Aruru. Shalamu."

She quickly transferred Indur to her left side so she could use her right hand to free the inner latch to the door, then swung it wide to admit the *a-zu*.

"Shalamu, Lord. Nani and I are in the courtyard; Suba's with his mother." She thought a moment while she was re-locking the door, then said to him, "It's getting darker outside, must be even darker in her room. Could you take a kindling stick and light the torches?"

"That's thoughtful." He coughed again, turning his back to sniff and swallow. He walked with confident familiarity of the home to a cache of tapered palm splinters in a niche outside the pantry. He lit one from the lighted torch by that door, then walked through the passageway that connected the houses, lighting another hall torch on the way.

"Shalamu, Suba," he offered as he stood outside the bedroom, waiting for an invitation to enter.

"Shalamu, my friend. Thank you for attending to us."

En-me lit both the wall torches in the room, noting without having to think about it that one needed more oil. Now able to see the old woman as she lay on her bed, he asked, "How is she doing?" He listened to her breathing, rather than focusing on Suba's opinion.

Suba watched his mother's face intently, then answered, "She's so weak, En-me. I'd like to get her to eat something, maybe broth or a porridge. Do you think she can manage that?"

"May I touch her?"

A nod indicated assent, and En-me felt her forehead, then opened one eyelid briefly, searching her pupil and the white of her eye, which was actually pale yellow; he noted especially that she didn't turn her eyes to see him, just lying there passively. He used his thumb to help her eye close completely.

After placing his hand on Suba's shoulder and gripping it, he said, "Don't give her anything to eat or drink. It will just cause her more misery, and her body can't use it." He removed his hand and bent over to look directly into his face.

"She wants to die, Suba. Her spirit wants her body to die. Let her go; you'll grieve, but her suffering'll end sooner. I've seen this several times. It will be a gift to her." Then with finality he added, "The gods so chose."

Suba nodded, weeping.

"I'm going to go speak with Nani now. Zambiya's returned, and there's other news from the palace. I'll look back in before I leave." He hesitated before saying, "It shouldn't be very long, my friend."

He was able to leave the room and reach the hallway before sneezing with a force so hard it triggered a biting pain in his side that dropped him to one knee. He reached for the rough bricks of the wall under the torch to steady himself as he slowly stood up and the pain slowly receded. He rested with his back against the wall to let the pain subside further before he continued to Nani's courtyard.

————— • ● • —————

"Tikal wouldn't have allowed the palace and Isin to disintegrate into turmoil and chaos, and neither will I."

The king sat at the head of the banquet table, his wife seated next to him. Both wore regal costumes, white robes with crimson decorations, further adorned with gold trim. Ninegala had a light shawl over her shoulders, and her headband sported gold beads dangling in front of her ears down to her jawline. Unusually for him, Enlil-Bani wore a high crowned conical cap, with a lapis cabochon set in gold just above his forehead. It was clear to all that this was both a somber and formal meeting.

Now late in the evening, every torch in the room blazed. Seated around the table were officials of every important faction and institution of Isin, including the *Sangus* of both temples, the four most prestigious members of the Elders Council, the General of the standing army and his two most senior assistant generals, and both the Captains of the guards, one for palace defense and one for the civic patrols. Zambiya stood behind and to the left of Ninegala, while Muda was to the right of the king. Everyone's attention was fixed on the sovereign.

Although Zid-tara had provided an array of foods and both beer and wine, along with small silver dishes and flat-bottomed cups for each participant, there was little appetite for partaking.

"I want all of you to know that Tikal had every confidence in each of you; he has expressed that to me on many occasions, and I have no changes in mind for any of you." The king at this point looked with particularity at the generals and guard captains, then turned to the priests and priestesses. "I expect the rites for Tikal to reflect the honorable man he was; present him to the gods with respect and know that I will be included in the ceremonies. There will be a day of mourning with a city-wide feast to be part of it, and it must be concluded within two days. The second harvest can't be delayed."

The king noted the shared looks of consternation between the religious notables. Raising his hand to quell any objection, he announced, "I know it is little time. You should already know what needs to be done, so see that it happens."

"Now," he announced, "there have been changes I've already made that all of you need to know. The first affects the palace itself; I've designated Zid-tara to oversee both the kitchen staff and those stewards who serve the maintenance and cleaning of the palace: he will be Chief of Palace Staff. He will no longer be cooking, but he assures me there is an able cook to replace him."

Enlil-Bani looked around the table at each of the functionaries there, then stood up. Everyone except Ninegala also rose, at first thinking the meeting was about to conclude until he raised his hand and motioned for Zambiya to come forward.

"This man, my son Zambiya, is now my Chief Counselor. He will attend me at every official function and will be in charge of our officials and emissaries, and be the liaison to you generals, as well as in charge of the civil and palace guards. Last, you men of the Council," he said looking directly at the four Elders, "you are to confer with him about each trial that you consider sending on to the palace for a decision. I've been asked to consider matters that could have easily been decided by your members; I'll ask you, no, direct you, to deliberate longer in the future."

One of the Elders, the youngest of the group, raised one hand and started to protest but closed his mouth, nodding assent.

The king turned and offered his hand to Ninegala, helping her stand up from her seat. Zambiya announced in a clear voice, "That is all." With Muda leading the way to the door, the royal pair left the room and retired to their respective chambers.

●

Two days after Tikal's death rites were concluded, Kusu sat in her palace apartment with Nisaba. With the king's permission his former Chief Counselor's body had been buried in Tikal and Kusu's family chapel in the palace, to be guarded by their household god.

"I can't tell you how grateful I am to *Ensi* for allowing me to stay here, at least for now." The women sat near one another on an ornately carved dark hardwood divan, well-cushioned; between them a bronze tray held a single dish of pitted dates stuffed with pine nuts and a bowl of beer.

Nisaba had brought her personal silver straw, and she leaned over and blew into the beer as she stirred to avoid the husks, then leaned her straw against the side of the bowl. Before responding she plucked one of the dates off the plate with her thumb and little finger and placed it into her mouth delicately, smiling and chewing with appreciation. She swallowed and wiped her lips with a napkin she had placed over her large bosom before saying, "I will share with you that when Enlil-Bani was made *Ensi* by the gods, I imagined he would be coarse and selfish, but he has proven himself to be honorable and sensitive to others. My daughter says the same."

"I was surprised and a little hurt that his daughter didn't attend the funeral rites for my husband. I've been told she has a slave who could have watched her child."

"Oh, but she's also caring for Zambiya's child you know, and furthermore her husband's mother died the same day as Tikal." Nisaba noted the look of dismay and sorrow on Kusu's face and quickly added, "I'm so sorry to remind you, dear lady."

Kusu patted Nisaba's arm and said, "It's not as if I can think of much else. I'm just raw from having Tikal taken by the gods so suddenly." She let out a low sob, but gathered her composure and continued on, saying, "I was pleased you were willing to visit with me so soon after Tikal's death. Many people, especially married women, avoid having to talk with a widow. I think it scares them to think about losing their own husband, and it's in the hands of the gods." She looked down at the floor covering at their feet, then took a deep breath and said rapidly, "That's why I asked for you to visit. I didn't do anything to comfort you when Erra-imitti died, and I owe you an apology for that. I think you've probably forgiven me by now, but I wanted to say it." She searched Nisaba's face for what the former queen was feeling.

"That was different, you must know." Nisaba drew a swallow of beer, then another, then confided, "My husband had become crude and lecherous years before he died, as well as fearful and slovenly. For me personally, his death was a shock, but not a loss." She waited a moment before adding, "I hope you're not shocked to hear me say that. Your husband was a good man; you've every reason to grieve for him."

"I thank you for saying so. He was a good husband, but now I don't know what to do with myself." She imitated Nisaba's process, blowing through her straw to get past the residue of barley floating on the beer, studied it and then took a long drink. "*Ensi* has allowed me to stay here in the palace, but I have no function here. As wife to the Chief Counselor, my job was to support Tikal and raise my son. Now I've no husband and no son."

As if saying that out loud breached a barrier in her feelings, Kusu turned away from Nisaba and began to wail, giving in to the pain in her throat and the pressure of her tears that wanted to spill over again.

At first Nisaba reached across the tray to pat Kusu on the shoulder, but soon recognized that her friend was suffering to her core in this moment, so she went to the other side of the divan and held her close, rocking her as she would an injured child. She thought to herself that Kusu also had an unborn grandchild by a foreign woman, but she suppressed the thought in favor of just being a supportive friend.

—•—

Half a moon later, Ninegala made a special appeal to join the king while he held his morning conference with Zambiya. The two of them shared a light breakfast on his veranda every day, now a routine. Their discussion again concerned the quality of the emmer wheat and sesame crops, due for harvest within days, because the grains and stalks were noticeably brittle; drying winds seemed to appear from across Buranun out of the distant desert every several days.

Isin's young queen knew this matter of the crops was always in the background thoughts of all the wealthy farmers as well as the temple administrators and her husband as well. This was as much from his previous duties when he was a commoner working for a temple as for his current responsibilities as king. Her concern was much closer to home, and could have been considered trivial compared to the status of the crops.

Ninegala sat to one side of a bench that held both her and the king, relaxing against a new striped bolster, crimson and cream in color, while Zambiya sat across from Enlil-Bani on a backless padded stool. She held a tall silver bowl of beer in both hands, drinking just small sips as she waited for the business of the city to be concluded. She had opinions, but refrained from comment.

This morning the wind held moisture, so the ordinary heat was tolerable. Zambiya stood and bowed to both his father and the queen as if to leave, but Ninegala sat forward and then moved closer to the king, saying, "Please stay, Zambiya. What I want to discuss concerns Neti's widow, the lady I met on the dock. I've not seen her since. Has she been banished from our city? She told me her name is Ila. Is that right?"

Enlil-Bani seemed shocked at the question, but answered for Zambiya, saying, "Banished? No! Certainly not. What made you think that?"

Zambiya explained, "I had Rangu, our interpreter, escort her to the Meluhhan village, so she could spend time with her own people and speak her own language. She was very stricken herself at the time. When we were coming home to Isin, she wondered all the time how Neti's parents would feel about her. And her baby, too." He held out his palms toward her, pointed toward the ground as he continued, saying, "It was only moments after she saw them that the gods took Tikal and struck his wife to the ground. I thought it was a good decision to not have her in the palace for a while. And probably better for Kusu as well."

"That was probably a good idea at the time," Ninegala offered while waving away a fruit fly from her dish. "Now, though, Kusu is past the double shock of losing both her son and her husband. She wanders around her apartment with no purpose. I've had several talks with her, as I've grown to love that lady like a mother. She tries to look into her future and sees nothing there. She needs a purpose, a reason to get out of her bed in the morning."

Zambiya looked chagrined and said, "I'm at fault here for not thinking about Ila and what she must be feeling. I sent her away to her people's village, a place where she only knows one person. She must feel abandoned by the gods and by me as well. She's a good person, and I know she deserves better."

The king took his wife's hand and looked into her face, saying, "Knowing you, I doubt that you wanted to tell us this and didn't have a proposal to make. What do you suggest?"

Ninegala smiled and said, "Kusu hasn't been out of the palace since the ceremonies for Tikal. I think she needs to meet her son's wife, and they need to know more about each other than the deaths that afflict them both."

Zambiya turned and walked to the outermost edge of the veranda. From here he could see part of the market square past the zigurrat steps, then turned back and said to Ninegala, "Let's arrange with both ladies to meet for a midday meal in the square. I'll make sure Ila is there. Ila speaks our language perfectly, so they will not have any problem with that."

"Couldn't they meet here in the palace, say at a banquet?" asked the king.

"In my opinion, *Ensi*," said Ninegala, "that would be too formal and carry the burden and expectation of a negotiation. I think Zambiya's right about the setting, sharing griddle cakes and beer together, perhaps a pastry. No other agenda." She hesitated, then asked, "When would be good? Just Kusu and me, and Ila and you, Zambiya?" She waved at the fly again, frowning.

"I'll be meeting with the owners of the large farms tomorrow, and the meeting will probably be long and contentious. Everyone needs water, and no one wants to share if they don't have to. Never mind. The next day, then. Just before the sun is at zenith we'll meet by the nearest beer parlor and decide which of the two parlors has the best food to offer." Zambiya thought a moment before adding, "Please excuse me for not attending to this matter sooner." He closed his eyes and held up his hand to signal that there was more, then looked first at Ninegala then at the king and said, "I'll share with you both another matter that's weighing on my mind, but at a later time."

───────── • ● • ─────────

"I'll remain in Isin a while longer if you need me, Zambiya. You've a lot on your shoulders now." Nabi and Zambiya stood together in full sunlight at the foot of the zigurrat steps late in the afternoon the next day, watching across the square at the market stalls. The beer parlors were already starting to attract early evening customers, and all the transient vendors had deserted their places for the day.

"That's true, my friend, but I've no need for you to delay your new life. I'll admit I expected to have your help with managing this part of the city, since you understand the rhythms of the market and know who's supposed to be here and who's likely to cause trouble. But leaving Isin? I'm actually shocked to hear you say it."

"I was shocked when Nisaba agreed to my proposal, though she refuses to marry me." Nabi motioned to Zambiya to walk with him toward the closest parlor, saying, "I'm parched. I usually watch the market from a shaded spot, but today I've been across the way observing from the avenue, and I'd like a beer. Join me?"

"Gladly. I've been inside most of the day listening to rich men argue with priests about how much more each needs canal water. Never felt sorry for Tikal before now. These endless squabbles were his life."

They strolled in the direction of the stalls while Nabi silently rehearsed how to explain his new arrangement. They agreed on a table with two short benches under the canopy, and Nabi motioned to an attendant to bring a pitcher of beer. Once it arrived and they had their straws settled in the drink, Nabi said, "I'll manage her farm, which isn't all that far from Isin. She told me that we'd have more time together if I wasn't on duty in the city, and even though we won't be married, we can share Inana's pleasures when we want to." He delayed further comment while he looked around to be sure there was no one close by, then confided, "She's a lusty woman, that one."

"What about her daughters? Both are married, one to the *Ensi*. Won't she want to spend time with them?"

"She says she just wanted them married and settled. I asked her if she wouldn't want to be around her grandchildren when they arrive; she actually shuddered. Said, 'Not if I can help it. Babies are an unending source of sounds and smells.'"

Zambiya mimicked Nabi's search for privacy, rising part way off his bench to look around, and in a low voice said, "Aren't you afraid she'll find out it was you who killed Aga? I'd be worried if it were me."

"How'd she find out? Who knows besides you and me? Tikal's dead, and only the three of us knew; Tikal told me he'd tell *Ensi* that Aga got suspicious and escaped. I don't talk in my sleep." He chuckled to himself.

Both men settled in their seats and concentrated on the pitcher in front of them, thinking. Then Nabi pointed across at a shabbily dressed boy who was skirting the edge of the main thoroughfare as he left the square. He commented, "I think that one is a thief, but I've not caught him yet. He's clever, but I've got time."

— •●• —

Kusu sat across from Ila at a shaded table large enough for six, with Ninegala seated on the same bench with enough space between them for another person. Zambiya sat across the table from her. Four guards arranged themselves at discrete distances from the queen and her group, facing away from them, and no other patrons were allowed to sit nearby. Polite greetings had been completed and now they waited while the proprietor himself arranged individual deep cups of beer, straws, and ceramic plates with fried cakes and fruit on the common trestle table in front of these special patrons. No one spoke until he had gone, and several moments then went by. No one paid any attention to the food or drink.

Then Kusu sighed an audible sigh and reached up to her left temple and loosed her veil from that side before saying, "Please, Lady, show me your face. Ila? The face my son loved." Her voice broke into a low sob as she finished her sentence, and she blinked hard to clear the tears from her eyes.

Ila reached across the narrow table to take Kusu's hand in her own, while removing her veil and placing it with its silver dangles on the table. "Ah, oh, Lady. I'm so sorry to bring such sorrow into your life. Neti and I had made such plans before he died. Ah, he was so looking forward to seeing you and his father." Ila's voice was strained with emotion, and she added, "I hate for you to see me looking like a professional mourner with ochre running down my cheeks." She pulled a linen cloth from her tunic and tried to clean her face, but since the cloth was already stained, it was no more than moderately successful.

"Let me help you, dear girl." Kusu removed a cloth of her own from where it was kept in her dress and immersed it in her cup of beer, removed the excess by holding it in her fist over the ground behind her, then flicked away the husks that adhered to the cloth. Standing up, she moved around the table and slid next to Ila, then tenderly cleaned off Ila's face, while Ila allowed her tears to flow while gazing at her mother-in-law the whole time.

Ninegala stood up and motioned to Zambiya to accompany her to a nearby table, saying simply, "Let's let them talk."

• ● •

Within three days, Ila had moved into the palace, sharing Kusu's apartment and occupying what had formerly been Neti's chambers. The two widowed women chatted often, conversing mainly about what Ila intended to do. Now that she no longer had a husband but had a child, her prospects as a trader now seemed more troublesome.

Enlil-Bani had welcomed her into the palace warmly, told Zambiya to be sure she had every comfort, and even instructed Zid-tara to inquire about her food preferences, though she was satisfied with whatever was presented, except in the morning.

She did her best to quell her nausea, which beset her for a full two moons before she could stomach more than plain baked barley cakes and water, but by early afternoon she was ravenous. Within half a moon's time, it was common for Zambiya to arrive at Kusu's apartment and invite both ladies to visit the market for a light repast; most often, it was only Ila who accepted, seeming to need time in the open air and sunlight.

———— • ● • ————

A few days after Ila became ensconced in the palace, Ninegala reminded the king that Zambiya had told them that he had a personal matter to discuss with them.

"What do you think it could be?" asked the king. The royal couple was walking from their chambers to the banquet room, Muda and a pair of guards several paces in front of them with another pair to the rear.

"Maybe he'll tell us tonight," she responded. She seated herself to the king's right side. Zambiya entered shortly after; he nodded to Muda and bowed to the king and his wife before sitting on the side of the table closest to his stepfather.

The king made a gesture to the leading attendant and the servers presented the dishes and drinks in a well-choreographed arrangement of platters and bowls, cups and straws, and napkins. Steaming roasted squabs lay on a bed of baked onions and garlic, these on a lower bed of mixed wheat and barley, with toasted sesame seeds and fried locusts sprinkled over the whole platter. Tonight's beer was flavored with cumin, and there was a pitcher of cherry wine available.

Once the royal trio had been served, the stewards stepped away, their backs to the walls, alert to any signal for service.

Ninegala pried the meat from her bird and lay morsels on a fried wheat cake on her plate, but once it had been prepared, she turned to Zambiya and stated, "I know you've been quite busy, but I recall a few days ago you said you had a matter you wanted to share with us. You gave us no notion what it might be. Would this be a good time to tell us?"

"Perhaps when there are fewer attendants close by," offered the king.

"No, now is good." Zambiya had just swallowed, and he took a drink of beer before going on. "What's on my mind is something Nani brought up with me as soon as I went to see Indur after I returned to Isin." He observed Ninegala with his peripheral vision while he spoke more directly to the king. "You know my son was born with his upper lip split. His mouth doesn't close completely and it's hard for him to get food to stay in his mouth." He waited while this picture formed in the minds of his listeners before he continued, saying, "Nani thinks En-me can repair Indur's mouth but En-me isn't sure he can do it, and he's not anxious to try. Not because it might anger the gods, but if he harms Indur, the law makes him subject to punishment." He took another portion of beer, then said, "That concern leaps out into my other thoughts like a lion pouncing on a gazelle. It's up to me; I can't ask Indur." He raised his fist toward the ceiling and declared, "Curse the god who did this to my son!"

Ninegala frowned, but then said, "I knew your son had been afflicted but I've not seen him." She turned to her husband and asked, "Can this be fixed? Has it ever been done?"

Enlil-Bani replied, saying, "I've met several adults who have such a mouth, and they seemed to adjust to their plight." He thought further and declared, "I've never seen anyone cured. Actually, Indur's mouth is better than some; the split doesn't go up to the nose and it doesn't affect his gums."

No one was eating. As they silently scanned the banquet offerings with their eyes, other images and fantasies occupied their consciousness. Finally, Ninegala said to Zambiya, "You're right, of course. It is your decision. But I'm wondering how you'd feel if En-me tried to repair your son's lip and it was no better or even worse. Would you want En-me punished?"

"No!" Zambiya's responded immediately. "I've thought about that as much as I've thought about what he might be able to do. If he agrees that he could even improve Indur's mouth, it would be my responsibility for him to try." He looked at the king and Ninegala earnestly, then said, "It helps to be able to talk about the decision. My thoughts when I'm alone are like a dog chasing its tail: no progress and no decision."

"What does En-me think he could do?" asked the king. "And wouldn't it hurt Indur?"

Zambiya held up one hand signifying that the royal couple should wait for a reply. Using his sharp table knife, he speared the meat on his plate and lifted it off the boiled grains, moving it off to one side. Then he moved and flattened the grains with the knife, creating a rounded edge, then split the edge to create a wedge-shaped separation. Using the knife as a pointer, he explained, "What En-me suggested could be done, and he said, 'perhaps,' and 'possibly,' is to cut the skin off the lip at the top," indicating the upper most wedge section by scooping a part of the division away and putting that section of grain on top of the pigeon meat, "and then sew those parts of the flesh together, so they would heal up closed." He demonstrated by pushing the grains together in the upper part, leaving the bottom division still separated. He finished his description moments later, concluding, "He would cut the lip so that the joining would be even with Indur's gum, and his teeth won't affect the wound when he has teeth."

Everyone at the table studied Zambiya's plate. Ninegala felt the inside of her lips with her tongue and shuddered involuntarily. The king felt his lips with his fingers. Zambiya had already imagined the proposed correction in his mind and by drawing on the ground on other occasions, and he just re-visited his fantasies.

Enlil-Bani raised his hand and felt the scar from an arrow wound on his shoulder, then asked, "That would have to hurt Indur beyond measure. Could you allow that for your son?"

"No, Father. Certainly not. En-me says they can give Indur so much beer, or even honeyed wine, that he will be asleep when the cutting and sewing is done, and we will have to keep him as close to asleep as possible for some days after. And he can't be allowed to touch his mouth, either." He let his gaze wander toward the ceiling, then added, "I wonder how to keep his tongue away from his lip."

Ninegala beckoned to a steward to pour her a cup of the wine; after two large swallows she ventured, "Why not do it all? Wouldn't that be better?"

Zambiya nodded to her and said, "I asked the same thing. En-me said the lower lip is much more active, and would not be likely to heal closed. This," he said, indicating his upper lip, "is the best chance to make an improvement that could 'possibly' work."

Zambiya pushed his grains back into a pile with the meat, now cold, on top. The royal family resumed their meal, deep into their respective fantasies, until Ninegala offered another comment. "I wonder if the gods will be angry if we try to interfere with what they've done. Would the priests know?"

No one responded to the rhetorical question.

CHAPTER TWENTY

PEAS IN A POD

*What curve of hip or flare of nostril, what shape of
eyes or lips, what brow or beard or scent or voice seizes
our attention and flavors with passion every other aspect
of our beloved, spreading into our very fibers, to imbue one
woman or one man an allure that eclipses all others? Do
even the gods know?*

"Ah, I'm going to resume trading, Zambiya," Ila announced. "Thanks to your help arranging for me to be transported to the *Meluhhan* village every several days, I've been able to keep in touch with those craftsmen who do the best quality work there. See?" She pointed toward her earrings. "Rangu was a great help also, even though his attention is diverted by preparations for his wedding." She chuckled and then added, "And after."

Ila and Zambiya made a slow circuit of the market square, waiting for their favorite beer parlor to start seating patrons. The aroma of baked goods wafted toward them, and Zambiya again looked in that direction even though he had no interest in food. As soon as he saw the rope barrier with its black pennant flags being gathered by the proprietor's portly wife, signaling the shop's opening, he guided Ila by the elbow in that direction, saying, "Look. They're ready. Let's sit in the front so we can watch the vendors set up. That's always entertaining."

As the couple skirted the vendors of vegetables and fruit, dried meats and fish and fresh eggs, they were greeted by the proprietor himself, an

285

aging man with a beard that looked as if it had never been trimmed, who called to them from several paces away from his stall. "Lord and Lady, Shalamu. May the gods bless you all your days, and especially this one. Let me show you to our best table."

He beckoned to them, hoping to guide them to a prominent place where they would advertise his parlor by just their presence; Ila was garbed in an exotic long russet colored tunic set off by long dangling purple faience earrings. Her veil was plain light linen with matching purple beads weighting the bottom. These were a new product of the *Meluhhan* village, which she hoped to make fashionable in Isin and beyond. Zambiya's attire was modest for his rank, though he wore his beaten silver breast insignia with its blue lapis cabochons plus a short sword in an intricately engraved and polished scabbard.

"Shalamu, citizen. This will be fine." Zambiya was impatient to be seated, served and left alone.

"Would you like to know what pastries we are offering today, Lord?"

"We'll just have a pot of fresh beer and two new straws, and soon," Zambiya answered, waving the man away.

Ila sat on the bench next to Zambiya so that they both faced the open bazaar area; as soon as the proprietor left, she let down one side of her veil, allowing it to droop.

"I was surprised to have you invite me to visit the market this early, Zambiya. We often come later." She adjusted herself on the bench, arching her back which was beginning to ache in the mornings. Placing her forearms on the table to support herself, she began idly turning the bronze and silver bangles on her wrists. Then she observed, "Ah, you haven't said anything about my continuing my trade. It was what I intended to do here in Isin. You knew that."

The proprietor's wife brought a tray with two newly-cut long reed straws and a deep bowl half filled with beer and sat it between them. She started to leave but turned back and said, "Lady, those earrings are lovely. I've never seen such work." She smiled at Ila with lips showing gaps in her teeth, then turned to leave.

"Thank you, Lady."

Zambiya waited for Ila to blow away the husks from the top of the beer, then did the same before saying, "I didn't ask you if you wanted anything to eat with your beer. Would you?"

"No. I'm not eating very much in the morning. The beer soothes my stomach, though, if I don't overdo."

Zambiya looked past Ila to the market, then sat more upright and rolled his shoulders backward, willing them to relax. He commanded them to slump and took a deep breath and slowly exhaled. He became aware of how tense his abdomen was, and let those muscles go slack as well as he inhaled slowly.

"I wanted to say something and I didn't want to wait," he said to Ila. He reached up to briefly touch the earring she had referenced, then lightly stroked her cheek before lowering his hand to take her hand in his. He looked into her eyes and huskily announced, "Ila, I want to marry you. No, I want very much to marry you. I know you're carrying Neti's baby, but I…"

He stopped speaking and held his breath when Ila started to cry, covering her eyes with her other hand, but holding tight to Zambiya's.

Ila tried hard to look at Zambiya but her tears continued flowing, so much that they dripped off her cheeks, wetting her tunic. "Oh…ah… Zambiya." She shook her head, willing her eyes to dry and her voice to obey her desire to speak. She took a linen cloth from a subtle pouch near her waist and wiped her eyes, then her nostrils. Trying to control her breathing to stop its gasping in trembling shudders, she finally spoke after slowly sipping and swallowing some beer.

"I never meant to make you cry." Zambiya's mouth was turned down and deep lines formed between his eyebrows. "I had no desire to cause you such distress by saying what I did. I'll escort you back to the palace when you're ready. I…"

Ila dropped her handkerchief into her lap and reached across the table to put her fingers over Zambiya's mouth, saying, "I can think of nothing I would like more than to be your wife. You're a good man, a strong man." She took Zambiya's hand in both of hers but searched his face for the truth of his feelings when she said, "Ah, but can you accept Neti's child as if it's your own? Truly? That matters more than my happiness."

"I answered that question for myself before I asked you. You've met my Indur several times now, and you're not repulsed. And he likes you; I can tell. We can be a true family, and even have more children, if the gods so choose."

Ila lifted Zambiya's hand to her mouth and kissed his fingertips, then said, "We must tell *Ensi*... and Kusu."

• ● •

Enmerkar lay still, hearing the sound of En-me snoring next to him but actually examining the dream that had wakened him. While it clearly concerned his family, he felt no tone of danger as previous dreams had contained, and he felt puzzled by the overall twin sensations of both calmness and imminent closure that pervaded him, as if a good event was needed to occur. He knew to attend to his feelings and noted there was no ache behind his eyes.

He attempted to re-construct the dream, but was further surprised to find that he was one of the figures, not just an observer.

His father the king stood next to Zambiya, holding his hand, while Nani held Zambiya's hand and Suba's, and he, Enmerkar, was grasping Suba's hand as well as En-me's. The six formed a circle facing inward, but it was not closed; a space was open next to Enlil-Bani. In the center, Lith-el walked from one to the other, smiling at each until she came to the vacant spot, at which point she frowned and made a clucking sound of disapproval. The scene was repeated three times, until on the third circuit Lith-el made, she stopped at the empty spot and gradually, very gradually, disappeared from view without having moved.

Enmerkar did his best to apply logic to the arrangement, noting that Suba and Nani were together, as were he and En-me. While he knew that Ila and Zambiya were planning to marry, their ceremony had been scheduled to coincide with a festival later in this moon cycle, so her absence was appropriate. The puzzle in his logical review involved Enlil-Bani, who was married; Ninegala was not present in the dream. Did the dream portend something ill happening to Ninegala? If so, why was his feeling so devoid of dread or danger?

He decided to share the dream with En-me after they were both awake. Looking through the narrow window of their bedroom he could tell that dawn was not imminent, and he turned over to resume sleeping, but also noticed that En-me's snoring occasionally stopped for extended periods,

288

but would then resume. He also determined to share that observation with his lover when morning came.

In fact, neither conversation took place. En-me woke the following morning with a wracking coughing spell that lasted for so long it left him weak. This was the first time that coughing brought up blood that showed on the bed cover, and Enmerkar sent word to the palace that En-me was too ill to attend that day.

———————— • ● • ————————

"Over there! Further!"

Ninmah commanded her guards to withdraw further from the table she shared with Zambiya.

This beer parlor was selected by Zambiya because it was not the one he and Ila frequented. While Ila had wanted to tell Kusu and the king, Zambiya felt a great need to remain on good terms with Ninmah, the priestess with whom he had shared so many romantic and erotic interludes. Now satisfied with the positions the guards had taken, well out of earshot, she engaged Zambiya directly.

"I've heard that you want to have En-me correct Indur's Asag-mouth. Is that why you want to see me? I had hoped you'd call for me much sooner, Zambiya. I still think of our last night together, before you went on the voyage to *Meluhha*." She looked into his eyes and put a morsel of pastry in her mouth, then slowly licked her lips as she put her hand over his forearm. Swallowing, she smiled and added, "I do understand that you're much busier since you've become Chief Counselor."

Zambiya moved his arm from under Ninmah's hand to reach for his wine cup. He drank and sighed, then raised both his hands toward the canvas canopy and looked up at it. He set his cup back down and took both of Ninmah's hands in his, then declared, "That's not why I wanted to see you. I've not settled on trying to fix Indur's lip; En-me is consulting with other *a-zus* about how to proceed, and wants to talk with a priest as well." He shifted on the bench, then said, "The gods have conspired to keep us parted, but I love you still. I've loved you from the day we met."

"You know I love you too, Zambiya." She lowered her voice and smiled, stroking his hand before asking, "Did you want to arrange another night of pleasure? Because you know I'll say 'yes'."

"I'm going to get married in ten days' time," he blurted out. "I'm going to marry the *Meluhhan* woman who came back with us, Neti's widow. Her name's Ila. I wanted to tell you myself. I can't marry you, and I need a wife, and Indur needs a mother. The woman Ila is with child, and she wants a father for her child." He settled back on the bench, as he had been leaning forward, still tense throughout his body. "But I value you and your friendship; I don't want that to ever change."

Ninmah withdrew both of her hands and crossed her arms over her bosom.

"You're very brave," she stated evenly while staring at him. "If I were to scream and say you threatened me, my guards would kill you as you sat there." She closed her eyes and then placed her hands in her lap. Opening her eyes, she looked into Zambiya's eyes and said, "But I meant what I said: I love you, too. Perhaps some day the gods will relent and allow us to be together as more than friends."

"I want you to meet her, Ninmah. She's a good woman."

Ninmah stood and motioned her guards to wait before joining her, then said to Zambiya as he stood up, "So we're to be friends again? Are we also to be lovers?" She made a dismissive wave of her hand as she turned from him, slowly shaking her head as she walked away from the table.

———— • • • ————

Ninegala sat next to Kusu in the latter's apartment while Ila and Zambiya were out of the palace sharing a light repast. Ila could still tolerate food only late in the morning, and Zambiya often escorted her outside for this meal.

"He promised me and my mother before I agreed to marry him. He's such an honorable man, and a compassionate one as well, so I know he'd keep his promise. I know he'll never touch me, Kusu." She waited a moment, then blushed and said, "But I want him to. I don't know what to do."

"Why in the name of all the Great Gods would he agree to that, Nina? He's not that old. And why would you?" Kusu sipped a strong berry wine from her cup, and just waited. She had determined that she would not speak until Ninegala had said something to explain this un-heard of anomaly in marital affairs. Then she renounced her own resolve and asked, "What has your mother had to say about this?"

Ninegala squirmed at her place on the divan and said, "I've not told my mother, but I did tell my sister, 'Rida. She had no suggestions." She thought a moment before adding, "You do know my mother's off at her farm. That's why I'm asking you for advice, but mostly because you're the wisest woman I know. And I can't tell anyone else." She stood up and turned her back to Kusu so she couldn't see the widow's reaction, then told her what had happened to her with the Chaldean those months ago.

Kusu looked about her sitting room, over at the walls and up at the ceiling, then stood up and walked up to Ninegala's back and held her, weeping softly. Understanding more, she sighed before proposing, "Would you know how to seduce him?"

Ninegala gasped, then said, "No. I think if I got into his bed completely nude, he'd go sleep somewhere else. Truly, I think he would. And I'd be so embarrassed I'd have to kill myself."

"Drastic, dear girl. Drastic." Kusu thought some more, then proposed, "I've only one other idea. See him alone and tell him how you feel about him and that you don't want to hold him to his promise. I can't think of anything else."

• ● •

"I'm sorry to be late, Ensi," Ninegala explained as she entered the throne room from the rear. "I know you like me to attend trials with you, but we've not had any for many days, and Sud just told about this one when I came back from visiting with Kusu. She sends you blessings." Ninegala raised the hem of her ankle-length pink tunic as she ascended the three steps to the level of the throne, showing her slender calves, then settled onto her chair next to the king, looking out over the spectators.

The king leaned over and quietly assured her that the trial was just about to commence. He noticed the aroma of the queen's perfume, a scent that combined flower petals with a hint of musk, but was only vaguely conscious of the sheen of perspiration on her bare arms and shoulders and that her palm was moist when she tenderly caressed his forearm.

She smiled at him warmly before asking, "Why the large audience, husband?"

In addition to Zambiya, who as Chief Counselor would be presenting the matter to the king for a decision, there were six members of the Elders'

Council, Nabi, plus Enmerkar and En-me, the latter looking healthier than he had for many days. Muda, of course, stood to the right of the throne.

Then she saw the subject of the trial standing between two guards off to one side of the room, a slight adolescent boy, tall and gangly, who stood quivering with fear. His hands were bound in front and a length of hemp rope girdled his slender waist to make it easier to control him if he should try to bolt or attack. One of the guards held the rope at the boy's back.

"Oh. I see that boy. What could he have done?"

"He's accused of theft. Let's listen to why he's been brought here, instead of having the matter handled by the Elders." The king gestured to Zambiya to proceed.

"Bring the prisoner forward, guards," the Chief Counselor said, and waited no more than three breaths before continuing. "This youngster's been the subject of two hearings this morning. Nabi caught him in the market stealing onions, and two tribunals have already determined that he stole them. That's no longer a question; he is a thief." The youngster hung his head at this pronouncement; his knees quivered and he writhed with his shoulders, one after the other. "The question has to do with punishment," Zambiya continued. "The exalted king Lipit-Ishtar declared years ago that the penalty for theft was to have the right hand severed, so that all will know this is a thief." Zambiya paused for effect, then continued, "Even though he's tall, both tribunals failed to agree that a boy this young should be treated this way, but no alternative punishment seemed to fit. The Elder Council begs for *Ensi* to decide."

Throughout Zambiya's presentation, Ninegala watched the youngster intently, again noting the rolling of his shoulders, as if he were trying to rid himself of the filthy tunic he wore. She leaned toward the king and gestured toward the boy, her face serious and animated as she spoke to him in a whisper.

Enlil-Bani asked the nearest guard, "Do you think there are enough guards here to keep that boy from attacking me?"

Shocked at having been addressed at all, the guard stammered, "Of... of course, my *Ensi*."

"Then take off that rope around him and take off his garment. Then turn him around. I want to see his back."

The guard who had been addressed hurried over to where the boy stood and helped his two guards comply with the king's order.

"*Ensi*, uh…uh…the cloth is stuck to his back."

"En-me," the king said. "First, welcome back to the palace, I'm glad to see you here. Tell us what is causing this."

En-me walked to where the boy stood and examined the youth's back, then gripped his shoulder and carefully peeled the cloth away from his skin in several places, dabbing the new blood that oozed from the wounds with the boy's tunic. He stood away from the boy and motioned for one of the guards to bring a torch from the wall.

"*Ensi*, he's been beaten with something sharp. There's both blood and pus in these sores." En-me held up the torch to allow the king to see. Everyone except the king and the members of the king's family were surprised when Muda left his usual post and walked up to examine the boy for himself, remembering his own punishment with a knout the day before he was purchased by Enlil-Bani.

"Turn around and come here, young man," the king ordered. "You two guards," he said to the pair that had been assigned to him, "bring him up closer."

"Explain what has brought you to this point in your short life." The fear on the boy's face was clear; he tried to answer the king, with his lips moving but with no sound above a whisper, unintelligible.

Ninegala stroked the king's arm to get his attention and with gestures, gained permission to address the prisoner.

"Boy, tell *Ensi* why you steal so he can both hear you and understand you." She saw him struggling to control his voice then added in a reassuring tone, "I don't know how you could be in worse trouble than you are at this moment."

The boy took a deep breath then blurted out as rapidly as he could, "I have to steal, *Ensi*. Uncle beats me if I return to the house without food, the same with all us boys." He raised his tied hands and pulled down his lower lip, displaying a gap where two teeth had once been. "See? I'm punished every day I don't bring back enough. It's not my fault I steal. If I told you who my uncle is, he'd kill me. It's certain."

Zambiya turned to Nabi and asked quietly, "Do you believe what he said?"

"I could well believe it," Nabi replied. "Look at his back. I think I've seen this uncle but I've never seen him take anything."

"After *Ensi* has made his decision, find this 'uncle,' Nabi." Zambiya looked up and added, "I think Muda would like to speak with him." Muda nodded in assent.

The king turned to Ninegala and smiled, saying, "Once again you've noticed the deeper meaning behind the obvious actions." Addressing the present witnesses he said, "This boy is the agent of a thief. Not a thief. But he did steal."

En-me spoke up from where he had returned to sitting with Enmerkar, with whom he had been conferring in low tones after having first spoken to Nabi. "*Ensi*, may I speak?"

"Yes, En-me. Were you wanting to treat his wounds?"

"Yes, that too. But allow me to propose an alternative to cutting off his hand. No one wants to do that; it doesn't seem just." En-me waited three heartbeats, then said, "Instead, declare him to be a slave and assign him to me." He quelled a cough that was threatening to erupt, turning away to sniff and clear his throat. Turning back to address the king he said, "Nabi tells me the boy is very deft, very alert." He hesitated before explaining, "I would like to train a new *a-zu*. Isin lost many *a-zus* during the *mutanu* plague, and if this boy has talent, he could earn his freedom and learn a valuable trade. I was a slave when I learned to be an *a-zu*. Everyone gains."

Enlil-Bani spoke directly to the youth, saying, "You have no say in what happens to you, but this offer by my personal healer seems to be the best for you, too. It's my decision to make." Looking out at the audience, he announced, "I agree. It is so ordered." He stood up from the throne and offered his hand to Ninegala; they both descended the stairs and exited at the rear of the room, accompanied again by Muda and two guards.

En-me had bowed to the king before the royal couple left the room. He went up to the boy and said, "Come with me. I'll take care of your back and then we'll get you some food." By this time Enmerkar had limped up to them and was introduced, although the youngster looked disoriented and in shock. They led him toward the public entrance to the throne room where most of the citizen audience was leaving.

There the newly pronounced slave was met by Nabi, who assisted the guards in removing the rope from the youth's waist and wrists before telling him, "I will see you tomorrow, boy. When I do, you will take me and a couple guards to where this 'uncle' lives. Oh, and Muda will be with us." Nabi smiled in anticipation.

* ● *

The royal couple dined together that evening, after the king's usual visit to the temples atop the zigurrat. Sud stood attentively near the doorway, ready to provide more food or wine or beer. Ninegala had made known that she favored fruit wines with her evening meal, so a pitcher was ready for pouring.

Enlil-Bani pushed the morsels of broiled gazelle away from him with a wheat cake, saying, "I'm not very hungry tonight, Nina. I've been thinking about that boy at the trial. I wonder how many other children are in such predicaments; they have no control over how they're treated, even by their own parents."

"He was not much older than a child, certainly." She turned in her chair to face him more directly and put her hand on his cheek, adding, "You made a wise and thoughtful decision, agreeing with what En-me suggested. That boy's life will be much better now. He has both of you to thank."

The king turned his head away from Ninegala, the executions of the Chaldean and the killers of Lith-el appearing in his mind's eye, then he looked back at her and said, "Tikal and I spoke on different occasions when I was feeling that I had been too harsh in ordering a criminal to be killed. He told me those times were justified and even desirable, and that I could be merciful at some other time. I think this was a good time to be merciful."

"It was, husband. It was." She gestured to Sud, pointing at her cup; Sud brought the wine and poured a third portion. Ninegala drank half, then indicated that Sud should refill it. She waited until it was poured and Sud had returned to her place again, then turned back to the king and pivoted in her chair to face him almost directly.

"*Ensi*, husband, I want to talk about our marriage, and your promise to me and my mother those several moons ago."

Enlil-Bani stopped breathing for two heartbeats, then took his straw in his hand and drew up a large swallow, then turned to face his wife. "I expected this day would come, Ninegala. So you've found a young man who excites you? I'll be honest; I will miss your sensitive counsel in the throne room. I've come to depend on your thoughts."

Ninegala put up both palms toward the king and said, "You misunderstand me. There's no other 'young man' I think about. I think about you! I want to release you from your promise to never take me to your bed. I'm a woman and I want to be your wife in fact as well as in name." She reached with both hands to take up her cup of courage, but realized she didn't need it any longer, having said what she wanted, so she put it back on the table.

"After that horrid man defiled me it was as if the sun never shone again; every day was gray and every sight and feeling was dull. It was like my heart had shriveled. Like having beer that was half water, no taste worth drinking." She breathed deeply, then continued. "Since we've married, my days have been full of color and good people." She looked directly into Enlil-Bani's eyes and said, "But not complete."

The king regarded her with wonder, deep lines between his eyes and furrows on his brow. "But I've seen over twice as many flood times as you. I'm not old, but I'm certainly older than you." He took another large swallow of beer, then turned far enough to take Ninegala's hands in his. "I never expected to have such feelings for any other woman after Lith-el. Whenever I've started to notice you in that way, as a woman, I remember my promise and try to stop the feeling." He hesitated to confess, "When I wake in the morning, it's hard knowing you're in the next room. But even if I hadn't made my promise to you, you're so young I would have felt like an old fool to think you could feel anything for me except possibly friendship."

"You've never acted the fool, husband, and I've never wanted a young impetuous man. I'm certain about my feelings for you; I've consulted the gods, and especially the goddess." She removed one hand from his grasp and lightly brushed his lips. "If you want me as a woman, I want to be your wife."

Enlil-Bani reached up with his hand and felt the softness of Ninegala's cheek at the same time inhaling her perfume. For the first time he allowed himself to be honest and acknowledge his desire to be with her. Throatily, he asked, "Are you certain, Ninegala?"

"This desire of mine is not new, my husband. I've not known how to let you know before now. Kusu told me to just be honest with myself and with you. I am certain."

Enlil-Bani stood up from his chair and helped Ninegala to stand. Still looking at his wife and holding her hands, he announced, "Sud. You're done for the evening. Leave the food and the dishes and don't wake up my wife in the morning. She won't be in her room."

Puzzled, Sud watched the royal couple exit, hand in hand, through the door leading to their quarters.

The end of part two.

ACKNOWLEDGMENTS

Foremost, I want to thank my wife, Marilyn, for her encouragement, patience, editorial acumen, and most of all for her love.

I also want to thank Kym Dupont, my editor, for her attention to detail and helpful suggestions.

I would be remiss not to recognize the help of Ashley Whitman, convener of the Blacksburg Library Writers workshop, and its participant writers. This workshop is an offering of the Montgomery County, Floyd County, and Radford City Library system in the New River Valley of Virginia.

REFERENCES

Ancient Cities of the Indus Valley Civilization (1998) Kenoyer, Jonathan Mark

Assyrian and Babylonian Chronicles (1975) translated by A.K. Grayson

Sumer and the Sumerians (1991) Crawford, Harriet, Cambridge University Press

Civilization before Greece and Rome (1989) H.W.F. Saggs, Yale University Press

The Timetables of History (1963) Bernard Grun, based upon Werner Stein's *Kulturfahrplan* English Edition Published by Simon and Schuster

The Atlas of the Ancient World (1992) Margaret Oliphant, Simon and Schuster

Mesopotamia (2007) Eyewitness Books, D.K. Publishing, Inc.

Ancient Mesopotamia (2004) Virginia Schomp, Scholastic Inc.

The Sumerians: Their History, Culture, and Character (1963) Samuel Noah Kramer, University of Chicago Press

Splendors of the Past: Lost Cities of the Ancient World (1981) National Geographic Society

The Oldest Cuisine in the World: (2004) Jean Bottero, Translated by Teresa Lavendar Fagan, University of Chicago Press

The Cosmos News: (5-26-13) Snake Invasion and Attacks kills (sic) 60 villagers in southern Iraq

Handbook to Life in Ancient Mesopotamia: (2003) Stephen Bertman, Oxford University Press

National Geographic Magazine: (January 1951); Ancient Mesopotamia: A Light That Did Not Fail; E.A Speiser

The Literature of Ancient Sumer: (2004) Translated by Jeremy Black, Graham Cunningham, Eleanor Robson and Gabor Zolyomi, Oxford University Press

Myths from Mesopotamia: (Revised 2000) Stephanie Dalley, Oxford University Press.

Printed in the United States
By Bookmasters